Saskia Sarginson was awarded a distinction in her MA in Creative Writing at Royal Holloway after a BA in English Literature from Cambridge University and a BA in Fashion Design & Communications. Before becoming a full-time author, Saskia's writing experience included being a health and beauty editor on women's magazines, a ghost writer for the BBC and Harper Collins, copy-writing and script editing. Saskia lives in south London with her partner and four children.

Visit Saskia online:
www.saskiasarginson.co.uk
www.facebook.com/saskiasarginsonbooks
www.twitter.com/SaskiaSarginson
www.instagram.com/saskiasarginson

By Saskia Sarginson

The Twins
Without You
The Other Me
The Stranger
How It Ends
The Bench
The Central Line
Seven Months of Summer

Seven Months of Summer

Saskia Sarginson

PIATKUS

PIATKUS

First published in Great Britain in 2023 by Piatkus

1 3 5 7 9 10 8 6 4 2

All characters and events in this publication, other than those clearly in the public domain, are fictitious and any resemblance to real persons, living or dead, is purely coincidental.

A CIP catalogue record for this book is available from the British Library.

ISBN 978-0-349-42874-1

Typeset in Goudy by M Rules
Printed and bound in Great Britain by Clays Ltd, Elcograf S.p.A.

Papers used by Piatkus are from well-managed forests and other responsible sources.

MIX
Paper from responsible sources
FSC® C104740

Piatkus
An imprint of
Little, Brown Book Group
Carmelite House
50 Victoria Embankment
London EC4Y 0DZ

An Hachette UK Company
www.hachette.co.uk

www.littlebrown.co.uk

To Cassidy Jackson Jessiman.
Who came into the world at
the same time as this book.

It is not time or opportunity that is to determine intimacy; it is disposition alone. Seven years would be insufficient to make some people acquainted with each other, and seven days are more than enough for others.

Jane Austen, *Sense and Sensibility*

I sow'd the seeds of love

Folk song (1689)

PROLOGUE

Kerala, India

15 January 1993

Kit wobbles on his bicycle, just missing a deep pothole, and puts his foot down to look at the road ahead. It's a busy highway, full of lorries and SUVs. A motorbike swerves around him, beeping. There are two children crammed onto the seat behind the driver, a length of scarlet fabric fluttering like a red flag.

He grimaces, knowing that Summer imagined the way to the next village would be a quiet back road winding along by the sea, not this congested route dense with fumes and the sound of blaring horns and revving engines. The guy hiring out the bikes at the hotel said it was a thirty-minute ride. Don't be a wuss, he tells himself, it's not much worse than cycling around Marble Arch at rush-hour. He pedals off, keeping his head down, looking for the next pothole or stray rock. An elaborately painted lorry roars past, wheels so close he sees the tread-pattern on the tyres; he steadies the bike and curses as the backdraught pushes him off balance.

He keeps going, one foot after the other, damp hands slipping on the handlebars.

He tastes sweat and dust on his lips, the acrid stink of diesel. The sun throbs, a pulsing ball of energy. His legs are heavy. It's not just the heat, he realises. His whole body is weighted down with a sense of wrongness. Every time he pushes on the pedals it takes him further from her. He stops again, putting his foot on the tarmac, and glances behind at the road that leads back to Summer. Being with her is more important than getting paid for a few sketches. This is a mistake. He's going to turn around.

It takes him a while to get to the other side of the road. He has to grab his chance when he sees a gap between two lorries. He dashes across as they bear down on him, horns sounding wildly. Trembling on the verge, he pauses to take a water bottle from his bag, downing it in one long drink. He wipes his face on his arm, smearing sweat and water into his stinging eyes.

He imagines how horrified she'll be when he describes this crazy road. She'll be glad that he's returned safely to her, secretly pleased he didn't go to the dance festival. They can spend the afternoon on the bed, talking. There's so much more he wants to know about her. It's the first time in his life he's had someone he wants to take care of, tell his thoughts to, share the details of his day with. He needs to understand everything that matters to her. Later, maybe they'll take a wander along the cliff path as the sun goes down. He noticed a pretty necklace in one of the shops, a delicate rope of twisted silver with tiny green stones hanging from it. It will go with the colour of her eyes, match her earrings.

They can call in at their favourite café and sit at the little table overlooking the ocean. They'll order an extravagant supper. Other girlfriends have picked at salads, pretending they're not hungry, all the time eyeing his meal with wistful expressions. Summer will happily take mouthfuls from his plate as well as her own, gesturing for him to help himself to her food too.

He can't wait to go through the door into the shuttered cool of their room and find her asleep on the bed. He'll wake her with a kiss.

He's cycling under the shade of banana trees as a scooter accelerates past. It pulls ahead, and he glimpses the man driving, sees a woman in a fluttering sari sitting side-saddle, a large basket clasped on her lap. He wonders how she can sit like that, calm and balanced, while the scooter dodges left and right. She's not even holding on. He feels a nervous admiration. A single-decker bus sways around the corner towards them, and at the same time he hears the grate of gears behind him, recognising the rumble of a diesel engine, signalling a lorry close on his heels.

He holds the handlebars steady and braces himself for the ordeal of it overtaking. The scooter is just up ahead. The woman's sari is blue. She turns and smiles over her shoulder. Up ahead, something leaves the shadows of the banana plantation and his pulse accelerates as his brain catches up with his eyes – it's a dog, trotting straight into the traffic.

The scooter swerves sharply to avoid the animal. The woman tumbles back, falling as if in slow motion, the basket bouncing away, her sari an unfurling sweep of sky.

He's trying to stop, his fingers jamming around the brakes.

The woman is stretched out on the road. The scooter and its driver are still attached to each other but moving on their sides as if being dragged along by a giant toddler. The scooter and driver slide straight into the path of the oncoming bus. The bus gobbles them up, machine and man churning under its wheels; the bus swings across Kit's path, the side of it rearing like a wall. Faces stare out of windows. Terrified eyes. Open mouths. He hears nothing, not even the lorry as it goes past him, headlong into the oncoming metal and glass. He is caught inside the dusty hot breath of heavy things in motion. His fingers are rigid around the brakes, his back wheel going from under him. He hits the road, sliding across asphalt. He sees his hand before him, reaching through space.

A white stillness holds him at its centre.

He thinks of Summer, of her sleeping face.

The bubble bursts and there is the high-pitched screaming of living creatures, and the other kind of scream when metal clashes with metal and windscreens shatter into fragments.

Pain explodes inside him.

He sees the liquid gleam of something dark, and the darkness pulls him into itself like a friend pulling him from the sea.

Kerala, India

15 January 1993

Summer checks the silver men's watch she's wearing. It's too big for her and slips around her wrist bone. She twists the face upwards and catches her breath. He's been gone ages. She remembers him confessing his habit of missing appointments and deadlines. As he said it, he'd rolled his eyes, poking fun at himself. She'd thought his inability to keep track of time was endearing, part of his artistic, easy-going nature. But not now, not when she needs him.

It's claustrophobic in their little hut at the top of the cliff, but as she steps out into the dazzle of light, she feels her skin sizzle. The plastic of her sunglasses leaves a rim of sweat on her cheekbones. Beads of perspiration prickle her forehead. She sits on a stone wall next to a dried-up ornamental pond, flapping the neck of her shirt to try and catch a breeze, her suitcase by her feet. Every time the door to the reception opens, she looks up expectantly. But it's never him.

The minutes tick on, and there's a tightness at the back of her throat as she understands that she'll have to leave without seeing him. She can't wait any longer. She could die if she doesn't get to the hospital. In a sudden panic, she grips the handle of her suitcase and stands up. Immediately, the world sparks and rushes away from her, so that she has to sit back down with a bump to stop herself from falling. She puts a hand to her head, waiting for the dizzy spell to pass.

In the air-conditioned cool of the reception, she asks for some paper and a pen. It'll take her a while to sort things out, she might be there for hours. She writes: *Kit, I can't wait any longer. I have to go. Please come and find me at the airport. I'll be trying to get on the first available flight home.*

She shoves the paper across the desk at the receptionist. 'Can you give this to Kit Appleby? I need a taxi please. It's urgent.'

The driver is a young man. He gets out of his Padmini to open the door for her, and she notices he wears no shoes. 'I need to get to Cochin International fast,' she tells him.

'Ah, I am very sorry, but we will have to take small roads,' he says. 'The main road is closed. But don't worry,' he adds quickly. 'You will be there in a lamb's tail. No doubt about it. I am the fastest driver in Varkala.'

She slides onto the back seat, and the car pulls away. She stares out of the window, not seeing the painted lorries rumbling past, the darting motorbikes, the elephant on the back of a truck. She's imagining the spires of Cambridge, the cold of an English winter, and a hospital where they're waiting for her.

JANUARY

One month of Summer

1

Summer

Seven days earlier . . .

Even before breakfast, the hotel barometer measures eighty-two degrees Fahrenheit. But it'll take more than the heat to get Summer onto an air-conditioned bus with the rest of the Trojan Tours group. As of this morning, she's free. No list of tourist sites to visit or schedule to keep to. She sets off alone along a dusty road in Fort Kochi, plaits bouncing over her shoulders, red flip-flops slapping the ground, a rush of joy bubbling inside her chest. This is how she imagined she'd feel, all those months ago when she opened the envelope Dad gave her for her twenty-sixth birthday.

It had been an unassuming rectangle of beige, the kind usually containing dull, official letters. The first thing that fell out was a plane ticket to Madras. Dad laughed, delighted by Summer's confusion. 'You deserve it,' he said. 'I know how hard things have been – how much you've had to give up.'

Summer was booked onto The Majesty of Southern India,

by Trojan Tours. Part of the itinerary included visiting two national parks, where elephants, bison, whistling dogs, leopards and tigers lived. She imagined watching a herd of elephants at sunset by a watering hole, her camera to her eye. Perhaps if she was very lucky, she'd spot a solitary tiger.

Emerging out of arrivals in Madras, there'd been a skirmish and clamour of people grasping at her luggage and shouting over each other for her attention, the honking of taxi horns, the stink of burning rubbish and, beyond everything, the velvety ink of the night, deeper and wider than any she'd known before. 'I'm here,' she'd whispered, a shock of dusty air blow-torching her lungs, as she'd grabbed the skin on her wrist between finger and thumb, and pinched.

But the national parks had been disappointing. No tigers. No leopards. A glimpse of a tusker behind fronds of green. The tour guide, Tony, hurried them through every attraction, as if they were late for a train. Everybody in the group had a camera, and the sound of clicking erupted whenever the bus stopped. It felt as if they were watching a film, rather than having an experience. Parting ways with Tony and Trojan Tours was the best decision she'd made since arriving.

Fort Kochi seems a laid-back town, full of cafés and groups of young Europeans with guitars on their backs. Houses shimmer in blues and yellows; lush vines sprout against walls in more kinds of green than she'd thought possible. She pauses under a wide-spreading banyan tree. She loves the way that a single street can accommodate a Hindu temple and mosque. That in another heartbeat there will be a white stone Catholic church, and then a Jain temple, where doves rise at the sound of each tolling prayer bell.

She squats in the dust to watch a common langur monkey

at the side of the road. It turns its intelligent face to observe her, elegant hands dissecting a rotten mango. She brings the camera up, holds her breath. Light shimmers on the pale sable of the animal's coat as her finger squeezes the shutter release.

Further down the road, a goat sleeps on the foot pad of a parked scooter. Smiling, she swings her camera up and snaps twice. Tuk-tuks bounce past, tourists crammed onto the back seats.

Stopping to check the map, she realises she's wandered onto Vasco Da Gama Square. She gazes at the water and the famous Chinese fishing nets. The square is bustling with activity. Stalls sell fish that come straight from the nets, and people gather to barter, slender cats threading in and out of legs, eyes glittering with desire. Summer sniffs the mix of brine, smoke and charred fish, and her mouth waters. Three or four young waiters compete with each other, trying to corral her into a seat at one of the little alfresco cafés. She allows herself to be escorted to an empty table by the least pushy one. Moments later, a plate of catch, hot from the flames, arrives with a glass of lime soda.

She sips her drink, looking around the bustling square. Out of habit, she touches her earrings. Tiny silver hares dangle from her lobes. She takes three postcards from a paper bag and composes one to her best friend Laura: *Wish you were here – we'd have so much fun!* One to home: *Kochi is amazing, pink dust, burning sky – so much to photograph!* and then, biting the end of her pen, starts another to Adam. Except she can't think what to say. He'd loved her. Then, without warning, it was over. He'd slept with another girl. 'Thing is, I'm not ready to settle down,' he'd said, and it was as if he'd landed a punch in her heart. 'I still care about you, Summer, but . . . we're too young.' They'd been together for five years, and he'd let go of her so easily.

She'd bumped into him before leaving for India – that was the problem with living in the same town. At least he hadn't been with his girlfriend. 'Send me a postcard,' he'd said, as if he hadn't broken her heart. And she'd agreed, just to escape. She taps her pen on the table, frowning. She and Adam split up three years ago. She should be over it by now, and yet, there's been nobody since him, no one important.

Two stray dogs hover, gazing at her hopefully. One of them has lost half an ear. Summer thinks of the dogs in Cambridge with their designer collars and expensive haircuts and wishes she could scoop up these feral creatures and give them a bath and a proper meal. They pad closer, noses sniffing. She drops pieces of fish on the ground. The dogs pounce. She can see their ribs through their dusty coats. The one missing an ear sidles forwards. She puts her hand out. 'Go on then, boy,' she murmurs, 'take it. You look like you need it more than me.'

The dog snuffles the food from her fingers. 'What happened to your ear?' The dog cocks his head, as if he can understand. She strokes his sun-warmed fur. 'Don't worry,' she tells him. 'You're still a handsome fellow.'

She snaps a couple of photos of him as he looks up at her, his eyes gentle and hopeful.

'Oi, you!' An English voice booms, making her startle. The dog freezes. She looks up as a giant of a man in a Hawaiian shirt, paunch jutting over baggy shorts, strides towards her, mirrored glasses glinting. 'Don't feed them!' He waves his arms. 'Shoo! Bugger off!' The dog cowers, crouching by her side, ragged ears flat against his head. The man aims a kick. There's a sickening thump as his toe finds the dog's ribs.

'Stop!' She's on her feet, chin up.

The dog disappears into the crowds, tail between his legs.

'What are you doing!' Her voice trembles. 'What's the matter with you? He wasn't doing any harm.'

'Filthy creatures. They should all be shot.' He shakes his head. 'People like you, encouraging them . . .'

'People like me?' she says, standing on her toes and broadening her shoulders. 'You want to shoot me too?'

He makes a twirling motion next to his ear with one pudgy finger and gives a short laugh. 'Calm down, love.'

'Don't tell me to calm down!' She clenches her hands, fury knotting the words in her throat. 'How . . . how would you like it if I kicked you!' she blurts out.

'Whoa!' A tall young man steps between them, arms raised. He turns to the angry man. 'You should go,' he tells him in a steady voice. 'It's really none of your business if she feeds the dogs.'

'Are you all right?' The same voice floats somewhere above her head.

Her heart is racing, adrenaline firing. She's too upset and angry to talk.

'Fine,' she manages, turning away. She scoops up her belongings and walks off, nearly falling over a bucket of iced fish, but rights herself and strides on.

'You sure?' she hears him call.

She raises a hand, not looking back.

She stops around a corner, out of sight. Squints against the glare of the street. It replays in her mind: the man's toe catching the hoop of ribcage; the impact lifting the animal off the ground.

She starts to walk towards the hotel – at least she hopes she's going in the right direction. The sun is a dazzle of white – a wall of brilliance that confuses her. She can't remember which is the turning. She keeps moving, on feet swollen with heat; sweat pools between her breasts.

It's only as she steps into the hotel lobby that she realises she forgot to pay for her lunch.

2

Kit

Kit Appleby watches her leave. She's obviously upset. She weaves her way unsteadily through the crowd, red trousers fluttering. There's a moment when she nearly falls; he tenses himself to run and help.

He calls out, 'You sure?'

She doesn't turn her head.

When she's out of sight he returns to his table, glaring at the man in the lurid shirt, who ignores him, inscrutable behind his mirrored glasses. From the waiter's concerned expression and the owner's waving arms, he realises that in the kerfuffle the girl's forgotten to pay her bill; he presses the money for her meal as well as his drink into the waiter's hand, before he gathers his sketchpad, downs the dregs of his iced coffee, and leaves.

Could he have done something to make her stay? He can't actually remember what he said now. It happened so fast. He'd been sketching the fishermen, trying to capture the lilt of their bare feet treading bamboo poles. It's become his habit since arriving in Kochi, to sit at the same café table every morning, eking out a coffee, drawing for an hour or two. There's so much to see in the square.

As he sits and sketches, strangers come and go from the tables adjacent to his own – tourists from different parts of the world. He likes to try and guess where they're from before he hears them speak. He noticed her as soon as she sat down. She had an air of quiet calm, a self-contained independence that seemed at odds with her round, freckled cheeks and large eyes. He guessed she was Dutch. Although maybe that was just the blonde plaits. She started to feed the dogs as soon as her meal arrived, sharing it with two scruffy, skinny creatures. Most people ignored them or shooed them away.

It's not in Kit's nature to jump into a conflict. He's happiest with his pencil and sketchpad, sitting on the edges of things. But he had to intervene when that man was suddenly towering over her, shouting, threatening.

He wonders where she's staying. Fort Kochi is a small place.

He's wandering down narrow streets with no real idea of where he's going. He turns into the overgrown garden of the Dutch Palace. There's a flight of steps webbed in a triangle of shade. He heads straight for it, sitting with his back against a door, pulling his toes into the curve of shadow. He would have liked to have had a chance to draw her before it all kicked off. Quite literally. He opens his sketchpad and idly flicks through, each page filled with memories of places where he's travelled. There are temples, elephants, women washing clothes at a riverbank. On the first page is a quick portrait made before he left England. He's caught his mother's angular features; she's only forty-eight – but looks years older. He sighs, gazing at the picture. Bitterness lives in her face, carving discontented grooves between mouth and nose, forging a zigzag of worry between her eyebrows.

It was always the same. Life was against her. Nothing was fair. And it all came down to his father. The bastard, she called him. The bloody bastard. Everything that went wrong was his fault. And every time Kit behaved in a way that displeased her, she made the comparison.

The sun has moved. His left leg is no longer in shadow; heat burns his knee as if an iron is pressing on it. He shifts along on the step, inching his way back into the shade. He doesn't want to think about his mother. He thinks about the blonde stranger instead, and tension melts from his chest. The way she'd stood up to that bully. She must have been half his size, but she'd shown no fear. She'd been a bright blaze of gold – a small warrior – a sword of justice.

He remembers that she'd spoken English. Perhaps she wasn't Dutch after all. Although the Dutch he's met on his travels invariably speak English with a flawless accent. He slips a pencil from his pocket, and holding the pad on his lap, he starts to doodle, trying to sketch her from memory, his fingers working to describe the curve of her cheeks, her generous brows, her freckled nose.

3

Summer

She likes exploring the narrow streets, watching people going about their life. But this is her second day in Fort Kochi. She's trying to decide where to go next; maybe up into the Western Ghats, where there'll be more animals, more opportunities for photographs.

She clutches her Discman in her hand as she listens to her favourite album, singing along to it. She knows all the lyrics.

A hand descends on her shoulder. The unexpected human touch makes her let out a yelp. She spins around, wrenching her earphones out, and finds herself staring up into a face she recognises.

The guy looks mortified, backing off, hands in the air, 'Shit, sorry! I didn't mean to startle you!'

She swallows, her heart still thumping. 'No. Sorry. Overreaction.' She manages a smile. 'I was miles away.'

'You're English!' he says, as if he's surprised.

She nods.

'What are you listening to?' He gestures towards the dangling earpieces and Discman.

She switches it off and puts it in her bag. 'Kate Rusby.'

'Who?' He makes a puzzled expression.

'She's a folk singer. It's a compilation album.'

He raises one eyebrow, 'Aren't you too young for that?'

'Compilation albums?' She allows her voice an ironic twist. She knows what he means.

'Folk music.'

Here we go, she thinks. 'I suppose you'd prefer me to listen to Madonna?' She takes a breath. 'Folk music's timeless. It's not all long beards and floral skirts.'

'I should hope not,' he says with a wicked grin. 'Nobody with a long beard should wear a floral skirt.'

She refuses to capitulate. 'You say *I'm* old-fashioned,' she scowls, 'but *you* think someone with a beard can't wear a skirt.'

'It was a joke!' He throws up his hands. 'Can we start again? Pretend this conversation never happened?'

He's very tall. She notices that his T-shirt is on inside out. He runs his hand through his hair, making it stick up. She relents. It's not his fault that folk music is a sensitive subject.

'I saw you . . . the other day . . .' he's saying. 'You were facing up to that bully who kicked the dog.'

'It *is* you. I thought it was.' She feels guilty for jumping down his throat. 'Thanks for trying to help.'

The tips of his ears flush. 'No need to thank me. Think he was secretly terrified of you. I just gave him the excuse he needed to slink away.'

She smiles. Playing down his role in the whole episode makes her like him even better. Especially as she knows she has something else to thank him for too.

'Did you pay my bill?' she asks. 'I went back to apologise, but they said the young Englishman paid for me.'

'Yeah.' He rubs his nose. 'No big deal.'

The heat of the day penetrates her hat. Prickles of sweat make her scalp itch. She's always really careful about avoiding direct light.

She gestures towards the sky. 'We should get out of the sun. We . . . um . . . we could get an iced coffee or something?' she suggests. 'I owe you.'

He's already nodding. 'I know a nice place just around the corner.'

The café has a courtyard, and they find a table surrounded by cactus plants in bright pots.

'It *is* nice here,' she says, settling into her seat.

'Yeah,' he says, heaping sugar into his glass. 'Kerala feels different from the rest of India.'

'Have you been travelling in other parts too, then?'

'Uh huh.' He ducks his chin, and his hair flops into his eyes. 'Been here a while. Started in Delhi, then made my way through Rajasthan and Uttar Pradesh.'

She sips her iced coffee, sneaking glances at this well-travelled, blushing stranger. He has a nice face. Not drop-dead gorgeous, as her friend Laura would say, but open and warm. His eyes, framed with golden lashes, are an unusual colour – tawny is the word that comes to her mind. His mid-brown hair has sun-bleached streaks. Some women pay a fortune to have highlights like that, she thinks. But this guy obviously doesn't give much attention to his appearance – he's well over six foot, with broad shoulders and long, lanky limbs that are uncoordinated. He's already tripped up twice since she met him. His Celtic-fair skin has turned a reddish tan. He's wearing cut-off shorts to his knees, an old, faded, inside-out T-shirt and flip-flops.

'I'm Summer,' she says. 'Summer Blythe.' She puts out a hand. His hand swallows hers. Tucked inside his palm, her skin fizzes, as if they're generating an electric shock between them, and she lets go quickly. His eyes widen, as if he felt it too.

'Kit Appleby.'

She puts her hands in her lap. 'So, Kit Appleby, how come you can swan around India like this?'

He clears his throat self-consciously and shifts on his chair. 'I'd been saving for a car since I was a teenager, but decided to use the money for travelling instead. I've been away for,' he screws up his face, 'about . . . eleven months – but I've begun to wonder if I should go home . . . do something with my life.'

'What are the options?'

'Study to be a dentist or keep on with being an unemployed and impoverished artist.'

'Hang on,' she wrinkles her forehead. 'A dentist?'

'Unlikely, I know.' He takes a sip of his drink, rattling the ice cubes at the bottom of the glass. 'My mother's idea, not mine – only in the end, I couldn't go through with it. Five years of study and a lifetime of looking into people's mouths?' He makes a pantomime horror-face. 'I did a fine art degree. But of course, when I graduated, I wasn't being paid a fortune for pickling a shark, I was taking dead-end jobs and painting portraits that nobody wanted. One day I thought, what am I doing? I bought a plane ticket and . . . took off.'

'If your money's lasted this long, you must have been saving for a flashy car?' she says.

'I am a bit of a classic car nerd, I'm afraid, and I had aspirations for a Ferrari Dino 246 GT . . .' He pauses, as if she might comment. But she has no idea what that is. He goes on, 'I was going to get one that needed restoring. The only way I could ever have afforded it.' He blinks and looks away. 'The Ferrari money has lasted me so far – but it's getting a little thin now. What about you?' he asks, looking at her again. 'Have you been travelling long? Are you on an extended adventure, or is this a holiday and you have a job to get back to?'

She sits back in her chair. 'That's a lot of questions.'

He raises his large hands in a helpless gesture. 'Sorry. Only answer the ones you want – or none at all.'

She smiles, 'It's okay – I'm not that easily offended.' She notices that he doesn't fidget like most people, or stare over her shoulder at his surroundings and other customers. He appears to be giving her his full attention. 'I've been here nearly a week, and I have just over one more left,' she tells him. 'I was on one of those guided tours, but it felt like I was going through the motions, ticking things off. I wanted to explore a bit on my own.'

'A wise decision,' he says gravely.

Sudden anxiety clutches her heart. 'The thing is, I . . . I don't know when I'll ever be able to do anything like this again.' She takes a breath. 'So . . . I need to make the most of it.'

They've finished their coffees, and she thinks that this is the moment they'll stand up and go their separate ways. Only, she doesn't want either of them to go anywhere. It feels as if she's known him for much longer than the hour they've spent in the coffee shop.

She pays the bill, despite him trying to contribute his half, and he pauses as they step out of the café into the glare of the street. 'Would you . . . would you like to get something to eat later?' He pushes his fingers through his hair and glances at his feet. 'I know a nice place . . .'

'Another nice place?' She smiles, teasing him, and then nods quickly in case he thinks she's refusing. 'I'd like that.'

They look at each other, his pupils expanding like ink stains. She has that prickle again, down her spine. It's as if she's falling towards him. She blinks and drops her gaze.

'Where are you staying? I'll pick you up at seven p.m.' His voice sounds hoarse. 'If that's good for you?' he adds quickly.

She gives him the name of the hotel and they loiter awkwardly; she thinks he's as uncertain as her about whether to give a hug or do the air-kissing thing. She steps away without doing either, lifting a hand. He echoes her wave and walks in the opposite direction.

She feels odd, as if she's unbalanced by leaving him. She shakes her head. How crazy. He's a stranger. A conversation comes back to her; one she had with Dad years ago after Mum died. How did he know that she was 'the one'? she'd asked. He'd stared into the distance for a moment, his blue eyes watering, and then he'd turned and said, 'I just did. Almost immediately, before we'd even spoken. It was a feeling inside me. Very strong. Completely without reason.' And he'd laughed, 'Me. A man whose life is built on reason.'

She'd convinced herself that Adam was 'the one', but it turned out she'd been wrong. Now she understands how rare that love-at-first-sight thing is – how easy it is to be duped into believing in it and ending up disappointed. Mum and Dad had been lucky. All she knows is that, with Kit, it feels as if she's met a long-lost best friend. She'd wanted to reach across and take his hand, not just for pleasure, but for the comfort of touching him. She'd had an urge to run her thumb over his big, reddened knuckles, link her fingers with his.

Being here makes her want to take a chance. She feels free

for once. All her senses are open and alert to the beauty around her, to the possibilities in every moment. She's lived under the shadow of death for a long time, but this tall, untidy stranger has helped her out from under it; and even if it's only for a little while, she wants to know what it's like to live without limits.

She longs for the evening to come, for the moment when she'll see him again.

4

Kit

He stops as soon as he gets around the corner, staring up into the Indian sky. He almost expects to see a banner floating inside the iridescent air announcing that he, Kit Appleby, has met Summer Blythe, and she's agreed to have dinner with him. Trumpets, please!

Shit. Maybe he's getting ahead of himself. He needs to calm down.

But she likes him, he knows she does. She kept meeting his gaze and holding it. She sat with her body mirroring his. There's none of the doubt and confusion that sends him into a stomach-dropping rollercoaster of emotions: the up and down of trying-to-play-the-game and second-guess another person. Instead, it's as if they both share a secret – and without discussing it, they can both tell that the other one understands completely. They know the secret too.

He's dizzy with his good fortune. This beautiful woman, with her slightly crooked teeth and large, expressive, sea-coloured eyes, this brave woman, who he knows so little about, and yet who he has an instant affinity with, is interested in him.

She's sitting across from him now, in the open-air restaurant he discovered on his first night here. It's a family-run place. Chairs sit at drunken angles on an uneven earthen floor. There are bright plastic colanders serving as lampshades, candles on each table, and the cook is busy grilling fresh fish and vegetables on a giant smoking griddle in the corner. On a low stage, a four-piece band dressed in shiny jackets are enthusiastically rendering their own cover of 'A Horse with No Name'. Under the table, a small dog sleeps on the dirt, curled into a circle. Summer, he notices, has kicked off her shoes; she leans on her elbows smiling at the band. She twirls one of the little silver creatures hanging from her ear. 'I love it here,' she says.

'You haven't tasted the food yet!'

'I don't have to,' she says. 'Listen to that music.' She glances around her. 'The décor. The dog. I've never been anywhere like it!' She lowers her voice, 'And we're nearly the only tourists. Most people here look like locals. That's a good sign.'

He grins at her pleasure, feeling a glow of satisfaction that she likes his choice of restaurant. He takes a deep breath of night air, laced with delicious cooking smells, and another aroma that might be coming from the dog. But really, he thinks, nothing can spoil this.

'What do you do?' he asks. 'For work, I mean.'

'What do I do?' She stares at him for a moment with a non-plussed expression, and he's just beginning to feel embarrassed about asking such a dull, predictable question, when she clears her throat. 'Journalism. I . . . I work for magazines.'

'Magazines?'

'Magazines. Newspapers. I'm a photographer and . . . I write features,' she says.

'That sounds like an exciting job.' He remembers the camera around her neck when they'd met earlier. 'What kind of articles do you write?'

'Anything to do with nature and wildlife.'

'So, you take the pictures to go with your features?'

'Yes.' She blinks and glances at her hands.

'And you make a living from it?' He sits back. 'That's impressive.'

She picks up a fork and turns it between her fingers. 'I work mostly for local publications at the moment. And I have my own business walking dogs.'

He rubs his nose, realising that she's ambitious and talented as well as everything else. He's trying not to feel inadequate. 'I thought you must be a dog whisperer when I saw you feeding those strays.'

She laughs, 'Dogs are easy, compared with people.'

He half closes his eyes, 'I'm getting an image of you surrounded by dozens of hounds.'

'Not quite,' she smiles. 'My usual pack are three black Labs, a spaniel, and a lovely cross-breed. Five is my limit, otherwise you can't keep an eye on them when they're off lead.'

A young boy comes over and puts their plates and drinks on the table. They wait for him to finish.

'Going back to your pictures. Why animals?' he asks. 'I mean, I can tell you love them, but why do you like taking photos of them?'

'It's their honesty,' she says. 'They're always true to themselves. But I suppose . . . well, I'd like to think that maybe one of my images might change someone's mind about the animal in the photo, so they see them as an individual, instead of a meal, or a pest – or target practice.' She takes a breath. 'Enough of me.' She gives a small self-conscious laugh and takes a sip of her drink. 'You said you're thinking of going home,' she says. 'Where is that? Home, I mean.'

'Truth is, I don't know any more,' he says slowly. 'Mum lives in London, but I don't feel connected to the city, and it's an expensive place to be an artist.'

She swallows a mouthful of food and makes a noise of approval. 'Oh, God,' she puts down her fork and sighs. 'That's good.'

She scoops up another spoonful. 'Just taste this,' she offers. Feeling self-conscious, he leans forwards, opening his lips, and she bends across the table to put the food into his mouth. The act is incredibly intimate. Heat suffuses his face, and to his horror, he stiffens with desire. He sits back quickly and drops a napkin onto his lap.

'I've been in Cambridge as long as I can remember,' she's saying. 'Moved there when I was little, because Dad's a maths genius.' She tries a mouthful from his plate, without asking permission, pausing to make an expression of considered bliss. 'He taught at one of the colleges. It's a nice city, and the Fens are good for wildlife.' She smiles, 'I spend an awful lot of time waiting around in wet grass for a badger or fox to show up.'

Having recovered enough to be able to speak in a normal voice, he gestures towards her ears. 'And rabbits?'

She touches her earrings. 'These aren't rabbits. They're hares.' She leans on her elbows. 'My favourite animal. Grantchester Meadows at dawn, that's the place to find them. By the way, you never really explained why you gave up your car and spent the money travelling.' She pushes rice onto her fork. 'Was there a reason for taking off like that?'

He puts food into his mouth to give himself time to compose an answer. He chews and swallows. 'I hoped it might be good for my art – you know, finding inspiration, getting out of my comfort zone. And . . . actually, I do have my first commission,' he admits. 'Someone saw me drawing and asked me to sketch at a festival in Kollam.'

'That's brilliant,' she tucks her hair behind her ears, making the little hares swing at her lobes. 'Congratulations.'

He wants to take her hands and press his lips into her palms.

The band are covering 'Ain't No Mountain High Enough'. The dog under the table starts to scratch enthusiastically behind his ear with a back leg.

'Shall we get the bill?' she says.

All evening he's been wondering what it would feel like to kiss her. They walk back to her hotel and pause just outside the gates. He puts his hands on her lower back and gently pulls her close, reading her body language, checking that she's happy about being pressed against his chest. She holds herself still in his embrace for a moment before she puts her arms around his shoulders, her cheek against his chest.

And then they are kissing. And the moment stretches and intensifies, and all that exists is the kiss, and the two of them inside the kiss. When they break apart, they are both breathless.

'I'm going away tomorrow,' he says in a rush. 'The commission I told you about? It's a dance festival – I've been asked to sketch the dancers. It's only down the coast. I've booked myself into a beach hut in Varkala for a week. I know it might sound a bit . . . sudden. But. Come with me?' His pulse has revved into overdrive. He holds his breath.

She steps away, staring into the night. He notices she's biting her lip. His heart drops like a broken elevator. Shit. He's got it wrong.

Then she's nodding. 'Okay,' she says. 'Why not?'

'Yes?' he can't stop himself checking. 'That's a . . . yes?'

'Yes!' She's laughing and nodding. 'Yes! I'm probably crazy. But I'll come with you.'

He wants to shout with joy and sweep her off her feet into a bear hug, but he manages to stop himself, nodding enthusiastically instead, 'That's . . . that's great.'

She fiddles with her hair, her expression sobering, 'I mean . . . obviously I'll need to book a separate room.'

He's taken aback for a second. But then he's nodding again, 'Yeah. Of course. I'll call them soon as I'm back at the hotel.'

They kiss, losing themselves inside a longer, slower exploration of tongues, lips, teeth.

One day, he'll recount this story to some interested person, he thinks. And to their question of how they met, he'll tell them that on their very first date, he asked Summer to stay in a hut with him on an Indian beach. The friend will be surprised, shocked even, but they'll also be bowled over by the sheer audacious romance of it. And he'll say, but you see, I just knew straight away. We were meant to be.

He can't speak any of this aloud – she'd run a mile, and he wouldn't blame her. But he can't argue with this feeling inside him.

5

Summer

The kiss did it. As his lips met hers, heat flickered through her body, igniting a fire in the pit of her belly. Emotions whirled through her, making her want to cry and laugh; she quivered all over, and when they pulled apart, they were both breathless. She looked into his eyes and knew he felt the same. There was only one answer to his invitation.

She feels less certain when he picks her up from the hotel next day in the cool of the dawn. Plunged into shyness, she can hardly meet his gaze as she stands to greet him in reception. When she does, she can tell straightaway something is wrong by his awkward body language. 'I rang the beach hut place,' he tells her, heaving his bag off his shoulder. 'But they're fully booked.' He wrinkles his eyebrows. 'I'm sorry. Maybe it's the dance festival. I rang a couple of other places nearby to see if they had spare rooms. Everything is chock-a-block. I'll understand if you want to pull out. Or . . . I'm happy to sleep on the couch or . . . something.'

She dithers for a second. Can she really judge this man after knowing him for a couple of hours? She looks at his open, anxious face, his big hands, his mop of hair. 'All right,' she says. 'But I'll take you up on your offer to sleep on the couch.'

She sneaks glances at him as he gazes out of the train window. He turns his head and catches her eye. 'What?' He's not being combative, she realises, just curious, a little teasing.

She blushes. 'Nothing.' She clears her throat. 'Just wondering if I could tell how mad you are.'

'Mad?'

'You must be a bit, to invite me along on your trip.' She smiles to show that she's joking. 'But I meant . . . what unreasonable things you're prone to – phobias, temper tantrums – disgusting habits, like picking your toenails . . .'

'Ah,' he smiles. 'You want a run-through of my most annoying habits?' He brushes a hand through his hair, leaving bits sticking up. 'Fair enough. Let's see . . . what faults can I confess to? Okay. I lose my cool when I can't find my stuff – you know, keys, wallet, et cetera, getting myself into a panic because I'm late for something.' He leans forward, forehead wrinkling in thought, as if he's enjoying the confession. 'Actually, that's probably my worst fault. I'm not great at timing. I'm always missing deadlines, appointments. Buses. Trains.' He sits back in his seat. 'I made a big effort not to be late today.' He grins, 'Huge.'

'That's it?'

'Yeah. Otherwise, I'm completely perfect. Your turn.'

'I could write an essay . . . but the ones you need to know for the next few days . . .' She screws up her forehead. 'I'm probably . . . okay, I'm *definitely* obsessively tidy.' She counts on her fingers. 'I do not like chaos. Also, I need to eat breakfast before I do anything.' She pushes her long braid behind her shoulder. 'I get grumpy if I go hungry for too long.' She widens her hands apologetically. 'Low blood sugar.'

'I'd better make sure you never go hungry, then.'

She smiles. 'No danger of that.'

Their tickets are numbered, and he has the seat across from her. She wishes he was next to her. The train winds slowly through the dusty landscape, past sudden drops to big rivers where children swim and banana trees make lush green shapes. There are little dwellings. She watches a flock of slender white birds rise, long necks stretched out. Ibis. The name comes to her. Water oxen yoked to a cart. A line of women walking through a field, their saris fluttering, brilliant as butterflies.

'The hotel will have a phone, won't it?' she asks, remembering with a stab of anxiety that they'll be staying in a beach hut.

'In reception,' he says. 'Is there someone you need to contact?'

'Oh . . . one or two.' She avoids meeting his eyes. She doesn't want to explain – not yet. 'Life doesn't stop because you're away, does it?' she adds with a shrug.

She gets out her guidebook and buries her face, turning to the page about Varkala. She reads about the beach they're staying at. The Pearl of the Arabian Sea. Also known as Papanasam Beach, which means to wash away sins.

'I'm too far away over here,' he says, getting up and slipping into the empty seat next to her. 'Better.'

She feels centred again; the bulk of his shoulder warm against her. She leans into his side, brushing away her earlier fears. When the train pulls into the station, Kit hoists his huge, battered rucksack onto his shoulders and grabs her bags too. The crowded, bustling platform is a shock even though she's prepared for it. Porters shout and barter with passengers. A man with a large suitcase on his head steps in front of her, blocking her view of Kit, and she has to duck around and scurry to catch up. Families sit on the ground, reclining against bedrolls. Tea vendors clank aluminium kettles and cups. There are shouts of 'Chai, chai! Hot chai!' She spots a couple of monkeys on the opposite tracks, tails like question marks, and wants to photograph them, but Kit is disappearing into the crowd.

She hurries to catch up. She opens her mouth to tell him that she can carry her own bags, but Kit walks ahead with a determined, confident swing, as if he knows exactly where he's going. She follows in his wake, noticing a ragged scar on the back of one of his ankles. She wonders how he got it. It hits her again; she has no idea who he is.

He turns and waits, holding out a hand, shifting both bags into his other one.

She hurries forward. 'Give me at least one,' she says.

Wordlessly, he passes her the smallest bag. 'Right,' he says. 'Let's find this beach, then.'

'The Pearl of the Arabian Sea.'

He looks at her, eyebrows raised. 'That's its name?'

She nods, and they chorus at the same time, 'Romantic.'

He laughs. 'Let's see if it lives up to its promise.'

The pit of her stomach drops, as if she's stepped off a cliff. In a way, she has – jumping feet-first into a situation romantic enough for any starry-eyed honeymooner. But perhaps he's thinking this is just a few fun days at the beach. It doesn't matter. She wants this. She wants him. She did from the moment he stopped her in the street.

Summer grips her bag and Kit's fingers. This is her only chance to be reckless and wild. Her last chance.

6

Kit

Kit throws the door of the hut open and stares into the gloom. The cheapest accommodation in the whole of Varkala; he booked it before he asked her to come with him. The room is small and round. There are two windows without glass, just bamboo shutters, which are closed. After dropping the bags on the floor, he tries to open them, but the catches are stiff and he struggles, cursing under his breath, trapping his finger before he can fling them wide. He turns to examine the interior with trepidation.

The curved, ribbed walls are brown and oily-looking – some kind of lacquered bamboo, he thinks. A large bed takes up most of the space, a grubby mosquito net looped into a knot above the dark cover.

He swallows and turns to look at Summer, worried he'll see disappointment on her face, even horror. But she's pulling open a narrow side door and stepping into a flood of brilliance. He squints, confused for a moment.

'The bathroom has no roof!' she calls in a voice full of

delight. 'Look! We could be hit on the head by a coconut in the shower. Even worse, on the loo!'

He follows her into the tiny room and gazes up into open sky, fringed with fronds of coconut trees. There's a shower, rickety basin, and an old – but he notices with relief – European-style toilet. A crudely painted mural of waves spirals around the walls, a pink plastic washing-up bowl sitting on the cracked tiles.

'Not exactly five-star,' he says gruffly to cover his embarrassment.

'I love it.' She walks back into the bedroom and stands in the doorway, gesturing towards the sea, 'It's got a five-star view.'

He joins her at the threshold, sucking his finger where a bruise blooms. She's humming under her breath. Their round thatched hut is one of several identical ones in an enclosure with a dried-up ornamental pond in the middle; narrow paved paths run between the huts, leading to the reception and exit. By a stroke of luck, their hut is closest to the top of the cliff and has an unobstructed view of the ocean glittering below. Just outside the fence is a footpath that winds along the edge of the cliff.

'We'll be on the beach,' he says. 'Most of the time.'

She murmurs an agreement, picking up her braid from the back of her neck and twisting it on top of her head, perhaps hoping for a breeze; he can't resist kissing the soft area of exposed skin. She laughs and drops her plait, turns and kisses him briefly, hands on his chest. 'Okay,' she says. 'I'm going to reception to make a phone call. Then I think we should find somewhere to get lunch, don't you? I'm starving. We can unpack later.'

He likes the fact that she's clear about what she wants – proactive. He can imagine that proactive might edge into bossy at times, but he finds it endearing.

After she goes, he lets himself crash out on the bed, sprawling across it, star shaped. He wonders who she needs to call. Work, perhaps? He imagines her talking to someone at a magazine news-desk, getting her next assignment. She's connected to the real world, unlike him. 'Life doesn't stop because you're away,' she'd said, shrugging, as if he understood. But that's exactly what's happened: his life at home has stopped. He hopes she doesn't think he's a hopeless dreamer. He has the commission, he reminds himself.

It's sweltering in the hut. There's no air-con, but a large, dilapidated-looking fan is fixed to the ceiling. He finds a switch and the fan revs into action. He resumes his position on the bed, wafts of warm air ruffling his hair, brushing his skin. The roaring noise is punctuated with clicks as the blades revolve. He closes his eyes. The early start is catching up with him. His limbs relax, tension seeping from his shoulders.

As he slips into unconsciousness, he remembers her enthusiasm for the open-air bathroom, and smiles. Lots of people would be sulky or shocked or resentful when faced with the basic realities of the hut, but she looked for the positives.

He wakes, bleary, sticky-mouthed, disorientated, and blinks, remembering where he is. The fan is whirring and clicking above him. The mosquito net has been unknotted and falls around the bed in a pale haze. A blonde head rests in the hollow under his shoulder. She's undone her braids and gold spills around her sleeping face; her cheeks are pink, eyes closed, her parted lips moving slightly as she breathes. Something in his chest releases as he looks at her. His shoulder is aching a little from the weight of her head. He carefully manoeuvres to get more comfortable without waking her.

He squints down, taking in the tilt of her nose, the sprinkle of freckles, the dusty length of her eyelashes against her cheeks. He wants to keep lying here looking at her, to hold the weight of her skull against him, feel the damp warmth of her skin through his T-shirt, listen to her breathe. He watches as she twitches her nose like a mouse, then rubs it with her eyes still closed.

Her lids flutter open. They look at each other for a moment in silence.

'Hello,' she says.

'Hello, you,' he kisses her salty forehead. 'Did you get through – your phone call?'

She nods and yawns. 'You were fast asleep when I got back. What time is it?'

He lifts his arm with some difficulty, as her head is pinning it down. Screwing up his eyes, he stares at his watch, 'Looks like . . . four o'clock.'

'No wonder I'm hungry,' she says, sitting up beside him, her hair falling in tendrils down her back. Her cheek is creased from the folds of his T-shirt. For a second, he imagines her old, with wrinkles instead of creases, her beauty weathered and softened, her skin familiar as his own.

He's not hungry for food. It's her he wants – to kiss her sleepy mouth, run his hands down the lines of her body, inhale her, taste her. But he remembers what she said about low blood sugar. He remains lying down and rubs his thumb over the sleep-lines on her cheek. She puts her hand over his fingers, holding them still against her skin, looking down at him with a steady, questioning gaze.

His heart slows; his breath stops. The moment shivers, full of possibilities. Then, without breaking eye contact, she turns her head and slowly kisses the centre of his palm. He feels the rub of her tongue, cat-like against his skin. He lets out a faint groan.

'You were right,' she says hoarsely, 'about this place. There is a problem. I've just noticed it.'

'A . . . a problem?' He can hardly speak.

'Yes,' she whispers, leaning down, holding herself above him, 'there's no couch.'

Then her mouth is on his. The power of their kiss sends shock waves through his centre, and they are kissing hard, removing their clothing at the same time, tugging at waistbands, pulling T-shirts over heads, fumbling with buttons. And at last, the relief of being naked, the joy of her pressed against him, skin to skin, hot and sticky and sweaty. He maps out her body with the span of his hands, savours her on his tongue. They roll across the bed, getting tangled with the mosquito netting, laughing. He loves the way she fits against him, her curves rounding into his harder planes, her limbs shorter than his, her toes brushing his calves as she lies beneath him.

Then she's on top of him again, her hair falling around them in a gleaming curtain. He hears her breath at his ear, the swell of it like waves. She tastes as salty as the sea. His heart is huge inside his chest. The strength of his feelings overwhelms him. It's painful, this surrender, this falling, this drowning inside her. But if this is death, he thinks, bring it on.

7

Summer

The golden-pink path of the sun's dying rays leads directly to them, as they sit on stools at a round table, sipping iced beer and eating crispy samosas. Her fingers and lips are slippery with oil; the beer cold and bubbly in her mouth, tickling her tongue. The side wall of the café is open; sea and sunset fill the view.

Her body sings, her skin sensitised and tender, lips slightly bruised. They took a shower afterwards, standing under the shadowy fronds of coconut trees, the water hardly more than a cold dribble, making them gasp.

A young, smiley couple come in with a baby strapped to the father's chest – the mother and father are tanned with blond dreadlocks.

'Bet they're German,' he says, seeing where she's looking.

'It's brave of them to bring a baby.'

'Yeah,' he nods, putting his beer down. 'But that's how I'd like to be, if I had a kid. You know, take them on adventures, show them the world.'

'Do you want children?' She blots her mouth on a paper napkin.

'Definitely – do you?'

'I haven't thought about it much but – when the time is right – at least one.' She glances at Kit and wonders what their child would look like.

He's staring at his hands. 'I'd try and be a good father, play with them, make them tree houses, tell them stories.' He looks up. 'I think it's important to talk to kids and listen. Listening's probably the most important bit.'

'So, no Victorian parenting for you, then.'

She's teasing, but he doesn't smile. 'It's just that words are important,' he says quietly. 'Speech is a gift. It's easy to take it for granted.'

A brief look of pain flits over his face, and she leans across the table, 'This sounds personal?'

'I stopped talking when I was four years old.'

'Completely?'

'Yeah. Totally silent.'

She stares at him, trying to imagine a silent four-year-old. 'What made you stop?'

'Nothing in particular. I just . . . couldn't get any words out. I kind of froze when anyone expected me to say something.'

'How long did it last?'

'Nearly a year.'

'God . . . how frightening.' She wishes she could go back in time to comfort him. 'Is that when you started drawing?'

He nods. 'I've always been happiest with a pencil and paper. When I'm sketching . . . I'm myself.' He reaches across to take her hand. 'Can I draw you?'

She feels her cheeks flush. 'Me? Yes, please. I'd love it.'

His book is poking out of his bag, and she reaches down and puts it on the table. 'Can I see?' She wipes her fingers before she turns pages, squinting down. She is silent, pausing at each one. 'These are wonderful,' she says as she reaches the end. 'So full of life and energy. I knew you'd be good. But these are incredible.'

'Thanks.' He seems pleased and embarrassed.

She's impressed by his talent, almost in awe of it. It must be much harder to make a drawing or painting than to take a photograph. 'You capture people really well,' she says, trying to give him the confidence he seems to lack.

'Nobody wants them,' he says. 'There's no money in it.'

'Really? I can't believe that.'

'Right now, the money's in conceptual art. And I'm inspired by old masters – Rembrandt and Vermeer. I aim to paint realistically, but not with the photo likeness that's popular at the moment.' He frowns. 'I want my work to look like paintings not photos. I want to discover what's under a person's skin – bring their character and experiences to the surface.'

'That's exactly what I see in your sketches. Honestly. You can't give up.' She closes the book. 'You're a proper artist. And . . . and don't forget you've got your commission,' she remembers. 'Someone else has recognised you too.'

'Guess I got lucky there.' He gets up to order more drinks.

'It's talent, not luck!' she calls after him. He turns and grins. She picks up the pencil and doodles a heart on the back of the sketchbook in a corner, then she writes in tiny letters: 'Actions speak louder than words! But both are best of all.' Kerala, 1993, Summer xx.'

Kit returns with two Star beers. They clink bottles, toasting each other. 'To us,' he says.

'To our amazing good luck to be sitting here in the most beautiful place on earth,' she says.

'With six more days,' Kit adds.

As they lie together in the dark, under gauzy netting and the noise of the fan, Summer presses her nose into Kit's neck and inhales, wanting to imprint everything about him upon her, to absorb him, make him part of her. The tiny details seem of utmost importance: the whorls in his fingertips, the scar on his ankle, the smell of his skin just below his ears.

'You haven't mentioned your dad,' she says. 'Only your mum?'

'They split up when I was a baby,' he says.

'Oh . . . I'm sorry,' she wriggles closer.

'My mother was a ballet dancer before she got pregnant. After he left her, she never really recovered – said her career was over, her body wrecked.' She feels him tense up. 'She tried to make me hate him too. For abandoning us. For ruining her life.'

She says nothing, waiting for him to continue.

'Thing is, it was me that was the problem. It took me a while to work it out. Must have been about twelve when I realised that *I'd* destroyed her body and her career – *he* got her pregnant, but I was the unwanted result that ruined everything.'

His voice is raw, and she tightens her arms around him. 'Do you see your father at all?'

'My dad?' He clears his throat. 'Yeah,' he says. 'Despite what Mum says about him . . . he didn't abandon me. Always remembered my birthday, took me on holidays. And we have a . . . a great relationship now.'

'I'm really glad,' she whispers. Tears prick the corners of her eyes. She can't bear to think of how it must have been for him as he grew up: his disappointed mother grieving her lost opportunities, blaming the father, and making her little boy blame himself too. No wonder he'd stopped talking. 'Does he live in London too? Your dad?'

'No, he's in Wokingham,' Kit says. 'Suburban bliss.' He kisses her forehead. 'What about you?' he asks. 'Are your parents happy?'

'They were,' she admits. 'Mum died when I was fifteen.'

'Oh, God. I'm so sorry.'

She swallows, not wanting to dwell on her loss, not when he's had such a hard time. 'There was a lot of laughter and singing and being silly in our house,' she says. 'Even when Mum lost her hair and couldn't get out of bed, the tenderness and humour never went away.'

'That's . . . wonderful,' he says, and she hears the catch in his voice.

'I was lucky.'

He kisses her then, and they take longer this time, exploring each other's bodies, discovering what pleases the other. Kit takes her by the waist to slide her further down the mattress, so she doesn't bang her head on the headboard, lifts her hips and slips a pillow under them.

Afterwards, she relaxes in his arms, leaning into him. She has a crick in her neck from resting on his shoulder but doesn't want to move. A song has started up inside her head, words tracing themselves onto her mind.

'What are you humming?' he asks over her shoulder.

'Sorry.' She grins. 'I do it all the time.'

'I've noticed,' he says. 'What's the song?'

'"The Seeds of Love". A folk song. Really ancient. From the sixteen hundreds.' She sings the first couple of lines softly, without lifting her head, so that vibrations move from her throat into his chest.

'I like that idea,' he murmurs. 'Planting the seeds of love . . .' His voice trails away.

She lies awake for a few moments more, listening to his breathing deepen and the rush and sigh of the sea far below on the dark beach; the ballad continues in her head, lyrics weaving themselves through her mind, the old story of love and betrayal playing out.

But it doesn't have to be like that, she thinks. Sometimes there are happy endings. Sometimes flowers grow and bloom and have their time in the sun.

8

Kit

Every day after breakfast, they make their way to the beach, passing tiny boutiques selling handmade jewellery and colourful slippers, signs advertising yoga classes and Ayurvedic massages, then down a narrow, steep path winding along the side of the cliff.

Today, she's singing as she walks ahead of him, carrying her towel, a sarong twisted around her hips. Her voice is beautiful. Strong and pure.

They find their usual spot, spreading towels next to each other. Kit hires a striped umbrella and positions it carefully, digging the pole in deep. The sand is white, fine-grained, the sea a tumultuous blue, waves crashing onto the shore. Body surfers ride the breakers; swimmers wade in, shrieking as they're turned over by a rush of water. Sitting under other umbrellas are Indian families, the women immaculate in saris, the men in neatly pressed chinos, taking tea and watching the tourists with amused incredulity.

There's so much to look at, and his fingers itch to hold his pencil. But the person he wants to draw most of all is lying beside him in a scarlet bikini.

'Your voice is beautiful,' he says. 'Must feel amazing to be able to make that sound.'

'Singing makes me feel free,' she says.

'Painting does the same for me.' He makes a concerned face. 'You know, you *might* even be changing my mind about folk music,' he smiles. 'Do you perform at folk conventions or something?'

'Um. Yeah. Sometimes.' She rubs her nose sheepishly and gazes out to sea. 'Just open mics . . . evenings in pubs.'

He thinks it's adorable that she's so modest. 'One day someone's going to sign you to a record deal.'

'I don't think so,' she laughs. 'It's possible that you're biased.'

He closes his eyes, listening to the noise of the waves, the endless, cyclical push and pull – a call and response, like her song. The air is redolent with brine, fresh with breeze, despite the burning sun. He lets his mind drift, and it circles back to Summer. He doesn't want to pretend with her, not ever. He'll have to take a risk and tell her how he feels. They need to work out how to keep seeing each other after India. Come up with a plan. But maybe she'll think it's too soon for that?

He's aware of a shadow behind his lids and opens his eyes into her smiling face. 'Swim?

They yelp at the scorching temperature of the sand. He grabs her hand and they run straight into the waves, wild spray flying up into their faces, droplets of crystal exploding in the air. The sea swallows them as they dive in and under. They lose each other's fingers. The world becomes liquid. A swirling, eddying place where he turns in confusion, not knowing which way is up and which way is down, tumbling in gravity-free somersaults. Seeing sun-dazzle, he thrusts towards it and breaks through the ocean with a gasp.

She surfaces next to him, gasping. They play in the rolling breakers, body surfing, jumping the waves, flailing and snorting with laughter as they're dunked over and over before they stagger back to their umbrella and sit down, dripping, panting. She towels off her hair, rearranging the straps of her bikini. He tilts his head from side to side to try and remove the water inside his ears.

'Leftovers from breakfast,' she says as she offers him an orange.

He peels it, enjoying the tangy juice on his tongue.

'Can I sketch you again?' he asks, swallowing the last segment.

'You're not bored yet?' She sits cross-legged.

'Never,' he says. 'If you could just get into a comfortable position? I'll do a few quick sketches to get the feel of you.'

'Think you did that last night,' she murmurs, eyes wide and innocent.

He grins. 'Don't distract me.'

He makes some lines on the page, looking at her differently now that he's drawing her. He examines her legs from this perspective, how the curve of her thigh joins the angle of her hip; and then, moving his gaze upwards, he draws the three small rolls of flesh at the shortened inner bend of her waist, created by the way she's leaning on her left hand. She has a roundness to her, a generosity, a wholeness that he finds aesthetically pleasing – and a big turn-on.

He finishes the sketches and lets her see. She examines them with noises of approval and admiration. 'Can I keep one?' she asks.

'Of course. Choose whichever you like.'

After tucking the picture carefully into her bag, she drags her towel out from under the umbrella. 'I'm going to have fifteen minutes in the sun,' she says, yawning. 'It's lovely and cool with this breeze.'

He yawns too and lies back under the umbrella. He's sated from sun and sea, from the satisfaction of drawing her, the intensity of his working gaze. The only thing he'd change right now is to be next to her. But he's too sleepy to move.

When he opens his eyes, he's dozy and confused. And thirsty. His skin is itchy with dried salt. The sound of the sea reminds him of where he is, and he sits up. Summer is sprawled in direct light, fast asleep with her straw hat over her face. He checks his watch – they've been sleeping for at least an hour, maybe longer. He lifts the edge of her hat and blows on her cheek, 'Summer? Wake up. We fell asleep.'

She sits up, looking groggy. 'Oh God … how did that happen?' She crawls back under the umbrella and finds her water bottle, tilting her head to gulp, wiping the overspill away with the back of her hand. 'Hope I haven't got burnt.'

Her skin has turned neon pink. They take a cold shower, and he tells her to lie on the bed, so that he can massage her with the aloe vera gel she's found in her washbag. She radiates heat like an oven. 'Drink more water,' he insists, pouring her a glass from the bottle of mineral water.

'Damn,' she says, after she's drunk the whole glass. 'How could I have been so stupid?'

'You're not stupid. It wasn't your fault you fell asleep.'

'It's just …' She swallows and looks away. 'My mum. She died of skin cancer,' she says, her voice wobbling. 'How could

I go and turn myself into a lobster? And . . . and we only have a few days left.'

This is his cue. Speak, he tells himself. 'We . . . we don't have to say goodbye just because the holiday ends,' he says quickly. 'Do we? I'd . . . I'd like to keep seeing you when we're at home . . . if you would too?'

She stares up at the knotted mosquito netting, 'I'd like that.'

He lets himself breathe again.

'Except . . .' Her eyebrows kink. 'It's not always going to be this easy.' She waves her arm around the hut, 'This isn't real.'

'Yes, it is,' he says, trying to sound positive rather than defensive. 'It *is* real.'

'We'll be different at home – different people.'

'Not really,' he counters. 'Our feelings will be the same.' He frowns, sitting on the bed next to her. 'It's hard to talk about this stuff without sounding like an idiot.'

'Hey,' she says quietly, slipping her hand into his. 'I understand.'

He wonders why it's so hard to voice his real feelings. Fear of rejection. Embarrassment. He doesn't want to be a coward, like his father. They are silent for a while, and he thinks he should try again, explain exactly how much he wants to keep seeing her, tell her about the sense of belonging he gets just from being near her, but as he prepares to speak, she's already talking.

'I know where I'll be,' she pauses. 'I'll be back in Cambridge. But . . . where will you be?'

He startles. He hasn't even thought about it. 'All I know is . . . I don't want to stay in London, especially not with my mother,' he says slowly. 'I need to find a place of my own.'

'I've always had a dream of moving to the Suffolk

coast.' Her voice brightens. 'My mum grew up there. Around Woodbridge and Leiston. It's my favourite place in the world.'

'What makes it so special?'

'There's the sea, of course . . . the wild, dark North Sea, but there's heathland too, which is rare in Europe, and freshwater marshes, reed beds and rivers.' She sighs. 'It's beautiful in a bleak way – not rolling green hills; it's flat, with shimmering light, huge skies.'

'Sounds ideal for painting.'

'Yes.' She turns to face him. 'I've heard it's popular with artists.'

'Oh, yeah?'

'Yeah – I've read about some quite famous artists' colonies based there. Maybe you should check it out, if you're looking for a place to live?'

He smiles at her enthusiasm. 'It would be even better if you were there too.'

'I will,' she says. 'One day. But Suffolk and Cambridge aren't so far apart, about an hour and a bit by train . . . if you moved there, we could visit each other?'

He feels a rush of happiness. It's as good as a plan. 'Sounds perfect.' He props himself on one elbow to see her better. 'I'll check it out when I get home.'

'Great,' she says quietly.

He scoops her to his chest, kissing her. She kisses him back and then breaks off. 'Ouch!' She winces.

'Shit! Sorry.' He lets go, careful to avoid her flaming skin.

She makes a regretful expression. 'Don't think sex is going to be possible tonight.' She passes him the bottle of aloe vera.

'Mmm,' he agrees, tipping a pool of gel into his palm and spreading it over her thigh. 'But . . . just out of interest . . . how long does sunburn generally last?'

She clicks her tongue at him in mock disgust.

9

Summer

Light comes through the wonky shutters in glancing shafts of dusty gold. She winces as she moves on the sheet. Turning her head, she sees the pillow is empty next to her. The door to the bathroom is open. He's not in the hut.

She remembers their conversation last night, and her insides clench. He wants to keep seeing her, which is exactly what she wants too. But it means a confession on her part. And she's frightened of losing him when she's only just found him.

He comes in with a tray laden with food. 'Thought you should eat breakfast,' he says, standing in the open doorway.

She absorbs his broad smile and tousled hair, the little flourish he makes as he kicks the door shut behind him with a flick of his heel. The thought of losing him makes her breath stick in her throat. She forces a smile and sits up as he places the tray on the bed. There are two cups of milky coffee, frothy pineapple juice, a basket of croissants, and sliced papaya with lime. She uses a teaspoon to scoop up some of the cool fruit. He perches on the edge of the mattress and dunks a croissant into his coffee, glancing up, 'Sorry, disgusting habit.'

'Dunk ahead.' She blows a wisp of hair out of her face. 'Fine by me.'

They eat hungrily in silence. He's dropped crumbs on the sheet and there's a moustache of pale froth on his top lip. She's learning how messy he is. She reaches over and wipes it away with one finger, licking it clean. She pauses. This. Happiness floods her, filling up every cell in her body. She can't imagine waking up in the morning without him.

'You okay?' he asks.

She blinks. 'Just wondering if I can eat a third croissant.'

'Course you can,' he says, passing her the basket. He glances at his wristwatch. 'Suppose I'd better get going if I'm going to make the dance festival.'

She'd forgotten he was doing that today. Dismay coils in her belly. Damn. Her confession will have to wait until he gets back.

'You're not really up to coming with me, are you?' He's looking at her burnt skin with a worried expression.

'No . . . I think I should stay here.'

'Will you be all right?'

She prepares her face before she looks at him, 'Of course I will.'

'If you're sure . . . then I'll go . . . just for a couple of hours.'

'Good,' she touches the curve of his forearm, hoping she sounds positive.

'It's my first commission,' he says, earnestly. 'First chance to feel like a real artist.' He gives a short self-deprecating laugh, but she knows how important this is to him.

'How are you going to get there?'

He looks doubtful.

'They hire bikes at the hotel,' she suggests. 'It's only in the next town.'

'You are determined to get rid of me, aren't you?' He's obviously relieved that she's encouraging him to go.

'Yes!' She gives him a little push. Her acting skills better than she thought.

'Okay! Okay!' He holds up his hands in surrender. 'For a couple of hours. Then I'm coming straight back.'

'Understood.' She reaches up to kiss him with a swimmy sense of deep familiarity – as if they've fast-forwarded thirty years. She wonders what he'll be like when he's fifty-six. Perhaps they'll look back at this day, and she'll be able to admit she didn't want him to go. But this commission could be the start of his career, and that's what they'll remember it for, not her lies.

She gets onto the bed, listening to him taking a shower and cleaning his teeth. He comes back into the room and pulls on his shorts and a T-shirt from the chair, runs a hand through his damp hair, 'Will I do?'

'Nicely.' She manages a grin.

She has a sense of urgency, a need to tell him everything. Get it over with. If she's honest about who she is, she can also be honest about how she feels about him. *I love you, Kit.* She tastes the words on her tongue.

He swings his bag onto his shoulder and goes to the door, then comes back and leans down, careful to avoid her sore patches, and kisses her again, a longer, lingering kiss. His hands go to her face, holding her between his palms. Her stomach knots with lust. She wants to pull him onto the bed with her, never let him go. But she sits back, touching her mouth with her fingertips. 'You'll be late.'

He rolls his eyes, 'And you forgot to mention you were bossy.'

She feels homesick for him already. 'Stop prevaricating.' She waves a hand, smiling. 'Go! Make amazing art.'

Just before he leaves, she blows him a kiss, and can't stop herself calling out, 'Don't be too long!'

After the door closes and she can no longer hear the slap of his flip-flops on the path outside, she lets her expression fall. Her stomach churns with anxiety. She doesn't know how he'll react when she confesses. He'll be hurt and confused. She expects that, even anger – but what if he changes his mind about her? She turns towards the cooling whirr of the fan above.

It's strange to be alone in the room.

She imagines him cycling through the lush Keralan landscape, his sketchbook and pencils in his rucksack. He might pass an elephant or a herd of water bison. There will be monkeys at the side of the road. To any onlooker, he'll be unmistakably English, as if he's stepped out of an E. M. Forster novel: a young man who plays cricket, who looks good in a dinner jacket. And yet none of that is true – except the dinner jacket part. He would look handsome. But he's not aristocratic or mannered or privileged. His height and the width of his shoulders belies the vulnerability in him. The silent child inside. But she can see it, and it makes her want to protect him.

Meeting him is the best thing that's ever happened to her; she didn't want to ruin these precious, shining days. He might have felt sorry for her, pitied her, and she couldn't have borne that. She wanted to be different here – to be the self she imagines she could be – strong and confident, fulfilling her dreams.

When he's back, she'll tell him who she really is.

*

She wakes, not knowing how long she's slept. Even with the fan on, the room is muggy and close. Her eyes feel gritty and her head pounds. She glances at his watch – left behind on the bedside table. He must have forgotten it after his shower. He'll be at the festival by now, she thinks, sketchpad on his knee, pencil moving skilfully over the page. She loved it when he drew her – although she'd felt oddly invisible inside the focus of his gaze. She had ceased to be herself, she thought; had become instead the sum of her body, each sinew and muscle, every flaw and detail; all of her physicality magnified and recorded in the strokes of his pencil. But when she'd looked at the drawings, she'd understood that he'd seen so much more. He'd witnessed something of her inner self, her mood, her longings. Her fear was there too, large inside her eyes. It had taken her breath away.

Her ears are alert for the sound of his feet on the path outside, the noise of the latch lifting. She calculates the hours ahead, trying to guess when he might appear. Squeezing out the remains of the aloe vera tube, she rubs her burns, remembering Kit doing it, how gentle his hands had been, how careful he'd been not to hurt her. She wants to have him here beside her. Her body yearns for his, every bit of her alive with an ache more acute than the sting of sunburn. She allows herself another glance at his watch, slipping it onto her own wrist. He'll be here soon.

There's a polite knock on the door.

At last! She fights the urge to run and fling it open, and instead wraps herself in a sarong and walks towards it, a broad smile stretching her mouth.

The knock comes again.

'Why, how very formal of you, Mr Appleby . . .' she's saying as she pulls the door open.

The manager of the hotel stands there looking serious. 'Miss Blythe.' He inclines his head, rubbing his hands together. 'There is a phone call for you in the lobby. It is most urgent, the gentleman says.'

She clutches the receiver tightly. 'Yes?'

The line crackles and hums. 'Summer?' It's Dad's voice on the line, faint, whistling across continents.

Her heart tumbles from a great height. 'Oh God,' she steadies herself. 'It's Effie, isn't it? How bad is she?"

'It's . . . it's urgent.'

'I'll try and change my flight for today.'

'She's on dialysis at the moment . . .' There's a shuddering intake of breath. 'She went downhill fast.'

'I'm a match,' she says. 'A good match. She's going to be okay. I'm on my way. Hold on, Dad.'

'Come quickly,' he whispers.

She puts the phone down with trembling fingers. Her mind is racing. Her heart thrums, but not with panic. She knew this day would come. She's been preparing for it for years. They've done all the tests. She's been afraid for so long, but now she feels weirdly calm.

She goes back to the hut and gets dressed, throwing things into her case, grabbing her stuff from the bathroom. For once in her life, she rams everything in, without a thought for order. Where is Kit? He should be here. She can't leave without seeing him.

She sits on the bed, feet flat on the floor, spine straight, listening for the sound of his flip-flops. The dark walls of the hut are like a cage. She opens the door and paces up and down over the crazy-paving path under the flaying sun. Every time someone appears through the door to reception, she startles and blinks at them through the confusing wall of light. Slow seconds pass. Her sense of urgency tightens like a mangle, wringing out her insides until she can hardly breathe. She's going to have to leave without seeing him. She goes back into the hut and writes her address and phone number in capitals.

Kit- here are my contact details in case I have to leave before you get back. My sister is very ill. Kidney disease. I have to go home. I'm her donor. I'm sorry I didn't tell you before. I'll explain everything when I see you.

She leaves the note beside a bedside lamp. Then runs back and adds:

I hope you'll forgive me. X

She carts her case towards reception but doesn't go in; she lingers a bit longer in the scrubby garden by the dried-up ornamental pond. He'll have to walk past her to get to their hut. She sits on a low stone wall, her suitcase at her feet like a patient dog, her gaze on the door, willing him to appear. She bites her thumbnail, thinking of Effie in hospital, attached to that machine.

Where is he? And she remembers him saying how bad he was at timekeeping, how he missed appointments and deadlines. She touches his watch, hanging loose around her wrist. He doesn't even have a way of telling the time.

In the cool of the reception, she asks for some paper and a pen. She writes:

Kit, I can't wait any longer. I have to go. Please come and find me at the airport. I'll be trying to get on the first available flight home.

She shoves the paper across the desk at the receptionist. 'Can you give this to Kit Appleby? I need a taxi please, to Cochin International. It's urgent.'

She sits in the back of the Padmini, and stares out of the window, not able to see anything, wishing herself home, longing to be with Effie. She puts her hand on her stomach, over her gift, her life-saving cargo.

10

Kit

He drifts, weightless, at the bottom of a dark, nowhere place. Voices come to him, flickering bursts of static, saying things that make no sense, talking in words he doesn't understand. He remembers the sound of sirens. He remembers lying on his back, and moving down a bright corridor, masked faces staring at him. But now he's trapped in this dim fog, where only a dull aching pain connects him to a body and he has no sight, no voice.

Then, as if a blindfold has been removed, he begins to see. At first, there is a confusing jumble of shapes, a light that makes him wince and blink. He has a prickling, sharp sensation in his nose – disinfectant or bleach, he thinks. The strange landscape he's arrived in makes itself known to him. He's in a narrow, raised bed, his arm inside plaster, one leg encased in white and raised by a pulley. He has a needle stuck in the back of his hand. A thin tube tethers him to a machine. Another tube is connected to a bag of saline hanging above his head. He notices another appearing out of the sheet with yellow liquid seeping through it. A nurse's kind, round face comes close.

She smiles at him and takes his pulse, his temperature, checks the information transmitted through the screen above his head. She's wearing a red and blue tunic, and blue pyjama-type trousers under a white cotton coat. All the other patients and staff are Asian too. His mind shapes the word ... Kerala. And then: Summer.

'The doctor will see you soon,' she says. 'Don't try and get up.'

'How ... long have I been here?' he says. His voice sounds odd – thin and weak. The words scratch.

'Two days,' she says.

She walks away, and he lies back against the pillow. Two days? He frowns, closing his eyes. Does Summer know he's here? Does she know about the accident? The accident. He squeezes his eyes shut. He's falling backwards inside his mind, landing on a burning road, gripping handlebars, feet pushing pedals. Dust in his eyes and mouth. Flying metal, shards of glass.

He struggles for air, forcing the images away. He stares around the ward, at the strangers in beds, the hum of hospital life. Outside the window, the sky is an unbelievable blue, and he sees a jumble of buildings, the tops of palm trees.

A gaggle of doctors are making their way through the ward. They hold clipboards. They approach his bed. One of them is obviously the most senior. The others listen to him intently.

'Good day, Mr Appleby.' He's an elegant man, with liquorice eyes. He doesn't look as though he would ever get his hands dirty or raise his voice. 'I am Dr Sharma. You are a fortunate man. The accident you were involved in was most serious indeed.' Kit can't keep up with the flow of words. The consultant nods towards the plaster cast enveloping his lower right arm. 'A laceration ... fracture.' Kit struggles to listen, but he's thrown by a technical word he doesn't understand. 'Cracked ribs. Broken wrist.' The list of his injuries continues. His head is thick with congealed information. 'Femur,' the doctor's saying. 'Open fracture. Surgery . . . screws . . . plate.'

Kit waits for him to finish speaking, 'When . . . when can I leave?'

There are looks of gentle disbelief amongst the group; nodding heads. Someone gives a quiet titter, silenced with a stern flash of Dr Sharma's dark eyes.

'Patience, Mr Appleby,' the doctor says. 'It will be weeks yet. We will arrange more X-rays to see how you are healing.'

He falls back onto the pillow, exhausted. A nurse hovers by his bed as the others leave. She gives him a sympathetic glance.

'Has someone come to see me?' he asks. 'A blonde girl?'

She shakes her head.

'Where are my things?'

She gestures to the cabinet next to the bed. When he manages to tug the rucksack out of the cabinet and onto the bed, it's scuffed and torn, but contains the stuff he'd been carrying with him the day of the accident; he roots through. There's his sketchpad, pencils tied together with an elastic band; some broken, but still useable. He pulls out a ripped T-shirt, his shorts. At the bottom, there is a pair of flip-flops, stained with something that looks like oil. His watch is missing – maybe it got smashed in the accident. He finds coins, his wallet, passport, a matchbox with the name of a hotel inscribed in red: The Beach Hut Hotel, Varkala.

Could she still be there? She was supposed to go home, he remembers. She has a job to get back to – but maybe she's been able to extend her holiday? She must know that something's happened to him – maybe she heard about the accident and realised he was caught up in it?

He opens his sketchbook and flicks clumsily through pages using his left hand, stopping at a drawing of their small hut with the thatched roof. He turns another page and finds the sketches of her. She smiles at him with her slightly crooked teeth. She is all curves. She is beautiful. He runs his fingers over the pencil lines. Her expression is warm, happy. But there is sadness too. He doesn't know where the sadness comes from. Underneath he's written: Summer.

His heart expands. He feels her breath on his face, sees her smile. Her sea-coloured eyes. He moves his left hand, remembering how her hair twisted and slipped between his fingers, a tumble of silver, gold, and bronze.

He looks again at the drawing of the hut. The round room with the dark, lacquered walls. He can visualise the bed with the mosquito netting. He can hear the sea boiling against white sand, smell suntan lotion on her warm skin, see her beside him in a red bikini. As he struggles to put the sketchbook in his bag, he notices something written in a corner of the back cover. 'Actions speak louder than words! But both are best of all.' Kerala, 1993. Summer xx.' He rubs his fingers over the tiny letters.

FEBRUARY

Two months of Summer

11

Kit

They take out the catheter and antibiotic drip; he's no longer tethered to the bed, but frustratingly he can't use crutches because of his wrist, so he has to rely on someone pushing him in a wheelchair.

There's a payphone on the wall in the corridor. One of the patients from the bed next door, a young man called Anil (fractured shoulder from a motorbike accident), agrees to wheel him to it. The corridor is full of people waiting. They crouch on the floor, take up all the available chairs. Women in saris handing out food, children running up and down. Anil weaves the wheelchair in and out as if he's driving his motorbike. Kit reaches up and dials the number on the book of matches. He pushes coins into the slot.

'Can I speak to Summer Blythe?' he asks, his heart pounding. 'Room twenty.'

There's so much noise around him, Kit can hardly hear. He clamps a hand over his free ear. 'Sorry. What?'

The voice on the other end tells him that Miss Blythe has checked out.

‘When?’ Kit asks, swallowing his disappointment. ‘When did she leave?’

There is a rustle of pages being turned. ‘The fifteenth of January.’

Kit frowns. ‘You’re sure?’

‘Perfectly sure, sir.’

He frowns, confused. She left the same day he went to the dance festival – the day of the accident.

‘Can I help you with anything else, sir?

‘It’s Kit Appleby speaking,’ he admits. ‘From room twenty. I’m sorry I haven’t been back . . . haven’t done a runner, honestly – I was in an accident . . . I don’t need the room any more. I’ll be there when I can to collect my stuff and settle the bill, I promise.’

He puts the greasy receiver back in its cradle.

The fact that she left the hotel on the day of his accident feels like a betrayal, and yet, he doesn’t know why it should. There must be a good reason for her going early.

‘No luck?’ Anil asks. ‘Your girl – she wasn’t there?’

Kit shakes his head.

‘Some women,’ Anil says. ‘They are all about tricks and things. Not steady. Reliable. Not wife material. Maybe you should forget her. Go back to England. Plenty of other pretty girls there, heh?’

‘No,’ Kit shakes his head. ‘This girl’s different. She’s not someone I can forget.’

‘You’re speaking about love?’ Anil clicks his tongue and clutches his heart, making a face. ‘I feel sorry for you, my friend.’

Kit tries to answer with a smile, but if she’s not at the hotel, he has no way of contacting her, not while he’s stuck here. But she will have left him a message, he reassures himself. It’ll be okay.

'I just need to make one more call,' he says. 'My mother.'

Panic pushes against his sternum; his throat tightens, the old fear swelling through him again.

He must have been about four years old. It was bedtime and he was barefoot and sleepy in his mother's room. She was sitting on the edge of her bed, wearing a pair of shoes he'd never seen before. They were the bright red of his Lego bricks. He liked the colour. But he didn't like the thin spiky heels. She stood up, growing taller and taller, her head reaching far above him. He had a beaker of apple juice in his hand, and as he stared up, the beaker tilted forwards.

His mother gasped, her face flying down towards him, her mouth open so that he saw her pink tongue and the dark gleam of metal in her back teeth.

'Jesus! Look what you did!'

The red shoes were spotted with darker red. Juice dripping from the spout onto the leather toes.

'Can I never have a moment of peace?' she was shouting. 'Do you have to ruin everything?'

He backed away. She was taking off the shoes. 'Go to your room,' she was yelling. 'Go to bed.'

As he turned to obey, a shoe flew past him, thumping against the wall. He took another step, gasping as something bit his ankle. Shock and pain whooshed through him, fireworks sparking in his brain. He turned to look down, expecting a shark or alligator or snake. Another red shoe, heel sharp as a blade, lay nearby. His skin was welling with red, oozing down the back of his foot onto the carpet in a ribbon of colour.

His mother was kneeling next to him, her eyes wet; she pulled him against her chest saying, 'Kit . . . I didn't mean to, I didn't mean to. I'm sorry.'

And something inside him closed like a door.

'Does it hurt?' she was asking. 'You might need stitches. You mustn't say Mummy threw the shoe, okay?' She gave him a little shake. 'Okay?'

He stared at her. *Yes, Mummy*, he knew he should say – but each word stuck to his tongue like fluff. They clung to the wet inside of his mouth. He felt sorry for the balled-up words. They didn't like it outside. They were frightened of all that space, of making other angry, bigger words slice them into pieces, or squash them down into nothing. They were safer inside his head.

Anil is discharged and he leaves with a crowd of relatives, including his elderly mother and father, a host of helpers to carry his things, escorting him from the building with wide smiles. He gives Kit a cheerful thumbs up as he leaves the ward. As soon as the bed is changed, another patient takes his place. He arranges several brightly coloured icons on his bedside table; Kit recognises the physician of the gods, the four-armed Dhanvantari. A favourite in the ward.

Kit has carefully torn the sketches of Summer from his drawing pad and stuck them to the side of his bedside cabinet. The nurses admire them when they give him bed baths: 'Such a pretty girl,' they say. 'What a lucky man you are.'

Summer, the drawings of you are the first thing I see when I wake up, and the last thing I see before I go to sleep. Not that I sleep much in this place. It's never dark enough or quiet enough. Do you know what happened to me the day of the festival? That I was involved in an accident? A terrible pile-up on the road to Kollam. I'm *not sure how I avoided death, but my leg got messed up pretty badly. I broke a few ribs, smashed my arm, fractured my wrist. My drawing hand, so I'm worried about that. Now I'm stuck in a hospital bed. I miss you. I wonder where you are and what you're doing, and if you are thinking of me. I know you've left our hotel. I hope you don't think I've abandoned you. I would do anything to be able to speak to you right now, to see you, hold you.*

The weeks pass. Kit gets to know other people in the ward; but none of them stays as long as him. Flocks of noisy relatives and friends visit patients, laughing and chatting, passing babies over beds, bringing ropes of yellow flowers and stacks of silver containers containing food; delicious smells of curry and spice linger in the air. Sometimes they offer him bowls of rice, neat folds of warm bread. He smiles, nodding his head, hands together in a gesture of thanks. '*Nandi*,' he says, which is thank you in Malayalam. It makes them laugh. But his aloneness swallows him when they turn back to the patient they're visiting.

He has more X-rays. Thank God for travel insurance, he thinks as each day passes. They remove the cast from his arm with an electric saw, vibrations tickling. His wrist is newly lumpy, thicker, his fingers stiff. He learns to use crutches, managing to swing and lurch his way clumsily around the ward. He still feels as though he's been run over, but then he remembers the driver of the scooter. Why wasn't he, Kit, the one to hit the dog, to be crushed by the bus, the wheels of the lorry? It comes down to numbers, he thinks; an invisible, accidental calculation of time and space. Unseen laws of physics had been working around him. It was as if he'd fallen through a gap in time, an escape-hatch. He shakes his head. He's not sure what to call it: a miracle, fate, luck.

That's what he feels, as he hobbles and lurches, the crutches digging in under his arms. Despite everything, he feels lucky. He's seen death here, seen the poverty and desperation of others waiting in the corridors. Not everyone can be saved. Not everyone gets the care they need. He's got hope. He's getting better. And every day brings him closer to her.

12

Summer

Summer and her father pause at the open door into the private room. Effie is asleep, dwarfed by the machine beside her, a tangle of wires connecting her to the metal bed. There's a line inserted into her neck; a small, dark bruise blooms at the entry point. Summer turns to her father, whispers, 'What happened to putting an AV thingy in her arm?'

'No time,' Dad whispers back. 'It was an emergency.'

A sheet of ice slides through her. Her little sister looks worse than she's ever seen her – yellow-skinned, bone-thin. Effie's lids flutter open, her eyes huge and unnaturally dark in her face, but her mouth stretches into a smile. 'You're here,' she whispers.

'Hello Little Bear,' Summer slips into the chair next to the bed. 'You're going to have a brand new kidney – I've been keeping it safe for you.'

'Sorry,' Effie's voice is hoarse. 'I . . . didn't want to make you . . . come back early.'

'Silly,' Summer says. 'I'd fly to the moon for you. You know that.'

She gets a lip balm out of her handbag and dabs some onto Effie's chapped mouth. She can't show her fear. Statistics are on their side. Only one in five hundred donors die. The odds are not quite so good for the recipient. There are instances of patients' bodies rejecting the new organ, bleeding, blood clots, death.

Don't think about that, she tells herself. Stay positive.

There's no reason why it won't be a textbook transplant. Her kidney – her left one, they've told her – will find a new home in her sister's body, and will do its job of filtering, purifying and balancing, allowing Effie a normal life, free of pain for the first time.

Summer is allowed to spend the night in Effie's room. She and Dad will take it in turns, so that Effie will always have one of them with her. They put out a cot. But there's no chance of sleep, not with the hum of machines, and the noise from the hospital corridors, the constant visits from nurses checking Effie's stats.

'Summer?' Effie's voice floats over the edge of the bed.

She sits up, 'I'm here. Can't you sleep?'

Effie moves her head on the pillow. 'I'm scared.'

Summer slips onto the bed, easing herself onto the edge of the mattress, lying next to her sister, careful not to dislodge any of the equipment. 'I'm a bit scared, too,' she admits. 'But this operation's going to change your life. It's the beginning of exciting things. You can plan to go to university, be independent.'

'But if I die . . .'

'You won't die.'

'But if I do,' Effie insists. 'Then you have to promise to do all the things you want to do – your photography, writing, singing ... maybe you could go to university. I know you wanted to ...'

'None of that matters—'

'It does,' Effie says fiercely. 'You've given up so much to look after me.'

Summer says nothing, her throat is tight.

'Promise,' Effie says. 'Promise me you'll live your dreams?'

'Okay. I promise,' Summer manages.

Effie falls asleep, her breathing laboured and uneven. Summer stays on the mattress, stroking her sister's forehead.

The next morning, Summer slips into the bathroom to wash and clean her teeth. When she gets back, Effie is awake.

'Have they told you when it's happening?' she asks. 'The op?'

'I just need a few more tests, apparently,' Summer says, wrapping her fingers around Effie's hand. 'Just to bring everything up to date. One final hurdle, and we're on.'

'Cool,' Effie whispers in a hoarse voice. 'And then I can eat what I like. Drink gallons of Coke. And party, party, party ...'

Her eyelids droop. Summer can sense Effie slipping under the surface, and it reminds her of Mum when she was close to dying; that loose, dreamy, falling-away from the moment, the dipping in and out of two different worlds. It terrifies her.

'Stay here, Little Bear,' she whispers. 'Hold on. We're going to fix this. Everything's going to be fine.'

Underneath her anxiety about Effie, the hurt she feels over Kit's silence burns deep down. Maybe he met someone at the festival? She pictures a lithe, dark-eyed dancer, or a tourist; someone who got chatting to him when she saw him drawing. Maybe, she worries, there was always a girlfriend in the background – and that's why he was travelling in the first place, to have time to think, to have a break from his serious relationship, before he went back to her. She remembers that he'd seemed reluctant to answer when she'd asked what made him change his plans and use his money to travel instead of buying the car he'd always wanted.

She can't look at any of it; can't allow herself to remember those days on the beach, those nights inside the fall of netting, his skin hot against hers. This is her punishment for lying to him, for imagining, even for a moment, an existence without her sister. She squeezes her eyes shut. Guilt slips into her heart, sharp and unforgiving as a blade. Why did she tell Kit about living on the Suffolk coast? Why did she think she could continue to see him after lying to him? It was all nothing but a fantasy. Her life is with Dad and Effie. They need her. They have since she was fifteen years old.

13

Kit

He's moving around more easily – the crutches don't feel as awkward, now that he's got the hang of them. Under his cast, his skin itches like crazy. At night, his thigh aches with a deep, throbbing bruise of pain, but his leg is healing. Metal plates and screws fusing into bone. He's getting stronger.

Free of the plaster on his wrist, he's using his right hand again, making sketches of the people in the ward: doctors, nurses, patients, visitors. His fingers are stiff, his wrist sore, but the relief of being able to move a pencil over paper is revitalising; it returns him to himself, allows him to lose himself in observation. Like a kind of meditation. Hours speed past when he's sketching.

Patients and visitors gather around his bed to look at his drawings, and he tears sketches out of his book and gives them to anyone who asks. People lift their children up to get a better look. Kit draws cartoon characters, creates little graphic short stories, making the kids laugh. Soon people request portraits, and he obliges; someone fetches extra paper, handing it over with an expectant smile. One elderly man, a frequent visitor to a brother with two broken legs, nods appreciatively when Kit shows him their joint portrait, and gives him some money. Kit tries to refuse, but the man insists.

Summer, today I heard the rushing chatter of a big crowd and hobbled over to the door of the ward to see what was going on and saw a huge gathering of people all dressed in white filling the corridor – they were like a sea in their pale robes. Turns out they were the relatives of a patient thought to have died. Premature mourners. A junior doctor was set the task of breaking the happy news to them, that no funeral was needed – and encourage them to disperse. A few looked rather disgruntled.

Later on, a young girl came into the ward, and threw herself at the feet of one of the senior doctors. She was kissing his shoes, and he was trying to get her to stop, obviously embarrassed. Two nurses came and helped her up. I think the doctor had saved her mother's life.

The hospital is overcrowded. There are long queues. The staff are frantic, rushed off their feet. But the people are kind. They have the gift of sharing. I love the way they express themselves – so much more fluently and honestly than we do in the UK.

I'm drawing again, and luckily my wrist works fine, just a bit stiff. It's good to be using my hand. My sketches have become a bit of a novelty in the ward, and I'm often asked to draw someone, and usually have an audience when I do! Someone actually insisted on paying me for a portrait today. My first paid commission!

But my healing is taking a very long time, and all I want to do is get out of here and find you. I miss you, Summer. I miss you so much.

14

Summer

After her mother died, Summer sometimes caught a glimpse of her, as if she was really there, alive: Mum at the stove, long bare feet under flared jeans, a rollie between the fingers of one hand and a wooden spoon in the other. When Summer got back from school, her mother would emerge from her pottery studio, wiping her clay-dusty hands on her apron to cut fat slices of bread, spreading them with honey. She'd put the plates in front of them both and ask about their days. She had a knack of remembering the important details. She made their house into a home. Summer couldn't even make a meal without burning it.

While she chopped vegetables for supper, she dreamed about her 'before' life: at a disco with her friends, giggling under the flickering lights, wondering if Adam would notice her. In that life, she'd be painting her nails glittery purple, watching *Top of the Pops*, eating food made by her mum, her school uniform clean and folded in her drawer, put away as if by magic.

But in this life, dirty laundry piled up in the basket on the landing, spilling onto the floor. There was a grey tinge to the sink, toothpaste trails around the plug. All the sheets on the beds needed changing.

In this life, if she didn't cook, nobody would eat. Dad was more hopeless in the kitchen than her.

'Look after Effie,' Mum had said.

I am, she told her inside her head. *I'm trying, Mum.*

But there were Effie's medications to be managed, hospital appointments to write on the calendar on the wall so Dad didn't forget them, and Effie needed a special diet: not too much or too little potassium or protein. Summer was scared all the time about getting it wrong and being the person who stopped her sister's kidney from working.

Upstairs, a bundle of laundry in her arms, she heard noises from behind the bathroom door.

Effie was at the sink, scrubbing something with the nail-brush, her thin shoulders shaking with hiccuping sobs, her bottom half naked. The familiar sharp smell of ammonia spiking the air.

'It's okay,' Summer said quickly. 'We can put them in the washing machine. It's not your fault.'

She tugged her sister away from the sink, dried her soapy hands, blotted her face. 'I miss Mum,' Effie said, her bottom lip quivering.

'Me too, Little Bear.'

She scooped Effie into her arms; a girl made of paper and sticks.

She curls on her bed, her thoughts returning to Kit, trying to understand why he's abandoned her. Perhaps he's angry – it would have been a shock to discover the scribbled note she'd left him. She remembers kneeling astride him on the bed that first afternoon, feeling powerful and seductive, bending low so that her hair fell around them. Kit had groaned, holding her waist, the compass of his fingers and thumbs fitting exactly under her ribs.

She hasn't taken his watch off since she got home. The heavy metal face bumps her wrist bone. There's a permanent mark there now, a small tenderness. Sometimes she presses it, just to feel the bite of nerve-endings connecting her to him.

A thought hits her, and she goes cold. Maybe he's been mugged, or fallen off his bike? She uncoils, lying straight. Why didn't it occur to her before? It's the only thing that makes sense, because even if he was angry, he'd never ignore her like this; not the man who held her face between his palms, who looked at her as if he could see right into her soul. And he wouldn't have gone off with another woman. At the very least, he would have told her.

She listens to her father moving around the house, the creak of his footsteps on the stairs. A rush and gurgle of water through pipes. He's about to leave for the hospital – his turn to keep Effie company. He calls out goodbye, and she answers. She waits for the sound of the front door closing. She counts inside her head. Dad often has to return for something he's forgotten. When she gets to two hundred, she pushes her feet onto the floor and goes down the stairs to the kitchen. She takes the receiver from the phone on the wall and calls international directory enquiries.

She jots down the number of the Beach Hut Hotel, and dials.

It rings and rings. She imagines it trilling on the reception desk. Through the window, the breeze will be sighing among coconut palms, waves crashing onto white sand below the cliff. The Pearl of the Arabian Sea.

'Good morning, Varkala Beach Hut Hotel.' The voice sounds thick with sleep. She wonders what time it is there.

'I'm calling to speak to Kit Appleby,' she says in a hushed voice.

'One moment.' There is a long pause. A hiss and crackle. She wonders if she's been disconnected or forgotten. 'He is not here, madam.' The voice is breathless.

'He's . . . he's checked out, then?' Hope fills her. Maybe he's on his way to Cambridge.

'One moment.' Again, a pause, filled with rustling. Echoes of time and space on the line. 'He has not checked out,' the receptionist sounds disapproving. 'There's a bill to settle.'

Tangles of confusion take over her mind. She can't think straight. He's all right. Not dead or injured. He's still living in their hut, so he must have seen her note. She slumps to the floor, holding the phone. 'Can you tell him . . .' She thinks of Kit in their room, the brown cover, the mosquito netting. What can she say? There's too much to explain. The only thing that matters is Effie. The fact that he hasn't even phoned, hasn't shown the slightest interest that her sister is critically ill, or that she, Summer, is about to undergo a serious operation, shuts a door in her heart. 'Nothing.' She struggles onto her feet, replacing the receiver quietly.

15

Summer

They wear matching green gowns and have matching intravenous drips in their arms. With their free hands, they hold each other's fingers across the gap between their trolleys. Her sister's hair, like her own, is tucked up under a cap. Effie's hollow face is pale, her freckles bleached out.

'Everything's going to be fine,' Summer whispers, her voice as steady as she can manage. 'A bit of me will always be with you now.'

Effie is wheeled away first. The girls uncurl their clasped fingers at the last moment, and Effie forces a smile. 'See you on the other side!' she says, raising a hand.

'You bet,' Summer calls out.

After the swing doors close, Summer turns to the orderly, 'She's the bravest person I know.' She blinks and swallows. 'Never complains. Since she was little, she's been putting on a cheerful face.' She stares up at him. 'She's going to be all right, isn't she?'

'You're in the best hands,' he squeezes her shoulder, 'both of you.'

They are to be in next-door operating theatres, so that Summer's kidney can simply be walked through at the right moment. Her operation will be shorter and less complicated – her surgery will start after Effie's, and she'll be out before her.

She lies flat on the gurney, feeling floaty from the pill they've given her, removed from her body. The anaesthetist looks down, eyes kind above his mask. 'You'll feel a little scratch,' he says. 'I'm going to get you to count back from ten.'

Ten . . . nine . . . eight . . .

Darkness folds itself around her, the drug a wave in her blood, dragging her under.

She wakes.

Something is wrong. Her chest tightens with fear. A nurse comes close. Summer moves tight lips. 'My . . . sister?' The words scratch.

The nurse checks her temperature. 'Try to rest.'

'She . . . she's okay . . .?'

The nurse touches her hand. 'Try not to talk.'

Summer's throat hurts. Her insides hurt. She moves her hands down over the blanket and encounters a swollen curve. Her belly is huge, still puffed up with gas from the transplant. She's weak and woozy, her eyelids impossibly heavy and, although she tries to keep them open, they are two traps snapping shut.

She surfaces again, out of a black hole of nothingness. Dad is sitting by her bed. He starts when he notices she's awake and leans close, taking her hand in his, 'Dearest?'

'Effie?' she whispers.

He doesn't need to say anything. His red-rimmed eyes hold her gaze.

She moves her head on the pillow, tears seeping under her lids. It can't be true.

They squeeze each other's fingers until it hurts. That small pain is something to grasp, a twig protruding from the side of a mountain as she dangles over a ledge, a roaring flood far beneath her. She hears its cold, rushing darkness. She will fall. She doesn't think she will survive.

16

Summer

They did everything they could, the surgeon explained. There was unexpected haemorrhaging. Her fragile heart gave up.

She remembers the nephrologist telling her that we have two kidneys for the same reason we have two eyes, two ears, two hands, two legs – a person can afford to lose one, she'd said, and with small adjustments, cope perfectly well.

But what about losing a sister? She had only one. One irreplaceable sister. There are no adjustments possible. No way of coping.

Despite not sleeping or eating, her body persists in carrying on, learning to manage with one kidney. The organ is growing in size, compensating for the loss of its twin.

But Effie is dead.

Home seems strange, smaller and shabbier than she remembers, as if she's been away for years instead of weeks. Each of Dad's collection keeps telling the time; pendulum, spring-driven, digital and electric, marking the passing moments. The house is filled with ticks and chimes, tiny hands inching forwards, numbers blinking. She'd forgotten the noise they make, a slight, mechanical scratching, as if clockwork mice are marching through the rooms.

She doesn't read the papers or watch TV, but she puts the radio on to mask the emptiness of the house. The news is mainly about the recession, and the hope that it might be nearing an end. Then she hears about a little boy found dead on railway tracks. Just over a week later, it's all over the news that two ten-year-old boys were responsible for the child's murder. She stops listening to the radio after that – the world has fallen into a darkness that matches her own.

Kit's watch lies heavy and cold around her wrist. Wearing it reminds her that meeting him happened, that he exists. Those few days together were real, even if it was only a holiday romance to him. But the heat and brilliance of India seem like a mirage here, in the middle of an English winter, in a land stripped of colour. With Effie gone.

The Cambridge house rattles in the winds howling across the Fens, straight from the mouth of a Siberian storm. She and Dad move around each other with careful, trembling steps, as if they are both invalids. She's glad of the aching pain in her belly – it is only right that her body echoes the hurt in her heart.

At the funeral, she enters the church with Dad on one side, Laura on the other. She's known Laura since primary school, ever since she saved Summer from the misery of playground isolation by commanding her to join a game of British bulldog. From that moment, the world had righted itself. Laura is the only person Summer knows who's bossier than her. The six-year-old Laura was sturdy and determined, with a mop of black curls and impressive scabs on her knees. Minus the scabs, the twenty-six-year-old version doesn't look much different.

It was Laura who helped her register the death and organise the funeral. They picked out hymns and readings together, a poem by Yeats. And for the beginning, when everyone is arriving, Summer wants a recording of 'Time of Your Life' from *Dirty Dancing.*

'God, she loved that track,' Laura sighed.

'And I'm going to sing,' Summer said. 'A folk tune. The one she liked best.'

'You sure?' Laura touched her arm. 'That's a big ask.'

Summer nodded. 'I want to. For her.'

When the time comes, and the vicar moves from the pulpit, Laura whispers good luck as she makes room for Summer to squeeze out of the pew. Summer's legs tremble. The church is packed. Every pew full. People standing at the back. She doesn't dare risk looking into anyone's face; she keeps her gaze on her feet, moving across ancient, worn stone. She's going to sing with no accompaniment, as if it's just the two of them: Effie propped against pillows, and Summer sitting on the bed. When Effie was sick, they spent hours listening to the radio, talking, playing board games. And her sister would ask Summer to sing 'to take away the pain', she said.

Summer stands with the altar behind her, looking above the heads of the congregation, her gaze falling on a coloured glass window at the end of the church. She imagines Effie, her elfin face tilted upwards, that wicked grin twitching the corners of her mouth. There's a hush of anticipation. She pinches the skin of one hand with the thumb and finger of the other. She won't let grief clog her throat. Nothing will ruin Effie's song.

'Why don't you sing in public?' her sister used to ask. 'You're not supposed to hide your light under a bushel – whatever that is. You should be out there making other people happy, not just me.'

'I don't have time for that,' Summer used to say. 'Too much to do.'

Truth was, she was scared. But she let Effie believe that looking after her and the house was holding her back from doing things for herself.

This is for you, she thinks, as she takes a breath and opens her mouth. Every syllable, every note, for you. The only apology I can think of for not saving you.

Forgive me.

Her chest expands. The old song flies out, words swelling to fill the air of the church, swirling around the rafters, over the heads of the mourners. When she reaches the end, she realises her cheeks are wet. She looks at the people in the front rows and sees they're crying too.

Effie's classmates and friends are here. Parents. A couple of teachers. Summer recognises one of the nurses who looked after Effie in hospital. Lots of their neighbours from Kimberley Road have turned up.

After the service, she takes Dad's elbow. He shuffles next to her, tremors shuddering through him. He has aged years in just a few weeks. On her way out of the church, she notices Adam sitting at the back. They catch each other's eye, his look like a warm hand squeezing her shoulder.

Walking into the grey chill of the churchyard, the vicar waits just outside; he takes her limp fingers. 'That was a beautiful tribute to your sister,' he says. Her face is frozen, her mind numb. She can hardly reply. Her mother is buried here too. Maybe they're together now. She'd like to think so, although she has no faith in the existence of a place after death. She has no faith in anything. Love wasn't enough to save her sister.

Before dawn, she wanders the house like a spirit, unable to sleep. She goes into her sister's room, touching everything, finding pink hair bobbles with long auburn hairs caught in the elastic. She picks up a pot of bubble-gum lip-gloss and electric blue mascara, remembering how excited Effie had been when she got them – she'd wanted to grow up so badly.

She discovers notebooks neatly arranged on Effie's bookshelf. Opening them, she finds her sister's brief comments about how she was feeling that day; no word of complaint, just facts.

Was sick again today. Couldn't eat. Felt too tired to do my homework. Another injection.

Why did Effie have to suffer? She was so brave and hopeful. Like Beth in *Little Women*. It's always the best people that have the worst luck, she thinks, with a twist of bitterness in her throat.

She discovers that some of the notebooks are covered with her own writing – stories she made up for Effie when she was little. She remembers Effie's present to her before she left for India – a pretty exercise book covered with a red and silver pattern, 'so you can do some writing while you're out there. You could put the two together – pictures and writing. You're so good with words.' Effie, her number one fan. Always encouraging, always positive. Summer stops, winded with guilt. The book is somewhere in her own room, hardly used.

There'd been moments when she had been filled with childish fury that caring for Effie meant she couldn't live the life she was supposed to live – *not fair*, she'd sometimes whispered to herself, as she'd made another meal, put the wash in the machine. She'd wanted to go to university like other teenagers, get drunk, have fun.

But it was Effie that life had treated unfairly, not her. It was Effie who couldn't do any of the things she longed for, who couldn't live as she wanted. But that afternoon in hospital, Effie had only been thinking of Summer. 'Promise me,' she'd said, 'you'll live your dreams.'

She kneels on the floor with Effie's fluffy slippers in her hands, their floppy ears, glassy eyes and noses an approximation of feline faces. Summer slips her hands inside to feel the imprint of her sister's slender feet, her bony toes. Effie knew all the actors' lines from *Dirty Dancing*, could sing all the songs. She must have watched the end dance a million times; the video almost worn out. 'Nobody puts Baby in the corner,' she'd murmur, smiling.

Summer gets into Effie's bed, hugging her pillow, inhaling the last traces of her scent, sobbing into the lilac mohair that Mum knitted the year she got ill. 'I'm sorry,' she whispers. 'I let you down.'

As the dawn chorus starts up outside the window, she goes into the bathroom. Lit under the sudden glare of light, her face is a gluey mess of snot and tears. But, apart from her tear-ravaged complexion, she looks the same. It's unbearable that life carries on as normal, that there is no outward sign to tell people of her loss.

She wants to look like she feels. She wants to punish herself for being alive when Effie is dead. She wants a ritual to express her misery. These are the reasons she finds for herself afterwards, but she has no real clarity as she picks up a pair of nail scissors from the toothbrush pot and cuts off a strand of hair at the roots; she just knows that it's something she has to do. She drops it into the basin, where it curls in on itself, glistening against the porcelain. Quickly, before she can change her mind, she slices through more, giving herself a quiff of spikes, like a nascent punk. Her fingers are trembling, the nail scissors too small to get through her whole head, so she goes downstairs and finds a pair of kitchen scissors, hacking off the rest without looking. When she's finished, her skull is lighter, her newly naked neck and ears strangely cool. She pats her head, feeling the blunt, wispy tufts, and scoops up the soft mess of her shorn hair.

She goes into the garden. She's wearing thin cotton pyjamas; her bare toes spread against slick, wet grass. She shivers, craning her neck to look up at the curve of inky blue, the far-off pinpricks of starlight, and she can't help thinking that these are the same stars that had shone down on her and Kit, except they'd been huge in India, brighter, warmer. He'd given her hope, and she'd accepted it greedily, as if it could be given as a gift. She opens her fingers, releasing clumps of hair onto the dark lawn, scattering it like handfuls of ashes. It feels like a kind of offering. A release. As she goes back into the house, she wonders if a bird or animal will take it for a nest.

Early next day, she cycles into the fen with her camera. She knows she's not supposed to be cycling so soon after the operation, but her own health seems an irrelevance. She takes it slowly along the flat, straight roads, wincing if she pushes too hard on the pedals; but she needs to be outside, in nature. There's a fox set that she knows, the home of a wise, old vixen. Summer has photographed her several times over the years, seen her mothering two litters of pups. She leans the bike against a tree, and walks into the fen, picking her way around a dyke, trailing her fingers across willow twigs, noticing they've turned orange for spring. Seasons keep turning, new life appearing.

Pushing through swathes of moor grass, she settles herself in a den of her own making. Her breath mists the air. She's wearing fingerless mittens so that she can use the camera. They are the softest sage, etched with cream embroidery. Effie gave them to her last Christmas. 'I know your favourite colour is red. But these won't frighten the animals,' she'd said.

She checks Kit's watch. An hour has passed. Her thighs ache and cramp grips her calves. She sees some rabbits, a stoat, but it's the fox she's come for. Effie had particularly loved a photograph of her with her pups play-biting her ears. 'They're like a cross between a dog and a cat, aren't they?' Summer had found a frame and fixed the photograph to her sister's wall.

A change in the atmosphere makes the hair rise on her arms. Something moves out there, a wind swaying through the sedges. As she looks, the breeze metamorphoses into a creature, a sleek flame flowing from the undergrowth, tail held low, ears pricked. A dark muzzle scents the ground. Summer stares at this cunning survivor. She raises the camera and lowers it again without taking the shot. The vixen gazes straight at the place Summer hides, and turns, slipping back into long grasses.

What's the point of taking pictures? How can she go on doing the thing she loves when Effie is dead?

It's hard to believe how carefree she'd been in India, how filled with life and love. That person has gone. She'll never be able to feel like that again – she's numb, dead inside. But she can't give up; she still has Dad to think about. She straightens, rubbing her arms, and cycles home wearily, her shorn head tucked against the wind.

17

Summer

Her father is in his study, staring at numbers, equations and algorithms. Although he's retired, he doesn't know what to do with himself if he's not puzzling out some new and complicated theory. He's tried to explain how maths is a voyage of discovery in a world built of logic.

He's blinking at her through his spectacles, eyes faded to a washed-out denim. There is something innocent about him, something that makes her want to look after him, as if the purity of maths keeps him apart from the thrust and greed of the rest of the world. Mum knew how to bring him down to earth, make him laugh. Summer can't manage the same trick. Disappearing into his world of logic is the only thing that's saving him now – but she's afraid he'll get stuck there and never come back.

'Dad,' she says. 'Can I talk to you?'

He turns slowly and stares at her, puzzled, 'What have you done to your hair?'

She touches the choppy tufts. 'I . . . I didn't want it any more.'

'Summer,' his voice wavers and he takes a step towards her, 'dearest . . .' He widens his fingers as if to touch her hair, and then lets them fall. 'Punishing yourself won't bring her back . . .'

'I hate myself,' she swallows, her throat closing. 'Why wasn't my kidney enough? Why couldn't I save her?' A sob breaks free, and she puts her face in her hands.

He pulls her to him. 'We just need to keep plodding on. Day by day, step by step, we'll make it through. Somehow.' He swallows. 'Effie would want us to. We need to be brave. And you are brave. I'm proud of you.'

'Dad . . .' She's crying big sloppy tears, and he holds her close. He's only a few inches taller than her; his shoulders feel delicate, smaller than she remembers. She closes her eyes, inhaling the familiar scents of Pears soap, sandalwood shaving cream, and the whiff of the moth balls he keeps with his shirts. He holds her until she stops.

She blows her nose and wipes her eyes and fumbles behind her to sit on the broken-down leather chair in the corner. He sits at his desk, swivelling to face her. She shuffles to the edge of her seat, hands caught between her knees.

'You wanted to ask me something?' he asks.

'Remember how Mum used to say that one day she wanted to go back to the Suffolk coast?'

He looks confused. 'Suffolk?'

She nods. 'She used to talk about the children's home she lived in, near the beach at Leiston?'

'She never liked being landlocked,' he sighs. 'She missed the sound of the waves and sea birds.'

'Why don't we go,' she says, 'the two of us, just rent a place?'

'You mean . . . to Leiston?'

'Anywhere along that bit of coast.'

'Leave Cambridge?'

'I can't bear it here . . . the house is so . . . empty.' She takes a deep breath. 'If we can get away for a while – I think it would be good for us.'

He stares into the distance, his eyes watery, and she can't tell what he's thinking. He looks at her. 'There's nothing to hold me here. But what about you? The dogs – you love them so much.'

Relief floods her. She realises she'd been holding her breath. 'I've had to tell my clients I'm unavailable anyway. With India and then the operation,' she says. 'Someone else is walking my usual lot. I miss them, but they're okay. Anyway, I was thinking of it as a kind of holiday – just to go somewhere for a while.'

He's shaking his head. 'Why would we want to come back? I'll put this place on the market.'

She bites her lip. 'You sure?'

'Everywhere I look I see them. Both of them.' He stands up. 'I even smell them sometimes. It's unbearable. You'd think it might be a comfort. But it's not.'

She touches his hand.

'So, you're right. It's no good for us here.' He takes off his glasses.

'Don't put it on the market straight away,' she says. 'Let's give it a couple of months at least – I keep hearing how house prices have dropped, so maybe we shouldn't sell at all.'

'Estate agents are always putting leaflets through the door telling me how valuable and desirable places on Kimberley Road are, next to the river and Midsummer Common, close to town.' He rubs his cheek. 'I think we'd still get a good price. We could leave them to sell it for us while we're in a rented cottage.' He frowns. 'But not if you think we should wait. You're always the sensible one, Summer. Only, perhaps we should put our stuff into storage? Just in case?'

'Leave it to me, Dad,' she says, standing. 'I'll sort it out.'

'You always do,' he murmurs. 'I rely on you too much.' His voice cracks. 'You've been looking after me, when it should have been the other way around. I've been a selfish old man.'

Tears swell behind her lids again. 'Don't say that. I didn't mean—'

'Summer ... things need to change. I want to try and help you make the most of your future.' He reaches across and takes her hands in his. 'You're all I've got left.'

She squeezes his fingers tightly, and neither of them say anything. She can't speak because of the hard knot in her throat and suspects it's the same for him. Packing up the house will give her something to do, something to focus on, keep her sane. Nothing will mend the hole Effie's left in her heart, and she wouldn't want it to, but now she has a reason to pack up her sister's things. If they go to a charity shop, at least other people will get pleasure from them.

She'll keep Effie's ridiculous cat slippers and favourite glittery pink hair bobbles, the lilac mohair jumper, and some of her school exercise books with her familiar neat handwriting. She'd wanted to be a normal teenager, to go to parties and flirt with boys; she'd wanted to run and dance and one day go to university. It hadn't seemed too much to ask.

MARCH

Three months of Summer

18

Kit

Dr Sharma appears the following day and sits on a chair by Kit's bed. The nurse draws the curtain around them. Mr Sharma folds his hands neatly in his lap. 'You will be discharged tomorrow. My advice is to return to the UK and attend hospital there. I will write a letter for you – send it ahead.' He nods. 'You'll need to have the remaining cast removed when you get home, and physiotherapy arranged.'

Kit wants to kiss him.

Summer, this is it! Finally, I get to leave this place and come and find you. I have no idea where you are, but I'm guessing you are at home in Cambridge, back into your busy life. If you'll have me, then I'll be with you as soon as I can. Wait for me. Please.

He takes a taxi to Varkala, to the entrance of the Beach Hut Village, and makes his way along the narrow path towards the main building, the rhythm coming naturally now, thump, swing, balance, thump, swing. The man behind the desk looks at the crutches, his plastered leg, and raises his eyebrows in concern.

'I'm the one who owes you money,' Kit says. 'I was involved in the accident on the road to Kollam. I've been in hospital.'

'Mr Appleby.' The receptionist clasps his hands together. 'That is terrible news.'

'The girl I was with, Summer Blythe, when I rang before, they said she'd checked out on the fifteenth of January. Is that right?'

The man opens a ledger and flicks through. 'This is correct,' he says. He cocks his head and holds up a finger. 'It was me on reception that day. She was in a hurry. Said she needed a taxi to the airport.'

'Did she . . . say anything else? Did she leave a message for me?'

He bends down under the counter and straightens up with a piece of paper in his fingers. 'Yes. Yes. Here, sir.'

His heart leaps, and he unfolds the note, scanning brief sentences:

Kit, I can't wait any longer. I have to go. Please come and find me at the airport. I'll be trying to get on the first available flight home.

It makes no sense. 'Nothing else?'

The receptionist looks under the counter, peers inside the ledger, and then holds up a finger again. 'Wait one moment.' He disappears and returns with a bag. 'Your possessions.'

Kit's chest sinks with disappointment. Another member of staff appears, noticing Kit with a small jolt; he confers with the receptionist in hurried low tones. The receptionist looks back at Kit with a mournful expression. 'Ah, I am very sorry, sir, but my colleague has reminded me that there is another outstanding bill.'

Kit raises his eyebrows questioningly.

'A bicycle. Hired and not returned.' He gazes past Kit's shoulder as if hoping to see the bike parked outside the door.

Kit remembers the feel of handlebars, the blare of horns, the sun blinding him. Panic flares, and his heart kicks into overdrive. 'I'll have to pay for it – I was riding it when . . . when I was . . .'

The receptionist widens his eyes in horror. 'No payment needed. It is forgotten.'

'Can I see inside number twenty?'

The man consults the large book. 'It has been cleaned and used several times since you checked out. Do you think you left something behind?'

Kit shrugs and opens his palms. There are small callouses on them from the crutches.

Kit takes in the dull brown cover on the double bed, the drooping twist of mosquito netting hanging above, and grimaces. He's surprised she didn't abandon him as soon as she walked into this place. The lacquered shutters are closed; he struggles to pull them open, letting in the dazzle of the morning. He touches the bed, and a memory comes back so fast it makes him sink onto the mattress.

Summer on top of him, her hair falling in a gleaming curtain. The scent of her skin – almonds, sea salt, citrus tang; the feel of her lips on his.

He heaves himself up, leaning on his crutches, and begins a search of the room, looking for a note or a clue that the cleaners or the previous guests have missed. He pulls open the rickety drawers in the chest, reaching into every corner, runs his hands under the mattress and pillows, hops into the bathroom and gazes up at the square of open sky above, remembering her laughter.

He shuffles slowly across the floor, scanning the surface. The cleaners haven't done a great job; there are clumps of dust in corners, crumbs on the rug. It gives him hope that they might not have swept everything into the rubbish. He finds an elastic band with a couple of long black hairs attached. Just as he's about to give up, a gleam of silver catches his eye. A tiny silver tip protrudes between two planks of wood, almost invisible. He pokes it with the point of one crutch. He'll have to get down onto the floor. He uses the bed and manages to lower himself into a sitting position, the plaster cast straight out in front of him. He can't get his finger inside the crack; he takes a pencil from his pocket and uses it to lever the silver item out from its snug hiding place. A tiny hare emerges.

Summer sits across a table from him, smiling. She touches the little hares hanging from her ears, twirling them.

He cradles the earring in the centre of his palm, wondering if she still has the matching one. He tries to stand up, his good arm reaching for support; but his plaster cast is heavy as a boulder, and his crutches fail to get purchase. Panting, he tries again and again, finally managing to stand upright, swaying on one leg, wiping the sweat from his brow. He has a last look at the room, this simple space they'd inhabited together. He imagines them lying on the bed, wrapped in each other's arms under the mosquito netting, her nose pressed into his neck. The wooden blades of the fan revolving above, creaking in the darkness.

Could she really believe he'd leave without telling her?

The first step to finding her is to get a flight back to England. For whatever reason, she'd decided to go home. He hobbles into the afternoon. Her note had been puzzling, but one thing was clear: she'd wanted him to meet her at the airport. It wasn't him she was running from.

19

Summer

Laura is on the doorstep, a bag of takeaway food in her hand. 'Didn't think you'd feel like cooking,' she says. 'Thought this might be useful, too,' holding up a bottle of wine. Then she does a double take. 'My God! Your hair!'

Summer shrugs.

Laura's expression is pained. 'Give me some sharp scissors and I'll try and tidy it up.' She walks into the hall, the smell of Chinese food entering with her. It makes Summer feel sick. Laura puts the foil containers on the kitchen table, getting out bowls and forks. Summer watches her heap food into a bowl and take it to her father in his study.

'At least he started to eat after I put the food in front of him,' Laura reports, when she returns, 'which is more than I can say of you.'

Summer grimaces. 'Can't swallow anything,' she says.

She sits on a stool with a towel around her shoulders while Laura combs her hair, snipping and sighing. 'I'll do my best . . . but I'm not an expert . . . looks like you used the garden shears.'

'Just wanted to get rid of it.'

Laura stops cutting hair, and touches Summer's shoulder. 'I know everything feels pointless now,' she says quietly. 'But life goes on.'

She pours out a glass of wine and puts it in Summer's hand. 'Effie wouldn't want you to punish yourself,' she squints as she slices through a stray tendril. 'You gave her your kidney.'

'But it wasn't enough.' Summer drops her head into her hands.

Laura crouches beside her, wrapping her arms around her. 'You were a wonderful sister,' she murmurs. 'The best.'

Summer hugs her back, sniffing. She sits up, 'Laura, I've got something to tell you . . . we're leaving Cambridge.' She wipes her eyes on the edge of the towel. 'We're going to rent somewhere on the Suffolk coast. I don't know how long for.'

'You're moving?' Laura straightens, her expression startled. 'Wow, I'm really going to miss you.' She swallows, blinking. 'But . . . but I think it's a great idea.' She bends to trim around Summer's ears. 'A new start. What about your job – the dogs?'

'It's all sorted. I'll look into getting some kind of work when we're settled.'

She'd walked dogs because it was flexible. The job gave her the time she'd needed for Effie and running the house. Now that Effie is gone, she has no idea what to do. Her dream of being a wildlife photographer and writer seem completely unrealistic – her only qualification is the short photography evening course she did at the local college. Her sister encouraged her, admired her photographs, told her she'd be discovered by *National Geographic*. But it was a game really, something to keep Effie's spirits up.

Laura is regarding her with her head tilted to the side; she sucks in her cheeks. 'You've worn the same clothes for days on end.' She clasps Summer's hand, 'You're not looking after yourself properly.'

Summer shrugs. Her tired body and numb mind are only able to cope with the most basic chores: she can clean her teeth, but flossing is out of the question. She can drag on the clothes she took off the night before; but choosing anything else to wear is impossible.

They pour the last of the wine into their glasses, as water chestnuts and stir-fried vegetables congeal in silver containers, and jasmine rice goes cold. The alcohol makes Summer feel loose and heavy; it dulls the pain. She tilts her glass, swallowing.

'I met someone,' she says. 'When I was in India.'

Laura shoots her an alert, interested look.

'Kit.' She stares into her empty glass. 'I really liked him. More than liked.' She roots through the cupboard unsteadily and finds another bottle of red, opens it. 'We only spent days together, but I thought he was . . . "the one".'

'The one?' Laura holds up her glass for a refill.

'Yeah,' Summer leans back in her chair, her head swimming. 'Stupid, right? There's no such thing. Not for most people. But I really began to believe I'd got lucky. Anyway – big reality check – he disappeared. Went off to a dance festival and never came back. Not until after I'd got on a plane, anyway. I left him my number. Address. He hasn't called. Nothing.'

'Where is he, then? Don't you know?'

'Maybe still in India,' Summer sweeps her arm, the movement feeling oddly liquid-like. 'When I called our hotel . . . appran . . . rently . . . ' she struggles with the word. 'Apparently . . . he was still there. Staying in our room.'

'Call him again.' Laura says, rising unsteadily to her feet.

'Come on. You need to speak to him. Fuck sake. This sounds important.'

'Laura. No. He has my number. What if he doesn't want to speak to me?'

'But he fell for you, too? Right?'

'Yes,' she whispers. 'But if he's at the hotel, why hasn't he called me? I'm scared he's gone off me or ... met someone else ... I can't face any more rejection ... any more loss.' She takes a breath. 'The thing is – I didn't tell him about Effie. And I made stuff up. Told him I was working as a journalist, a photographer. Talked as if I was on the folk singing circuit or something.'

'What? Why?' Laura is staring at her. 'That's not like you.'

'I don't know,' her face is flaming, and she grips her wine-glass stem. 'I suppose it all seemed like a dream being there with him – the truth would have burst that bubble ... I regret it now.'

'Well,' Laura frowns, 'you made a mistake. Did something out of character. But it wasn't malicious or anything. I'm sure he'd understand if you could explain. I really think you need to speak to him.'

With Effie dying, every bit of hope has drained from her. But Laura is looking at her expectantly and, suddenly, she knows she has to try one more time.

When she's eventually put through to the Beach Hut Hotel, the line is crackly and faint. 'Is ... is Kit Appleby there?' Her stomach lurches.

A pause. A hiss. 'No, madam. Mr Appleby has checked out.'

'Oh.' Disappointment falls through her. 'Did ... did he get my notes?' she asks. 'I left one in our room, and another at reception for him. I'm Summer Blythe. We were staying there together.'

'Just a minute.'

The receptionist must have put the receiver down. There's a busy silence, the whoosh of time sliding forwards, echoes of palm trees, wave-wash, the whirring of green wings. Then someone clearing their throat. 'Mr Appleby was given the note in reception, madam.'

'Oh,' she says again, holding the receiver tightly. 'He was? Thank you.'

If he was given the second note, then he must have got the one in the hut too. He must know why she left, and where she is. She feels nauseous. She was right the first time – he's moved on. She presses her hands to her temples, squeezing, wishing she hadn't drunk so much.

'Well?' Laura demands.

'He's gone,' she opens her palms. 'It's over.'

Her head is full of Kit, smiling, laughing; then looking at her, suddenly serious. The golden colour of his irises, darkening to chocolate around his pupils. Kit under the umbrella on the beach, his sketchbook on his knee, his gaze burning away the rest of the world, looking at her in a way she'd never before experienced.

It wasn't real. It was another world – one that doesn't exist any more. This is real. Effie's death. Dad to look after. A house to pack up and a cottage to find to rent.

20

Kit

London. The cold hits him in the chest. Everything is dim, grey, muted. His eyes struggle with the lack of light. He leaves his big bag in storage at Heathrow – an expensive necessity. He'll go back for it when he's mobile.

It's tricky to manage the escalator on his crutches. He has his small rucksack strapped to his shoulders. On the tube, he sits in silence with the other passengers, rocking with the movement of the train as it hurtles through tunnels. He notices people snatching sideways glances at him, realising he must look odd and out of place in his shorts, a grubby cast encasing his leg from foot to thigh, his one flip-flop. The only footwear he possesses.

When he gets to his house, he rings the bell instead of using his key. His mother opens the door, and her expression contorts with shock. 'Kit!' She takes him in, her eyes flicking up and down. 'You're back – why on earth didn't you tell me when you were arriving?'

'I just . . . sorry . . . I didn't think.'

'I've been worried about you. Stuck in hospital on another continent.' She puts a hand over her chest, shaking her head. 'Those roads must be a death-trap. I never understood why you wanted to go to a place like that.'

He notices that her lashes are heavy with gloopy black, red stuff is smeared over her cheeks and lips. Her blouse is undone to show the top of her cleavage. He wonders if she's met someone new.

She opens the door wider. 'Come in.'

She gives him a brief, tight embrace, the sherbet smell of her perfume a familiar shock, her lips brushing his cheek, leaving a sticky smear. 'I think you've got even taller,' she says, as he hobbles inside after her. 'How long has it been? Over a year?'

The house is cramped, overheated, overfurnished. He has a sense that his head is nearly brushing the ceiling, and that any movement from him will sweep the Royal Doulton ballet dancers off their display surfaces and send them crashing to the floor. Stooping, he sets his rucksack down carefully. She shows him into the sitting room and gestures towards the sofa. 'Tea?'

He nods, dropping the crutches and sinking down. He's exhausted from moving and travelling, negotiating stairs and steps, and crowds. Crowds are the worst. He could be pushed off balance at any moment by the clip of an elbow, the brush of a hip, a casual swing of a bag. He's as precarious as one of his mother's ornaments.

She comes back and hands him a cup and saucer. It's green and white. Part of a set that's always been in the kitchen cupboards. He's been drinking from it since childhood.

He perches on the edge of the seat and sips the hot liquid as she watches him from a chair in the corner. The tea burns his tongue. He meets his mother's gaze and the hairs on his arms stand up. What is he doing here? How did he go from being with Summer in Kerala, to sitting in this house with his mother? The shiny ballerinas regard him with disdain. His hand jerks, spilling the tea. Drops darken the pale blue of the sofa fabric.

His mother leaps up. She disappears and comes back with a cloth, getting onto her knees to scrub at the spreading mark. By the time she's finished and put the cloth back in the kitchen, tut-tutting under her breath, he knows he can't stay.

'What are your plans?' she asks, lighting a cigarette, and crossing her still-elegant legs. 'Now you're home.'

'I don't know yet. I met a girl, but . . . we got separated. I want to find her before I decide anything else.'

'What makes you think she wants to be found?' she says, in a voice that clearly says he's yet another deluded man. 'Maybe she got "separated" from you on purpose?' She makes quote marks with her fingers.

Cold slides through him. Why does she always try and make him doubt himself? 'No,' he says, 'it's not like that. Something came up, and she had to leave. She left me a note. Wanted me to meet her at the airport.'

'People lie, Kit. You're too trusting. You shouldn't take the word of someone you've only just met.' She blows out a stream of smoke. 'Anyway, if she lives over here, why don't you just ring her?'

'I don't have her number,' he admits.

'And you don't have her address?' She raises one eyebrow.

'But I know her name,' he counters. 'She lives in Cambridge. If I can borrow the phone, I can look her up.'

'For heaven's sake, Kit.' She raises her eyes to the ceiling. 'You've got a good brain – can't you see she's left you?' She stubs out her cigarette. 'Don't go chasing after some girl when your own life's a mess.'

'Can I?' he asks. 'Can I use the phone?'

'All right,' she sighs. 'But no long-distance calls. And keep it short. You should know, I'm with Terry now. He lives here – and he doesn't like extravagant behaviour.'

Kit puts his cup and saucer down on one of many nests of side tables. He could be only moments from hearing her voice. He heaves himself onto his feet, saving himself from toppling over by digging the crutches into the carpet.

In the hall, he calls directory enquiries. There are three Blythes listed in Cambridge. His heart hammers at his chest. He calls the first number, finger trembling in the dial. 'Nobody called Summer here,' a man says. The second one is answered by the high, whispery voice of a child; they laugh and hang up on him. The last number rings and rings, without being answered.

He has no idea if she lives alone or with other people. Maybe she has flatmates. His questions fill him with doubt, a familiar little voice telling him that Summer is too good for him – she's got her life together, she's juggling careers, she's ambitious and gorgeous, why would she want someone like him?

He's angry with himself for allowing his mother's words to get to him. He'll go to Cambridge. He needs to find her, read her expression, talk to her in person.

'No luck?' his mother asks when he hobbles into the living room.

He shakes his head.

'You're staying for a while, then, are you?'

'Not long.'

'Don't be difficult. You have to admit you've behaved badly – disappearing off like that. Only two postcards in a year. Can you imagine how worried I've been?' She blinks. 'People ask after you, and I don't know what to say. It's embarrassing. Terry doesn't believe you exist.'

There are letters addressed to him on the hall table. He has an appointment booked to remove his cast at St Thomas's Hospital in three days. Can he wait three days before he goes to find her? He glances through a chink in the curtains. It's dark outside and raining hard. The pavements will be lethal for his crutches. He'll have to negotiate escalators and trains; and he doesn't know where she lives, or even if it's one of the addresses he's jotted down. He knows the sensible thing is to stay in London until he has the cast removed. As soon as he's mobile, he'll go straight to Cambridge.

'Stay as long as you like. This is your home,' she says, when he finds her in the kitchen. 'I'll get on with making dinner. Terry should be back soon. Be polite, all right?'

He goes upstairs with difficulty, thumping and shuffling to his old room. It's been stripped bare. He stares around, confused. He opens drawers, finding them empty. He puts his hand to his throat, feeling the familiar sense of constriction. There are bulging black bin bags stuffed into the bottom of the wardrobe. He hooks one out with a crutch and delves inside, digging out a jumper. Searching deeper inside a tangle of fabrics, he unearths some socks and a pair of sturdy boots. He sits on the edge of the stripped mattress and struggles to get one sock onto his left foot. He has no strength left. He drops the boot on the floor and flops backwards onto the mattress.

21

Summer

'You've lost weight,' Laura says. 'You have to eat.'

They are packing furniture to go into storage. The cottage that Summer's found to rent comes unfurnished, but it won't take much to fill the tiny two-up, two-down. The girls wrap china in newspaper, clear out drawers, pile books into boxes. Since coming back from India, Summer's lost her appetite. And now the food she does put into her mouth tastes of nothing. Ashes. Dust. The flesh has fallen away without her noticing.

'Tell me more about this guy, Kit,' Laura says, flicking through records, Dad's jazz collection ranged on shelves in alphabetical order. She's picked up a Bix Beiderbecke album.

'Leave those,' Summer says. 'He'll want to pack them up himself.'

She puts the record back. 'But … Kit?' Laura stands up, brushing dust from her fingers. 'Or … don't you want to talk about him?'

Summer rubs her thumb across the glass of the watch face. She can't take it off, despite everything. The ticking is like a tiny heartbeat. 'He's … he's funny and talented,' she says. 'Hopelessly untidy. An artist. He made lots of sketches of me while we were on the beach.'

Laura looks interested. 'Do you have any of them?'

'One.'

'Can I see it?'

Summer goes up to her bedroom and slides the sketch out of a book. Downstairs, she hands the paper to Laura silently. Laura considers it for a long time, and then she looks up. 'He really got you, didn't he?'

Summer nods, concentrating on taping a packing case shut. She can't trust her voice.

'You said he's not at the hotel any more.' Laura sits down, her chin in her hand. 'Do you think he's back in England?'

'He was thinking of coming back,' Summer admits, 'but I have no idea where he'd be – his parents don't live together. Haven't since he was little. I think they're divorced. His mum is in London … can't remember where he said his dad lived.'

'Whose name does he have – his father's or his mother's?'

'I think his father's … Appleby.'

'Why don't you look him up?'

'Laura, he's chosen not to contact me. I can't chase after him, can I? It's humiliating.'

'But you don't really know what happened to him, or how he's feeling, do you?'

'Why are you so keen on me tracking him down?' She can't help a note of frustration in her voice.

'Because you said you thought he might be "the one". And I have a gut feeling about it.' She leans closer. 'For the last three years I've watched you go on dates and never follow any of them up … because you always put Effie first. You never said so, but after things finished with Adam, I could see you'd made a decision not to get close to anyone else. Not to let a boyfriend come before your duties at home.'

'Effie wasn't ever a . . . a duty,' Summer says quietly.

'I know,' Laura says quickly. 'I didn't mean it like that. All I'm saying is I understood why you didn't jump into another relationship. But now . . . if there's a chance of contacting this man, Kit, a chance of making it work with him . . . then you should.'

Summer bites her thumbnail. 'I suppose . . . I suppose his father will know where he is – he might even be staying with him.'

As she says it, a tiny flicker of excitement sparks. She thinks back to the conversation where he threw out the name of a place, joking about suburbia.

'Wokingham!' She drops the roll of tape on the floor. 'That's it. Where his dad lives.' She stands still, hands steepled over her mouth. She wants to believe Laura. 'I'll try direct inquiries.'

'There's an Alan Appleby.'

Alan Appleby. Wokingham. It has to be Kit's dad. Summer's body thrums with anxiety. What if Kit's there? She looks at Laura. 'Does this make me a mad stalker?'

'Absolutely not,' Laura backs away. 'I'll get out of your way – make a start on the bathrooms.'

The phone rings in the house of Kit's father, and Summer wants to slam the receiver down. She anticipates and dreads hearing a voice on the other end. It might be Kit himself who answers. 'Hello?' It's an older man.

Summer freezes, unable to speak.

'Hello?' the voice repeats.

'Mr Appleby?'

'Yes.'

'I wondered . . . if your son was with you?'

'Who is this?'

'You don't know me. My name is Summer. I met your son on holiday – and . . . and we got separated.'

'You met my son on holiday?' The voice sounds incredulous.

Summer swallows. 'Yes.' She grips the receiver. 'Is he there?'

'I don't know what you're playing at,' the voice continues, with a steely edge. 'But this isn't funny.'

She falters. 'I'm sorry . . . I don't . . .'

'My son is nine years old.'

Summer nearly puts the phone down. She hesitates. 'But I thought . . . I'm sorry. I thought you were Kit Appleby's father.'

There's a pause, and a long-drawn-out sigh. 'I don't live with Kit. I live with my son from another relationship.'

'I see.' She can hardly speak. The knowledge falters and takes hold. 'Do you have a number or address for him? I mean, for Kit.'

'I'm not his keeper.' The voice is cool. 'Last I heard, he was travelling.'

Summer sits down. She stares at the phone in its cradle. Alan Appleby's voice held no love when he mentioned Kit. But this is the father he has such a good relationship with? A sense of unease makes her hands tremble. She folds her fingers, clenching them tightly.

Laura puts her head around the door. 'Well?'

Summer shakes her head. 'It was him. His dad. But he doesn't know where Kit is.'

Laura's face falls. Summer gets up and puts her arms around her friend's shoulders. 'I know what you're doing,' she says, gently. 'But it's OK. I don't need distractions, and I don't need him. I have you and Dad. And moving to the coast.'

'Guess we'd better get on with the packing then.' The doorbell rings. Summer grimaces. 'Oh god, not sure if I can face talking to anyone right now.'

'Shall I get rid of them?'

Summer shakes her head. 'I'll deal with it.'

Adam is on the doorstep, holding a bunch of white roses. 'I just wanted to say . . .' He pauses, and his thin face contorts, his button-brown eyes watering. 'Fuck. I'm so sorry, Summer.'

'Thanks.' She swallows hard and takes the flowers. He's remembered they're her favourite. 'Laura's here. Do you want to come in?'

'I saw you at the funeral,' she says as he steps through the door. 'Thanks for coming. It meant a lot.'

He stops dead, looking at the packing case. 'Jeez.' He stares into the half-empty rooms. 'Are you moving?'

'Yes,' she inhales the sweet scent of the roses, 'we're going to Suffolk.'

She stoops to move a box out of the way. 'Hey,' he puts his hand on her arm gently. 'Haven't you just had a major operation? I'll do that.'

He pushes the case to the side and straightens up, taking in her new look with a puzzled frown, 'You cut your hair?'

She touches her head, still surprised by the feel of it.

Laura comes down the stairs and puts her hands on her hips, 'How did you know we needed a bit of extra muscle?'

He holds up one arm and squeezes his bicep ruefully. 'Not sure I qualify. But if you need help?'

'Don't let her bully you,' Summer says. 'You're not obliged to do anything.'

'I'd like to help,' he says, pushing dark hair off his forehead. 'If that's okay?'

She bashes the ends of the stalks and puts the roses in a vase. Adam rolls his sleeves up, making more jokes about his lack of biceps, and the three of them get to work. As they wrap and pack, they talk about Effie, remembering funny stories, recalling the things she liked to say, how she could be stubborn as the devil when she wanted. Tears drop off Summer's cheeks without her bothering to sweep them away.

All the clocks chime the hour. A cacophony of trills and gongs. Nine o'clock. 'Want me to see if there's anything left to cook in your kitchen?' Adam offers.

'Yes, please,' Laura and Summer chorus.

'I'm starving,' Laura adds.

The house smells of frying butter, thyme, cheese. Summer remembers that Adam is a good cook. At least, he makes a great omelette. They used to sneak into his parents' kitchen late at night, and she'd sit on the table while he mixed up eggs, scattering in herbs like a professional. After eating, he'd walk her home along the river. It had felt like just the two of them in the world, with the mist rising on the water and the sky above the spires turning silver. A school romance, her first love. She blinks away the memories.

She sets some plates out, glasses of water, salt and pepper, and calls her father down from his study. He shuffles in and gazes around him at the packing boxes and newly bare shelves. He seems confused.

'Are you OK?' Summer asks.

'A child dying before a parent. It's turned the order of things upside-down.' He looks at the packing cases, his mouth trembling. 'But we have to believe that out of every ending, there's a beginning.'

Summer manages a few mouthfuls; it's strange to chew and swallow, feel the food moving through her body, heavy in her belly. Effie had longed to be able to eat whatever she wanted. She'd fantasised about salty chips, melting Brie, guacamole and fat green olives. Eating belongs to the living, the lucky. She remembers reaching across and taking food from Kit's plate, as if they'd known each other for ever; sensual mouthfuls, tastebuds tingling, all the better for sharing with him.

After the meal, Laura and Summer do the washing-up and her father goes off to bed.

'Your dad's a wise old owl,' Adam says.

'I hope I've done the right thing.' Summer bites a nail. 'Hope he's going to be all right, in a new place.'

'Suffolk's not far on the M11,' Adam says.

'Are you angling for an invitation?' Laura teases. 'You are the ex, remember.'

Adam scratches his nose and looks away.

'I'm counting on you both visiting,' Summer says quickly. 'It'll be strange, not knowing anyone. I've lived here as long as I can remember.'

The three of them keep going, working late into the night, labelling boxes, wrapping ornaments and taping up cardboard. At regular intervals, Laura bustles off to put the kettle on for tea, Adam entertains them with a supply of terrible jokes, and Summer is grateful for their company, their practical kindness, the comfort of old friends.

22

Kit

He has the cast cut off at St Thomas's, the plaster cracking open to reveal his leg, paler and thinner, but whole again. A pink scar, thin as wax paper, twists around his knee and over his thigh. They make him appointments to come back to have a last X-ray, and physiotherapy. He says yes to everything. But all he really cares about is having his freedom.

He can walk unaided, although his leg is weak and stiff. He's been told to take it slowly, bathe his neglected skin every day, do the prescribed exercises. Rest.

When he gets back to his mother's, Terry is in the living room, the television blaring. 'Want to watch the football with me?' he calls. 'Bring me a beer, will you? A cold one.'

He takes a can from the fridge and hands it to Terry over the back of the sofa. He's a sturdy, short man with halitosis and a scrub of grey hair poking above the collar of his shirt. The thought of him touching his mother makes Kit feel queasy. But she seems happy enough when Terry squeezes her bottom or nuzzles behind her ear.

'Sit down,' Terry pats the cushion beside him. 'You may as well watch it – you're not going to be playing it for a while, are you?' He laughs as if he's said something amusing.

Kit remains standing. 'I'm going to Cambridge,' he says. 'I might be gone a while. But I'll stay in touch.'

'Off to track down that girl?' Terry asks. 'Don't listen to your mum. I'm sure what's-her-name has still got the hots for you. Good-looking lad like yourself.'

'Summer,' Kit murmurs. 'Her name is Summer.'

He gets off the train at Cambridge, the two possible addresses on a piece of paper in his hand. He walks slowly down Station Road, wincing when he has to step up onto a kerb. As he reaches the centre of town, the pale stone facades of college buildings appear around him, walls pockmarked with age, open gates showing glimpses of green quadrangles, like something out of a costume drama. Students pass him in groups, laughing. The air is full of spring – scents of jasmine and the watery dank of the river. He could run into her at any moment, around any corner. His mouth is dry with anticipation as he looks at every approaching blonde. Sometimes a pair of eyes will look back, their owner giving him a small, questioning smile. He walks on.

At the first address, the woman who opens the door has never heard of her, and a child, probably the one who'd answered the phone, sticks out her tongue from behind her mother. The second and last possibility is a house near the river, just over a bridge that leads onto Midsummer Common. Kit walks up a tiled path and rings the doorbell. It chimes inside the house, the peals echoing back to him. He cups his hands over his eyes to peer through the coloured glass panels, making out a shadowy hallway. He can't see any signs of life. He steps across the little patch of front lawn to a bay window and looks in, feeling like a snooper. The room is empty, apart from a roll of packing tape nestled in one corner. Sunlight lattices the wooden floor.

He returns to the pavement and stands back, tilting his head to look up at the second-floor windows. He plunges his hands into his pockets, rocking back on his heels. Curtains are drawn across one of them, but he's pretty sure the place is deserted. His fingers find the small shape of the earring in the bottom of his left pocket. 'Where are you?' he murmurs.

Without his watch, he has to rely on asking people for the time or finding public clocks. But his stomach is telling him that it's past lunch. He goes into a café and orders a sandwich and tea, choosing a table by the window so he can look into the street. He takes a big bite of the cheese and pickle on wholewheat, remembering Summer's unabashed passion for food, her way of picking things off his plate. It could have been annoying, but instead it made him feel as if he'd known her for ever. He stares through the glass as he chews, dizzy from scanning faces. At the next table, a young mother is feeding her grizzling toddler, strapped into a high chair. The woman cuts up a banana and offers a slice to the little girl, making aeroplane noises, zooming a fork into her child's mouth.

It was a special treat to go to a café. He swung his feet into the space below his chair, heels going thud, thud against the wooden seat. He had a chopped-up banana on the plate in front of him. He didn't like touching the slippery, gooey discs. One skidded through his grasp and dropped onto the floor, and he glanced at his mother quickly to see if she'd noticed. But she was staring at the door.

'When he gets here, answer him when he talks to you,'

Mummy was saying, leaning down. She scrubbed his cheeks with spit on a screwed-up hanky. He tried to duck out of the way, but she held his face with pincered fingers. 'I know you can speak if you want to.'

She put the hanky in her purse. 'And call him Daddy. Don't forget.'

Then she was smiling, lowering her eyelids and touching her hair all at the same time, and a man was bending over the table saying, 'Hello, Margaret.'

The man pulled out a chair and sat opposite them. His long, reddened fingers undid the buttons on his coat. He reached across and pinched Kit's cheek. 'How are you, son?'

Kit stared at him. He remembered his deep, loud voice, and the shape of him in a room; how he took up all the space, all the air. Remembered being lifted up to ride on his shoulders, so he was almost as high as the moon, and how safe he'd felt then, holding onto his daddy's ears.

Daddy laughed, 'Cat got your tongue?'

His mother's hand had snaked under the table, sharp fingers twisting his thigh. 'Answer your daddy, Kit.'

His tongue lay sleeping in his mouth. There were no words for him to spit out. They were tucked up so deep inside him that he didn't know what they were, what they would say, even if they dared to creep into his throat.

'He's still a mute, then?' Daddy said.

'Give him a chance . . .' Mummy gave a choking laugh. 'He hasn't seen you for two years.'

Mummy's voice had changed from her normal one into something sweet and pleading, like a cat curling around and around asking for milk. Kit lowered his head to the problem of the banana. He knew he'd be in trouble if he didn't finish it.

Mummy and Daddy were ignoring him, talking at each other with words that were getting sharper and harder. He pushed the banana slices over the side of the plate with his finger. One by one, they left snail trails as he nudged them along the surface of the table until they tilted over the edge. Far below, they made yellowy-brown blobs on the floor.

He shakes himself. He's not here to reminisce about his childhood. It's not good to dwell on the past, on things that can't be changed.

He pays at the till and uses the café's facilities. He stares at himself in the mirror, trying not to feel disappointed. Her phone number obviously isn't listed or isn't under her name. Maybe it will take longer than he'd thought to track her down. But she's here, somewhere in the city. It's not as if he doesn't know anything about her. He's squeezed his memories dry, going through their conversations, filtering them for information, extracting clues.

He goes back into the café and asks the woman behind the till if she knows of a cheap bed and breakfast nearby.

23

Summer

She watches the removal lorry trundle away, flexing sore fingers, rubbing at her dirt-smudged face. Their new home is a cottage, sitting in a row of eight others, detached from each other, facing a desolate stretch of shingle beach and the far reaches of the North Sea. It's a windswept hamlet close to the mouth of the Ore, where the river, meeting the sea, creates a cross-hatching of currents. Signs warn swimmers away.

The cottage is a quarter of the size of the house in Kimberley Road. The front door leads directly into a sitting room, with low dark beams and a worn wooden floor; there's a neat kitchen next door, the window over the sink looking out at the beach. A narrow creaking staircase leads from the kitchen up to a small landing; two bedrooms and a tiny bathroom are tucked under the eaves. Despite half their stuff being in storage in Cambridge, this place will be bursting at the seams once the unpacking is finished. Dad's brought his clock collection and his record collection.

The sound of Thelonious Monk reaches her. Summer rolls

her eyes. His records weren't on the list of things to unearth first. She leans on their whitewashed picket fence, and tilts her face into the breeze, watching the play of sky and water over the stones. This place had looked idyllic in the pictures on the brochure: a higgledy-piggledy, white clapboard cottage, with sunflowers in the garden, at the edge of the beach, a short walk from the sea. Gazing around her at the barren spit of land, lashed by the waves of the North Sea, she hadn't quite understood how isolated it was.

Glancing along the length of beach to her right, she sees the bulk of a Martello tower; Dad said it was constructed as a lookout back in the Napoleonic wars. It presents a stony face to the sea, narrow windows like those in a medieval castle. Down by the shore, she can make out the huddled shapes of a couple of fishermen, and there's a figure moving in the landscape: a woman wandering along, stooping every now and then to examine the shingle. Summer can't see her face because she has a beaten trilby pulled low. She picks something up and puts it in her coat pocket, straightens, and seems to be looking right at her, so Summer raises a hand and waves. The woman remains very still, and then turns away. 'Okay,' Summer murmurs. 'Just being friendly.'

She goes inside to help Dad. When enough boxes have been unpacked to unearth the necessities, the two of them sit down to a supper of baked beans. There's no toast to go with the beans. The cupboards are bare. The only food they've brought with them are a few tins and a packet of tea. She'd donated the rest of their food supplies to a couple of elderly neighbours before they left. The nearest supermarket is miles away. She'll go tomorrow and stock up, while Dad sorts out a few more boxes.

They clink two mugs of black tea together, 'Here's to us,' Dad says. 'And to taking it step by step.' They eat in silence. The wind has got up, and the windows rattle.

'We've got a wood-burning stove,' Summer says.

'I grew up without central heating. Had to chip ice off the inside of the windows,' Dad says, cheerfully. 'And, do you know, none of us was ever ill.'

Later, cleaning her teeth in the bathroom, she stands at the window above the sink and looks out into the night. The sky is huge and dark, sprayed with stars. On the horizon, there are other orbs of brilliance, strung out like Christmas tree lights. She squints, trying to make out what they are, realising they're the lights of huge container ships.

She has a twinge of anxiety that she's done the wrong thing, moving them to a windswept beach, miles from the comfort and familiarity of home. Far from shops and doctors' surgeries and dentists and friends. She rinses and spits and puts the brush down on the enamel, pushing a hand over her eyes. She's just tired. She was certain it was the right decision before – she gives herself a little mental shake – everything will look better in the morning.

Her bedroom has no curtains yet, and moonlight falls through the glass, making shapes on the floor. She slides between cool sheets. She can't sleep. A mix of excitement and anxiety squeezes her chest. To help herself relax, she spins a series of memories through her mind: Effie giggling, reaching for a hug, lying in sun-dappled grass. She realises that so many of the best memories have Adam in them too. When they were dating, Adam never excluded Effie: the three of them watched films tucked up on the sofa under a blanket; they took picnics to Midsummer Common or punted down the river to

Grantchester, with Adam serenading them in a silly voice. He'd made her sister laugh with his constant supply of jokes: 'What does a cloud wear under his raincoat?' Effie shaking her head in suppressed delight, waiting for the answer. 'Thunderwear!' 'Tell me more,' Effie begged, and he had, until Summer put her hands over her ears, and Effie said her tummy hurt with laughing.

She'd opened her window before she got into bed, and there's salt in the air, the clean, fresh snap of the ocean. The sound of the waves against the shingle is soothing, the rhythmic pulse of the water, rising and falling, like the steady breathing of a huge creature. She closes her eyes. Tomorrow, she'll do more unpacking, get some food supplies. Tomorrow is her new start.

24

Kit

After a restless night in an uncomfortable bed, Kit stands in the dingy hallway of the B & B and calls every local newspaper and magazine listed in the book. 'Do you have a journalist working for you called Summer Blythe?'

'She's a photographer and writer,' he explains. 'Specialises in wildlife.' He slots in coins. More coins. His pockets nearly empty. 'Sorry,' each person on the other line tells him. 'She doesn't work for us.'

He replaces the warm receiver in its cradle with a dull sense of disappointment, and something else, a sick feeling creeping into his stomach. Her journalism had been his main clue. But he has others. She told him that she sang in pubs. He just needs to discover the pubs that put on folk evenings. One of them is bound to have a list of performers.

He walks into the pale, cold morning, an icy wind making him shove his hands into his pockets. It's too early for pubs to open, so Kit decides to follow another clue. He heads for Midsummer Common.

Everywhere he looks dogs are gambolling, sniffing at trees, peeing, playing and barking. He walks along the path that follows the line of the river; elegant spires reach above the trees, bare branches just beginning to gather new green. A slender boat skims the surface of the river, powered by a quad of strapping young men, their bodies opening and closing over their oars like clockwork figures.

He stops, hands deep in his pockets, scooping the earring into the warmth of his palm. He squeezes it for luck as he stares across the green space, searching for a young woman with long golden hair and a pack of dogs at her feet. He sees a couple of black Labradors playing together in the distance and his heart leaps. He sets off towards them, cutting across the grass. He's halfway across a footpath, one heel peeling from the surface, when he catches a blur of movement out of the corner of his eye and jumps back just in time as a cyclist whizzes past, shouting, 'Idiot!'

Kit stops, pressing his palms over his eyes, struggling to breathe. Panic skids through him, shutting his lungs, closing his throat. He's back on a burning road, a lorry trundling past, time slowing into snapshots: a bus rears up in front of him; mouths scream as glass shatters.

He forces the memory away. When he's able to move, the two black dogs have gone. He blinks, turning his head, scanning the park. He breaks into a stumbling run, twisting his head back and forth. He can't see the animals, or anyone who looks like Summer.

He slows to a walk, limping. He takes off his jacket, wipes his brow with the back of his hand. The disappointment is back, heavy in his chest. He takes one more look around. She's not here.

*

He wanted a dog when he was little. A scruffy one with a patch over its eye. But his mother said that a dog would make a mess, and who would look after it? Not her. But Kit kept hoping she'd change her mind. Leaning over his drawing pad, he sketched a bouncy, friendly terrier with short legs and a little, waggy tail. He called him Scruff and used a black felt tip to give him a wet black nose and teddy-bear eyes. Then he drew himself running next to the dog, a big smile on his face. He put in a blue sea and a fat, round sun to complete the picture. His mother had just got back from work, dumping a bag of shopping on the hall table. 'Look Mummy,' he'd said. 'Me and Scruff at the seaside.'

Her mouth twisted. She snatched the drawing from him. 'You're never going to have a dog,' she said in a wobbly voice. 'Can't you understand? Stop this now.'

She ripped the drawing into tiny pieces, bits fluttering to the floor. He crouched, picking up the scraps. Scruff had become a puzzle of eye, paws, ears, tail. He screwed the ruined picture into a ball, throwing it from him as hard as he could. It rolled under the sofa.

A banging of saucepans sounded from the kitchen.

Kit stands by the river, watching the moorhens hurry across the water, necks out, chasing off ducks. It's hard to ignore the suggestion whispering in his mind that Summer has lied to him. Why would she do that?

The bar is crammed with a Friday-night crowd. He pushes his way through and orders a beer. He's walked around every pub in Cambridge, asking if they have folk nights. The ones that do told him they'd never heard of her. This one, The Fox and Hounds, said they were having an open mic this evening, including folk music. So here he is, with pint in hand, waiting for the entertainment to begin, scanning the door every time it opens.

There are tables of rowdy twenty-somethings laughing and joking, faces shiny with drink. Kit sips his pint slowly, leaning against the bar. He's trying not to let himself admit to the disappointment and confusion that's gathering inside him. He's trying to stay optimistic. But there's a well of hurt threatening to burst free and overwhelm him.

An Irish guy, acting as compère, kicks off the open mic with a couple of jokes before introducing the first performer, a lugubrious man who sings an interminable ballad. Some of the students start to heckle before he's finished. Then a pretty girl with a sandstorm of freckles gets up and plays guitar, singing in a slight voice. She gathers a round of relieved applause. The performers get up, one by one; some are terrible, most are reasonably good. A couple are brilliant. None of them is Summer.

He remembers the way her voice had sounded as she'd walked ahead of him down the path to the beach, the sweet, pure truth of it, and how he'd complimented her on her singing. She'd brushed off his compliments, almost bashfully, but she'd said, she'd definitely said, that she sang at folk nights and open mics in Cambridge.

25

Summer

The next morning, there's a postcard on the mat. Summer turns it over, to find it's addressed to her in Laura's familiar writing.

> Happy Moving In! Will visit when I can. Miss you already. Love to your dad. And big hugs to you, my darling. L xxx

She runs her finger over the words, feeling an ache inside. It's going to be strange not being able to pop out to the pub for a drink with her, meet her for a walk on the common, chat over coffee on Sunday mornings.

She unpacks the rest of Mum's ceramic tableware, and puts them on the rack over the dresser, polishing each one first. They are made of robust stoneware, weighty and solid, glazed in sea green, teal, rust, and cream. All of them were once shaped by her mother's dextrous fingers, coaxed from a lump of clay into something lovely, friendly and useful.

She stands back and admires them, the plates placed in neat

circles on the shelves, bowls on the next shelf down, mugs arranged on hooks beneath. Immediately, the tiny kitchen feels more homely. But it's a home without a scrap to eat. She sits at the table with a drink of black tea in her favourite mug and writes a long shopping list.

After calling goodbye to her father, she walks the crunching shingle path that leads past the row of cottages towards the Martello tower and the narrow lane that leads in and out of the hamlet. Summer notices that some of the cottages have pieces of driftwood, old lifebelts and faded buoys outside them, collections of pebbles heaped up in decorative piles on outdoor tables, steps and windowsills.

She stands for a moment, her hands out wide, letting the wind buffet her, and it feels good. She thinks of Varkala – the heat, the azure, crystal waves, the Hindu pilgrims in yellow robes. And Kit.

She frowns; she can't let herself go there. Can't let him inside her head. She's reached the end of the path, where there's space for parking next to a red phone box. She's glad to see their old blue Renault – a familiar reminder of home. She strides over, unlocking the door and sliding in behind the wheel. Kit follows her in. Damn. Too late for control. Her mind has slipped into forbidden territory, because now she's imagining him under their beach umbrella, and how he'd fed her segments of orange, wiping the juice from her chin with his thumb, how he'd run his hands over her back, spreading oil into her shoulders and down the length of her spine; long, deft strokes, kneading and circling her skin.

She turns the key. The engine stutters into life. Damn. Damn. She can see him in front of her, holding eye contact with his tawny gaze, cupping her cheeks with his palms, as if he's trying to tell her something. She rams the gearstick into reverse, grabs the steering wheel with both hands, and presses her foot to the accelerator.

The car lurches backwards, and there's a sickening crunch of metal, the shock of a collision. She's hit something solid. Fuck. She must have backed into the phone box. She throws the door open and gets out to take a look. The frame of a bike is jammed under the Renault's back wheels. Summer gasps, hands flying to her mouth. She hurries into the car and inches it forward, then rushes to pull the bike into an upright position. It lurches like a drunk in her grasp, the front wheel curved into a bow, the central frame crushed and twisted.

She wonders how to find out who it belongs to, as she drags it into the grass and lays it down on its side.

'Hello! You there!'

She looks up to see a figure marching towards her, the tails of a raincoat flapping behind, a battered trilby pulled low. As the person gets closer, Summer recognises her as the woman collecting stones on the beach.

Close-up, she's weather-beaten and lined, with pale hazel eyes, a bold nose and wide mouth, wisps of bottle-red hair escaping from under her hat. Summer guesses she must be in her early sixties. The woman lets out a howl of horror when she sees the bike and crouches down, putting a hand on the bent-up metal frame. 'Esmerelda.' She strokes the distorted machine and straightens up, glaring at Summer, 'You ran her over?'

'By mistake,' Summer says. 'I'm so sorry. Of course, I'll pay—'

'Oh, you people,' the woman spits. 'You think everything can be fixed with money. You think you can buy whatever you like – a community, a life, a . . . bicycle.' She pats the handlebars.

'I've had this bike for twenty years, looked after her, oiled her, replaced parts and kept her going, until you come along.'

The phrase 'you people' repeats in Summer's head. A cog in her chest tightens.

'As I said, I am very sorry,' she says slowly. 'If you let me know how much you need to mend or replace . . . Esmerelda—'

'You can't just come in here and start throwing your weight around,' the woman scowls. 'You need to respect this place. Tread carefully.'

Summer turns away, opening the car door, deciding the best tactic is to ignore her. She can hear Laura's voice in her head – don't encourage her; mad people love to talk.

But the woman follows, close on her heels, 'You turn up for weekends when the weather's nice, tramp all over the fragile vegetation, leave litter on the beach, and then you roar off in your big expensive cars.'

The cog turns again, and something snaps. Summer swings around. 'Does this look like a big, expensive car?' She gestures to the Renault. 'You're obviously unhappy about us moving here for some reason. But we're not going anywhere.'

The woman takes a step back. 'It's not a weekend cottage?'

'We've rented it for six months. And we might extend the lease or buy somewhere after that.' She frowns. 'Not that it's any of your business.'

The woman is rubbing her face with her hands. Her nails are painted yellow. 'Forgive me,' she says in a husky voice. 'My temper gets the better of me sometimes.' She shakes her head. 'I got the wrong end of the stick. It's not unknown, to be honest. But as a long-time resident here, I am angry about the amount of city folk who think they can buy a place and leave it empty until they feel like coming down for the three sunny weekends of the year.' She takes off her hat. 'I'm sorry to have thought you were one of them. I can see now that you are not.'

'It's okay.' Summer's shoulders relax. 'Maybe we can start again,' and she remembers Kit saying something similar on a dusty Indian street. She pushes the thought away as she offers her hand, 'I'm Summer Blythe.'

'What a marvellous name,' the woman says, giving her fingers a hearty shake. 'I might have to pinch it. I'm Loretta Miller. Cat lady. Writer.'

'What kind of writer?' Effie asks.

'Romantic novels,' she says with a wink. 'I write for the older woman. Plenty of armchair sex.'

Summer laughs. 'I've never heard that expression before.'

'Probably because I just made it up.' She plonks her hat back on her head, and glances over her shoulder at her bike. 'I'd better sort this poor love out. I'll get her back to my place and see if anything can be done.'

'I'll help.'

'No, no,' she waves a hand. 'You get on – you must have a lot to do. You've only just moved in, haven't you?'

'Yes. It's two of us, me and my father, Donald.'

'Come over and have a drink one evening. Bring your father. I'm in the blue cottage at the end.'

'Any evening?' Summer asks.

Loretta nods. 'Six o'clock is my favoured hour.'

26

Kit

His fingers are freezing. He wasn't expecting it to be so cold. His body is still in shock from leaving India. He makes his way along The Backs, away from the city through flat countryside. The roads are quiet, and mist rises from the fields. Grantchester is a village of thatched cottages, a pub, and a famous tearoom. On his right is a broad green flood plain, long grass silvered with dew, ancient oaks with branches spreading over the winding river Cam. He goes through a kissing gate into the meadow.

As he wades through thick grass, his shoes and the bottoms of his trousers are quickly drenched. As far as he can tell, there's not another soul here – animal or human. He finds a spot under a tree and slumps down between the crooked fingers of some exposed roots. The ache in his leg is back. He tries to concentrate on the scene before him, the movement of the grass, the glint of light on water. *Best place to spot hares*, she'd said.

Did she lie about everything?

But she wasn't the only one to hold back the truth. He

didn't tell her the real reason he spent his savings on a plane ticket to India.

His father had forgotten to send a card on his twenty-sixth birthday. That was no big surprise; he hadn't been in contact for years. But it occurred to Kit for the first time that there was nothing stopping him from just going to see him. He knew his father lived in Wokingham.

He took a train, and for the whole journey rehearsed the things he'd say when he got there.

He walked from the station. It was the summer – a heatwave making the tarmac soft, an acrid smell of asphalt spiking the air. The pavements were hot and dusty; leaves drooped on the trees. He walked slowly, sweat prickling his neck, stinging his eyes. He checked house numbers, feeling nervous, suddenly wondering if he was doing the right thing – it wasn't too late to turn around. The houses were large, set back from a busy road behind dark shrubbery and high fences. Most had several cars parked in spacious driveways. He heard children playing in gardens, the sound of hosepipes, the whirr of lawnmowers. Number fifteen was called The Laurels. The wide metal gate stood open. Kit paused, sick with anticipation.

Then he saw it – a black Ferrari Dino 246 GT parked in the driveway next to an estate car. The sight made him gasp. He stepped forward across the gravel drive, nerves forgotten as his hands hovered over the gorgeous curves and lines, the slightly flared wheel arches, the perfect proportions. One of the most beautiful cars in the world. At first, considered a poor relation by snobs who said it wasn't a Ferrari. But Kit knew it had been made by a grieving father in honour of a much-loved dead son.

They had the same taste in cars, exactly the same. He

couldn't wait to tell him, and he knew that this was a sign that everything was going to be all right – they'd laugh about the coincidence, and his father would take him for a spin. Maybe he'd even let him take the wheel. They'd listen to the perfect, small engine purr, grin at each other knowingly as they talked about the car's fingertip responsiveness, how nimble it was, how elegantly it cornered. And then his father would explain what had happened to separate them all these years. He'd apologise. Make things right.

He was walking past the Dino towards the house, which was actually a big, sprawling bungalow, when the front door opened.

Kit threw himself into the nearest bush, whipping headfirst through a tangle of thin branches and waxy leaves. Landing on his hands and knees, he crouched on the earth, heart exploding through his ribcage. Instinct. Fear. He wasn't sure what made him dive for cover. He untangled himself from a clutch of twigs, pushed a leaf from his face, feeling like a fool. Now he was going to have to crawl out of the bush and explain himself. Through a mesh of green, he saw his father appear out of the house, older, smaller, and losing his hair, but definitely the man he remembered. He tensed his thighs, ready to stand up, when bounding after his father came a boy, a red-cheeked child.

'Let's get our skates on, Harry,' his father was saying. 'Or we'll be late.'

The boy looked up, grinning. He couldn't have been much more than ten. The boy said, 'Can we take the Dino, Daddy? Please?'

And his father rolled his eyes and glanced behind at the house, 'All right, but don't tell your mother, OK?' He reached over and tousled the boy's head. 'She won't notice when she's on the phone to her sister. Got the present?'

The boy – Harry – waved a neatly wrapped box, and they both climbed into the black car, and with a roar of 195-horsepower engine, and a skid of gravel, they drove past Kit's hiding place.

He stayed there, under the leaves, hands pressed against dirt, the taste of exhaust fumes on his tongue. Then he got up and walked back to the station and caught the next train. He bought his plane ticket for India a few days later.

Kit blinks into the morning. Thinking about that afternoon makes him feel sick. He can't bear to have the memory inside him, wishes he could scrub it away.

The dew has evaporated from the meadow, the sky gathering blue into its depths. A quickening in the grass catches his attention. He can't focus properly at first – the noise of the Dino's engine still roars inside his head – but he realises he's looking at a pair of long black-tipped ears. They quiver, making a 'V' shape. He's motionless as the animal lopes towards him, and he can see what Summer meant when she said that a rabbit and a hare are completely different creatures. The hare is larger than he expected, with huge, muscular back legs. He can sense the energy thrumming through the elegant body. Amber eyes seem to encompass the world.

Kit stares, mesmerised. Another hare approaches, and suddenly, they are dancing. The two of them upright, on long back legs, chests almost touching, front paws moving like boxers. Silken ears fly behind them, paws darting in and out. Back legs shuffle and hop. Kit holds his breath.

A splash. A shout. And the hares are down, noses twitching, alert for danger. He blinks. And in the time it takes for the skin of his lids to slide across the curve of his eyes, they have taken off like wingless birds.

Three young men are swimming in the river, shouting and calling to each other, thrashing the water, churning it up with their limbs.

Kit uncoils himself, his leg cramping under him. He uses the sturdy strength of the tree trunk to help him stand, rubbing his muscles to try and get the circulation going.

The only truth is the hare. Everything else was a lie. He knows it now, and there's no unknowing it. The girl in India was a stranger.

The sky, the huge and spinning sky, wraps itself around him, binding him tighter and tighter, until he can't breathe, can't get air into his lungs. Blue clogs his mouth, stops his eyes. His body is filled with unbearable blue. His heart is drowning in it.

He comes to, flat on his back, looking up through a fringe of grass into concerned faces. The swimmers, dripping wet and wrapped in towels, clasp his shoulders and haul him into a sitting position.

'Think you fainted, mate,' one of them says.

'Are you all right?' Another voice. 'Do you need us to tell anyone where you are?'

Kit swallows. He opens his mouth. Nothing happens. Air whistles through his throat. He whispers ghost words.

'What's that?' One of them leans closer.

His friend is saying, 'Maybe he's foreign?'

Kit tries to get onto his feet. Several pairs of strong hands help him, grappling, heaving him up. When he's upright, he staggers to the side, regains his balance and looks at the young men. He tries to speak again, to thank them, but the simple words are stuck in his chest like stones. He shivers and shakes his head. He gestures, trying to indicate that he's all right, that he's leaving.

They stand around, half-naked, their bodies slick with river water, confused expressions on their blunt, open faces. They are probably students, just a couple of years younger than him, but he feels ancient in comparison.

As he opens the front door, his mother is there, dishcloth in hand, talking at him before he's had time to take off his jacket and remove his shoes.

'Kit! You're back. You could have let me know.' She raises her shoulders, shrugging at his constant ability to fulfil her worst predictions. And then, calling out from the kitchen, running the tap, 'Terry said you'd gone off to find that girl?'

Reluctantly, he follows her into the room. He doesn't want to talk about Summer, but his mother has lost interest in the subject.

'I'll have to put some more potatoes on,' she's saying, not looking at him. 'I suppose you're hungry?'

When he tries to answer, broken sounds emerge in squeaks and rasps, odd syllables catching on his tongue. He puts a hand to his throat. 'Don't . . . worry about me.' He coughs. 'I'm not . . . hungry.'

'Have you caught a cold?' She stops, hands on hips, accusing.

'Just . . . something in my throat.'

'That's public transport for you,' she says, ignoring him. 'Full of germs. And I'll do those potatoes because you need to eat. You look terrible.'

Their conversations are full of holes and misunderstandings. He didn't tell her about the day he went to visit his father and has no idea if she knows about Alan's new wife and son. She wouldn't understand about Summer. He wishes he'd never said anything.

He goes up to his room to drop his bag. The afternoon light catches one of the shiny patches on the wall where his mother must have ripped his posters off, and he wonders if she's thrown them away. All through his childhood he collected prints of classic cars, admiring the brilliance of design and mechanics that had gone into his favourites, paying homage in front of posters of Maseratis, Lamborghinis, and the Ferrari 275 GTB/4 owned by Steve McQueen. He promised himself he'd own a classic car himself one day – and every penny he earned from his paper round and his Saturday job, he stored in jam jars hidden inside his wardrobe.

There's a garage two streets away. A small place under the railway arches, run by a Portuguese man. Moteo was 'old school', could turn his hand to anything. When Kit was a boy, he spent as much time there as possible. The place stank of old oil, brake dust and dirt. Cars were jammed in, bumper to bumper in the windowless workshop. Engines were taken to pieces and laid out on cardboard to be checked, cleaned, renewed and reassembled. He'd got a Saturday job there when he was eleven. Spent afternoons making cups of tea, polishing metalwork, washing tyres, sweeping the oil-stained floor. Moteo's wife sat in a tiny cubbyhole they called the office, knitting baby booties for a seemingly unlimited number of grandchildren, unfazed by the topless girlie calendar hooked onto the wall above her. Whenever the phone rang, she would get up with a lurch, placing the knitting carefully on her chair. She was the one who added up the bills stuck onto skewers on the desk, muttering to herself in Portuguese. He left the place at the end of the day with smudges on his face, clothes and hands filthy, smelling of petrol. Moteo didn't talk much – and his accent was strong when he did – but his speech was of cars and engines and Kit hung on every word. He thrilled when Moteo addressed him directly, shivered like a dog when the man patted his shoulders in passing. Mrs Moteo tweaked his cheeks so hard it hurt; told him he was a 'good boy'.

Later on, Moteo taught him about mechanics, pointed out the intricate workings of engines, let him tinker with cylinder bolts and crankshafts. He'd shown him how to weld, and Kit discovered he had a feel for it, loving the smell of melting metal, the hiss of the MIG, the way he could transform something damaged into something whole.

He'd been looking forward to driving around to the garage in his newly restored Dino, taking the old man for a drive. But then Wokingham happened, and everything changed.

It occurs to him that he should visit Moteo anyway, even if he doesn't have a restored classic car to show him. He hobbles downstairs, calling out that he's going to visit the garage, and won't be long.

'Oh, it's not there any more,' his mother says, coming to the door. 'The old man passed when you were away.'

'Passed?'

'Heart attack. The developers seemed to move in overnight.'

He stands in front of the railway arches. A brand-new coffee shop has taken the place of the dark, greasy cave he remembers. Instead of the faded sign for the garage, there's a famous logo, a list of drinks, and the scent of coffee and sugar replacing the stink of oil and petrol. There are tables on the pavement, and customers sipping from tall cups, staring at the world through sunglasses.

Kit's chest tightens with sorrow. Moteo was the closest anyone had come to being a father figure to him. And now he's gone.

'So,' his mother asks, passing him the bowl of peas. 'What are you going to do? You can't hang around here for the rest of your life.'

'We'll have to start charging you rent,' Terry says, taking a mouthful of sausage and mash.

Kit stares down at his plate. 'I'll be out of your hair in the next couple of days. I haven't decided where I'm going yet – but I'm going to try and make it as an artist.'

His mother shakes her head, looking at Terry. 'He could have been a dentist. Could have been anything he wanted. Always got A's at school.'

'Your mother says you're good with your hands.' Terry wipes his mouth with a napkin. 'The building trade is solid – plumber, electrician. You'll never go without work.'

Kit says nothing. He doesn't want to argue with them. He pushes his food around. After the meal, he collects the plates and takes them into the kitchen. 'I'll wash up,' he calls over his shoulder. 'You two can relax.'

He hears the television go on, the snappy jingle of an advert. He's glad she's happy with Terry, but he can't wait to leave this house with its chemical atmosphere and frozen dancers. They've always given him the creeps, his mother's tribute to her lost past.

He could go anywhere in the world. Back to India. Maybe travel through Asia; he's always wanted to visit Vietnam, Cambodia, maybe go trekking in Patagonia. Of course, there is the problem of money. He could get a temporary job here and earn enough for a plane ticket, but then he'd need to stay at home and pay his mother rent while he collected enough cash. He doesn't want to do that. England then, or Scotland, or Wales. He likes the idea of finding a hut halfway up a mountain, becoming a hermit who paints and takes solitary walks. But he needs to eat.

Upstairs in his room, he takes the sketches of Summer from their hiding place, and sits on his bed, leafing through them, remembering how she'd felt in his arms, the silky texture of her honeyed skin, the push of her tongue against his when they kissed. He thinks of her describing the Suffolk coast: a home by the sea; a place full of like-minded people. She'd mentioned a town: Woodbridge. There's nothing stopping him from going there – finding a job in a pub or restaurant, or maybe he could find work in a garage. She said there were artists' colonies. It should be cheaper to live, and he doesn't need much, as long as there's time to concentrate on his painting. He begins to pack his rucksack, tipping in clothes. As he empties his drawers, he finds the hare earring under a tumble of socks; he looks at it for a moment before sliding it into his pocket.

APRIL

Four months of Summer

27

Summer

She washes up their breakfast things, wiping soapy hands on her jeans. Her father looks up from the table, where he's reading the paper, a coffee by his elbow.

'Apparently, eighty per cent of the population are unhappy with the way John Major is running the country,' he says.

'Yes, we need change,' she agrees. 'A big change.'

'You've stopped humming,' he says, closing the paper. 'It makes me sad not to hear you any more.'

She turns to face him, leaning against the counter. 'I don't even know what the tune is most of the time.' She attempts a smile. 'Probably really irritating.'

'Not at all. It's part of you.' He gives her a small, sad smile.

She looks out of the window at the beach, the long slope of shingle, the sea cabbages and yellow grasses. It's so different from Midsummer Common with its cyclists, children and dogs. She wonders how her dogs are getting on, who's throwing balls for them. She hopes they're getting affection, that someone is keeping an eye on them properly, knowing that Frankie doesn't like her ears touched, and Mabel won't come unless you shout 'goodbye' at her.

'You've never shown me any of the photos you took in India,' Dad goes on.

She keeps her face averted, looking out to sea. 'There hasn't been time to develop them.' She doesn't think she could bear it – being reminded of their hut, of him.

'But now there is,' he persists. 'You could set up a temporary dark room in the bathroom.'

'No,' she says. 'I don't think so.'

'Please,' he says quietly. 'It would mean a great deal to me.'

So here she is, surrounded by the familiar stink of chemicals, all her equipment arranged around her: loupe, puffer brush, focus finder, tongs. She's wearing her safety glasses and gloves, following the procedure she was taught when she did the photography course. She's strung a line between the door and the blacked-out window. Her trays are positioned in the bath, sitting in an inch or so of warm water. She's chosen her negatives. At first, she'd thought she'd avoid developing any pictures of Kit. But she's let herself have one. The room is bathed in the warm, red glow of the safelight. The smell of chemicals is metallic, pungent. It stirs an excitement in her chest, the thrill of the unknown. Watching images appear on the paper never fails to amaze her. Even though she understands the chemical process, the science behind each step, the process retains a sense of alchemy, a magic. And each time, there are always surprises.

She uses the tongs to take a piece of photographic paper out of the final fixing bath and drops it into a container of water to rinse it clean. Then she pegs it up on the string to dry. By the end of the afternoon, the line is clipped all along with rectangles of paper.

She unclips them when they're completely dry, and places them carefully on the board she's put across the bath to act as a wide shelf. Then she pulls down the blackout material, letting daylight into the room.

She leans over her finished photographs. And to her surprise, the excitement of seeing the images outweighs the heaviness in her heart. Here is the monkey eating the mango in Kochi, his long fingers cocked like a duchess taking tea. Here is the one-eared dog, looking at her with his head tilted to the side. Here is the tusker glimpsed through palm fronds, stippled with shadows. She moves from one picture to the next, assessing, critiquing.

Kit is the last one. It's a close-up, taken on the beach, and he's smiling at her, his eyes fixed on hers, full of warmth, intense with feeling. She studies his long, dusty lashes, the sunrays of his irises, his wide smile, his slightly chapped lips, the small bump in the middle of his nose. She goes back to his eyes – and notices a figure coiled inside the mirror of his pupils. Her own shape, shrunk to minuscule proportions, the camera to her face, caught at the heart of his gaze.

Kit.

Her throat tightens. Longing rushes through her. She turns the picture over and pushes the heels of her hands into her eyes, takes a deep breath.

The phone is ringing and Summer rushes to it, snatching it up, hoping to hear a familiar, friendly voice. She's not disappointed. 'Laura!'

'Hey, how do you feel about a visit? Not too soon to arrange one?'

Summer's voice chokes with tears of gratitude. 'When? When can you come?'

'In a couple of weeks? It's the earliest, I'm afraid. Work is crazy.'

'Seems ages away, but it's something to keep me going, knowing you're coming. And you'll stay? Saturday night. Maybe Friday, too?'

'Yes, please! Can't wait.'

Summer puts down the phone with a sense of relief and goes to find her father to show him her photographs, all except the one of Kit.

She gets up early, taking her cup of tea into the little front garden to catch the first hint of sun, watching the waves rolling in from the horizon. There's a haul of flotsam and jetsam in the garden. Dad returned from his evening stroll with things he found at the shoreline: a twist of bleached rope, a pale curve of wood, a plastic yoghurt pot refined into something beautiful by the pressure of water, and a handful of white shells.

She yawns. She'd been awake for hours last night. She'd found the notebook Effie gave her with the red and silver cover, had turned its blank pages, promising her sister that she'll write in it now. She ran her finger over the serrated edge of a missing page; torn out for the note she wrote Kit in the hut.

A figure appears across the shingle, wisps of red hair flying out from a shiny, tight black cap – Loretta, marching towards the sea, wrapped in a dressing gown and clutching a towel. She sees Summer and waves, changing direction to come over.

'Just off for my swim – want to come too?'

'I thought it was too dangerous to swim here?'

'Oh, it is further up towards the river mouth. Lethal currents there. But just here is fine.'

Summer prevaricates. She's not the strongest swimmer. 'Really . . . at this time of year? Won't it be freezing?'

'It'll do you good,' Loretta says. 'It'll clear your head, revitalise your organs. I swim every day, summer and winter.' She grins, circling her face with a finger. 'How else do you think I defy time?'

Summer returns her smile. 'All right. Just give me a minute to change and grab a towel.'

The shore slopes dramatically down to the water's edge. A steep bank of shingle rolls under Summer's feet as she lurches and winces over stones to the water's edge. She dips her toes in and snatches a breath, 'It's freezing!'

'Best to get it over with fast,' Loretta calls over her shoulder, as she submerges herself in the waves. 'And watch out because it drops quickly.'

Summer forces herself to take a couple of steps; she's up to her knees immediately, her skin flinching at the arctic temperature. Another step and she's up to her thighs. The cold snatches oxygen from her lungs. It makes her laugh. A shock of joy shoots through her. Her mind is blank, spinning, laughter bubbling out of her. She's still laughing when she steps off a shelf into a void. Her eyes open into swirling grey. She struggles to the surface, spitting out water, gasping with something like hysteria.

'Keep moving!' Loretta calls, as she powers away with a strong front crawl. Her shiny head looks like a seal's.

The experience is so different from swimming in the Arabian Sea that Summer can't hold the comparison for more than a second. This sea demands her attention, numbs her mind and body, tricks her feet, blinds her with its opaque depths. She begins to swim, her arms scooping out a half-doggy-paddle, half-breaststroke, legs flailing. She stays close to the shore, resisting the current that's trying to push her further out. She swims up and down, her chin raised, swallowing salt water as she gulps air.

She staggers out of the sea. Loretta comes out after her, grinning.

'See what you mean about it being invigorating,' Summer laughs. She looks down at her thighs, mottled purple blue. Her fingers are quilted. Her skin feels electrified, her mind clear.

She picks up her towel from the beach and wipes her face, rubs her head. Her short hair still surprises her – but it's certainly easier to dry.

'Cold water cures most things,' Loretta gasps, wrapping herself in a voluminous robe. 'It releases happy endorphins. And the ocean's full of magical health properties – biorhythms and things.' Her teeth chatter, as she towels her hair vigorously, head on the side. 'So, has it helped?'

'Sorry?'

'Whatever was worrying you before?'

'Oh,' Summer looks at her. 'How did you know?'

'You have one of those faces, my dear. Transparent. It's rather rare nowadays.'

'I was . . . remembering someone I've lost,' Summer admits. 'I met him in Kerala. We were only together for days, but . . . I thought we were going to keep seeing each other . . .' She shivers and wraps her towel tightly. 'I suppose part of the problem is that I never really knew who he was . . . we didn't have enough time.'

'If you want my advice,' Loretta says, 'don't dwell on the past. Don't get hung up thinking that some guy is the only one who can make you happy.' She waves a hand. 'The kind of books I write aren't real. Life isn't like that. They're fairy tales for grown-ups. But there are still plenty of love stories waiting to be written. You need to throw yourself into the fray once more.'

Loretta pats Summer's cold knee. 'You're too pretty to mope.' She squints her eyes, looking out to sea. 'Wish I had my binoculars with me.' She points to some birds hovering above the waves. 'See those? Kittiwakes.'

'What are kittiwakes? Seagulls?'

'There's actually no such thing as a seagull,' she says. 'There are many types of gulls, and not all of them live by the coast – a kittiwake is one of the more common ones, and they *are* coastal gulls.'

'I didn't know that. About seagulls.'

'It's one of my hobbies – birdwatching. It's a good excuse for taking long walks. There's always something interesting to see.'

'Could I come with you one day?' Summer asks. 'Unless . . . I'd be in the way.'

'My dear, I'd be delighted.' Loretta heaves herself up off the stones. 'Right,' she says briskly. 'If I don't get into a hot shower, I might lose some toes and fingers.' She's banging her arms around herself. 'I advise you to do the same.'

Summer hurries back up the slope of shingle, clutching her towel around her, going through the open gate and the dove grey door, the paint under her fingers coming off in ragged slivers.

Going through the living room, her teeth are chattering, and she's looking forward to the heat of the shower when the phone starts to ring. She frowns but picks it up.

'Summer?' a familiar voice asks. 'It's Adam.'

She holds the receiver tight, bringing the sound of him closer.

'How are you?' he asks, and then, 'Sorry. Silly question.'

'No. It's OK,' she reassures him. 'We're managing. Dad and I made a kind of pact to keep going, one foot in front of the other,' she says. 'I've been swimming in the sea. It's unbelievably cold.'

'Outdoor swimming in April?' He sounds impressed. 'Rather you than me. Your sister would approve.'

She wraps her towel tighter. It's good to talk to someone who knew Effie.

'Anyway,' he goes on. 'I was wondering if you have a free weekend soon. I'd like to come and visit?'

They agree on a date and, as she puts the phone down, she realises that she's hungry, properly hungry for the first time in a long time. She goes into the kitchen, her gaze sweeping over Mum's ceramic plates, the old Raeburn, and the colourful rag rug on the mellow red tiles. The place really does feel like home, especially with Dad's clocks ticking from walls and shelves. She pulls out the biscuit barrel and picks up a digestive, takes a bite of the sweet crumbly biscuit. No more thoughts of Kit, she thinks sternly, as she glances out of the window at the beach. She'll throw herself into the North Sea every day if she has to – if that will keep her from remembering him.

It's a week later when she finds Dad on his hands and knees in the little shingly front garden. He's laying white shells on the ground, making swirls and lines. He has a bucket of shells next to him. He is so engrossed that he doesn't notice her until her shadow falls across him.

She crouches beside him, studying the patterns. 'That's lovely.'

He smiles, 'I've collected so many, thought I'd better do something with them.'

He attempts to get up, and she helps him with a hand under his elbow. He was fifty when she was born, newly married to a woman nearly twenty years his junior. He'd been an academic and a bachelor his entire life – but Mum changed all that.

'I said we'd pop over for a drink with Loretta later. Is that okay?'

He nods, looking distracted. 'I have something to tell you, Summer.' He moves from one foot to the other in an anxious dance. 'Let's go inside.'

They get out of the glare, and she blinks, blinded by the shadows of the house. Dad is standing in the tiny living room under the low ceiling, clasping his hands. 'The estate agent's been in contact,' he says. 'They have someone who wants the house. They didn't even need to advertise. It's a good price. A very good price.'

'The house is sold?'

'Not yet,' he says quickly. 'I can tell them no.' He looks at her, 'What shall we do?'

She goes over and takes his hands, holding them steady inside her own. 'We should say yes,' she says. 'It's time. We've done the hard bit, and it's feeling more and more right to be here every day.'

'Good. Good,' he says, moving away from her. He bends down, lifting something up from behind the sofa. A package wrapped in brown paper. A substantial box. 'On the strength of all that lovely cash coming our way – I got this for you. I've heard you talking about it, and . . . and I knew you'd say no, so I went ahead.'

He hands her the box. Puzzled, she pulls off the paper, and sees the image on the box. Pulse hammering, she opens it.

'Dad,' she gasps. 'It's ... it's a Canon SLR. With a telephoto lens!'

'It is the right one, isn't it?'

She hugs him. 'It's perfect. Exactly what I've always wanted.'

He squeezes her, 'I know you haven't used your camera since we got here – but those pictures you took in India are extraordinary, Summer. You have a gift.'

Her fingers itch to explore the beautiful, shiny machine. She wants to go straight outside and find something to photograph.

Six o'clock, and with all Dad's clocks whirring and chiming behind them, they crunch over the shingle to Loretta's cornflower cottage. It's bigger than theirs, with sliding glass doors opening onto decking. As she goes through the gate, she spots a table covered with different pebbles, arranged by colour into piles with bits of interestingly shaped driftwood and turquoise sea glass. She runs her fingers over them.

Loretta is sitting in a wicker chair, a novel open in her lap. A black cat is sprawled in the sunshine, basking. Another one sits in the shade of a plant pot.

'I like your collection,' Summer says.

Loretta puts her book down and stands up. 'I pick up anything that catches my eye when I'm walking,' she smiles. 'You'll get the habit too, I expect. Everyone who lives here does.'

'I'm Donald – Summer's father.' He steps forward and Loretta takes his hand. 'I've already caught the habit,' he says. 'With me it's shells. White ones.'

'The whelk shells.' She's wearing a long, floating purple dress, and bright pink earrings that clash spectacularly with her scarlet hair. 'How strange to choose those when there are so many beautiful and unique stones. Aren't they a bit boring?'

'Each one is slightly different,' Dad looks defensive. 'And the precision of the whirls and spirals is intriguing.'

'Dad's a mathematician,' Summer offers.

'Maths isn't a language I speak,' Loretta says with a slight toss of her head. 'Numbers tumble through my head like sand through a sieve.' She touches one of her earrings. 'Now then, martinis for everyone?' She disappears through the French window. Summer stares after her into a sitting room. From what she can see, Loretta's home is a comfortable muddle of antiques, piles of books and magazines, cat litter trays, ornaments, and colourful fabrics thrown everywhere.

Loretta comes back with a silver cocktail shaker. Summer sinks into a chair, and Loretta places a cold drink in her hand, garnished with a twist of lemon.

Loretta holds up her glass in a toast. 'To you both – I'm so glad to have interesting neighbours.'

There's a brief silence as they sip their drinks. 'You said you write romantic novels?' she prompts Loretta.

'Indeed. I've been doing it for the last … goodness,' she laughs, flicking her red hair over her shoulders. 'I've lost count … must be over twenty years.'

'And you make a living from it?' Dad asks, as another cat slinks out of the house and leaps into his lap. The creature butts her head into his hand, and he gives her an absent-minded stroke behind the ears.

'You could say that.' Loretta shoots a cool glance in his direction. 'I've won romantic novelist of the year five times; my books have been translated into twenty-five languages. One of them was made into a film a few years ago – with Debra Winger. It was rather good.'

Dad looks a little dazed. 'Well,' he mutters in an undertone. 'That told me.' The cat jumps off his lap and wanders away to lie the shade.

The silence stretches and tightens. Summer pinches the thin stem of her glass. She's trying to think of a safe topic of conversation. 'I'll put some music on,' Loretta says in a strained voice. She goes into the house. The sound of Ella Fitzgerald's voice singing 'Lady Be Good' floats out to them.

Their father salutes Loretta with his drink as she comes back. 'One of my favourite Ella songs,' he says.

'Ah-ha,' she says, sinking into her seat. 'Something tells me I've found another jazz fan.'

'That's an understatement,' Summer says with a relieved smile.

'But the 1947 version is the only one worth listening to,' Dad goes on. 'Her scatting is genius on that – I find this version a little bland.'

'Really?' Loretta says with a sweet smile. 'I completely disagree.'

'I've been trying to persuade Dad to get into the sea,' Summer says quickly. 'Loretta swims year-round,' she adds. 'You love it, don't you?'

'I swear by it,' she says. 'If you pluck up the courage,' she tells Donald, you'll feel like a new man.' She turns to Summer, 'Join me tomorrow?'

'Sorry,' Summer says. 'Not tomorrow. I'll be out at dawn with my new camera. But Dad – can't we tempt you? It's incredibly invigorating.'

'I have no desire to feel like a new man,' he says. 'I'm happiest on dry land.'

Loretta leans towards Summer. 'Pebbles and cold water aren't to everyone's taste.'

'How many cats have you got?' Dad watches a large tabby stroll into view.

'Twelve at last count,' Loretta says. 'I take in waifs and strays. Try to find them new homes.'

'Twelve?' he repeats in a faint voice. 'Lucky your books do well; that's a lot of mouths to feed.'

'Luck doesn't come into it, my dear Donald,' she says over the rim of her glass.

They chat about other things, but Summer is painfully aware of a jarring between the two older people. No topics seem safe.

'You know, I think it's time we went home,' she says, standing up. 'I have an early start.'

Dad unfolds himself from his chair, and she holds his elbow to steady him as he stands. Seeing him in company makes her realise how out of practice he is at social niceties. He's become set in his ways, almost cantankerous.

They make their goodbyes, and tramp back across the shingle.

'Didn't you like her?' Summer asks. 'I thought you'd get on.'

'A bit too brash for me,' he says.

'Shame. It would be good for you to have a friend here.'

'I don't need anyone else. I have you,' he says, and he strides ahead, his white hair blowing in a sudden breeze. He seems eager to get home.

She has to hurry to catch him up.

28

Kit

He gets out at Woodbridge Station, heaving his rucksack onto his shoulders, attempting to tuck his folded-up easel under his arm. He walks up a gentle slope towards the centre. It's a small market town with pretty painted houses, some of them Elizabethan, and a surplus of antique shops. He calls into cafés and pubs as he passes, asking if they need staff. Nobody does, although one takes his CV, tells him to come back in a couple of weeks. He needs a job and a place to stay – he has enough money to keep him going for a couple of days, but his savings are dwindling.

He finds the library, a modern building that's almost brutalist compared to the chintzy prettiness of the rest of the place, and takes a seat in the window, flicking through the local papers, checking small ads and job vacancies. Nothing for a mechanic. He jots down a few possibilities. There's a community board by the front desk plastered with cards – he scans them for anything interesting, his eyes moving over adverts for a grand piano, and a washing machine, free to anyone who'll collect it.

There's a note for a gardener; he tears off the telephone number. How hard can it be to pull out some weeds and mow a lawn?

Outside, on the pavement, he sees a phone box at the corner of the street and pulls open the heavy door. He calls up about the gardening position, but it's already taken. He tries a couple of the other job vacancies, but they've all gone. He pushes out of the box, thinking he'll find a cheap B&B, continue looking again tomorrow. Maybe he'd have better luck in a bigger town like Ipswich, more chance of him finding work as a mechanic. But he wants to settle on the coast next to the wild North Sea that Summer told him about. He hasn't even seen it yet.

He retraces his steps back to the station and the river. He'd glimpsed water through a small forest of clinking masts when the train pulled in, heard seagulls. He crosses the railway tracks by way of a tall, narrow metal bridge and goes carefully down the other side to find himself next to a small marina, yachts and barges moored to the dock, wobbly wooden planks bridging the gap across the water. Some of the boats look as if they haven't moved for years – pots of geraniums on board, unfolded deck-chairs, bikes. He spots a tabby cat looking out of a porthole.

There's a greasy spoon housed in a caravan next to the metal bridge; the smell of frying food makes his stomach rumble. He joins the short queue, and orders tea and a sausage sandwich. He sits on a bench with the easel propped beside him, rucksack at his feet, and takes a sip of hot liquid from the polystyrene cup. The river is a wide body of water, bobbing with buoys and boats at anchor, alive with ducks and swans. He hears snatches of conversation as couples wander along the river wall just behind him, a mother with a flock of small children, a man calling his dog. On his travels abroad, he'd loved the freedom and anonymity of being a stranger in an unknown place, but the chatter of his own language, the everyday sounds of people's lives, makes him feel isolated, invisible.

He takes a big bite of his sandwich and chews. Things always seem better on a full stomach. He's aware that the pitch of someone's voice has risen – recognises a twist of fear, 'Gramps, watch out!'

Looking to the right, he sees an elderly man balancing precariously on a tumble of rocks that seem to have been placed as a kind of flood defence. The tide is high, and dark water laps at the man's feet. A woman has taken hold of one of his hands and is trying to guide him back towards the bank, but the man resists, wobbling. There's a look of panic on his face.

Kit leaves the remains of his lunch on the bench, shoves his rucksack underneath it, and goes down to them, jumping onto the nearest, flattest rock, landing with a sharp pinch in his leg – it must be nearly a three-foot drop; he's not sure how the old man made it. 'Can I help?' he calls.

The woman turns, her cheeks flushed. She's young, he sees, probably early twenties. Long black hair swings around her shoulders. 'Can you grab his other hand?' she gasps in frustration. 'Come on, Granddad. It's not safe here.'

Kit takes the old man's hand, and smiles, 'Hello. Shall we get off these rocks back onto the path?'

'I need to feed the swans,' the old man says in a wavering voice. 'She always did, you see. Every Saturday.'

'Just step where I'm stepping.' The man's bones are long and frail. Keeping gentle tension between them, Kit manages to get him over the rocks to the raised side of the bank. He lets go and clambers up onto the path, before reaching down again for his hands. 'On the count of three,' he says. 'Ready?'

Kit looks into watery pale eyes, a mouth gaping between

sunken cheeks. He hauls, while the girl stays on the rocks, pushing from behind. Together they get him back onto the path. Kit steadies him, and helps him sit on a low wall, then reaches down and clasps the woman's hand in his own and pulls her up. She's light and springy, and the surprise lack of resistance makes him stagger back, still holding her hand, so that they end up jolting against each other, her face squished into his chest.

She's laughing, pushing the hair out of her eyes. 'Thanks for that. God knows how I'd have got him onto the path without your help.' She turns to the old man. 'You gave me a fright! Leaping about like a man half your age.'

Kit glances back towards the bench to check that his bag and easel are safe. A large seagull is perched on the bench, and it flaps away in slow motion with the half-eaten sandwich in its beak. Kit grimaces, and shouts after it. 'Greedy bugger! That's my lunch!'

He goes back to reclaim his bag and easel and puts his cup in the nearby bin. 'I'm sorry,' the girl's saying. 'Let me buy you another.'

'No,' Kit says. 'I'd eaten most of it.'

'Don't be daft,' the girl says. 'Least I can do.' She brushes some dirt off her jeans. 'I'm Sally-Ann Fisk, and this is my gramps, David.'

Kit puts out his hand, 'Kit,' he says. 'Kit Appleby.'

She squints at him through narrowed eyes. 'You're not a local,' she says. 'Are you?'

He shakes his head. 'New in town today.'

'You staying here, in Woodbridge?'

He shakes his head. 'My plan is to get to the sea. I want to find a place along the coast.'

'What, for a holiday or something? You a rambler? Birdwatcher?'

'No. A painter.' He glances at the easel in his hand. 'I'm hoping to settle for a while. I'm looking for part-time work. A place to stay.'

'Really?' She puts her head on one side as if she's thinking, 'How about a village on a river that's very close to the sea? Would that do?'

'Yeah,' Kit agrees, not sure where this is heading. 'That kind of thing.'

'And you want part-time work, like bar work?'

'Uh-huh.'

They're walking now, back along the river wall towards the station. She has her grandfather's arm firmly linked with her own. 'My dad runs a pub in Orford. We're looking for extra staff.'

'Seriously?'

She laughs at his expression. 'Yeah – and I can put in a good word for you, if you like.'

'Could you give me the address? The telephone number?'

'I can do better than that,' she pats her grandfather's hand. 'We're going home right now, aren't we Gramps?' She turns to Kit. 'I can give you a lift, show you the place, introduce you to my dad?'

'That's . . .' he stumbles over his words in his surprise, 'that's . . . kind.'

She shrugs. 'Serendipity or whatever you want to call it – right place, right time. Sometimes life works like that, doesn't it?'

'Sometimes,' he agrees, thinking of Summer, and the unlikely scenario of an angry man and some stray dogs bringing them together.

She offers again to get him a replacement sandwich from the café, but he manages to dissuade her, and she tosses her head, 'Just don't tell me you're hungry later.'

He accompanies them to a battered, mud-splattered Land Rover Defender parked in the station car park, throws his rucksack onto the hard back seat and clambers up beside it. Gramps heaves himself into the passenger seat, and Sally-Ann gets into the driver's side. She's tiny, with slender legs in tight jeans, and the shoulders of a child. She can hardly see over the wheel. But she cranks into gear with confidence, reverses out of the space like an expert. Now that the engine has roared into life, sounding like a diesel bus, it's impossible to hold a conversation, so he braces himself, and cranes his neck to watch the landscape slide past, his teeth rattling every time they hit a bump.

They drive out of town, over a bridge and through a pine forest, along narrow roads that pass under a canopy of ancient-looking oak trees. He sees pigs rooting in big, muddy fields. They drive through small hamlets consisting of a few cottages; some have vegetables and boxes of eggs for sale, next to honesty boxes.

It's about half an hour more before they enter a large village, driving past a pretty market square and gracious, stone church with a square tower. The houses seem mostly Georgian in style, faded red brick, with climbing roses and thick swathes of lavender growing in front gardens. The Land Rover winds down a slope towards a quay. He glimpses a sweep of water beyond rooftops. They pull up next to a low, whitewashed pub called The Anchor. Seagulls perch on the tall chimneys.

'This is it,' Sally-Ann says, as she climbs out.

Kit helps get her grandfather down from the passenger seat.

'Gramps, Mum's in the kitchen,' she tells the old man. 'She'll give you a cup of tea. Come on,' she calls to Kit over her shoulder. 'Let's see if Dad's around.'

The pub is dim inside, low-ceilinged, with dark, smoked beams, an inglenook, a huge brick chimney breast and a fireplace with the grate swept clean. It's empty of customers at the moment, but it's the picture of what a homely country pub should be, Kit thinks, looking around.

'We serve food – simple stuff. Ploughman's. Sausage and mash. Fish and chips, of course,' Sally-Ann says, gesturing around her. 'We'd want you to serve behind the bar and help in the kitchen, empty glasses, take out the bins, pretty standard stuff. There's a local lad, Jack, who works weekends. Mum and I are the chefs.'

'Sounds good,' Kit says, wondering where he'll be able to find a cheap room to rent close by. Not having his own car could be tricky. This place is miles from anywhere.

She opens a door into a back room, and a couple of large dogs burst free, barrelling past her with a scrape of claws, hot breath and snapping teeth. He stands his ground, letting teeth and hair and barking resolve into two German shepherds banging up against his knees and snorting at his feet. He waits for them to settle before offering his hand for them to sniff.

She snaps her fingers, and they pad over to her. 'Sneezy and Doc.' Sally-Ann points to them in turn, then gives him an approving nod, 'You passed that test, then.'

A short man with a shiny bald head and the bow legs of a jockey bustles through the front door, and eyes up Kit with a questioning look.

'Dad,' she says quickly. 'Meet Kit. He saved me and Gramps just now, in Woodbridge. He's a hero. And he needs a job.' She gives Kit a look. 'He's got loads of bar experience.'

Kit is uncertain at first that there is a job. Her father seems confused and a little irritated to find a strange young man standing in his pub, cluttering up the place with a large rucksack and easel. But he's clearly besotted with his daughter, and her charm-offensive works. After quizzing Kit on what bar experience he's had, he sticks out his hand and takes Kit's in a vice-like grip. 'Paul,' he says. 'Looks like you've got yourself a trial run.' He nods towards the ceiling. 'There's a room if you want it, though I'll take lodgings and food out of your earnings.'

Sally-Ann shows him upstairs. 'We don't live here,' she explains. 'So, you'll have the place to yourself at night. We have a house a few doors down. Gramps lives at the almshouses. There's another room at the back that we let out for B & B guests sometimes, and the other rooms are used as storerooms.' She throws open a door. 'This is the nicest one. You get a view of the river.'

He heaves his stuff through the door. 'I can't thank you enough,' he says. 'You're my saviour.'

She grins, 'Save your thanks till you've survived a few Saturday nights.'

Kit unpacks his few possessions into a wobbly chest of drawers. Most of the bag is taken up with his pencils, paints, brushes and sketchbooks. He unfolds the easel and sets it up in the corner, a reminder of why he's here, a symbol of intent. He rubs his aching thigh and sits on the narrow bed. The modest room is under the eaves, wallpapered in a faded floral design; one casement window opens over the quay. Across the stretch of river, he can see a spit or an island. The dark swell of movement beyond that must be the North Sea. He leans out away from the whiff of dog, the lingering aromas of alcohol and fried food, to inhale the clean, sharp tang of salt, the iodine scent of seaweed. In his pocket, his fingers close around the tiny silver hare. The warmth of his skin makes it feel almost malleable, alive.

29

Summer

She waits at Woodbridge Station. The little platform is deserted. The train appears on time, snaking slowly along the track by the river. Summer curls her fingers in anticipation, watching the passengers get out. She stands on tiptoes, craning to see over heads, and there she is – a small, dark-haired woman in jeans, chambray shirt and white plimsolls, her face beaming as she spots Summer.

Out of her work hours as a lawyer, Laura likes to get as far away from formal suits as she can – slouchy denim and men's shirts are her usual choice. She's hurrying forwards, one hand dragging a wheelie weekend bag.

They collide in a hug, Laura pulling her into a tighter embrace. Summer breathes in her friend's familiar musky scent.

'I've missed you,' Laura's saying.

'Me too,' Summer laughs.

They get into the Renault, and Summer drives them out of the market town, through country lanes, verges thick with sprays of white cow parsley, scrambling chickweed and the faces of moon daisies.

As they drive through the pine forest towards the coast, they catch up on each other's news, Laura throwing out question after question. Summer tells her about Loretta and her cats, and the early morning swims in the grey North Sea.

'You're swimming at this time of year!' Laura exclaims. 'Are you insane?'

'I know it sounds crazy,' Summer laughs. 'But it makes you feel amazing.'

'Well, you won't catch me going in any time soon,' Laura says. 'So don't get any ideas.' She smiles. 'Have you been out with your camera?'

'Dad got me a new one, with the zoom I've always wanted.'

She's pleased with her latest shots: a family of seals basking on the mud; a fox trotting through a smokescreen of mist; the underside of a gull, wings outspread, talons gripping a fish, the light and the angle making it look as though the bird has caught a miniature sickle moon.

Summer is looking through the windscreen, but she can sense Laura's assessing gaze. 'How are you holding up?' Laura asks quietly.

Summer tightens her fingers on the steering wheel. 'I miss her. Terribly. All the time.' She takes a big breath. 'But me and Dad – we're doing all right.'

They've reached the end of the road, and Summer parks the car next to the phone box. Laura gets out and gazes at the stern fortress of the Martello tower, turning to survey the expanse of shingle, the rolling waves. 'Wow – this place is remote.' She stares around her. 'It's like the edge of the world.'

'Come on,' Summer links her arm through her friend's and grabs her bag. 'Let's go in. I want to show you everything. Dad's longing to see you.'

They make their way along the shingle path to the small, whitewashed cottage. Laura's still exclaiming over the shell design in the garden and how charming and higgledy-piggledy the cottage is, as they walk out of the sunlight into the kitchen.

Dad is at the table, reading the Saturday paper, mellow jazz playing in the background. 'Laura! How lovely to see you!'

'And you, Dr Blythe,' she kisses his cheek. 'You look really well. Sea air suits you.'

Dad laughs, rolling his eyes. 'I've been asking you to call me Donald for nearly twenty years. I'll put your bag up in your room,' he says, brushing off Laura's protests that he doesn't have to. He ducks his head to go up the narrow stairs, carrying the bag.

They've put a camp bed on the floor of Summer's room, and Summer has insisted that Laura take her own bed. 'It's all made up for you,' she says, sitting down on it, and watching Laura go over to the window to look at the view.

As Laura turns, she notices the box of photographs on the dresser. 'Are these your latest?' She's rifling through. 'You and your hares,' she says. 'You've always loved them.'

'They're magical creatures.'

She looks at her, 'But you're not wearing the earrings?'

Summer's fingers go up to her ears automatically. 'I lost one in India.'

Laura notices a last photo in the box. 'And what's this?'

She's picking it up before Summer can stop her. The picture of Kit. 'This is him, isn't it?' She stares at Summer and Summer can't meet her gaze. 'You haven't got over him, have you?' she says, her voice softening, accusing.

'I have.' Summer glances up, 'I just need time.'

Laura nods. 'But how are you going to meet anyone else living in the middle of nowhere?' She widens her eyes.

'Don't look so worried!' Summer laughs, 'I'm not ready to rush into another relationship.' She takes the photo from her and slips it to the bottom of the pile, putting the lid on firmly. 'I'm happy being single.'

Laura does go in for a swim, although it takes a lot of cajoling and persuading, and she screams so loudly that Summer thinks someone might call the police. Afterwards they sit on blankets by the sea, hair salted into tendrils, their bodies hastily towel-dried, then wrapped in layers of sweaters, with coats piled on top. Laura shivers, 'I can't believe I just did that.' She grins, 'Nobody else but you could have got me to.'

'Feels good, though, doesn't it?' Summer huddles into her jumper. 'Like a happiness drug.'

They munch sandwiches and crisps and pour hot, sweet tea from a flask, clutching the warm beakers with blue fingers. Summer spots a white shell amongst the stones and picks it up, putting it in her bag to add to Dad's collection.

'Tell me about you,' Summer says, finishing her last mouthful. 'What's going on?'

'I've met someone,' Laura says, a smile breaking over her face.

'What? You've kept that till now to tell me? And?'

'She's called Charlie. Another lawyer.'

'Have you been seeing her for long – why didn't you say anything before?'

'Only a couple of weeks. I didn't want to jinx it by bragging. And we're keeping it quiet at work – you know what it's like. People judge.'

Summer nods. She knows how difficult it's been for Laura

to be true to herself in public – especially once she started at the law firm.

'But it's … really good. We just fit together, you know? I mean, not just physically, but emotionally, spiritually. I'm optimistic about this one.'

Summer touches Laura's arm. 'I'm so pleased for you – that's great.'

Laura smiles and stretches, 'Yeah – I want you to meet her. You'll love her. She's very cool. Clever. Funny. She's got a wolf tattoo over her back. And without going into too many details … she's incredible in bed. She has this knack of—'

'Enough already!' Summer pretends to put her hands over her ears. 'Don't forget I'm living like a nun here.'

'Time for you to meet someone else, then,' Laura says with a wicked grin.

'I told you, I'm not in a hurry.' Summer gives her knee a playful slap. 'And as you said yourself, not so easy, in the middle of nowhere.'

'Well, don't think you have all the time in the world, because you won't be a sexy young thing for ever,' Laura throws her hands up. 'Just saying!'

Summer unfolds herself from the ground, 'If you don't shut up, I'm going to drag you back into the sea.' She reaches down for her, as if she's really going to do it.

Laura pretends to resist, flapping her arms and then, with a sudden move, grabs Summer's hand and pulls her back down beside her, laughing. Summer sprawls on the pebbles, laughing as well, and heaves herself into a sitting position. 'Sneaky.'

'It suits you here,' Laura says, as her laughter becomes hiccups. 'You're still too skinny – but you have colour in your cheeks. You look good. You were right to move. Even if there is a dearth of men.'

'Wish you were here, too. Then it would be perfect.'

'Life isn't perfect, though. Unfortunately,' Laura says. 'But it's pretty bloody good.'

'Hmmmm,' Summer agrees, throwing a pebble into the sea.

'What are you going to do, now you're settled?' Laura asks. 'Are you going to get your photographs published?'

'I'd like to. I might try sending some to local magazines.'

'I always thought you'd do something with your writing,' Laura muses. 'I remember at school you were top of the class in English. You used to write all the time.'

'Funny you should say that ... Effie always encouraged me to write ... I have started to scribble things down again,' she admits. 'I found a notebook she gave me before I went to India. It reminded me to write again.'

'That's great. What are you working on? A novel?'

She shakes her head. 'Mainly observations about the landscape, thoughts about animals and birds,' she shrugs. 'I'm really enjoying it. I'd like to write articles one day, but I'm not sure if my jottings would be good enough, or if anyone would want to read them.'

'I would,' Laura says staunchly.

She's missed Laura. Showing her around, introducing her to the cottage and the beach, has been the final thing that's made it feel properly like home. And Summer remembers with a flicker of nerves that, next weekend, Adam will be here.

30

Kit

He's worked behind bars before, but this one is different. The locals ask for odd concoctions he's never heard of, like port and lemon: a measure of ruby port, served over ice, topped up with fizzy lemonade, and a slice of lemon. This is always for the women sitting in the snug at the back, nursing their drinks, handbags snapped shut in their laps, muttering to each other, while their husbands perch at the bar looking morosely into pints of strong, dark ale. During the week, the place is mainly full of these taciturn locals, who spend the evening slurping their pints in silence, staring into space, although they have a habit of surprising Kit with occasional ironic comments, delivered in dead-pan Suffolk accents. The two dogs lie by the fire, a mound of heaving fur; they slap their tails against the floor when Sally-Ann walks past and seem to take it turns to release foul eggy smells into the room, but however deeply they appear to be sleeping, each one opens one eye whenever a new customer appears.

At the weekend, tourists and weekenders arrive, easily

recognisable by their brand-new Barbours and taste for gin and tonics; sailors from the local sailing club flow through the door with ruddy faces and swollen hands, gathering in groups; he hears snatches of their conversation ... *bit of a chop today ... we were really heeled over ... tide was running fast.* The pub becomes crammed, noisy, hot with flames from the fire, full of cooking smells and dog breath.

His evenings are split between serving at the bar and helping with the food orders, running from the kitchen with plates of haddock and chips balanced on his arms; he's busy all night clearing the empties, stacking the dishwasher, pulling pints, and then the final clearing up after last orders. In the morning, there are deliveries to oversee, refills and cleaning to do. He's finding that Paul is a brisk but fair boss, who doesn't waste words. Sally-Ann's mother, Jenny, is a large, bleached blonde with roughened hands, scarred from the deep fryer, and a kind smile. He's never seen her without vibrant lipstick, and often a smudge of coral or scarlet finds its way onto one of her large front teeth.

His afternoons are his own – but, frustratingly, he hasn't got into the swing of painting yet. He's unpacked his paints and brushes and got as far as standing before the easel with brush in hand, but his room is small and lacks natural light after midday. He worries about dripping paint onto the carpet. He wonders if he could find somewhere else to work – an old outbuilding or shed, perhaps.

He's started to ask people if they know of anywhere that he could rent but hasn't had any luck yet. He's polishing glasses on a weekday evening, when he asks the same question of a couple of the regulars, 'Well ... Digby's got some arty types on his farm,' one of them says.

'Digby?'

'Gerald Digby. Big landowner around here.'

'You mean he's renting land or buildings to these … arty types?'

'He is,' the other man agrees, staring into his pint. 'Won't come to any good.'

'So … what's going on there?' Kit tries not to get too hopeful. 'Is it like a collective, you mean? Or a colony?'

One of them rubs his chin, 'Don't know anything about colonies or collectives.' The two men glance at each other and shake their heads. They look at Kit dubiously. 'All we know is Gerald's renting out a couple of his barns – good farm buildings gone to waste.'

'Won't last long,' the other one says. 'He'll come to his senses.'

Kit puts down the glass and cloth; he clears his throat. 'Could you give me the address of this place?'

Next day, Sally-Ann lends him an old, rusted bike. He has directions on a folded bit of paper in his pocket. He cycles up the hill, past the castle. As he's riding out of the village, along a narrow lane, he hears the roar of a lorry approaching from behind, and a gale of adrenaline whips through him, making him sweat. He has to get off the bike and drag it up onto the verge, letting the huge vehicle churn past. The horror of the accident is still embedded into his nervous system, firing warnings, triggering palpitations. He stands trembling, knee-deep in nettles, knuckles white.

His instinct is to turn around and go back to pub, walking the bike all the way. But he can't let his fear stop him. He gets back on, pedalling with shaky legs. He has to check out this Digby place. It's all very well, earning his keep tending bar, but if he's not careful, he'll end up stuck in a dead-end job again – which is exactly what he promised himself wouldn't happen.

There are sheep grazing in neatly fenced fields. At a sign to the Digby farm, he turns off the main track, down a rutted lane. As he enters the farmyard, he notices some machinery left beside the fence, grass growing around it. A red-faced man with his sleeves rolled up over freckled forearms is standing by a barn, overseeing another man up a ladder.

'Hello,' Kit says, getting off the bike. 'I'm looking for Gerald Digby.'

'You've found him,' the man says, without turning his head. 'Can I help you?'

'I heard that you might be renting your barns out to artists?'

Gerald calls up to the other man. 'Can you come down, Bob? I need a word with this young man.'

Gerald turns to Kit, 'You heard right. I'll show you around.' He takes Kit inside the first one. The large, lofty interior has been sectioned off into smaller whitewashed rooms.

'Great spaces,' Kit says.

'The idea is to offer them to local craftsmen for a fair rent. I have a couple of people interested already. A wood engraver and a jeweller.'

'Not farm stuff?' Kit says, thinking of the two men in the pub.

Gerald shakes his head. 'My wife was a painter – she always said she'd like to create an artists' colony here.'

'What kind of painting does she do?'

'She's dead,' he scratches his ear. 'Died last year. Watercolour was her thing.'

'I'm sorry,' Kit says quietly.

'Thought this would be a good memorial to her.'

'Definitely,' Kit says. 'I'm a painter, too. Oils.'

‘If you’re interested in one of the spaces,’ Gerald looks at him with a steady gaze. ‘I’ll only charge what you can afford.’

‘Thank you.’ Excitement buzzes in Kit’s chest. ‘I’d like to take one,’ he says. ‘I could move my stuff in right away.’

‘My wife would approve,’ Gerald says, putting out his hand to shake Kit’s.

It feels meant-to-be, he thinks, cycling back to the pub slowly. Ever since he set foot in Suffolk, his luck has turned, things falling into place.

He’s lugged as much of his painting equipment as he can over to the barn, even managing to transport his easel, balancing it on his handlebars, the bike wobbling underneath him. He looks around the little studio, thinking he’ll need a table and chair. Outside in the yard, he rescues a discarded newspaper from a bin, and finds an old wooden crate, wisps of hay sticking to the rough surface. He brings it in, spreads the newspaper over the top, and gets out his paints and arranges them on it. He’s running low on ultramarine blue and lampblack. He decants some turps into his empty jam jar and picks up the fibreboard he’s brought with him, already primed. He places it on the easel, imagining Summer’s face, her snub nose and generous eyebrows, the way her eyes took on different shades depending on the light or what she was wearing – sometimes Portland grey, sometimes cerulean blue, sometimes green gold.

He sketches the outline of her features in soft pencil, then takes a slim brush, beginning to paint onto the board. His pulse slows with concentration. Nothing else exists except this – the brush and her face, appearing in dabs and strokes of colour, blocks of light, tracings of shadow. Maybe this will be a therapeutic process, he thinks, a way to paint her out of his heart.

He glances at the little alarm clock he's started to carry around with him and checks the time. He should really replace his watch, but it was a one-of-a-kind, an antique, a classic Seiko from 1976. The stripe of white on his wrist has long melted away, turning the same burnished shade as the rest of his arm.

At lunchtime, he perches on the edge of an old stone cattle trough, empty of water, filled with plants; he recognises sage, rosemary and mint. As he brushes against the leaves, they release sweet, herby scents. He unwraps the sandwich he brought with him.

'Howdy.' A tall, weathered man has rounded the corner. He wears a Stetson and cowboy boots, a cigarette stuck to the corner of his mouth. He stops, and takes a last drag, stubbing it out on the barn wall and putting the stub in his pocket. 'You one of the artists?'

'Yes,' Kit says. 'Painter. Just moved into a studio in the end barn.' He smiles. 'And you?'

The man shakes his head, 'I'm a mechanic. Got a garage round the back,' he tilts his head towards the first barn. 'Used to work on the refineries. Retired now. I run a small workshop, just a few local jobs.'

'Sounds like you've been here a while?'

'Ten years.' He gestures behind him. 'I live in a caravan just over there. Gerald's a good landlord.'

'Good to know,' Kit stands up, offering his hand, 'I'm Kit.' He smiles. 'Kit Appleby.'

'People around here call me Blue.' The man takes Kit's hand in a firm grip and tilts his hat.

'I used to work with cars,' Kit says. 'I always feel at home with the smell of engine oil.'

'Then you come along with me,' Blue says.

Kit follows him around the side of the first barn, along a dry lane rutted with stiff mud. There's a simple structure with a corrugated-iron roof. Blue strides inside. An old BMW is jacked up above a pit. Kit sniffs appreciatively, inhaling the rich, dank smell of motor oil, the coppery scent of metal, the sweet odour of petrol. There are huge antlers nailed to the wall, and instead of the ubiquitous topless calendars, there are posters of cowboys riding into the sunset, herding cattle over dusty plains.

Blue sees where Kit's looking. 'Some of us just got born in the wrong life,' he grins. 'Not that I'm complaining. But if God gave me a choice, I know where I'd want to be.'

Kit looks at the BMW. 'If you ever need a hand,' he says. 'Give me a shout.'

Blue pats him on the shoulder. 'Well, I sure do appreciate the offer.'

Kit goes back to his seat on the trough and resumes eating; as he chews, he notices part of a green bonnet and bumper in a lean-to opposite. Finishing his mouthful, he wanders across and investigates. He pulls aside an old tarp and, removing some hay bales, discovers an ancient, rusted Mini Moke. He gives a low whistle, running his hands across the car's blunt bumper and cracked windscreen. There are small holes in the floor, the soft roof has rotted away, but the seats are intact. He opens the rust-mottled bonnet, leans in. Everything is lightly coated in gritty rust. But it's all there. If he could flush the radiator, change the oil and petrol, and connect a battery, with luck it would start.

'Found the old girl, I see.'

Kit straightens up. Gerald has appeared behind him.

'Hope you don't mind me taking a look. Such an iconic car. How long have you owned her?'

'Going on twenty years,' Gerald says. 'Couldn't bring myself to sell her for scrap.'

'What's the problem?'

'Various things – mainly overheating. I replaced her with a quad bike and a Land Rover – one is faster for getting about the farm, the other better for rough terrain and mud.'

'You get a roof over your head, too,' Kit laughs.

'There is that.'

Kit lingers by the Moke, fingers itching to investigate further. 'You haven't asked Blue to work on her?'

'Never occurred to me.' He shakes his head. 'I suppose I don't have a use for her any more.' He gives Kit a keen look. 'Are you a car man?' he asks. 'Because if you like getting your hands dirty, you're welcome to try and get her back on the road. If you manage that – she's yours for however long you stay in Suffolk.'

Kit stares at him. 'Really?' He pats the dusty bonnet. 'That's a deal. Thank you so much.'

Gerald waves a hand, 'It'll be good to see her being used.'

Kit gives the car one last pat. I'll be back, he promises. He wipes his hands on the pockets of his jeans and goes back inside the barn.

He spends another couple of hours painting, before the alarm clock tells him it's time to get going. He washes his brushes, cleans his palette, takes off his overalls and folds them up, leaving them next to the packing case. Before he closes the door, he looks back at the half-finished portrait of Summer; the surface of the board shows through her features, as if she's floating across it, not quite in the world, a ghost or spirit.

In the pub, Sally-Ann squeezes his bicep, 'I have a surprise for you.' Her fingers linger on his arm. 'A commission.'

Kit gives her a quizzical look. Table five are waiting for their ploughman's and crisps. There's a queue at the bar.

'My gran. Gramps is lost without her – but if you could paint her from a photo, then my family want to give him her portrait as a surprise present. Could you do that?'

'Yeah,' he moves away. 'Of course. I'd be honoured. Thanks.'

She grins. 'Great.'

'Talk details later, OK?'

He's humming under his breath as he delivers the plates to table five. He catches himself, isn't sure what the tune is.

'Someone's happy,' the customer says, looking up, amused, from his glass of wine.

'Sorry. Didn't know I was doing it.' He puts the salt and pepper on the table. 'Anything else?'

They shake their heads, picking up knives and forks. He makes his way back to the bar, stepping over one of the dogs stretched out on the floor, the tune vibrating in his throat.

31

Summer

Outside Loretta's cornflower blue cottage, two figures stand together. Summer puts up a hand to shield her eyes from the sun and realises it's Dad and Loretta. They seem to be talking. Good, she thinks. They got off to a bad start, but hopefully they're getting on better now. Except there's something about their body language that alerts her to trouble – Dad's shoulders are up, his chin poking out, and Loretta is gesturing too much.

Summer hurries to interrupt, smooth things over if necessary. She arrives, panting slightly.

'Ah, there she is,' Loretta swings towards her.

'Everything okay?'

'Of course,' Dad says, not meeting her gaze. 'I was just heading home.'

Loretta's cheeks are flushed. Summer hopes Dad hasn't been rude. Both she and Loretta watch him walk in the direction of the white cottage.

'Are you . . . okay?' Summer checks.

'Yes, yes,' Loretta seems flustered. 'Now then,' she changes the subject. 'We should get going.' She nods towards the camera bag at Summer's hips. 'Hopefully, you'll get some good shots today.'

A couple of families have set up camp by the sea's edge, with windbreaks and picnic blankets. A little boy is walking backwards, holding onto the string of a kite: a brightly coloured plastic bird hovers above him, the wind making the wings rustle and snap.

Loretta glares. 'They're trampling all over the vegetated shingle.' She frowns, 'It's extremely rare and delicate.'

Summer looks at sea kale, their thick rubbery leaves like bouquets of giant green roses, the feathery grasses, long and yellow, seed heads a blur of delicate colours. She's not sure how anything grows in the barren shingle. 'It's a shame if they get damaged,' she agrees. 'But at the same time, it's so beautiful here. You can't blame people for coming.'

Loretta looks unconvinced. They walk along the river wall, between fields of grazing sheep on one side, and on the other, shingle sloping down to the sea. Loretta stops every now and then to lift the binoculars to her face. Sometimes she hands them to her. 'Just there,' she'll say softly, guiding the glasses to the right place. 'Can you see that? It's a marsh harrier.'

Loretta keeps up a surprisingly fast pace, stopping suddenly when she sees an interesting bird. Summer has to concentrate to avoid breaking an ankle on the rough, tussocky ground.

'Avocets,' Loretta whispers. 'They hadn't been sighted here for a hundred years. They came back in 1947, when the marshes were flooded to defend against the Germans.'

Summer follows the flight of the little birds through her camera, framing them against the gleam of water. Marsh and reed beds stretch away as far as she can see, a flat and watery landscape. The narrow river is empty of sails; Loretta explains that it's shallow and difficult for boats to navigate. She grabs her arm. 'A seal,' she says. She points out the shiny head ducking under and then coming up again. Summer peers through the lens of her camera, and the creature pops up in her sights, giving her a close-up of its cat-like, whiskery face. Huge liquid eyes look right at her. She holds the Canon steady, and snaps.

Loretta points ahead to a rise of land. 'Burrow Hill,' she says. 'Used to be a hill fort in Saxon times. It was an island once.'

They find a spot to sit, in the shade of an abandoned building on a small jetty, and dangle their legs over the edge, looking over the river, eating their sandwiches in comfortable silence. Summer realises with a jolt of surprise that she's content in the moment, that somehow, she's survived, despite losses she thought would kill her.

On the way back, there's a man in a hat walking jauntily towards them. Summer squints, not quite able to make out why he looks odd. As he gets nearer, she realises that he's completely naked, except for his boots and hat. But just as she's wondering what to do, he whips the hat off his head and holds it over his groin. 'Good morning, Colin,' Loretta says cheerfully, as they meet.

'Good morning,' he smiles. He's weather-beaten, bronzed, with curling grey hair and a beard. Summer guesses he's in his sixties.

'I don't believe you've met my new neighbour,' Loretta pauses, making the introduction as if they were at a cocktail party. 'Colin, meet Summer. Summer, this is Colin.'

'I would raise my hat,' he says, with a straight face.

'Oh, please don't!'

He and Loretta laugh. He walks on. Summer glances behind and realises that she's looking at his naked buttocks, tanned as the rest of him. She's beginning to understand that this part of the world is full of eccentrics. Dad will fit in perfectly. It's just a shame he and Loretta don't get on.

'Lovely man,' Loretta is saying. 'He's quite famous around here. Always knows the right moment to use the hat.'

Saturday, and Adam arrives after breakfast. They have a whole day stretching before them. She'd been looking forward to it. But now she's feeling apprehensive. For two years, it was Summer and Adam, the couple most likely to stick together, according to the sixth-form yearbook, followed by three years of managing a long-distance relationship when he went to uni. Then after their split, three years of trying to avoid him. She hadn't expected that they could be friends – but she still cares for him. She's known him since she was eleven.

'Can we go for a walk?' he asks, looking around him. 'I'd like to stretch my legs after the journey.'

She takes him along the route that Loretta showed her, setting off along the beach, following the river wall towards Burrow Hill. She points out a spoonbill, and some bitterns. He attempts to be interested, but she knows him too well. It occurs to her that he hasn't once mentioned his girlfriend, Isabel. She wonders if she should ask, to be polite, but it doesn't feel right.

When they reach Burrow Hill, they climb the long slope to the top and stand in the breeze, looking out at the glittering river below, where the Vikings would once have come in their longboats. Across another river, close by, there's a famous burial mound. She's read about the boat that was uncovered there, filled with treasure, including the helmet of an ancient Anglo-Saxon king.

'Have you heard of Sutton Hoo?' she asks. 'It's near here. Outside Woodbridge.'

Adam stands close to her, and she can feel his body gathering a new alertness. History is his subject. He teaches it at the same school they went to together in Cambridge. He's much more interested in ancient kings and tribes of Saxons than he is in plants and birds.

'Maybe next time we could visit?' he says.

She notices the casual 'next time', and wonders if she wants him to come again. To make a habit of it. She's not sure, now that he's here, because it's their relationship that should be history – with all her feelings for him safely past tense, consigned to memory. But it doesn't feel entirely normal to be standing alone with him. It was different the night he came with the roses; Laura had been there, and her father. Now she feels exposed, nerve-endings a little raw.

'It's over between me and Issy,' he blurts out.

There's a moment of awkward silence. 'I'm . . . sorry,' she looks down, unsure of what else to say.

'It's OK,' he shrugs. 'Hadn't been right for a while.' He fumbles for a cigarette in his pocket and lights it, taking a drag and releasing the smoke slowly. 'It was, as they say, mutual.'

She nods. 'We should get back,' she says. 'I'll make some lunch.'

'Can't we sit for a while?' he asks. 'Enjoy the view?'

They sink onto the grass. He sits with his legs out in front of him; holding his cigarette between thumb and forefinger, he inhales deeply, narrowing his eyes. Summer arranges herself, cross-legged, beside him. She remembers the first time he'd kissed her, all those years ago. It had been in the rain, outside the sixth-form school disco. One of the rare social events she'd been able to attend. She'd come across him standing under the shelter of a tree when she'd stumbled outside, needing to cool down after some hectic dancing. God, how she'd danced that night, making up for lost time. He asked her for a light; she didn't have one, wished she did; she couldn't believe he'd finally noticed her. He cadged a light off someone else but came back to her under the fir tree, and as she was trying to think of something witty or cool to say, he'd leant in for a kiss, his mouth smoky and delicious.

She senses his bare arm close to hers, his black hairs shimmering in the sunlight, and remembers the details of his skin – the brown birthmark below his right ear, shaped like Iceland; his long toes, the taut curve of his hollow belly.

He stubs out his cigarette, slipping the butt into his pocket, gets to his feet and leans down, offering his hand. He pulls her up but doesn't let go. She stands uncomfortably, wanting to tug her fingers back, caught in his grip. She smells the nicotine on his breath.

'Summer,' he says. 'I've only loved two women in my life. And you're one of them.'

Shock sweeps through her, tiny sparks igniting. She swallows. 'I . . . I don't know what to say . . . I—'

'You don't have to say anything,' he lets go of her hand. 'Your expression is doing the talking for you.' He turns his back, gazing at the distant water. 'I was an idiot. I didn't know what I had.' He shrugs, 'Guess I was just too young.'

'We both were,' she says quietly. 'We needed to go our separate ways – experience more of life. I don't blame you for what happened. Five years is a long time at that age. But . . . it was sad . . . the way it ended.'

'Yeah.' He turns, his eyes downcast. 'I know I hurt you.'

'Can we be friends?' she says. 'I mean,' she clarifies, 'I'm asking the question. I don't know if we can.'

'It depends,' he says. 'Do you still have feelings for me?'

'You were my first love.' She looks at her feet, and then at him. 'But . . . things feel more complicated now because I met someone else.'

'Who?'

'He's called Kit.'

'Are you with him now?'

She shakes her head.

He gives her an assessing gaze. 'What went wrong?'

'I don't really know . . . we met in Kerala, and when he was away from the hotel, Dad called to tell me about Effie . . .' She stops, bites her thumbnail. 'He didn't come back. I had to leave without seeing him.' She looks out over the river. 'I left him a note, explaining. But I never heard from him.'

'Damn,' he says. 'So, he knew about Effie – the transplant?' He shrugs, 'Well, he's a fool for not calling you. Worse. He's a heartless fool.' He gives a half-smile, 'But . . . if you're single, then I'll let myself have a little bit of hope. If that's all right with you?'

She swallows. 'I don't think that—'

'Shhhhhh,' he touches her mouth with his finger, and she shivers involuntarily. 'Don't spoil it. Let me have this.' He tilts his head to the side. 'Don't look so serious.' He points down the hill, 'Come on, race you.'

He gives her a head start, and she's flying along, the slope giving her crazy momentum, blood pumping through her as her heels hit the earth, jolting her spine, setting off a rising hysteria.

She reaches the bottom and spins around to face him, snatching at oxygen.

He's bending over, catching his breath, wheezing. He

straightens, wiping his forehead with the back of his hand. 'God, I should really give up the fags.'

'I've been telling you that since I met you.'

'True.' He gives her a resigned look, and then squints at her, 'Hey, you didn't ask me who the other woman is. Aren't you curious?'

'You don't have to tell me.'

'I do,' he says, mock-seriously, pausing for a beat. 'It's my mother.'

She gives him a look, and then they burst out laughing. 'You're such an idiot,' she says. 'Can't you ever be serious?'

They walk back to the car, and he takes out a packet of mints, the extra-strong variety he always buys, offering them to her. She shakes her head, and he pops one in his mouth.

'What you said before. Can I have some time?' she asks. 'I wasn't expecting it . . . I was just getting used to the idea of us being . . . friends.'

'Of course,' he says quickly. 'I meant what I said. I do still love you.' He nudges her shoulder. 'See. I can be serious. When it matters.'

She laughs. She's finally feeling relaxed with him, almost normal. They'd both needed to voice what they were thinking and feeling. 'There's a castle in a village near here,' she says. 'We could fit in a visit after lunch, if you like.'

'Now you're talking my language,' he says.

She makes a tomato salad for lunch, chopping the ripe red fruit, yellow seeds sticking to her fingers; she boils new potatoes, bought from one of the local cottages. Under the thick coating of dirt, they have pale, waxy skins. She sprinkles them with mint, adds a glug of olive oil. There are cold cuts in the fridge, and she sets them on the plate – puts everything on a tray. It's warm enough to eat outside, and they go into the little front garden, where Dad has laid the round table.

As they take their seats, Loretta walks past. She pauses at the gate, her gaze moving over their meal, 'Looks delicious.'

'Plenty here, if you'd like to join us?' Summer says.

'Thanks,' Loretta shakes her head. 'But I'm expected elsewhere.' She waves a regal hand and walks on.

'Thank goodness,' Dad says in a low voice. 'I was afraid she'd take you up on that and we'd have to put up with her for the whole meal.'

'Dad!' She rolls her eyes. 'You two just got off on the wrong foot.' She turns to Adam. 'She's actually really lovely – and eccentric in a good way.'

They eat, and Adam entertains them with stories about the naughtiest kids at his school, throwing in a couple of new jokes that make them groan.

'What's the difference between a hippo and a Zippo? . . . One's really heavy, and the other's a little lighter.'

Summer gives a snort of laughter, remembering, in a flash, the moment he'd bent his head to the lighter in another boy's cupped hands outside the disco, and how he'd looked at her as he'd straightened and taken the first drag, his eyes never leaving her.

Summer drives them along country roads, hugging the coast, although the sea itself is invisible, until they reach Orford and pull up on the market square. They get out of the car, and wander down the sloping road together, feet moving in easy rhythm, shoulders bumping. Adam inhales sharply as the castle comes into view, 'God. A perfect keep.'

She smiles, pleased at his reaction. 'Want to go in?' She

sets off towards it. 'It's my first time here, too. Loretta told me about it.'

As they approach the castle, towering above on a low hill, Adam gestures to the rolling green banks around it. 'These must be the remains of the outer fortifications. There would have been a curtain wall, with flanking towers, and a gatehouse.' He squints his eyes, 'Can you imagine what it would have looked like then?'

She shrugs. 'Sort of. But go on . . . what are you seeing?'

'Soldiers in chainmail, and women in long medieval dresses. Goats, a pig. Horses stabled over there,' he points to a bush. 'Kids running around in the mud. Little lean-tos where a blacksmith works. Storerooms, probably.'

His enthusiasm is infectious. His pupils are lucky; lessons with him must be fun. They climb up the outer stone steps, into the stale, dank interior. The walls are thick, the air dim, most of the windows are open slits, but there are bigger glass windows, which Adam says would have been the height of luxury. Summer finds it difficult to imagine what it would have looked like when it was occupied. She supposes there would have been wall hangings – even so, it must have been freezing and full of draughts in the winter. At the top of the building, they climb a steep, winding staircase, ducking under a lintel, out onto a small flat roof. They stand at the low wall, breathing heavily, gazing out over the river to the sea beyond.

He puts an arm around her shoulders, squeezing her close, and twists his head so that he's nuzzling her hair. She closes her eyes. She can feel the circle of his breath, smell his familiar scent of freshly ironed cotton. It feels natural to stand like this, no need for words.

'We'd better get back,' she murmurs, as she lets go to stoop into the darkness under the low doorway, making her way down the vertiginous, narrow stairs.

'Watch yourself on these steps,' he says, close behind her. 'They're treacherous.'

The stairwell is like a tunnel: confined, airless and musty. She puts her palm flat against the cold stone wall, steadying herself, Kit's watch a heavy silver weight at her wrist. As they leave the castle, blinking into the sudden light, Adam is just behind her, and she turns to wait for him, reaching for his hand.

MAY

Five months of Summer

32

Summer

The weather report is for an early heatwave, and the temperature is already building. Summer crouches and places her hands on the pebbles – each one warm as a new-laid egg. She squints across the expanse of beach. She likes how, from a distance, shingle blends into pale brown, but up close each pebble is distinctly individual – translucent white, inky black, terracotta red, jade green, pale fawn, or dusky pink.

She sits on the stones, staring at the waves, arms linked around her bent knees. She thinks of the moment Adam pressed his lips to her temples – she wanted that connection, the comfort of it. Can she trust him? He'd hurt her badly. Then after allowing herself to trust Kit, she'd ended up hurt again. Maybe she should stay single and concentrate on her photography – her attempts at writing. But Adam has apologised, and she can tell he's genuinely sorry. After spending so many years together, doesn't their relationship deserve another chance? She remembers how he rustled up omelettes for them the night he stayed to help pack; she thinks of his kindness to Effie, his silly jokes, the fact that he coaches a kids' football team first thing on Saturday mornings, even though he hates getting up early.

She gets to her feet, staring out towards the horizon. Shakes herself and begins to trudge slowly along the coastline, walking without any sense of a destination.

Five minutes later, she's got away from the fishermen and the picnickers. This part of the beach is deserted. She wonders if she'll see the seals at the mouth of the river. Further ahead, she makes out movement in the waves, and cranes her head. She squints against the dazzle, making out two swimmers; further up the beach, her eyes pick out puddles of colour left on the shingle.

One of the swimmers is making for the shore: a woman, staggering to her feet. She's plunging through shallow waves. Even with the sun in her eyes, she recognises Loretta's familiar determined movements, her black swimming cap, tendrils of wet hair stuck to her shoulders. Summer opens her mouth to call, when she notices the other person – a man, wincing as he staggers calf-deep in water, struggling to catch up with her.

Summer gasps.

The man reaching out his hand to clasp Loretta's, giggling like a teenager, is her father.

Loretta helps him up the last bit of incline. She scoops up his towel, pressing it into his arms.

The sight is so strange that Summer freezes. Her heart bumps in her chest – why didn't her father tell her he was meeting Loretta for a swim? He refused Loretta's invitation before. The two of them don't even like each other. She walks closer, crunching over the shingle with uncertain steps.

The couple teeter on the pebbles, towelling themselves,

laughing and chatting as if they've been best friends for ever. And then her father leans forward and kisses Loretta.

Summer's body clenches in shock. 'Dad?' Her voice is sharp.

They turn, expressions falling. Her instinct is to bolt, and she spins on her heel, stumbling in the opposite direction, back towards the cottage, blinking as if she could erase the sight of them – the familiarity between them; their complicity in this secret.

'Summer!' Dad's voice.

Her face is hot. Her throat tight. How could they? Behind her back? Their lie isolates her, makes a fool of her. She keeps walking quickly, uncertain about where to go. She can't face them, not yet.

She hurries past the cottage, past the Martello tower. The parking area is filling up with holiday-makers' cars. People spill out, kids lugging blow-up rings, parents hauling picnic baskets and folded windbreaks.

How long have they been seeing each other? Did they think it was funny, to keep up the pretence? Have they been laughing about it?

She keeps walking, fury and humiliation powering her legs. As she leaves the beach, the sea breeze disappears, and the heat is like an iron on her scalp. She should have worn a hat. Her feet move against the hot surface of the road. Sheep doze inside the shade of a tree in the meadow on her left. A couple of cars pass her, going in the other direction, heading for the beach, open windows letting out bursts of music.

She ducks under a fence and strides out across a meadow dotted with cow pats. There are no rabbits or hares to be seen, no other living creatures. The heat has driven everything, apart from insects, underground or into the shade. Something bats against her mouth, spinning away in a buzzing arc. She wipes her lips, tasting sweat.

As she reaches the far fence and slips through, she hears a noise. It comes again. A low moaning. She stops, her senses prickling. It sounds like an animal in distress. Her insides clench with anxiety. The moaning seems to come from a clump of bushes to her right. She stoops under thick swathes of holly, swearing softly as leaves stab her bare shoulders and arms. The green gives way, letting her into a small, dark clearing. In the middle, tied to a branch with rope, is a dog.

He's a grey, rough-coated lurcher, with a fine, slender face. Even through the thick coat, she can see his ribs.

'Hello,' she says quietly, approaching slowly. 'What are you doing here?'

She crouches by the animal's side, running her hand over dusty flanks. His long, thin tail swishes in a weak attempt at friendliness. He droops under her touch, his spine a knotted string; she wonders how long he's been there, when he last had food and water. She unties the rope. The dog tilts his head to look at her, ears twitching.

She examines the worn webbing collar, but there's no name or address or number. The collar is tight. She undoes the buckle and loosens it, seeing sore, red skin underneath. A fist of anger gathers in her chest.

'Do you want to come home with me?'

She leads the dog out of the bushes, and he walks next to her, placidly submitting. She glances down, guessing that he's not a young dog; his expression seems to say he's past the point of caring what happens to him. Out in the field, he sits down abruptly and has a good scratch, using his back claws to work under his chin and behind his ears. He stands again and gives a shake.

They make their way slowly across the fields towards the lane, and she keeps her eye out for a possible owner, someone who will wave and shout, and accuse her of stealing their dog. Her fingers tighten around the rope. She won't give him up easily, not to the person who tied him up and left him in a collar that's too small.

She has to lift him over fences. He lets her gather him into her arms, resting meekly against her heart. He weighs almost nothing, all his bones sliding together like a folding toy. She leans over the wire, letting him down onto the ground on the other side. He waits for her while she climbs through.

When they get to the cottage, she runs a bowl of water and puts it on the floor for him to drink. He dips his head, and his tongue works noisily. She worries that he shouldn't drink too much, too fast, and lifts the bowl up.

'Dad?' she calls.

She hears him on the landing above, a creaking footfall, sees the bottom half of him descending the stairs, the rest of him appearing, his mouth preparing words to explain. He stops when he catches sight of the dog.

'I found him,' she says. 'Tied up.'

Dad stoops to pat his head. 'Poor thing.'

She shakes her head. 'He's dehydrated. His collar was digging into his neck, and look,' she kneels by the animal's side and touches his front leg, and then his flank, her fingers pushing his fur aside. 'He's covered in scars and cuts.'

'Well,' Dad says, looking grim. 'Let's see if we can find him something to eat.'

Summer warms up some mince, adds a spoon of yoghurt. The dog eats it quickly and with great concentration.

She sits on the sofa, in the cool living room, and coaxes

him up beside her; he stands on the cushions looking at her anxiously, half-turning to jump off, but when she talks to him softly, he lies down, puts his head on her lap, gives one shuddering sigh, and closes his eyes.

Dad has gone to fetch Loretta, in case she might recognise the dog. She comes in quietly and sits in the armchair, cocking her head, 'Never seen him before.' She leans forwards, frowning, 'Poor half-starved thing.' She sits back, and nods. 'He's been abandoned, I think. It happens around here sometimes. When a hunting dog gets injured or too old.'

Summer's throat tightens; she keeps stroking the coarse fur. 'Then we'll keep him. We can, can't we, Dad?'

'Looks like he's made himself at home already.'

'Let's call him Friday.'

Loretta stands up, giving her father a quick glance. 'I'll leave you to it.' She stops at the door. 'But you know where I am ... if you need anything.'

She disappears into a blaze of light, and the door shuts behind her.

Dad takes her place in the armchair. 'I'm sorry,' he says. 'I should have told you before.' He rubs his nose, 'about me and Loretta. But it took me by surprise. And I didn't want to say anything yet, in case ... I was ... mistaken ... by my feelings.'

'But you're not? Mistaken?'

He shakes his head. 'I like her. Very much.'

Summer takes a deep breath, and nods. 'I'm sorry, too. I shouldn't have run off like that. But ... it was a shock ... especially when I thought you hated each other.' She pauses, remembering, 'You said she was brash.'

He winces, 'I felt challenged by her. And I reacted like a child.'

'When did you change your mind?'

'After we started to talk, and I saw her differently. Instead of finding her difficult, I saw how passionate she is, how uncompromising. Afterwards I couldn't stop thinking about her, found myself seeking out her company.' He smiles. 'Being with her makes everything seem brighter.' Then he gives a short laugh, 'But Loretta says it's a typical love story trope. The protagonists taking a great dislike to each other – while all the time, they're falling in love.'

'And are you?'

He looks at her quizzically.

'Falling in love?'

He drops his gaze, and when he looks up, his expression is sad. 'Nobody will ever replace your mother. That kind of love is . . . rare . . . once in a lifetime. But with Loretta, I've found companionship, ease, laughter. A different kind of love.'

She nods.

'But . . . are you all right about it?' His forehead wrinkles. 'Because you know I'll stop seeing her if it upsets you?'

'No,' she says quickly. 'I want you to be happy, Dad.'

He lets out a breath, his shoulders falling. She sees how tired he looks and feels guilty about making him anxious. She's been selfish.

He's lived like a hermit since Mum died. They'd been an odd couple – Mum beautiful and gregarious; Dad older, academic and awkward. But there'd been a spark of magic between them. It hadn't occurred to her that he'd want to meet anyone new – that he's been lonely all these years. Loretta is right: there are plenty of love stories waiting to be written. She'll tell Adam she'd like to try again, see if they can make it work between them. They're both older and wiser. They have a solid history to build on, shared experiences and friends. Some love stories aren't written from scratch, she thinks, but are instead half-completed, just needing a few more chapters, a last, satisfying plot twist.

She gentles her fingers over the dog's bony head, stroking his soft ears. A lost sound rises into her throat, a low hum, like the murmur of bees. The murmur becomes a tune. Dad smiles at her. 'You're humming again.'

She keeps going, not sure of the song, just that it feels right.

33

Kit

Kit has jacked up the front of the Moke on axle stands. He's flat on his back, squinting up at the dirt-encrusted sub-frame. The exhaust is wrapped in spiders' webs, flecked with fallen rust flakes, and there's something that looks like a mouse nest tucked up behind a dusty front wheel. He shuffles out, wiggling shoulders and hips, grasping the edge of the car to slide the rest of the way, pushing himself up. He stands, brushing dirt off his backside, out of his hair. He's sourced some spare parts from Blue, replaced the radiator fan. He's confident he'll get it roadworthy. It won't have a roof – but hopefully the next few months will continue to be hot.

He wanders over to the disused pile of farm machinery he'd spotted when he'd first arrived, half-hidden in long grass. He nudges it with his foot and squats to examine it more closely. He thinks it must be an old plough. Kneeling in the dirt, he runs his hands over the heavy curves and lines, an idea forming.

*

In his studio, he stands back from the portrait he's just finished. Sally-Ann's grandmother looks at him. Three borrowed photographs of her are stuck up on the easel, and he's been careful not to damage them, not to let a blob of paint go astray. He takes them down, slipping them inside an envelope to return to Sally-Ann when she comes over, which should be anytime soon. He hasn't let her look at the portrait yet, withstanding her pleas and cajoling. *Just a peek!* And then, drawing her shoulders back, putting on a stern voice, *We're paying for it!* Actually, they're not. He wouldn't accept payment, not after Sally-Ann's kindness on that first day. Because of her he's set up in the pub, has a job and lodgings under one roof, and now he has somewhere to work.

He looks around his studio, feeling satisfied and hopeful. He loves the simplicity of the white walls, the one window that lets in a wash of sunlight. He found a decent bentwood chair and a solid oak table in a junk shop. Sally-Ann helped him get them back to the cell-like space in the Land Rover. He goes over to the table now, running his fingers over his tubes of paints, his cleaning rags, jam jar for brushes, linseed oil, gesso, and bottle of turps. There's no sink, but the outdoor tap is close by.

He waits outside the barn for her, leaning against the weathered wood, feeling the sun on his face. The barns are nearly full now with artists and craftspeople, just as Gerald's wife envisaged. There's already a sense of community, a gentle buzz of activity as people come and go, settling to their own particular skill. There's normally somebody taking a cigarette break in the yard or examining a piece of woodwork or half-finished canvas in the daylight. He supposes that some of the locals still think of them as cluttering up a perfectly good yard in their kaftans and paint-splashed overalls, talking nonsense about colour and inspiration, but Kit has learnt that Gerald won't be swayed by opinion.

As if Kit's thoughts have conjured him, he appears across the yard. 'How are you getting on?' he asks as he strides closer.

'Good. Thanks. And I wanted to ask . . .' he nods towards the old plough, 'I wondered if I could buy that from you – thought I'd see if I could do something with the metal. Blue said I could use his workshop.'

'Have it,' Gerald says. 'It's been lying there for years.'

Sally-Ann arrives, parking next to the first barn, a grin widening her narrow cheeks as she spots him.

'I'm going to close my eyes,' she says when she reaches him. 'Tell me when to open them.'

He laughs. She's always so enthusiastic. She turns her back, 'Put your hands here, then I can't cheat.' She takes his hands and folds them across her face. Her lashes tickle his palms.

'I might have wet paint on me,' he protests.

'Oh, I don't care.'

She's trapped inside his arms, the back of her head bumping against his chest. He smells something sweet; strawberries, he thinks, the chemical incarnation of them.

He moves them both slowly over to the barn, and into his studio. It's awkward to walk with her glued to his chest, his hands stuck across her eyes, but he manages not to step on her heels. Her relaxed spine and the stillness of her head spells out her trust in him.

'Right,' he says, as they face the portrait. 'Here it is.'

He takes his hands away, with a ripple of nerves.

She squeals and, for a second, he's not sure what the high-pitched noise means. Then she gasps, 'I love it,' as she spins on her toes and throws her arms around his neck, pressing her lips to his cheek.

It's the first time he's been kissed since Summer. The first time he's been embraced by another woman. Her mouth is moist, her hair brushing him in light, ticklish wisps. He's aware of her small breasts squashed against his ribs. He untangles her arms from him as gently as possible, putting two steps between them. 'Well, that's a relief!' He aims to sound practical. 'When do you want to give it to him?'

'Soon as possible,' she says.

'End of tomorrow? It needs to dry completely before we move it – usually I give it about twenty-four hours to be certain.'

'Can't wait to see his face.' She links her arm with his. 'My parents will be really happy.' She tilts her head quizzically. 'Are you still on for a quick dip before work?'

He nods. She maintains her grip on his arm as they stroll over to the cars. He feels as if he's shackled to her, as if she's arresting him; his elbow juts awkwardly. He doesn't know what to do with his hand. It flops down. God, he thinks. Loosen up. But he's relieved when she lets go.

When they get to Leiston, a sea breeze cools the temperature and goosebumps prickle his arms as he pulls off his T-shirt. Sally-Ann strips off her denim dress in one sinuous wriggle and is already running into the surf. The North Sea heaves in sullen, murky undulations. He wades in, wincing when he gets to a line of stones, his flesh withdrawing from the cold with a shiver.

'Come on!' Sally-Ann is calling from further out, waving an arm.

He dives under, into grainy darkness, then flips his feet, pushing up and out into the relief of oxygen, and sets off in a front crawl, testing the strength of his leg, feeling his arm muscles burning. He swims until he's exhausted.

They splash out together. She's coughing. 'Swallowed too much water,' she gasps, grabbing her towel and wrapping it around her narrow ribs. He picks his up too, rubbing his shoulders, his skin tacky with salt. She's attempting to step into her knickers, while holding her towel as a shield, and he turns his back.

'You are such a gentleman,' she's saying. 'It was my lucky day when Gramps got stuck on the rocks.'

While he waits for her, he stares straight ahead at the nuclear power station. A strange, pale globe against the skyline.

Sally-Ann bobs up into his field of vision, wet hair making damp patches on her dress. 'Actually, I should tell you something,' she bites her lip, looking at him from under her lashes. 'There never was a job. At the pub.'

He startles, and yet somewhere deep down he suspected as much. He looks at his feet. 'Hope your dad doesn't regret hiring me.'

'Not at all, silly,' she links her arm with his again. 'He said he couldn't do without you just the other day.' She blinks. 'None of us could.'

Kit shuffles his feet, uncertain of how to respond.

'It's okay,' she says in a teasing voice. 'I just wanted you to know. You don't have to say anything. You're not obliged or anything.'

'Thanks.' He swallows, 'I appreciate you saying that, and . . . thanks for getting me the job.'

'No problem.' She nudges him. 'Hey. You should meet the crowd I hang out with,' she says. 'You'd like them. There's a barbecue next week, on the beach. Want to come?'

He smiles, 'Sounds like fun.'

It's impossible to feel awkward around Sally-Ann for long. She says what's on her mind and is upfront about everything. It's refreshing. He can't imagine her telling lies. She'd never pretend to be someone she's not.

The Mini Moke is on the road at last. Kit's driven it through the pine forest, a herd of fallow deer leaping away over bracken; he's branched off down narrow country lanes, exploring the area. He's stood, at last, with his feet at the brink of the North Sea. He's visited pretty towns, fishing boats pulled up on banks of pebbles. One day, he followed his nose and discovered a little collection of cottages at a place called Shingle Street. The sea is wilder there, crashing onto a steep pebbly shore. When he told Sally-Ann, she said it wasn't safe for swimming.

Now he has the Moke, he's released from the fear of cycling. And it makes dividing his time between his studio, Blue's garage and the pub possible. He's never been busier. His fingernails are engrained with oily black, his hands speckled with flecks of paint; when he looks in the mirror, his skin is tanned, his arms lean and muscled from physical labour. Swimming in the sea is making his leg stronger – he can feel an improvement every day.

34

Summer

As soon as she told Adam that she wanted to restart their relationship, they slipped into a routine. He drives over at weekends, and they phone each other during the week. She's begun to write, too. Effie's notebook isn't big enough to contain everything she wants to say – and she's loath to fill it up completely. Keeping some spare pages is a kind of connection to her sister – an ongoing project that links them together. She's bought a new exercise book, and she's rapidly filling it with observations and ideas. Shingle Street is full of animals and birds, the weather creating and recreating the shoreline, and always the restless sea. There's so much to observe, so much to say. She has no idea if what she's writing is any good – but she finds herself opening the notebook every day. Hours pass without her realising.

They come, lolloping, nibbling grass, black-tipped ears moving in the wind like radar to detect the slightest whisper of trouble, tread of fox, breath of man, click of trigger. I watch through the lens, fingers focusing on amber eyes, their ears turning translucent as sunlight illuminates them.

The hare was considered sacred to the Saxon goddess of spring. She was the original Easter bunny, before the sweeter, cuddlier rabbit replaced her. The hare, it turns out, is a mix of contradictions, considered both holy and beloved of witches, a representative of purity, and yet also a symbol of fertility, sex, and love. I love this complex richness, all the contrasting meanings that mankind has attributed to this one creature.

She grabs a honey sandwich to shove in her pocket before she creeps out of the cottage at dawn, camera bag over her shoulder, her new retractable monopod clutched under her arm. She walks to fields, taking an old tarp to put down in the wet grass. The hour is golden, the landscape shimmering with rising mist, the edges of things softened. She nestles on the ground, staying upwind, wipes off the lens, and waits.

Back at home in the makeshift darkroom, she watches images surface onto paper, pegging them up to dry, and then examining what she has – sorting them into categories. When she's writing, taking pictures, developing prints, she feels most like herself. She remembers her promise to Effie.

She sends her best prints off to wildlife magazines, local magazines and papers. 'Dear Sir or Madam, please find a selection of my photographs enclosed.' She licks the gluey edges, sealing the envelopes closed, and pushes each one through the mouth of the red postbox in the local village with a sense of excitement. And waits.

A week later, there's been no reply, no response at all. She tries not to feel disheartened. She avoids mentioning it when she's on the phone to Laura for one of their regular catch-up chats, but Laura seems more interested in Summer's love life. She quizzes her on how it's going with Adam every time they talk. She was surprised when Summer first told her that she was back with him.

'Are you sure? He lied. Cheated.'

'That was a long time ago,' Summer said, and Laura had snorted, 'Really? Feels like yesterday that you were sobbing in my arms.'

Summer had held her ground. 'He's changed, Laura. He made a mistake. He still loves me.'

'I'm sure he does, but the important bit is, do you love him?'

Laura asks the difficult questions, always did, even before she became a lawyer. 'It's hard to know how I feel,' Summer had said slowly. 'Some days . . . I'm just numb. It's too soon, after Effie. But I'm beginning to come back to life.' She'd twisted the cord tight around her wrist. 'You were the one who said it would be impossible to meet anyone new here.'

'I think I said difficult,' Laura sounded remorseful. 'Not impossible.'

'But the point is, I don't need to meet anyone,' Summer had let go of the cord. There were white marks around her wrist. 'It was always Adam.'

She'd been worried about sleeping with him again, after Kit, but the first time he stayed over in her bed, Dad was in the next room, and the need to be silent had sent them both into giggles, reminding them of their days in the sixth form, sneaking around trying to find somewhere to be private. It broke the ice, and after that it felt natural to lie in his arms, to be naked with him. She knows the texture of his pale skin, the shape of his bones, remembers the smattering of freckles at the base of his throat; and he'd been gentle, stroking her face, telling her he loved her. Afterwards, she understood she'd crossed a boundary. The air around her felt different. The memory of Kit on her body had gone, erased as if a window had been opened, a breeze blowing through. She took off Kit's watch before getting into bed with Adam and hasn't put it on again. Not sure what to do with it, she'd put it in one of her drawers, under layers of folded tops. Her fingers sometimes make contact with it as she rummages for a T-shirt to wear, the unexpected cool of the metal a small shock.

She's walking back from an early photography session. The quality of light here is like nothing she's seen before; the vast sky, reflective sea, and shape of the pebbles pulls visual drama out of every weather condition.

She's been out since dawn, and as she approaches the cottage, her stomach rumbles, anticipating coffee and toast. There are two figures crouched on the beach outside the cottage and she realises it's Dad and Loretta. She crunches over to them.

Their heads are together, engrossed in something on the ground. Getting closer, Summer sees a line of whelk shells running across the shingle. It must be nearly fifty yards long, and they're busy making it swirl into concentric circles. The bleached white looks beautiful against the shingle.

'What are you doing?' she asks as she snaps a picture of the line, and then, raising the lens, of Dad and Loretta.

Loretta looks up. 'We were just sitting and talking,' she explains, 'when your dad took some shells out of his pocket and started to make a pattern on the shingle – like the ones he's made in your garden—'

'And Loretta began to add to the patten, extending it into a line,' Dad interrupts. 'We were doing it without really thinking.'

'But then we got excited about it—'

'And rushed back to the cottage to get my buckets of shells.'

Loretta grins, suddenly looking like a schoolgirl. 'We've been at it for hours.'

'Lovely, isn't it?' Dad gets to his feet with a lurch.

'It is,' Summer agrees, smiling at her father's enthusiasm.

'He was right all along about the shells, and I was wrong,' Loretta admits. 'I thought they were boring, but when you put them together, they make something unique.'

'Tell Summer what you said,' Dad prompts. 'Before.'

'Oh, well,' she adjusts her hat. 'A thought occurred to me as we were making the line. I remembered your dad telling me that you and he are coping with your sister's death by taking life one day at a time.' Loretta's voice has become serious. She gestures to the shells. 'I saw a similarity.' She puts up a hand, and Dad helps her to her feet.

Loretta links her arm with Dad's, and he pats her fingers. 'She's very clever,' he smiles down at her. 'Being a writer, she saw the metaphor – how we have the power to make our lives beautiful, even if we are just vulnerable, fragile humans. How life is a matter of gentle persistence. One step, one day at a time.'

'One shell at a time,' Loretta squeezes closer to his side. 'It's about hope, really. We're going to add to it every day.'

'But won't it get damaged,' Summer worries. 'By people and animals? The wind . . .'

'That's the point,' Dad says. 'Nothing is permanent. But maybe other people will start adding to it too, repairing it, changing it.'

'I see,' Summer says slowly. 'I love the idea of it evolving. I'll take some more pictures to mark the occasion of its birth.' She moves back to get perspective and squats down, concentrating on framing the shot with the coastguard cottages on the distant horizon, the shells in the forefront.

'Show me the photos when you print them, won't you?' Loretta says. 'By the way, did you ever send any to magazines? Your dad said that was the plan.'

'Yeah – but no luck so far.'

'Remember Colin?'

Summer lowers the lens, wrinkling her brow.

'The naked rambler?' Loretta prompts.

'Ah,' Summer smiles, 'he's unforgettable.'

'You'll be glad to know he wears clothes when he does his day job.' Loretta grins. 'He owns a bookshop in Woodbridge, but he also publishes a local magazine. It hasn't got a big circulation, but it's well-regarded. Why don't you try him?'

Summer touches the camera around her neck. 'Thanks, I will.'

Adam arrives on Friday evening for the weekend. They sit in the pub in Orford, sipping their drinks in a noisy, hot room. He'd wanted another look at the castle, but it was locked, so they'd walked around the earthworks, up and down the steep grassy slopes, rabbits scurrying away. Friday galloped after them enthusiastically, too slow to be any danger. He lies at her feet, his nose on her foot, snoring.

'I can see why you love this part of the world,' Adam says. 'You can really feel the past in the landscape. This pub is ancient too. I did some research, and apparently it was built in the late sixteenth century from wrecked ships' timbers.'

'Loretta says it used to be a smugglers' haunt.'

'Yeah, I'm sure there are some old pirate ghosts hanging around the place.' He smiles and leans across, kissing her, 'Here's to us, babe. To the future.'

He clinks his glass against hers and they grin at each other.

Babe. It was what he'd called her when they first went out in the sixth form – it had seemed sexy and grown-up then. Now it's sweet and familiar.

'Remember how we used to lie in my old bedroom holding hands and listening to *Tubular Bells*?' he goes on, looking wistful.

'How could I forget?' she laughs. 'Your mum was usually walking up and down the landing making as much noise as she could. Once she started vacuuming right outside the door. She really didn't like me.'

He rolls his eyes, 'She thought I should play the field. I think she was jealous.'

'It was hard not to take it personally at the time, but you're probably right. She would have felt possessive whoever you were with.'

'And now I have a lovely flat all to myself,' he leans back in his chair, sighing theatrically, 'with a king-size bed. And you're not there to take advantage of it.'

'It's a shame,' she shrugs. 'Life's like that, isn't it? Sod's law. I could still come and visit though.'

'So, what are you going to do for work, now you're here?' he asks, taking a sip of his beer. 'Another dog-walking business?'

'Since the house sale, as we're not strapped for cash at the moment, I'd like to see if I can get my work published before I commit to getting a job.' She pushes a finger against the table. 'I've sent some prints to magazines and papers.'

She blinks, warmth in her face from a mix of embarrassment and pleasure that she's told him her plan.

'That's great, Summer.' He grabs her hand and squeezes. 'I'm sure one of them will publish you,' he says quickly. 'You're really talented.'

'Thanks.' She lets out a breath, relieved that he didn't dismiss the idea.

'What about your writing? I know you've been scribbling away. Are you sending that off too?'

She shakes her head. 'I haven't been doing it for long and I doubt it's good enough to show anyone.'

'Yeah. Probably best to spend more time on it.' He grins, 'Practice makes perfect. That's what I tell my students.' He looks towards the bar. 'Fancy a packet of crisps? I'm starving.'

He slips out of his chair and disappears into the crowd. Her gaze wanders across the pub. The place seems to be full of sailors. A thin, dark girl is darting from table to table depositing plates of food. She glimpses the back of a tall man behind the bar with a tousled mop of tawny hair; her view of him is immediately blocked by a crowd of red-faced men talking about boats. One of the men moves, and she's looking at the back of the tall bartender's head again. Her insides squeeze together. He reminds her of Kit. She holds her breath, waiting for him to turn, but another sailor leans forwards, blocking her view.

'Summer?' Adam's reappeared. 'I got you salt and vinegar – that's right, isn't it?'

'Oh,' she startles, and nods. 'Yes. Thanks.'

She opens the packet and puts a crisp in her mouth, but her mind is still on the man behind the bar, and she cranes her neck, twisting to find him. There's an older man pulling pints. He runs a hand over a bald, shining head. She stares for a few moments, but the tall bartender doesn't come back. Of course, it's not Kit. As far as she knows, he's still in India, or travelling somewhere else, or in London. But he's not going to be in Orford, working in this pub. She almost laughs out loud at herself.

Adam is talking about the kids' football team he coaches, but she can't concentrate, and she plays with a leaflet on the table, restless fingers turning it, flicking the edges.

'Sorry if I'm boring you.' He gives her a hurt look, glancing at the leaflet.

For the first time, her eyes fall on the words written there:

Coming soon!
Only at The Anchor – their ever-popular
Folk Music Evening.
Book your slot for the open mic, or a table.

'Sorry.' She crumples it into a ball and looks up. 'You're not boring me.' She leans forward and kisses him briefly. 'It's just so loud in here. Can't hear myself think.'

'Yeah.' Adam stands up. 'You're right. Let's go.'

They walk on to the quay, Friday trotting next to her, his lead looped in her hand. Moonlight falls across the dark river, silver ripples quivering in the breeze. Boats moored to buoys look like paper cut-outs.

They stand with their arms entwined, gazing at the water.

'This is better,' Adam murmurs. 'Now I've got you to myself.' He pulls her in for a kiss, and she shuts her eyes, banishing Kit from her thoughts. She blocks out everything except the sensation of Adam's hands on her lower back, his warm, beery mouth – he's always had a lovely kiss, soft and giving. A flush of desire makes her tangle her hands in his hair, and their breath quickens, his fingers slipping under her top to find her skin.

35

Kit

It's a busy night in the pub. The sailing lot are in, their numbers swelled with other sailors from local clubs, after a day of dinghy races. There's a crowd three deep around the bar, most of them strangers. Paul is serving alongside him, when Sally-Ann appears.

'Mum's just cut her finger badly,' she says. 'Can you do the deep fryer tonight? Dad's fastest on the bar. Me and Jack will serve food and we'll pitch in with everything else.'

He's in the middle of serving someone, a dark-haired man with soft hands and a pale complexion – definitely not one of the sailing crowd, Kit thinks as he takes the money for two packets of salt and vinegar. 'Thanks, mate,' he says, dropping the coins in the till. 'What about the rest of the food orders?' he asks Sally-Ann over his shoulder.

'Mum's done all the prep – she can manage putting things in the microwave and plating up.'

He pushes through the swing door into the kitchen. Jenny sits at the table with her left hand wrapped in a bandage, a bloom of red soaking the fabric. 'Don't you need stitches?' Kit asks.

'Not on a Saturday night, I don't,' she says, grimly, scooping out ready-sliced tomatoes from a tub.

Kit gets to work, lowering baskets of raw chips into the boiling fat, the liquid sizzling and spitting. As the timer goes off, he lifts the basket, tips the chips onto the shelf above the fryer ready for serving, and fills another basket.

Next morning, there's a letter on the mat for him in handwriting that makes his heart sink. He opens it, reluctantly.

Dear Kit,

I hope you've settled in Suffolk and things are working out – I haven't heard much from you, so I'm hoping no news is good news. When are you coming home for a visit?

With my love

Mum

He folds the letter up, a sense of dread filling him as he thinks about going back to London. He'll have to ask for time off, abandon his painting and welding, leave the sea and his regular swims. He resents having to give up his life here, even for a couple of days.

'What's eating you?'

He jumps. Sally-Ann is standing behind him in the dark hall. 'Not bad news?' she asks, glancing at the folded letter.

'Nothing like that.' He shakes his head. 'Just my mother. Wanting to know when I'm going to visit her.'

'Don't you want to go?'

'Not really. We don't get on.'

'Well, don't go then.' She shrugs. 'Life's too short, right?'

He nods, but the folded letter in his hand is a rebuke. He

shoves it into his pocket, but it doesn't stop him feeling guilty. He'll ring her, he thinks. Soon.

He feels at home in Blue's garage – the smells, the blasts of heat, the banging and grinding, the roar of an engine. He bends over the curve of metal. Through his visor, he watches the welder as it bites through iron. He loves the intense glow, turquoise and gold sparking like fireworks.

He steps back, pushes up his visor. The sculpture is beginning to make sense. The essential form of the plough is still discernible, but out of it comes another shape. A hare. A sprinting hare, with ears flying back. The creature stands as high as Kit's knees. He imagines it finished – placed outside, in long grass, gradually becoming weathered by the elements, part of nature.

He has no idea if it's any good. The last time Sally-Ann found him in the workshop, she'd wrinkled her nose. 'Why are you messing around in here?' she'd asked. 'I thought you wanted to paint?'

He'd tried to explain that he hasn't stopped being a painter, but that he's always loved the physical aspect of welding, the heft and weight of working with metal, the solidity of it. He did a short sculpting stint as part of his foundation course, and now he's enjoying experimenting, playing around. But he gets lost in the process, just as he does when he's painting – it's the same creative urge, the same compulsion – just different materials.

But maybe she's right. Maybe he is wasting his time.

Blue is over at the other side of the garage, mending a hole in an exhaust pipe. He doesn't give his opinion on the sculpture. Dolly Parton is singing through speakers wired up to the rafters under the corrugated-iron roof, begging Jolene not to take her man.

Kit rushes through the pub door into the kitchen, knowing he's late. Jenny glances over at him, her fingers busy chopping parsley. The fryer is sizzling. A smell of burning oil in the air. 'Sally-Ann's about to open up, better get your skates on.'

'Yes, sorry,' he says.

'But, Kit,' she says, wiping her forehead, transferring a speckle of green to her skin. A plaster wrapped around her finger. 'I wanted to tell you how pleased we all are, with your portrait of Paul's mum. Gramps is beside himself, bless him. Has it right by his bed.'

A wash of pleasure goes through him, and he feels the tips of his ears flush. 'Thanks,' he mutters, hurrying into the bar.

'Where have you been?' Sally-Ann raises her eyebrows. 'The hordes are about to descend.'

He makes an apologetic face, grabs some glasses from under the bar.

'I'm kidding,' she says. 'It's a Monday. We'll be lucky if we see a dozen all night.'

He throws the polishing cloth at her.

She catches it in one hand. 'I have some good news,' she says, slinging the cloth over her shoulder and slipping behind the bar with him. 'Gramps has shown the portrait to all the other old folks – and guess what? Loads of them have said they want one, too. Of themselves, I mean. Although there might be one or two who want their departed spouses done.'

'Seriously?' He stares at her.

She nods, her face flushed with happiness. He takes her in his arms for a hug. He does it without thinking – a reaction to the moment – the neat little lines of her body enfolded in his larger frame.

As he releases her, she brushes at her clothes as if he's left dust on them, pushing strands of dark hair back, 'All right. All right. Don't get all soppy on me.' But going over to unlock the door, her cheeks are flushed and full with smiling.

Sally-Ann was right about the evening – it was a quiet one. After they've closed up, she gets out the diary. 'You've marked the nights you want off this month, haven't you?'

He nods.

She peers down, turning the pages. 'You're off on our next folk night,' she says. 'You sure you don't want to change that? It's usually a riot.'

'No.' He shakes his head. 'I'm good.'

'Oh, come on, don't be a spoilsport!'

He shakes his head again. 'I'm ... I'm not really into that kind of thing – open mics – always lots of dreary dirges, and some girl who thinks she's Joan Baez.'

Sally-Ann closes the book. 'Look who's the musical snob. Well, it's your loss.'

His words weren't him. They were mean and belittling, but he doesn't want to remind himself of his evening in the Cambridge pub, his eyes peeled to the door every time it opened. It would make him think of Summer. Her lies.

'I know what'll cheer you up,' Sally-Ann is saying. 'Tomorrow night – the barbecue I told you about at Shingle Street. I've booked you out of the rota. It's time you met some people your own age, and have some bloody fun.'

36

Summer

The day is slipping into the cool of evening. She ties a jacket around her waist and grabs her camera bag. The beach is busy with picnickers. Loretta and Dad's white shell line is still there. It's been extended to about two hundred yards long, winding across the shingle, coiling around plants, breaking into curves and hearts along the way. She's noticed other people adding to it, seen them taking photos. It's become a talking point.

She walks away from the hamlet, along the narrow lane parallel with the coast. Fields and hedges, trees and undergrowth; everything is lush, not yet burnt into embers, but hopeful, vigorous with life. She climbs a stile to get off the road and crosses a field full of sheep. Technically, she's trespassing. But she met the farmer through Loretta at Hollesley village shop, a red-faced man in the ubiquitous uniform of rust cords and checked shirt. 'A good sort,' Loretta had whispered before she'd introduced them, and afterwards, 'His wife died last year. He's become a supporter of the arts. I knew he'd be happy to allow you to take photographs on his land.'

She gets to the other end of the field, crawls under a barbed-wire fence and finds herself faced by a bank of feathery reeds. They are taller than her, and she tries not to break the stiff, smooth stems as she makes her way through them. She sees the glint of water ahead, and pauses to assess the width of black, speckled with algae, motionless as death. She makes a leap from a standstill before she can lose her nerve. Her trailing foot lands with a splash, soaking her foot with dank, muddy water.

On the other side, she's in a fallow field, empty of farm animals, and bright with the last of the evening light, dotted with daisies and cuckoo flowers. A flight of swallows dive-bombs overhead, gulping midges. She sinks onto her haunches, shielded by a clump of ragwort and thistles, the purple alive with bees. She gets out her camera, checking the exposure; then balancing the heavy zoom on a tree stump for stability, she waits.

She loses track of time as she fills a roll of film, and loads another. She sees a big rabbit thump its back leg on the ground and watches the rest of the colony scatter. She holds her breath as she squeezes the shutter release. A fox comes trotting low through the grass. A stoat appears, white-breasted, whiskers quivering either side of its small, inquisitive face. It sees something – a mouse, perhaps – and is suddenly bounding across the tops of the grass, a swift predator, spine arching.

She's aware that she's losing the light and slots a higher-speed film into the camera. She doesn't want blurry photographs. Even with the 300-mm zoom, there's a limit to what technology can give her.

She's got pins and needles in her shoulder and shifts her position. The sky has drifted towards night, more steel than blue. A moon swings high, surrounded by stars, and the dark fluttering of bats. She packs up her camera, blind fingers slotting pieces into the right places, making sure the finished rolls are safe in the film canister. She hadn't meant to stay out until dark. Dad will be worried. Crossing the creek at night isn't such a good idea. She'll try the other side of the field, get back to the lane that way.

She makes her way slowly, hands in front of her, testing each footfall. Clouds have moved across the moon, creating a void of nothingness around her. The temperature has plummeted. She stops to put her jacket on, zipping it up, checking that the camera case is fastened shut, repositioning the bag across her body to keep it secure.

She comes to another barbed-wire fence, and slides through the middle, her jacket catching on the top wire with a small ripping sound. She stands up, trying to see across the field. Everything is altered by the dark. There are inky crouching shapes and taller ones that are reassuringly tree-like. An owl hoots. Stumbling past a deeper darkness, the shape lengthens towards her, taking on the physical density of a living thing. She stops, heart thumping, as she catches the shine of an eye. She smells the treacly, manure scent of horse.

Relieved, she puts out a hand and touches a soft muzzle, reaches along the big head and pats the muscled length of neck, finding a thick, knotted mane. 'Wish you could tell me which way to go,' she whispers. 'I'm lost.' As she says it, she knows it's true.

Nothing for it but to keep on. At least the clouds have shifted, and she can see better in the moonlight. She stops. There's another light ahead. Manmade. Electric. She lets out a sigh of relief. A bright beam swings across the landscape, picking out details, the blades of grass, the rut of earth, tipping everything with silver. Someone with an electric torch, she thinks. She makes her way towards it, hearing sounds on the breeze, the sharp bark of a dog.

As she gets closer, the hairs on the back of her neck stand up. Her heart has begun to bang, heavy beats swirling through her blood. Something isn't right. She can see three or four vehicles parked together at the edge of the field. A group of men cluster together, breath like smoke in the damp air, and they have dogs, tall, slender, long-tailed dogs. One of them whines. The beam of light swings out again, and she ducks, not wanting to be caught in it. Lifting her head, she sees a familiar outline inside the shaft of brilliance. A hare is running, ears streaming behind, but two of the dogs are on it, and the one in front opens its jaws. There's a high-pitched scream.

She clamps her hands to her mouth. The light snaps off, and she can make out the dogs running back to the men. There's laughter, and the beam comes on again: an evil eye in the darkness, finding its prey, stunning it with the shock of light. The dogs run again, and again. One hare gets away, but two more are snatched up inside a hot mouth. It's unbearable to see their limp bodies swinging.

There must be a track somewhere behind their cars. A road nearby. Anger scalds her. She wants to rush at them, shouting, tell them to stop. But being a lone woman surrounded by hunters sharpens her adrenaline, makes her stealthy and afraid. She saw the outline of a gun, angled down, carried over an arm.

She creeps on hands and knees, crouching every few seconds to raise her head cautiously. She's aiming to circle past the men, tuck in behind the cars. Her knees are soaking, her hands cold. She hears the crack of a gun. Her body stills, her instinct to lie down, but she has to keep moving. She gets onto her feet and hurries forward in a scurrying, bent-over run. The light swings around, catching her for a dazzling second. There are shouts. An angry voice. Someone is running in her direction – their blunt silhouette barrelling out of the confusion of lights.

She's flying like a hare, blind, desperate. Sobs break free, every muscle on fire. She goes through a hedge, thorns tearing, slicing into her face and hands; she stumbles onto her knees in a ditch, and then she's up again, pushing through tussocks of grass, an ankle twisting. She stays inside the blank shadow of a hedge.

She hears the roar of engines, more shouting. Twin beams of headlights sweep the field in front of her. Then she's aware of a set of rear lights, smaller, further away to her right, blinking red before they disappear. Above the thunder of her pulse, her torn breath, she hears the murmur of the sea. It's the road home. She has to make a dash for it, hope she can elude the lights, the men. What if they set the dogs on her? There's a field of wheat between her and safety – a pale stretch, stirring in the moonlight like a strange ocean. She sprints, camera case bumping against her hip, as her body beats an opening through the thigh-high crop. The dry wheat swishes and sways, breaking under her. She gets to the boundary, skids under a wire fence, throwing herself headlong onto the road. She's blinded by headlights. Wheels grate against stones, brakes squealing as the car comes to a stop. She stays sitting on the tarmac, a hand up, shielding her eyes against the dazzle. The car door opens, and shoes land on the road.

'Summer!'

She struggles to her feet. Dad has his arms around her, 'My God! I've been so worried.'

Loretta is there too, wrapping her arms over Dad's, rocking Summer close. 'Whatever has happened?'

'Let's get you into the car.'

Summer climbs into the back seat, looking through the rear window across the fields at the distant shapes of two vans and a Jeep bumping away into the darkness.

She sits in the kitchen with a mug of steaming tea, doused with whisky. Loretta attends to the cuts on her face and hands with diluted iodine, dabbing gently with cotton wool.

'Sounds like they were lamping,' she says. 'I'm afraid there's a few people around here who go out at night, usually after hares and rabbits. Hares are considered more sport for the dogs.'

Summer shudders. 'It was horrible.' She looks up. 'Is it legal?'

'Not if they're trespassing on someone else's land.'

'Isn't there anything we can do?' Dad asks. 'Report them to the police?'

'They'll be long gone,' Loretta says. 'Need to catch them in the act. But I'll let Gerald know. Sounds as though it was happening on his land.'

Friday has got out of his bed to lean against her leg, his body a comforting weight against her knee. Summer strokes his head, and takes a gulp of her drink, the whisky burning through her throat, setting a fire in her belly.

The loss of the hares, tricked by a beam of light, hollows her heart, makes her ache through and through. She stares down into her drink. 'One thing I *can* do,' she says slowly, looking up at Dad and Loretta, 'is write about this.'

'The lamping?' Dad asks.

'Hares,' she says, already planning it; a piece about the way they're born with eyes open, ready to run. The fact that they have no burrow, no safe place to go. Speed is the only thing that can save them. It will be like a love letter to the fleeting beauty of nature. She wants people to feel the same way she does, to see through her eyes. She'll make a start on it straight away.

37

Kit

On the night of the barbecue, he drives Sally-Ann in the Moke, a crate of beer at her feet, buns and packets of burgers in a cool bag. They stop at the edge of the village to pick up a couple of her friends. Two young men climb into the back, exclaiming over how rad the car is, slapping Kit on the shoulder, telling him they're glad to meet him.

'Mike and Stuart,' she says as they settle into their seats.

'Hi,' he glances in the wing mirror as he puts the car in gear and accelerates away.

'Good to finally meet you. Sally-Ann hasn't stopped going on about you,' one of them shouts, his voice rising over the roar of rubber and blast of wind. Sally-Ann turns around to glare, and there's good-humoured laughter.

After parking under the shadow of the Martello tower, the four of them lug the beer and food along the shingle path by the cottages, then over the beach towards the sea, where a small group has already started an impressive bonfire. As they get closer, Kit hears music and laughter. Smells the charcoal scent of burning wood.

Sally-Ann introduces him to one person after another, and he's struggling to remember names, as they grasp his hand or lean in to kiss his cheek. He sees curiosity in their eyes, and remembers what Mike and Stuart said in the Moke. She's a few feet away, bending over a grill set up next to the fire, where sausages and burgers are cooking. She seems to feel his gaze, and glances up. He smiles and she smiles back, winking at him.

She's funny and kind. He likes her no-bullshit attitude. Her waist is small enough to encircle with two hands. And she likes him. She hasn't left him in any doubt about that.

The group settles on rugs to eat, swigging beer from bottles, passing burgers, packets of crisps. The sky has lost all trace of colour, is a dark, star-studded swoop above their heads. Flames light up features in a puzzle of flickering gold and bronze. He feels the heat burning his cheeks, the pleasure of the cool beer in his throat. The conversation is teasing and easy – they've all known each other since school, but they include him in the jokes, explain the back-story when he needs to know. Sally-Ann has nestled close, and he feels her willing him to get on with these people, wanting him to enjoy himself. He leans down and whispers, 'Thanks for inviting me. I like your friends,' and is rewarded by a huge grin.

When 'Everybody Dance' comes on the radio, people get up and start to bop around the fire. Sally-Ann stands, moving her hips, hair swinging around her face. He looks up at her; lit by the flames, her face is unearthly, beautiful. The music is high-tempo disco, and Kit's limbs twitch with the impulse to move. 'Get up, lazy bones,' she leans down and grabs his hand. He doesn't need an excuse.

He's on his feet, turning and twisting next to her, breathing in the intoxicating scent of wood smoke. He tilts his face towards the moon, moving over the shifting shingle. Someone turns the radio up. The wild dancing goes on, with beer breaks, as the fire leaps for the moon and the sea pounds the stones. Kit's forehead is skimmed with sweat, his chest heaving.

The radio DJ has switched the mood, playing slow, romantic tracks. The bonfire is dying, embers glowing blue and red. REM's 'Everybody Hurts' comes on, and a few people sprawl on the rugs, but Sally-Ann turns to him, leaning against his chest, so that it's natural to put his arms around her. They sway to the song, his lips in her smoky hair, her hands wrapped around his waist. She tilts her chin, eyes closed, and he bends to kiss her. She tastes of beer and ketchup.

He holds her, the small bones of her shoulders against the curve of his chest, the shape of her skull fitting under his chin. He realises he's happier than he's been for ages, since India. Music and smoke swirls around them. Then an angry voice slices through the moment, breaking the spell. Sally-Ann startles and turns towards the sound. A stranger has appeared out of the darkness, apparently to tell them off for lighting the fire. She stands with her hands on her hips, like an angry headmistress. The others get to their feet and put out the last embers with handfuls of stones as they clear up the remains of the party. Kit and Sally-Ann join in, shoving rubbish into bags, kicking more shingle over the glowing branches.

'It's irresponsible,' the woman tells them fiercely. 'The plants on this beach are easily damaged. Rare and delicate.'

'Silly old bat,' Sally-Ann whispers, as they lug the empties up the beach in the dark. 'She doesn't own the place.'

'Maybe we shouldn't have made such a big fire.'

'We were nowhere near the plants,' Sally-Ann retorts. 'We

were right on the shingle near the shore. Those pebbles have been around for thousands of years. Think they'll survive a bit of ash.'

But the atmosphere has sobered, and the group disperses with shouted goodbyes. He gives Sally-Ann and the other two a lift home, dropping Mike and Stuart first. She kisses him lightly before she goes inside, and he goes home to the empty pub, disposes of the bottles, and falls into bed, his head full of the REM song. They were a nice crowd. He'd felt welcomed by them. He thinks of Sally-Ann, her taut body softening inside his embrace. But should he have kissed her? They're colleagues, after all. Her dad's his boss. He shifts uncomfortably onto his back and stares up into the darkness – he doesn't want to do anything that will cause a problem, or hurt Sally-Ann. He rubs his eyes, remembering her probing tongue in his mouth. She's clear about what she wants, and it's time, he tells himself. Time to move on.

38

Summer

It's the first evening they'll have the cottage to themselves. Summer has put on her best underwear and changed the sheets on her bed. She's made a lasagne, and lit candles in the kitchen. Adam arrives as Dad and Loretta are leaving, off to see a film in Aldeburgh. He comes into the cottage with a bottle of wine and her favourite chocolates, and a grin which disappears as quickly as it came.

'My God,' he startles, staring at her. 'What happened to your face!'

She remembers the scratches and raises her hand to shield them. He puts the wine down and takes her wrist, turns it over to look at the cross-hatching of raised wheals. 'Jesus! Summer!'

She tugs her fingers back. 'I came across some lampers.'

'Lampers?'

'I'll explain in a minute. Come in.'

He ducks his head to follow her – he's not tall, but the cottage is all low beams and ceilings.

'Lampers?' he prompts. 'What . . . or who?'

'People hunting with a torch beam, lamping their prey. They set dogs on whatever the light has picked out. Usually, rabbits. Or hares.' She opens the wine and pours them two glasses.

'Shit.' Then his face tightens. 'Did … did they do … this to you?'

'No.' She's embarrassed. 'No. It was frightening coming across them on my own in the dark. I got spooked and took off.'

'I'm not surprised. Sounds like a scene out of *Deliverance*.' He makes a face, raising one eyebrow, and she knows he's going to start quoting from the movie.

'Don't,' she says. 'You know I hate that film.'

'I wasn't going to say anything,' he protests, palms up. He comes close and caresses her cheek with one hand, his expression serious, 'I just don't like the thought of you being frightened. Hurt.'

'One good thing that came of it,' she says quietly. 'It got me to write something. An article. I was so angry, I had to do something.' She looks up at him. 'I've even sent it off to a local magazine.'

Loretta had lent her an old manual typewriter; and despite blobs of Tipp-Ex and a malfunctioning letter 'b' that hit the page higher than all the other letters, it had looked reasonably professional. She doesn't tell Adam any of this, because his expression has become intense, misty-eyed.

Their glasses remain on the table, untouched. She leans into the touch of his fingers. 'I've made supper,' she murmurs.

'It's not food I want right now,' he says in a husky whisper.

She shivers. Then he's kissing her, and she kisses him back.

'Summer,' he groans. 'God … I want you.'

'Let's go upstairs,' she says. Although they have the place

to themselves, it doesn't feel right to start undressing in the kitchen.

Adam reaches climax with a loud cry, his body shuddering as he collapses against her. She didn't orgasm. It was too rushed. But the sheer physicality felt necessary, the push and pull, the salty skim of sweat on her skin, the tingle inside and outside her body.

They lie tangled on the narrow mattress, and he fiddles with her hair, moving his fingers through the short strands. 'I was devastated when you cut it,' he murmurs. 'But . . . it suits you. You seem different . . . stronger.'

'Mmmm,' she murmurs, beginning to drift into sleep.

'Babe . . . I was thinking,' Adam continues, waking her up, 'as we're a couple again, maybe you'd consider moving back to Cambridge?'

'Cambridge?' She startles. 'But . . . that was never the plan. I don't have a home there any more. And I couldn't afford to rent a place.'

'I know,' he says quickly. 'I'm just thinking aloud. It's just an idea . . . it's quite a long drive to do all the time.'

She bites her lip, 'I could come to you sometimes. We could share the journeys?'

'No, it's fine. I'd rather do the drive than worry about you on thc road.'

She opens her mouth to protest, but he's speaking again. 'Of course, another solution would be for you to move in with me. Not now, obviously. In the future. When we've given this,' he leans up on an elbow, gesturing to himself and her, 'a bit more time.'

'I don't know,' she says, sitting up and wrapping her arms around her knees. 'I really love it here.'

'Okay,' he kisses her ear. 'I don't want to pressurise you. Let's talk about it another time. I don't mind doing the driving for the moment.'

It's got dark, and the curtains are open, the window wide. Over the familiar rush and sigh of the sea, she thinks she can hear music. She throws on Adam's shirt and gets out of bed to look. There's a bonfire blazing down by the shore, a crowd of young people around the flames.

'Someone's having a party,' she says.

He gets up and stands next to her. 'Looks like fun,' he says. 'Are they allowed to have a fire like that?'

'I don't know . . . but if they're still here when Loretta gets back, I think she'll have something to say about it.'

Adam puts his arm around her, and they stare out at the fiery sparks rising into the night sky, the movement of bodies dancing through flickering shadows. She feels envious. She would like to be down there with them. She hasn't danced for ages. The last time she'd felt that kind of freedom was with Kit. From the moment she'd agreed to go to the beach hut with him, she'd come alive, properly alive, feeling everything more intensely in a richness of tastes and sensations, an abundance of being. Her body somehow made new through the lens of his desire.

'How about some wine?' Adam's saying. 'And I can smell something delicious in the kitchen.'

'Lasagne,' she says as she turns away from the window. 'Your favourite.'

'Great. I'm starving.'

They go down to the kitchen together, half-dressed, hand in hand.

JUNE

Six months of Summer

39

Summer

She sits at the kitchen table, fresh coffee in her favourite mug. The one with speckled moss-green over an egg-blue glaze, the shape just right between her fingers. Dad is out with Loretta, so she has the place to herself. Morning light seeps through the kitchen window.

Now that she's sent the hare article to Colin's magazine, she's begun to jot down other feature ideas. She practises on Loretta's huge manual typewriter, swearing when her fingers slip off the keypads, jamming in the mechanism. She has to bang on each letter so hard, the whole table shakes. She's had no response from Colin yet, but she's heard from other newspapers and magazines about her pictures – each one a rejection – and she feels helpless, a nagging doubt inside telling her that she's not good enough; it was only Effie, loyal Effie, who told her she could make it as a professional writer and photographer.

She puts down her coffee and bites her thumbnail. Maybe she should check that Colin has got her article – perhaps she needs to be more proactive? She has no idea how any of this works. She phones his office, nerves closing her throat. A girl answers. 'Colin's out,' she says. No, she doesn't know when he'll be back. Summer asks if he's read her article. 'Couldn't tell you, sorry.'

She puts the receiver down, imagining a huge pile of post towering on his desk. It's frustrating not to even know if he's looked at it. If only she could draw his attention to her submission, at least get some feedback.

A marmalade kitten rolls on her back under Summer's chair, batting at her ankles, playing with the frayed edges of her jeans. Loretta gave her to them yesterday, one of several recently rescued. Dad had picked up the fur bundle, holding her close to his face, 'I suppose we can't say no.' He'd regarded the kitten's wide blue eyes with his own faded ones. 'But I have a feeling your size belies the chaos you're about to unleash on us.'

The kitten, named Annabelle, already has a favourite game, involving dashing straight up the curtains, hanging near the ceiling by her tiny fish-hook claws. Long dangling threads now wave in the breeze, like octopus tentacles. Within hours of her arrival, she'd peed in Summer's slippers, broken a teapot, and fallen asleep inside the washing machine. Dad realised just in time, after switching the machine on, seeing Annabelle's mewing face tumbling through bubbles behind the glass door. Summer looks down at her now, 'It didn't put you off exploring though, did it?'

Friday lies in his bed, ignoring the cat. His bones no longer protrude through his fur, and the fear has left his eyes. Summer is glad that he can spend his last years in comfort, being loved. Meanwhile, Annabelle is showing her love in a trying fashion – batting his tail and biting his ears. He sighs heavily, nose on his paws, long-suffering.

There's a steady crunch of feet moving along the shingle path outside the cottages, but Summer doesn't take much notice. Dad and Loretta will be gone for hours yet, and she's not expecting a visitor. The knock on the door makes her startle; she sits up straight. Her heart speeds into a light flutter, as if she's been cornered. 'Damn,' she whispers as she stands up, reluctantly unlatching the door.

'Adam?' She stares at him. 'I thought you were coming tomorrow?'

'That's a nice welcome!' He leans in for a brief kiss. 'Can't I surprise my girlfriend?'

'Sorry.' She kisses him back, a long, passionate one to make up for her initial reaction. 'I was miles away.'

He follows her through to the kitchen. She takes down a mug, drops an Earl Grey teabag inside, sloshes in water. He pulls out one of the pine kitchen chairs and sits down. She gives him his tea, and slides into her chair, her cup between her hands, the remains of her coffee gone cold.

'I just wanted to see you,' he says, his voice thickening. 'I've missed you.' He looks at her earnestly. 'I've been going over our last conversation, and . . . I've had an idea that will solve everything.' His eyes gleam with suppressed excitement.

She holds her mug tighter. She was counting on having the whole morning to herself. She looks at his hopeful face. She's being mean. It's not as if she's got a deadline to meet, or any actual work. 'So,' she prompts, 'what is it?'

'I'm going to find a position in Suffolk,' he announces, his eyebrows dancing. 'Near here.'

She lets out a gasp, 'But . . . I thought you loved your job?'

'I do, but it's good to move on. I've already found something in Ipswich to apply for. Head of the history department at a girls' school.'

She gazes at him, 'You'd really do that? Move job and home . . . for me?'

'Of course,' he says. 'I don't want you to be unhappy.'

'It didn't occur to me that you'd even consider leaving.' She feels almost winded from his news – it seems such a big step for him to take. 'I know you really like your school.'

'It's not all on you,' he says quickly. 'So don't feel responsible. I can't get stuck in one place for ever. I'm looking for more responsibility in the next job.'

He laughs at her expression and pulls her in for a hug. She buries her nose in his neck, feeling overwhelmed, grateful, almost afraid. But if he gets a job nearby, they'll see each other more often, more easily, and she doesn't have to leave the cottage. Having her cake and eating it. The expression flits through her mind. She dismisses it immediately. She's always thought it was an idiotic one – what's the point of having cake if you can't eat it?

She and Adam go for a long walk along the river wall with Friday. When they get back, he chats to Dad in the living room, while she feeds the animals and throws together a spaghetti bolognaise, chopping onions, adding a tin of tomatoes, a pinch of oregano. She hears them laughing, and it makes her smile. Loretta comes over in time to eat, and the four of them sit around the bleached pine table, Adam pouring the wine, Summer dishing food onto plates.

'Did you send your article to Colin?' Loretta asks.

'Yes,' she says, 'but I haven't heard from him yet.' She puts her fork down. 'I tried calling his office, you know, just to check he'd got it. But he wasn't there.'

'There's one place you can usually find him,' Loretta says. 'He's a fan of folk music – like you.'

Summer remembers the leaflet in the pub. She strokes Friday's soft ears as an idea occurs to her, a plan beginning to form, one that will require her to swallow her fear. But it could work, she thinks. The conversation around the table has moved on to the new Channel Tunnel, opening next year.

'I don't like the idea of being under all that water,' Loretta is saying with a shudder. 'You won't catch me in it.'

'It's exciting,' Adam says. 'I'll be booking tickets as soon as it's open to the public.' He grins at Summer. 'We could do a weekend trip to Paris – what do you think, babe?'

'I'd be on for that,' she smiles. 'Sounds wonderful.'

Dad clears his throat, pushing his chair back, wood grating on tiles. 'As we're all here,' he straightens his shoulders. 'Loretta and I . . . we, we have something to tell you.' He glances at Loretta, and she smiles and gives him a little nod; and inside that discreet, silent beat of communication, Summer guesses.

'I've asked her to marry me.'

'And I said, "yes",' Loretta finishes.

Dad wrinkles his brows, a furrow of anxiety, 'We wanted you to be the first to know.' He looks at Summer. 'To make sure we have your blessing?'

Anyone who can make her father feel joy is someone Summer's profoundly grateful to, and she reaches both hands across the table to take a hand each of theirs. 'I think it's wonderful.' She squeezes their fingers. Dad's face relaxes.

'Yes,' Adam chimes in. 'Amazing news!'

'It will be a very small occasion,' Dad says.

'You want a bet?' Loretta smiles. 'You know how much I like a good party.'

'When?' Summer asks. 'Have you set a date?'

'We're going to have an open-air ceremony,' Loretta says. 'And then a party on the beach outside my place. And we're doing it at the end of July.'

'This July?' Adam says. 'Fast movers!'

'We're not getting any younger,' Dad says with shrug.

'Can we help?' Summer asks. 'With preparations and things?'

'Thank you,' Loretta says. 'I can deal with most of it . . . but one favour I did want to ask is . . . would you be my right-hand woman? We're not having a traditional ceremony,' she takes a gulp of wine. 'But we need two witnesses, and I'd love it if you could walk me up the aisle, although,' she pauses, blinking, 'there won't be an aisle, as such.'

She's nervous, Summer realises. 'I'd love to,' she says quickly.

'And I was wondering if you'd do me the honour of being my best man?' Dad asks Adam.

'It's me that's honoured,' Adam grins.

'Wonderful!' Loretta says, pouring out more wine. 'So that's all settled, then.'

'Just . . . one more thing . . . I feel it's important to say.' Dad takes off his spectacles and polishes them on his napkin. He puts them on again. 'At the start of this terrible year, we lost our beautiful Effie,' he swallows. 'And we miss her and her mother every day. But this wedding has given me hope – hope for the future,' he salutes them all with his glass. 'Even as life is at its bleakest, love can happen when you least expect it.' He looks at Loretta. 'Thank you for agreeing to be my wife.'

Loretta leans across and takes his hand. She kisses his knuckles, her eyes glistening.

Dad and Loretta have taken their glasses of wine and are listening to jazz in the sitting room. Adam and Summer have volunteered to do the washing-up. She washes and he dries. Adam moves closer, 'Did you know about this?'

She shakes her head.

'And you're okay about it?'

'Yes,' she says. 'I really am.'

'Good,' he says. 'I think it's cool.' He wipes a plate dry. 'Hey – maybe we'll be next?' He shoots her a look, eyebrow raised.

There's a stillness in the room, just the faint sounds of a saxophone floating from the sitting room, and Friday's snores. She doesn't know how to respond. Heat rushes into her face, and she turns away, bending to put a saucepan in the cupboard. 'We've got plenty of time,' she says lightly as she straightens, pushing her hair behind her ears.

Adam's expression is briefly crestfallen. But then he straightens his shoulders. 'Where will they live?' he asks.

'I don't know – Loretta's cottage is bigger. And she's been there for years. Maybe he'll move in.'

'So, you'll be alone in this place,' he muses. 'Seems a waste when I might be working locally?' He grins, dipping his fingers into the washing-up bowl, flicking soap suds at her.

She's relieved by his change of mood and splashes bubbles back at him, making a face. 'This isn't about us,' she whispers. 'For all I know they'll move to China.'

'Ha,' he grabs her around the waist, tickling her. 'I think that most unlikely.'

She writhes under his tickling fingers, and breaks away,

cupping another handful of suds to throw at him, needing laughter to dispel the lingering tension. But his question won't go away just because she's not ready to answer it. He'll ask her again, and next time he might be more direct, and there won't be a water fight to distract them.

40

Kit

As he works on the portraits of the residents of the almshouses, Kit recalls his mother – her beauty blunted, not through ageing, but through believing she'd been cheated out of the life she should have had. Yet these people, much older than her, have real beauty in their faces, a grace and wisdom that comes from accepting their lives and making the most of them. There's a lesson there, he thinks.

The intense sunshine of the last few weeks has faded, but the white walls of his studio reflect enough light for him to keep painting. He smudges violet onto his current portrait, using his finger to blur the edges. He's so immersed, he doesn't hear the door opening.

Sally-Ann appears beside him. He startles, the tip of his brush leaving a tiny, jagged line.

'Sorry!' she says. 'Didn't mean to make you jump.' She looks at the painting. 'Blimey – so lifelike. I don't know how you do it.'

He glances at the alarm clock he keeps on the table. It's his evening off. He wants to finish the portrait before the light drops.

'I won't disturb you,' she says, as if she can read his mind. 'I was passing, so thought I'd look in.'

She starts to wander around the small space, touching things, running her fingers over the tubes of paint, flicking the ends of brushes, and Kit feels his shoulders tense up. 'You've started doing landscapes?' She turns from the pastel sketch pinned to the wall.

He puts his palette down. 'Just trying it out at the moment. Seems a waste not to make the most of the light and scenery here.'

'You should take your stuff to local galleries – maybe you could get an exhibition?'

He nods, she's right. He should put his work about, see if anyone would be interested in representing him, an agent or a gallery.

'And who's this?' Her voice has tightened.

She's looking at the finished portrait of Summer, leaning against the wall. 'She's . . . pretty. Who is she?' she asks again.

'Someone I met in India.'

She gives him a considering stare, 'You mean . . . a girlfriend?'

He makes a noise of assent in his throat without looking up, focusing on cleaning his brushes. 'It was a holiday thing.' He breathes in, inhaling the bite of turps.

Her eyes are fixed on Summer's portrait. 'So . . . you're not in contact any more?'

'No.'

'What's her name?'

'Summer.'

'What happened?' she asks. 'I mean, you must have liked her a lot if you're still painting her?'

His heart accelerates until he thinks it will burst through his ribcage. He keeps cleaning the brushes, even though they're spotless. 'It's ... complicated,' he says. 'But it's over. I have no idea where she is – and I found out afterwards that she'd lied to me.'

Sally-Ann brightens. She slips her arms around his waist, tilting her head for a kiss, 'I'll make you forget her.'

Her lips are sticky with gloss. She pushes her tongue into his mouth, wriggling against his chest, then ducks away, smiling, 'Sure I can't persuade you to come tonight ... to the folk evening?'

He shakes his head, 'Sorry.'

'Some of the crowd from the other night will be there?'

'It's just ... not my thing.'

'Okay,' her eyes meet his, and she glances away. 'Well, better get back – it's going to be full on. See you later.' She gives him a last look under her eyelashes.

He shouldn't have left Summer's portrait out; Sally-Ann's curious gaze was always going to home in on it. Especially, he thinks ruefully, as all his other subjects are over seventy. He holds the painting and looks into Summer's sea-coloured eyes. He knows he'd fudged his answers about her, but how can he explain why their relationship ended when he doesn't understand himself? He puts the painting down, turning it to the wall. She did lie to him, he reminds himself. And it is over. That much is true. And maybe it's good that Sally-Ann knows about Summer. Everyone has history – emotional baggage.

He unlocks Blue's workshop. His sculpture of the hare is nearly finished, crouching on the grimy, blackened floor. He gets out the welding tools and puts on the helmet, pulling down the visor – he needs to lose himself in work tonight. He doesn't want to think about what's happening at The Anchor.

He concentrates on moving the welder, enjoying the hiss and spark, the alchemy of melting iron. The workshop is quiet without Blue working on an engine, without loud Country & Western songs, just the satisfying rasp of the wire brush as Kit dusts off the edges.

He stands back from the sculpture. The bare bulb overhead casts strange shadows, making the hare look almost alive. He touches the sleek, solid lines. He doesn't know what drove him to make it, but he's eager to find more abandoned metal and try again. He locks up and goes outside. The sky is blue-black, starstruck. He lifts his face, feeling the air on his skin. He smells tobacco.

'You still here?' Blue steps into the glow of the outside light, his lit cigarette a moving ember.

'Just wanted to finish the sculpture,' Kit says. 'Hope you don't mind. I've locked up.'

'Want a drink?'

Kit calculates that the folk evening will still be going on. He nods. 'Sure. That would be nice. Thanks.'

Blue's caravan is just a stone's throw from the garage, behind a copse of beech trees. As he follows Blue and his dancing circle of torch light, he hears the gentle whicker of a horse. A big, dappled grey is tethered in the long grass. Blue pats her neck, 'This is Texas,' he says. 'She's an old girl now, but she can still cover some ground.'

Kit strokes her soft muzzle. She twitches whiskery lips across his palm.

'Looking for carrots,' Blue laughs. 'Get away with you.' He gives the horse's flank a friendly push.

He opens the door of the caravan, and Kit steps up after him. The place is immaculate. A pair of worn cowboy boots are arranged neatly beside the door, a bridle hangs from a hook, an American saddle beneath it. A battered Stetson hat lies on the bench next to a small table. There's an acoustic guitar on the single bed at the end of the room.

'Sit down.' Blue gestures towards the bench at the table, scooping up the hat and putting it on a shelf. Then he's opening and closing cupboards, and Kit hears the clink of glass.

'You play the guitar?' he asks.

Blue slides onto the bench on the other side and puts a tumbler of amber liquid in front of himself, another before Kit. 'Simple chords – something easy to strum. Nothing too fancy.' He lights a new cigarette from the old one and inhales deeply.

'Have you always been into Western stuff?' Kit takes a sip, his eyes watering.

'Since I was a kid and I got to watch a cowboy movie at the local picture house,' Blue says, blowing out a stream of smoke. 'I never had a dad, and those men up on that screen, they seemed like the ideal role model to me – tough but fair, strong and noble.' He drains his drink and pours another. 'I dreamed of going over to the States, but I got my childhood sweetheart knocked up so, before I knew it, I was into the grind of paying the rent and putting food on the table . . . I got a job on the rigs. Paid well. But my relationship suffered.'

'I'm sorry,' Kit says.

'I talk too much to be a real cowboy,' Blue laughs. 'Can you imagine John Wayne shooting his mouth off like I just did?'

Kit smiles. 'You're not with your wife now?'

Blue shakes his head. 'She's with someone else – and my daughter, Darleen. She's married and lives in Australia.'

'I'm sorry,' Kit says, not knowing what else to say.

Blue waves a big, weathered hand, cigarette jammed between

his lips. 'Water under the bridge,' he says through a clamped mouth. 'I'm happy enough here. What about you? I notice Sally-Ann's been giving you the eye.'

Kit jolts. 'Yeah . . . we're . . . I don't know . . . we're kind of together.'

'Kind of?' He tilts his head to one side. 'She's a pretty little thing.'

'She's lovely. A lovely person,' Kit admits. 'I like her, but—'

'There's someone else?' Blue's eyes narrow.

'There was,' he admits. 'A girl I met on holiday.'

'Still got her on your mind?' Blue dips his chin. 'You listen to Chris LeDoux or Tanya Tucker, they got plenty to say on the subject of love. Funny, isn't it, how we humans just get hung up on that one emotion?'

Kit smiles, 'Life would be easier if we didn't.'

'But dull,' Blue grins back at him. 'Very dull.'

He stubs out his cigarette and brandishes the bottle of tequila. Kit refuses another, with a shake of his head. He has to drive. Blue picks up his guitar and begins to strum out a tune, beginning to growl the words to 'Take Me Home, Country Roads'. Kit finds himself humming along to the nostalgic melody, glad to be here with Blue, and not at the pub.

41

Summer

She looks in the mirror, running a hand through her hair. New growth makes it curl softly into the nape of her neck. Sun and seawater have bleached it almost white. Her face no longer has its roundness. She wonders if it's just the haircut, or being thinner, or losing Effie, that's given her a different expression, a little sadder, a little wiser.

Laura is waiting for her downstairs. 'You're really going to do this?' she asks, as Summer picks up her bag.

Summer nods.

'Good for you.'

Summer gets behind the wheel and Laura slides into the passenger seat. At the Hollesley junction, Summer indicates and takes the turning towards Orford.

'So, your dad and Loretta,' Laura says, 'that was a surprise!'

'Yeah,' Summer says, changing into third gear. 'They kind of went from nought to sixty. They're like young lovers.'

'And what about you and Adam? How's that going?'

'Good.' Her fingers tighten on the steering wheel. 'He's applying for jobs in Suffolk.'

She hears Laura catch her breath. 'Wow,' she says. 'And how does that make you feel?'

'Like he's serious about me. And if Dad moves in with Loretta, we could have the white cottage.'

'You'd live together?'

'Maybe not at first, but it's silly for him to pay rent somewhere else when I'd be alone in the cottage.'

'Seems like everything is working out for the best then . . .' Laura says, letting the sentence trail away suggestively.

'Yeah,' Summer says. 'Seems like it.' She allows herself a brief glance at her friend. 'I know what you're thinking,' she says. 'Stop worrying. I'm not rushing into anything – we're only talking about living together.'

'Okay,' Laura touches Summer's arm. 'Sorry. I know I'm an interfering cow sometimes.'

The pub in Orford is heaving, every table taken, the bar crowded with people, attempting to get service, or leaning against the wood, a drink in their hands. The small space is full of chattering voices, clinking glasses, and the smell of food and alcohol.

Laura holds her arm, 'Do you think he's here?'

Summer gazes around, 'I don't know . . . hope so.'

Laura fights her way through the scrum to the bar. Summer waits for her, looking at the busy staff serving drinks, wondering about the tall man with the tawny hair. She's curious to see his face this time. But he's nowhere in sight. It's just the bald man and a gangly boy who looks like a teenager. Laura returns, triumphant, clasping two drinks.

The women clink glasses. 'To your plan,' Laura says.

At that moment, Summer catches sight of the naked rambler. He's sitting at a table with another man. She recognises his sunburnt features and thick iron-grey hair. He seems smaller with his clothes on. She tries to erase the image of him walking away, his flat, tanned buttocks.

She nudges Laura. 'That's him,' she whispers.

'Then I guess you're going to have to go through with it,' Laura grins.

Summer takes a gulp of wine. Fear fizzes in her chest, and her legs feel weak. She wishes she could sit down. She realises she hasn't put her name on the list to sing – she hasn't thought this through properly. It's a stupid idea.

The pub quietens as a bleached blonde woman in her mid-forties clangs a bell. 'Thank you for coming to our folk night,' she says in a rich Suffolk accent. 'And now, without further ado, I have the first performer for you, with a song I think you'll all be familiar with.'

A thin woman with a guitar appears in the space in front of the bar and takes a seat on a bar stool. She bows her head over her instrument, long grey hair falling forwards. A thrum of melody, and she begins to sing 'Scarborough Fair'.

The pub is respectfully quiet, just the clink of glass and the muted shuffling of feet. As soon as the singer is finished, the compère, who must be the landlady, introduces a man and his son, singing in harmony. Summer waits, her body hot and tight with fear. If she's going to go through with this, then she needs to go next, otherwise her nerves will fail.

As the applause dies down, and before the landlady can introduce the next act, Summer takes a step forward. Her heart thunders, sweat prickling under her arms. She opens her mouth, and the lyrics to an ancient folk tune enter the air.

She closes her eyes. Words flow through her. Nerves leave her, her heart slows, and it's as if she's back in Cambridge, singing to her sister. When she finishes, the burst of applause shocks her. She stares around into beaming faces, hands a blur of movement.

The landlady is smiling and clapping too. 'That was a bonus performance from a surprise performer,' she's saying. 'What's your name, love?' she calls.

Summer shakes her head, ducking her chin. 'Too shy,' the woman goes on. 'We'll ask again later … And now a short break. Time to get some more drinks in before Mike Gooderham entertains us with "The Whole of the Moon".'

Laura takes her arm and squeezes it, 'You were bloody brilliant.'

Summer glances at Colin. He's looking right at her, and he raises his glass. She smiles at him, feeling a nervy satisfaction that she's succeeded in getting his attention. She'll have to find the right moment to approach him about the article.

'Honestly … you nearly made me cry,' Laura's saying, and then her eyes widen as she catches sight of something behind Summer.

Colin has appeared at Summer's side. 'That was a beautiful performance,' he says. 'One of my favourite songs.'

'Thanks,' she says. 'It's one of my favourites, too.'

'Colin,' he puts out his hand. 'Colin Black. I haven't seen you here before?'

'No,' she says. 'My first time singing. I'm Summer Blythe. I've recently moved to Suffolk. Actually,' a blush rises into her cheeks, 'I did meet you, briefly, on a walk with Loretta.'

He laughs. 'I remember now. I hope you weren't upset by my lack of clothes.'

'I was a bit startled,' she admits. 'But as Loretta says, you know when to use the hat.'

He laughs again. 'I've been rambling naked for a few years. People around here tolerate my madness.'

'What made you start? I don't think I'd have the courage.'

'I'm a nudist, have been for years, and one day I started to stroll along the shoreline on a nudist beach, and I just kept on walking. It was . . . an incredible feeling . . . so freeing. I've kept up with the habit.'

'I didn't even know it was legal,' she says. 'To be naked in public.'

'Oh, yes,' he says. 'It's fine as long as you don't do it to shock or offend. I tend to keep to quiet paths, and often go very early in the morning. The sense of being at one with nature is heightened by being unclothed.'

She feels Laura's finger poking her back. 'Talking of nature,' she says, coughing, 'I . . . I sent an article to you recently. I wondered if you'd had time to read it?'

'An article?' His forehead puckers. 'What was it about?' he asks, scratching his beard.

'Hares,' she says. 'I sent some photographs with it.'

'I'll look out for it when I'm back at my desk. I'm afraid my assistant is new, and things are in a bit of muddle.' He holds out his hand. 'I'll be in touch . . .'

'Summer,' she reminds him.

'Lovely name.'

She's trembling, elation rushing through her. The sound of the next song is already filling the space, accompanied by ringing guitar chords.

'Well?' Laura is by her side.

Summer gestures towards the exit, and the two women slip into the quiet of the night.

'You looked like you were getting on with him?'

'He's promised to read the article.'

'A double-whammy!' She links arms with Summer. 'And how did it feel? To sing?'

'Great. Once I could breathe!'

'Now you've broken the barrier,' Laura says. 'There must be other evenings like this one.'

At home, she tells Dad her news, while Laura makes them tea. Summer is still shaky, but releasing the song felt wonderful. Like dancing over the edge of a cliff and finding that gravity had no authority over her; she could glide through the air, buoyed up, effervescent with light. Flying.

Annabelle launches herself at her ankles, back arched, her throat buzzing with a purr too big for such a tiny body. Summer scoops her up, stroking her ears, pressing her face into the patchy coat.

'I hope you'll sing again?' Dad asks. 'I'd love to hear you.'

The kitten, already bored with being held, wriggles and squirms, and Summer puts her down gently.

'Sorry, Dad. I promise to tell you, if I do it again. Adam will want to come next time, too.'

'We can make a party of it,' Dad smiles. 'You know,' he says, placing a hand on top of her own. 'I've always liked Adam. He feels part of the family. He told me about his plan to move to Suffolk. I think it's wonderful. I'm so pleased for you.'

The blind is up on the kitchen window. She reaches across

glass jars of sprouting beans and a collection of pebbles lined up on the sill to lower it, shutting off her own reflection, and the restless swell of the sea.

42

Kit

Kit leaves Blue's caravan and gets back to the pub after closing. Sally-Ann and her mother are piling chairs on tables, sweeping the floor. Paul is behind the bar, doing a tally of the night's takings. The dogs are lying on the floor, looking hopeful, waiting to be taken home.

'Let me help,' he says, taking the broom from Jenny. 'Looks like it was a busy one?'

'Run off our feet all night,' Jenny says. 'The place was packed. A madhouse.'

Sally-Ann disappears behind the bar, stacking the dishwasher.

'Best night we've had in months,' Paul says. 'Perhaps we should have these nights more regularly. They bring in the crowds.'

'What was the talent like?' He sweeps the debris into a pan, drops it into the mouth of a dustbin liner.

'The usual lot. Mike's version of "The Whole of the Moon" had them on their feet,' Jenny says. 'There was a chap all the way from Norwich who didn't have a bad voice … and then there was this stranger – a girl – not on the list – who sang a beautiful song—'

'Mum,' Sally-Ann interrupts, sharply, 'can you help me with this?'

'What, love?' Jenny goes over to Sally-Ann.

'A stranger?' Kit is alert, his pulse thrumming through his body. 'A girl?'

'Lovely voice,' Paul says. 'We never got her name. She left before the end.'

'What did she look like?' His heart stills, waiting for the answer.

'Blonde,' Jenny says.

'Blonde?' He can hardly speak.

'She looked … desperate,' Sally-Ann snaps. 'And I don't know why you all thought she was so great – I thought she was kind of average.'

'You're a hard critic, Sally-Ann Fisk,' teases her mother.

'She was a frail-looking thing,' Paul says. 'Like the wind would blow her over. Never thought she'd have such a powerful voice.'

Kit's grip weakens on the broom, and he has to force himself to finish the job, pushing the bristles haphazardly, sending puffs of dust and grit scattering, missing empty crisp packets. There had been a moment when he'd been certain it was Summer they were talking about. He could sense her, almost hear the echo of her singing, as if she'd just left the room. But the description is all wrong.

'Leave that, Kit,' Paul says. 'It's your night off.'

He tips the last of the sweepings into the bag and doesn't argue like he normally would that he's happy to do the bins, or any of the other last jobs.

Upstairs in his room, Kit undoes his wallet and tumbles the little silver earring out into his hand. He looks at the running hare on his palm. The Summer he'd held in his arms was strong, with curves like a dolphin's back, sleek and smooth under his fingers, muscles dense and springy to touch.

He tips the hare back into his wallet. There's a knock at the door. 'Come in.'

Sally-Ann slips inside and closes the door behind her. 'Are you okay?' she asks.

'Yeah,' he pushes his hand through his hair. 'Why?'

'You looked a bit . . . rattled . . . when you came in.'

'Just tired, I guess.'

'Not . . . too tired?' she says in a low voice as she steps closer, placing a hand on his chest. Her knuckles are pink, her nails painted glossy purple.

He takes her thin, cool fingers and raises them to his mouth. She shivers. 'Kit,' she whispers. 'You know I fancy the pants off you, don't you?'

'What about your parents?' he asks, knowing they could still be downstairs.

'I'm a big girl,' she says, stretching up on tiptoes, and he suppresses a smile at the irony, lifting her off the ground. She weighs almost nothing. With one easy movement, he sweeps her up into his arms. She squeals and clasps her arms around his neck. He puts her on his single bed. She laughs, already wriggling out of her jeans, pulling her top over her head so that her inky hair crackles with static.

Summer belongs in his past. She's a memory that puzzles him, haunts him, despite his efforts to forget her. But life goes on – and Sally-Ann is with him now, here in his present, and maybe in his future, too. She's lovely, and she wants him. What's he waiting for?

'Come here,' she says in a husky voice, as if she understands his hesitation. And she holds out her arms.

He undoes his jeans, lets them fall, belt clunking as it hits the floor, and climbs onto the bed, lying next to her. They look at each other as he runs his hand gently over her ribs, her stomach. 'Kit,' she murmurs, kissing his throat, his chest. He sighs, burying his face in her neck. It feels good to be naked with another human being, to taste her warm breath, feel the rapid beat of her heart pressed against his.

43

Summer

Colin ushers her through into an open-plan space with shelves of books, a long table – covered in stacks of papers – before a French window, a typewriter with a piece of paper threaded through. 'My office and my home,' he says, leading her further into the room, where a sofa sits and something that Summer recognises as a Danish 'egg' chair. Colin tips a white cat off it, and gestures for her to sit. He pulls a glass coffee table close and says he'll make them some tea.

She watches him disappear into a galley kitchen, an embroidered shawl trailing over his shoulders. There's the whistle of a kettle.

'As I said on the phone, I liked the article,' his voice floats from the kitchen. He reappears holding a tray. 'I never knew that it was the Romans who first brought the hare to England.'

'Along with the chicken,' she says. 'And it's thought both creatures were revered in those days, considered sacred,' she says. 'Not eaten.'

'Fascinating.' He puts his cup on the glass. 'I've made some edits. I thought you might like to go over them with me.' He adds a spoon of honey to his drink. 'There's no doubt that you can write.' He stirs his tea. 'And your photographs are glorious. They speak for themselves.'

'So ... you mean,' she swallows. 'You mean you want to publish it?'

'In the next issue. We only publish four times a year.'

'That's ... wonderful,' she breathes, not wanting to ask anything in case it bursts the bubble – causes him to change his mind.

'We don't pay much, I'm afraid,' he says. 'But I'd be interested in seeing more feature ideas. And you should try other journals.'

'I have,' she admits. 'No luck.'

'Well, now you can mention that you've got something in *Suffolk Countryside*,' he says, 'that might help.'

She gets into the Renault and starts the engine, reversing out of the drive, her mind soaring with excitement. It's really happening. She's going to be published. Her photographs will be in a magazine – *her* photographs! Her ideas read – her passion for hares passed on to other people. She hopes her words might even make a difference, might help to protect them. Thoughts fall through her mind, nothing quite joining up, but her overall, arching feeling is one of air-punching, shouting-from-the-rooftops exhilaration.

As she reaches the crossroads, leading onto the Woodbridge Road, she remembers that they're out of coffee, and indicates left, driving into Orford. She parks in the market square and walks towards the little village shop. As she gets closer, she notices two German shepherds tied up outside. She approaches the dogs quietly, proffering the back of her hand for them to sniff. The introduction goes well; one of them nuzzles her pockets hopefully. She laughs, 'No treats, I'm afraid. But you're beautiful. You both are.' She strokes each one, fondles their soft heads as they rub against her legs, tails swinging.

She hears the shop door open and close behind her with a jangle of bell and is aware of the dogs pricking up their ears in eager recognition. She turns to find a thin girl coming towards them, a paper bag under one arm. The girl does a kind of cartoon double-take when she sees Summer.

Summer smiles, 'Sorry, I couldn't resist saying hello to your dogs. They're gorgeous. Must be quite a handful.'

'Yeah,' the girl agrees in a faint voice, untying them. 'They are a bit.'

She straightens, sweeping a stray lock of black hair behind her ear. 'You . . . you sang at the pub the other night, didn't you?'

Summer smiles, 'It was a spur-of-the-moment thing.'

The girl stares at her, then rearranges the bag under her arm, shifting her weight onto one leg. 'What's your name?'

'Summer . . . Summer Blythe. What's yours . . .?' she begins to ask, but the girl has pushed past her, muttering that she has to get on, untying the German shepherds and walking away inside a sea of shaggy fur.

Summer gazes after her. The girl had seemed upset or confused – and then going off like that in a tearing hurry. Strange. She shrugs. She's longing to tell Dad and Loretta about Colin, tell them the news that he's publishing her article, and then call Adam and Laura, and do it again on repeat.

44

Kit

He parks outside a cinema, turns off the ignition and gets out of the Moke. He hasn't been to Aldeburgh before. 'Filled with Londoners,' Sally-Ann told him. 'They love the pretty painted houses on the front. The delicatessens and gourmet pubs. You hardly hear a local accent.' She grinned, 'And there are four art galleries in the high street.'

They've spent the whole of the last two weeks together – working alongside each other in the pub, swimming at Leiston, a party at someone's house, and every night she's stayed in his room. He was worried at first that Paul and Jenny would disapprove, but their attitude towards him is as straightforward as ever. Sally-Ann wanted to come with him today, thought it would be funny to pretend to be his agent. But this is something he needs to do on his own. He's never been good at selling himself. He worries that what he thinks of as humility is actually just a fear of failure. He's got his best canvases with him, some portraits and his new landscapes, and at the last moment he included a snap of the hare sculpture.

'Maybe you shouldn't show them that,' Sally-Ann had said, wrinkling her eyebrows. 'They'll get confused. Your box says painter.'

'My . . . what?'

'Box.' She'd waved a hand, 'The thing that defines you. People like to know which one you belong in.'

Kit doesn't like the idea of being confined to a box. But that isn't the reason he won't show the photo. The sculpture is an experiment. He'd love a professional opinion, but he's not ready to try and sell it. He's been working on his painting for years, and he wants gallery owners to recognise him as someone who's serious about his art.

Sally-Ann thought he should wear a suit. But he doesn't possess such a thing. He's put on a blue shirt and reasonably clean jeans. He brushed his hair to try and persuade it to lie flat, but then ran his fingers through it to rough it up again, because artists are not supposed to look like they work in the City.

His portfolio is heavy. He hooks the strap over his shoulder, holding one hand to the side of it protectively as he gazes through the plate-glass window of the first gallery, seeing with relief that it's empty of customers. He pushes at the door, the sound of a loud buzzer making him jump. The cumbersome portfolio bangs against a small bronze sculpture of a mermaid, and he spins around to save it from falling.

A tall woman wearing a linen smock and matching loose trousers appears from out of the back. She looks at him with an annoyed expression.

'Hi, I'm Kit Appleby,' he says, settling the mermaid on the plinth and moving away. 'A local artist. I wondered if I could show you some of my work?'

'Do you have an appointment?' she asks, touching the long string of amber beads looping across her chest.

He stares at her blankly, heat building in his cheeks. Why hadn't he thought of ringing beforehand?

'Sorry. But if you're not busy?' He doesn't allow himself to look around the empty space, in case she thinks he's being sarcastic.

She sighs, and motions to him to put his portfolio on the desk in the corner of the room. He stands back from her, hands linked behind him, a schoolboy in front of a headmistress, while she looks at each painting.

'Hmmm.' She closes the portfolio. Her expression is blank, unreadable. 'Not for us, I'm afraid.'

He leaves, feeling the sting of humiliation behind his eyes. Not one word about his work. He stands on the pavement and pushes the back of his hand over his forehead. The temperature must be in the eighties, and his nerves are creating an internal furnace. The inside of his collar is damp, his spine itches with perspiration. It was a mistake to think he could be taken seriously.

He forces himself to enter the next gallery. There are a few people browsing, and he spots a man sitting behind a desk, looking at a catalogue. Kit approaches the desk. 'I don't have an appointment,' he says quickly. 'But as I'm here, I wondered if you'd have time to look at my work?'

The man glances up through Elton John-style glasses with tinted glass and huge pink frames. He closes the catalogue, 'You can put your portfolio on here. I'll just clear some space.'

He shoves clutter along his desk – a mug, a half-eaten packet of digestives, a potted plant and a framed photo of a smiling young man – then gestures for Kit to put his work out.

Kit waits while he looks through his canvases. The gallery owner pauses sometimes, tilting his head, making interested noises. Kit's mouth is dry. He shifts his feet, runs a finger around his collar, pushes his hair back from his forehead.

The man looks up when he gets to the end. 'You've really portrayed the inner worlds of your subjects.' He takes his glasses off, small eyes blinking, 'But I'm not sure if we could sell your portraits. Personally speaking, I like them, but to be frank, what you're doing . . . it's not fashionable.' He replaces his glasses. 'The landscapes are good, too. But we get so many of this sort of work, and I'm afraid yours aren't . . . unique enough for us to want to show them.'

Disappointment pulls at the muscles in Kit's face. He struggles to raise a grateful, polite smile. 'Thanks for your time,' he manages. 'And honesty.'

'What's your name?' the gallery owner asks.

'Kit Appleby.'

'Benjamin King.' The man puts out his hand. 'Leave me one of your cards, anyway.'

Kit fumbles with the door, getting his portfolio through without mishap and, just as the door closes, he thinks he hears Benjamin call something – goodbye or good luck, probably.

The next place refuses to see him, saying he must make an appointment; their diary is booked for weeks. The last one is friendlier, and take one of his cards too, saying they might be interested at a later date.

It's a glimmer of hope, and he hangs onto it, but when he gets to the Moke, he realises that he has nothing – nothing apart from four rejections. The act of going into the galleries, seeing other people's art on the walls, has made him hungry for success. But he's been going in the wrong direction. It's clear he has to rethink, find a stronger voice, a more interesting style. He feels daunted.

As he pulls out his car keys, glancing into the cinema's glassed-in noticeboard to see what films are on, he notices a small poster advertising a folk singing evening at a pub in Framlingham. He memorises the details. It's time to get over his problem with folk music. Maybe it would be a fun thing to go to with Sally-Ann; it would help to make up for letting her down before. He knows he hurt her feelings by refusing to go to the one at The Anchor.

45

Summer

When she told Adam about singing at the pub, he'd insisted she should do it again, on the proviso that he gets an invitation next time. Then Loretta announced that there was going to be another folk evening in Framlingham in a couple of weeks. 'It's a bigger venue,' she said. 'You should definitely put your name down to perform – and your dad and I are coming. No arguments.' So, Dad's idea of making a party of it fell naturally into place.

Saturday night, and Adam and Laura arrive at the white cottage. The plan is for all of them, including Dad and Loretta, to pile into one car after supper and drive to the pub in Framlingham. Adam is telling joke after joke. She's never considered before why he does it. Perhaps he puts himself under pressure to constantly entertain, or maybe it's just that someone else's humour is a cover for his own feelings of inadequacy. She slips her arm around his waist to reassure him, and he looks at her gratefully.

They eat supper squashed around the kitchen table, the conversation revolving around the wedding.

'We're hiring a small marquee,' Loretta is saying, 'to put over my decking.'

'Maybe Summer could sing?' Adam suggests. 'At the party?'

'Yes!' Loretta claps her hands together. 'Could you, Summer?'

She's torn between being annoyed at Adam for suggesting it without asking first and being pleased to contribute to the celebrations, 'If . . . if you really want me to,' she says, 'then, of course.'

'Are you having a honeymoon?' Adam asks.

'A night in a local hotel,' Loretta says. 'We don't need to go away when we've got such beauty on our doorstep.'

'And there'll be cake and speeches?' Laura asks.

'Definitely,' says Dad.

'This will be a party nobody will forget in a hurry,' Loretta smiles. 'Trust me.'

Loretta is pouring more wine into everyone's glasses. Summer puts her hand over hers. She needs a clear head to perform. She'd hoped conquering her fears before would have made it easier to do it again. But it hasn't.

She excuses herself from the table. 'I just need a few moments,' she murmurs.

Upstairs in the bathroom, she cleans her teeth and gargles, checks her eye make-up, adds mascara, dabs on lip gloss. She takes a deep breath and places her fingers over her stomach and does some voice exercises.

She's sitting on the loo when there's a short knock on the door, and Laura comes in. 'Don't flush,' she says. 'I need to go, too.'

Summer pulls up her knickers. 'Do I look all right like this?' She's wearing a long dress, poppies against a cream background; the skirt is cut on the bias, swinging out from her hips. It has buttons up the front, and she's undone the bottom three.

'Very folk heroine,' Laura says, considering her from her seat on the toilet. 'Disarmingly girlish. Your voice is going to knock their socks off.'

Dad has volunteered to be chauffeur for the night. As he drives, Adam throws a series of music-themed jokes into the car: 'How do you make a bandstand? . . . Take away their chairs.'

Laura groans. 'They get worse,' she says.

'I'm trying to distract Summer.' He finds her hand and squeezes.

Summer stares out of her passenger window into the evening fields, pink-tinged, heavy with gold. The heat is oppressive, a storm gathering out of the looming stillness.

Loretta is talking about her days at the grammar school in Framlingham when she was a girl. Summer winds the window right down, leaning her head out into the rush of wind, hearing the thrum of tyres against the road. The smell of hot tarmac is pungent. She likes its thick, dense scent.

When they arrive, Dad finds a parking space close to The Plough and the five of them walk up the slope of dusty pavement together. Winged ants swarm out of cracks, whizzing around their heads; one of them gets caught in Laura's hair and Summer stops to unravel it from her friend's thick curls.

'They're looking for a mate,' Adam says. 'This is it, their one chance to get laid.'

'In mid-air?' Loretta asks.

'Yup. So, the biology teacher, Lucy, told me. Loves to give me random biology info. If you look, some of the ants are larger. They're the females.'

The ant vibrates against Summer's closed fist; she opens her fingers, watching it fly free. The air pressure changes. Her ears ping. There's a faint rumble of thunder far away.

The Plough is a white building at the corner of the market square. At the far end of a deserted shopping street, Summer sees the ramparts of a castle. The sky behind the turrets has deepened to scarlet. Red creeps through blue, scorching the evening, turning clouds into glowing embers.

'Looks like a popular night,' Dad says, offering her his arm.

All those times her sister begged her to sing in public. If only she was here now, smiling and chatting, making the world radiant with her laughter – it used to surprise people to hear such an uproarious sound coming from her frail body. There'll be an Effie-shaped gap in her life for ever; on every occasion like this, the absence of her will hurt even more. She grips Dad's elbow tightly as they walk in together.

Loretta, Dad and Laura go off in search of a free table, and Summer squeezes her way between the crowd to find the person with the list for the evening. He ticks off her name. 'You'll be fourth up, love,' he says. 'Stick to one song. We're full tonight.'

'Anything for Dutch courage?' Adam asks, insinuating himself into the crowd stacked three deep around the bar. 'Maybe a small white wine, then,' she calls.

The others have claimed a tiny table and found enough seats. They perch uncomfortably on stools, elbows in, their backs continually jostled as more people crowd into the room, with nowhere to sit.

Summer's palms are clammy, and she wipes them over her skirt, pressing against her thighs. The first person up is a young woman, and she's good. She plays guitar well, accompanying herself. The audience are hushed, and clap appreciatively when she finishes.

She hardly hears the next two acts. She tries to remember the words to her song. The compère, looking stressed, calls her up to the microphone. She stands as if in a dream and makes her way through the crowd; they part for her, allowing her to get to the small space by the bar.

She licks dry lips, a pulse at her throat. She's hemmed in by spectators, a thicket of onlookers. There's a shuffling of feet and clearing of throats in anticipation.

She holds on to the thought of Effie – her promise to her.

I sowed the seeds of love,
And I sowed them in the spring . . .

She closes her eyes, finding the melody, diving deep into the texture of the song, allowing herself to go with it, to rise far above the heads of the audience. This is the song she sang for Kit that night in India.

The willow tree will twist
And the willow tree will twine . . .

As she reaches the end, she lets herself look into the faces of those around her.

I oftentimes have wished I
Were in that young man's arms
That once had the heart of mine.

Her gaze slides across strangers, the lyrics making her think of Kit, so when she meets his eyes, it's as if she's conjured him with her words. He's standing further back, towards the door. A gap in bodies reveals him. He's standing straight, alert, listening to her. She keeps staring at him, thinking that he'll disappear, fall away into nothing. His untidy hair, his steady eyes fixed on hers. Every detail of him so real.

That once had the heart of mine . . .

She stumbles over the last lines and there's silence.

The audience roars its approval, and Kit, her apparition of Kit, is clapping too. Those big hands; the long fingers that have held her body, touched her face.

Fear shoots through her like wildfire, scattering her thoughts. It's him. It's really him. After all these months. He's here. It's too incredible, too strange. As if her song has somehow pulled him through time towards her, a ghost from another world.

There's an ear-splitting whistle from the other side of the room. 'Summer!' Her family are calling to her.

She glances over. Adam has his fingers in his mouth, whistling, and behind him Laura, Dad and Loretta are all on their feet, clapping, beaming.

She looks back at Kit, but he's gone.

She searches the audience. But why on earth would he be here? What kind of a crazy coincidence would that be?

Her legs are trembling as she walks through the crowd to her table. Adam grabs her and kisses her on the mouth; his lips linger and he's a little unsteady on his feet. He tastes of beer and cigarettes. The others are patting her back, telling her that they're proud, that she was incredible.

'Summer?'

She swings round, her heart crashing through her sternum. She'd know that voice anywhere.

'What are you doing here?' He's standing close enough to touch. He looks uncertain, his forehead furrowed. He runs his fingers through his hair, just like she remembers him doing, and she notices splatters of paint on his knuckles.

'What ... what are *you* doing here?' Shock rings through her body. The room tilts. She puts out a hand to grab the back of a chair.

'Babe,' another voice at her elbow. Adam is leaning across her, stretching a hand towards to Kit. 'Hey,' he's saying. 'Don't think we've met. I'm Adam, Summer's partner.'

Kit shoots her an uncomfortable look as he takes Adam's hand. The tips of his ears glow pink.

'How do you two know each other?' Adam is glancing at Kit and then back at her, his expression neutral, eyes narrowing.

'We met ... on holiday,' Kit says. 'In India.'

'And now you're here?' Adam says. 'What are the chances, eh?' He takes Summer's hand and squeezes, gazing at her. 'Did you hear her just now? She's such a star. I couldn't be prouder.'

'Yeah. She was great,' Kit agrees, his voice faint. 'Well.' His golden eyes are blank. 'I'm with some people ... so ...' He glances behind him, obviously desperate to get away.

'Mate, good to meet you,' Adam says quickly.

'Bye,' Summer manages, watching him walk over to a lively group of young people, seeing him merge into them, reaching out to accept a drink from someone. There is laughter. He doesn't look back.

'Well, that was awkward,' Adam says. 'He's that guy you told me about, isn't he?' He stares at the back of Kit's head. 'What's he doing here?'

'I don't know,' she says, clenching trembling fingers. 'Can we ... can we go now?'

'He didn't follow you, did he?' Adam's frowning. 'He's not some kind of weird stalker?'

'Of course not. I think I mentioned that Suffolk was a good place for artists,' she says. 'I'm guessing he's here to paint.'

'Don't worry,' Adam says, pulling her close. 'We never have to see him again.'

'Yes . . . it was . . . a shock,' she says, feeling sick. 'Adam, I'm shattered. I really need to go.'

'Okay, babe, let's get you home,' he says, turning to call the others.

Dad, Loretta and Laura gather around her, sweeping her out of the pub in an excited chatter of voices. She glances over to where Kit stands, a tousled head taller than the others, talking to his friends, oblivious.

46

Kit

Somehow, he manages to pretend to join in with the rest of the group, listening to a couple more folk acts, laughing at people's stories, buying another round, while his mind scrabbles backwards to the moment he'd stood in front of her. He isn't sure what he said. He'd found himself blundering away through tight knots of people, the noise in the pub dropping into spinning silence.

Sally-Ann had been waiting, a pinched expression on her face. She'd grabbed his hand, clasping it tightly. 'Was it her?' she'd said. 'The girl in your painting? What did she say?'

Someone had handed him a beer. 'Nothing.' He'd taken a sip, forced his mouth to keep working. 'Her boyfriend did all the talking.'

'Boyfriend?' Sally-Ann had raised her eyebrows with a tentative smile.

He tilts his head, liquid moving through his throat in hard gulps.

Looking at her had been like diving into icy water – shock,

pain, breathlessness. He couldn't drag enough oxygen into his lungs. It was extraordinary that she was there, in the same room. Her new short hair revealed the lines of her face, making her appear vulnerable and older. She was thinner, fragile. He'd wanted to pull her into his arms.

She has a boyfriend.

The dark-haired man had chatted easily, but he'd been saying something different with his eyes, the force of his gaze like a physical blow as Summer stood mutely inside his embrace.

Shit. Kit drinks pint after pint, blurring the memory, the failure, the shock.

When they finally get ready to leave, he glances about. She's gone.

Outside, the storm has broken, and he and Sally-Ann run through the deluge, stumbling to her car. The wet, black world tilts and slides around him. He's more drunk than he realised. 'Told you it was going to pour,' she laughs as they climb into the Land Rover. 'Thank god we didn't take the Moke – would have been like sitting in a paddling pool!'

She drives them back to Orford, rain lashing the windscreen, blurring everything into a confusion of darkness.

They hurry into the back entrance of the pub, Sally-Ann yelping as she splashes through a puddle. Jenny appears from the kitchen with one of the dogs padding beside her. 'How was The Plough? Not as good as our folk night, I hope.'

'Not even close,' Sally-Ann grins.

He stands beside her, blinking in the overhead light, nodding, hoping he's making a convincing show of being sober, his hand flat on the hall table for balance. He needs to get to bed. The floor pitches beneath him, and he's beginning to feel seasick.

'Someone rang for you earlier, Kit,' she goes on. 'A gallery.'

The word makes him startle. He attempts to focus. 'Gallery?'

'Benjamin someone. He left the number.' She pokes a piece of paper at him. He squints down at a scribbled message. A beat of hope starts up inside his chest. He crams the fold of paper into his back pocket with fumbling fingers.

'Well. I'll be getting home.' Jenny turns, dog at her heels, and gives them both a cheerful wave, 'Night.'

'Night,' they echo.

'Come on,' Sally-Ann says, taking his hand. 'Let's get out of these wet things.'

His trails up the stairs after her, legs wobbling, and has to clutch the banister to stop himself from falling backwards. He shuts his eyes, snatches of the evening rushing back. Of course, she's with someone else.

He thinks back to his monosyllabic exchange with her. They said nothing to each other. After all these months. Nothing. She's here, in Suffolk. But . . . is she living here, or is she just visiting? The question bobs into his head, puzzling him.

He's outside his room, and Sally-Ann shakes her head. 'You're pissed, you big idiot.' He hears the smile in her voice. 'Come here. I'll help you.'

He stumbles into his room, stubbing his toe on the wardrobe, and crashes out on the bed. He can't move. It's like someone has piled a ton of bricks on his chest. He's vaguely aware of her pulling off his shoes, tugging the cover over him. 'Night, night.' A kiss lands on his forehead. 'Sleep it off.'

The click of a door closing. Darkness. But the bed won't stay still. It's cut loose from gravity, spinning through space, with him clinging to the mattress as it whirls and dips, nausea roiling in his guts, the taste of soured milk in his throat. Flashes of Sally-Ann, flashes of Summer, both of them looking at him with disappointed expressions.

The bed bucks, and plummets towards earth, and he goes reeling with it, eyes tightly shut, braced for the impact. For oblivion.

47

Summer

Adam's sprawled across the mattress in Summer's small double, snoring. She's squashed onto the edge. She nudges Adam and he rolls onto his side, breathing loudly. Wind howls around the house. Something bangs and rattles from the roof. The kitten jumps up and curls, purring, into the crook of her arm. Summer stares into the darkness. The events of the evening replay on a loop. The way they'd both gazed at each other, dumbstruck – the few meaningless words they'd spoken. And then he'd walked off, without a backward glance. Would it have been different if Adam hadn't been there? Would they have talked, explained? She could see that Kit was shocked by seeing her. But she hadn't been able to gauge what he was thinking or feeling as she'd stood hand in hand with Adam, embarrassment and frustration paralysing her.

Adam had fallen asleep as soon as they'd gone to bed. She knows he'll be apologetic in the morning. But it would have been hard to be physical with him when she feels like this. She'd answered with confidence when he'd asked why Kit was in Suffolk – but really, she has no idea. Kit had speckles of paint on his hands, so her suggestion that he was here for his art is probably correct. But he seemed to be with a group of friends, as if he's been living here for ages.

She wakes at dawn, with Kit the first thought in her head. The storm is over. She gets up and gazes out of the window at the beach. The light is violet, silver, misty. She can see driftwood tossed up on the pebbles, a dark twist of different types of debris the waves have thrown up in the night. Lost things returned.

She slips out of bed quietly, pulls on a pair of jeans and old sweatshirt and creeps downstairs in her socks, calling Friday softly. He stirs in his basket and gets to his feet, a little stiff, but tail wagging, eager for an adventure.

She sneaks a glance into the living room. Laura is asleep on the sofa bed. She'd noticed Kit last night, had witnessed the scene in the pub. Summer is already steeling herself for the interrogation that's bound to come as soon as Laura can get Summer on her own. But she doesn't want to talk about it, not even with Laura, who will ask the questions that Summer failed to ask herself.

She and Friday make their way slowly down the lane that runs parallel to the beach. He sniffs and lifts his leg to pee. Every few paces, he stops to inhale another bouquet of smells, his eyes half-closed. She waits for him, gazing over the flat fields stretching out on her left; hedgerows and branches shine with raindrops. The sheep in the field are wet-backed, steam rising from their thick coats.

Being so close to Kit after all this time has overwhelmed her with a muddle of feelings – pleasure and fear, anger and confusion. It had been hard not to touch him, press her fingers against his skin, just to make sure he was real. Was he angry with her? Did he still have any feelings for her? She pushes her hands over her face. She has to stop this, or she will ruin everything. She has a new life, one that Kit knows nothing about, one that doesn't include him.

Two days later, Colin phones with a commission. Her first commissioned article. The elation she imagined she'd feel at this moment is overpowered by her confusion about the other night; but she is deeply grateful for the work. It's what she needs to distract her. She sits at the kitchen table, Loretta's hulking old typewriter in front of her, and begins to draft an article about the pleasures of being a newbie birdwatcher. Her fingers jab at the keys, and every now and then she leans forward to erase a mistake with a blob of Tipp-Ex. She tries out sentences aloud as she writes:

> ... my body relaxes, a zen-like calm descending. Waiting to see wild birds is a slow game. While you wait, you become part of the landscape, willing yourself to be invisible, focusing intently on what's around you. And this is one of the wonderful things about the pastime: birds interact with insects and plants; they're influenced by weather and geologic formations. In other words, if you pay attention to birds, you quickly begin to understand the interconnectedness of all things...

She pauses and sips her coffee. It's making her more nervous than when she wrote about hares – that had been easy in comparison, because she'd been spilling out her passion; she hadn't been writing to please an editor. She finds she's constantly second-guessing herself. She rereads her words, frowning. She hopes it's not coming across as preachy.

Friday snores in his basket near the range. His paws twitch as he runs in his dreams. She wonders if he's chasing a phantom hare. Annabelle, prowling the kitchen, stops with her tail fluffed up, fascinated by the dog's moving feet. She looks ready to pounce, and Summer clicks her fingers to distract her. 'Leave him alone,' she tells the kitten. 'He's snoozing.'

Annabelle jumps onto her lap, purring. Summer sighs, 'How am I supposed to work with you in the way?'

'Coo-ee?'

It's Loretta. Summer sighs again and pushes her chair back to look through the sitting room towards the front door. 'Come in,' she calls.

Loretta glances at the typewriter. 'Sorry to interrupt,' she says. 'Won't stay. Writing time is precious.'

She strokes Annabelle and reads over Summer's shoulder. Summer can feel her shoulders and neck tensing up. 'You've missed off an apostrophe,' Loretta murmurs.

Summer takes a breath. 'Was there … something in particular?'

'I wanted to show you my wedding outfit while your father wasn't around,' she says in an elaborate whisper. She puts her capacious shopping bag on the floor and rustles inside, pulling something out. She shakes it free, holding it up against her, fingers spread. 'What do you think?'

It's a silky kaftan with matching trousers in a rainbow of vibrant colours, smudged together like an abstract painting. 'Too much?' she asks, gazing down at the clothes with a small frown.

'It's wonderful. Very you.'

Loretta grins. 'No point in pretending to be a shrinking violet at this stage.' She refolds the clothes carefully and puts them back. 'I've arranged to have a beautiful old Bentley to take us to the hotel after the wedding – it's a surprise for Donald.'

Summer smiles, 'He'll love that.' She doesn't think Dad cares much about cars, but he'll appreciate the thought; she feels a rush of warmth towards this woman.

'I was wrong, you know,' Loretta adds.

'Sorry?'

'When I gave you my advice on men. You remember, the first time I persuaded you into the sea with me?' She looks down at her clasped fingers. 'I'd forgotten what it feels like, you see. All those love stories, but I'd stopped believing in it myself.'

Summer's chest tightens. She can't speak. She manages a small shrug.

'Oh, and one more thing.' Loretta straightens and delves into the bag again. 'I wanted to give you this.' She thrusts a stiff embossed white card at Summer.

'The Suffolk Summer Art Show,' Summer reads.

'It's an invitation to the private view,' she says. 'Always great fun. Established and new artists. Your dad and I are going. Would you like to come?'

Summer looks at the invitation. 'Great – thanks.'

'Wonderful,' Loretta says. 'More the merrier. I'm friends with the organisers – bring Adam if he'd like to come.' She pats Summer's shoulder. 'I'll leave you in peace.'

Summer remembers the paint splatters on Kit's hands, and it occurs to her that he could be at the show, as an exhibitor or a spectator. The thought squeezes her throat shut. It would be torture to bump into him in another public space with Adam by her side. She couldn't bear to go through that again. But there's no real reason why he should be there, she tells herself. Suffolk's a big place. She's being paranoid.

She gets up and props the invitation on the mantelpiece.

48

Kit

He wakes next morning with a parched mouth. Before he's opened his eyes, the events of the previous evening come tumbling back, making him groan and grab his skull. The words of her song are repeating, coiling in an ear worm, as he stumbles out of bed, disorientated and heavy-limbed. Shut up, he tells himself. Shut up. He knows those lyrics, how they speak of betrayal. But it's her who lied to him.

It's only as he's pulling on his jeans from the night before that he remembers the scrap of paper stuffed into his pocket.

'I just wanted to check that the sculpture *is* your work?' Benjamin asks when Kit calls.

A hangover thunders through his skull. 'Sorry?' He frowns. He didn't show any of the gallery owners the photo of the hare. 'I think there's been a . . . mistake,' he says, hesitantly.

'The rabbit?' Benjamin persists. 'You dropped a photograph of it – looks like reclaimed materials?'

'The hare?' Kit is trying to get to grips with what Ben's saying – he had no idea he'd dropped the photo.

'Rabbit. Hare. Whatever. Wondered if I could see it?'

Kit drives out that afternoon to meet Benjamin at the barns. He's glad to have something to distract him from the unanswered questions spinning in dizzying circles. He's still in shock. Seeing her sing, seeing her with her boyfriend. He wonders how long they've been together. Maybe she had a boyfriend all along – even when they met in Kerala. The idea makes him feel sicker, but if she lied about everything else, why not that, too? He keeps seeing her face as she sang, her expression as she caught sight of him in the audience. It all seems unreal now. But he knows it happened, because Sally-Ann has continued to quiz him, checking that he felt nothing when he saw her, that he has no intention of seeing her again. 'I don't even know where she lives,' he told her. 'Maybe she was just here for the weekend.'

Kit takes Benjamin around the corner into Blue's workshop, where, under giant antlers and posters of cowboys riding into the sunset, Benjamin walks slowly around the sculpture. Crystal Gayle wails from the speakers, and there are intermittent bursts of angle grinder, but Benjamin ignores the distractions and examines the hare from all angles through his pink-framed glasses. He beckons to Kit to follow him outside.

'I'm organising the Suffolk Summer Art Show at the Maltings,' he says, brushing manicured fingers across his shirt, as if the air of the garage has left a stain. 'And I'd like to exhibit your rabbit.' He nods. 'Sorry. Hare.'

'Really?' Kit shakes his head. 'Great.'

*

Three days later, Sally-Ann announces that she's arranged a picnic to celebrate his news. They're going to Shingle Street. 'The place we first kissed,' she says, giving him a meaningful glance, then rolls her eyes. 'Hopefully the dragon lady won't turn up again.'

'As we won't be lighting any fires,' he smiles, 'we should be safe.'

He knows she's aware of his mood change since Framlingham. He's tried to hide how he feels, but he's been distracted. Snappy. And he hates himself, because she is thrilled about the art show and – in typical Sally-Ann fashion – she seems to have forgotten her original advice not to show the photo of the hare to anyone.

The Moke is packed with a picnic rug and hamper of food. He's got the keys in his hand and is halfway out of the pub when she comes running, breathless. 'Champagne,' she says, brandishing a bottle.

They pull up next to the old red phone box, and get out, crunching over mounds of pebbles, past sprouting sea cabbages, skirting the patches of lichen, down to the line of the sea. The water is glassy, hardly moving; a blue swell, as if giant lungs are breathing. There's a single line of white shells on the shingle. It runs for hundreds of yards in loops and swirls, shimmering in the sunlight. It ends in an arrow pointing at a white cottage.

Kit stops to crouch beside it, looking at the whelk shells, placed end to end. 'What a great idea.'

'Don't know why anyone would bother,' Sally-Ann shrugs. 'It's just going to get kicked about and messed up.'

He steps carefully over the fragile line and then, a little further on, spreads out the rug he keeps in the car. They sit down and munch sausage rolls and crisps, swigging the champagne straight from the bottle. 'You'll have to get used to this,' she holds up the bottle. 'When you're a rich and famous sculptor.'

‘A sculptor?’ He teases, ‘I notice you’ve put me in a new box?’

She laughs and pushes his shoulder. ‘I just want the world to recognise your talent. I don’t care what box you’re in.’

They finish the food, licking oily fingers, draining the last drops of bubbly. He’s been careful not to go over the limit, so Sally-Ann has drunk most of the bottle on her own. He leans back on his elbows, looking at the water. He sits up. There’s something out there. Moving, bobbing. Dark heads glinting in the sunshine. Seals? But then he realises they’re human swimmers; he can hear voices and snatches of laughter. He watches as they emerge, struggling through waves, holding hands, helping each other over the sliding banks of shingle.

It’s an older couple, a woman with red hair escaping a black swimming cap, water streaming from sturdy thighs as she powers up the slope, and a man, sinewy and pale, with freckled shoulders.

They stand together, drying themselves, laughing.

‘They seem to think it’s safe to swim here,’ he says, nudging her knee.

She glances at them and frowns, looking harder. ‘Isn’t that her . . . the woman from the other night?’ Her words slur a little. ‘The one who told us off?’

Kit looks at the woman again, and nods. ‘You’re right – it is.’

The man is rubbing his towel briskly over the woman’s shoulders, and she laughs and throws a large towel around him. She tucks it close, cocooning them inside it.

‘The old battle-axe,’ Sally-Ann grumbles.

‘She doesn’t look much like a battle-axe now,’ Kit says, smiling.

The couple are wrapped in a lingering, tender embrace. They sway together inside the towel.

'Yuck,' Sally-Ann huffs. 'They're way too old for all that. And in broad daylight.'

Something clicks in his memory and Kit startles. They're the older couple who were with Summer in Framlingham. He'd glimpsed them over her shoulder, part of the group at her table. That must be her father? She'd said her mother was dead. He watches as the couple make their way hand in hand over the sloping banks of shingle, towels slung over their arms, and wonders if they're heading for a car, or if they're going to one of the cottages at the edge of the beach.

Summer could live here too, at Shingle Street.

His heart hammers at his ribs. Automatically, he flexes his knees, starts to push onto his feet.

'Hey,' Sally-Ann says. 'Where're you going, mister?' She grabs his hand, twining her fingers with his.

He watches the couple disappear.

'I want ice-cream,' she's saying, tugging at his hand.

He remembers how Summer stood before him saying nothing, her boyfriend's arm snug around her waist, the awkward silence filled by the other man's fake friendliness. His stomach lurches, drops. What's the matter with him? It's irrelevant where she lives.

'Right,' he says with a forced smile, helping Sally-Ann onto her feet. 'Your wish is my command. But they'd better have pistachio.'

'Weirdo.' She's shaking her head and laughing. 'Why would anyone want anything except chocolate?'

She's more drunk than he realised. She slips her hand into his back pocket and snatches his car keys, making off with them, holding them aloft. 'And I get to drive the Moke!' she shouts over her shoulder, as she cackles and staggers away.

He powers after her, and she shrieks and dodges his flailing hand, until he grabs the straps of her dungaree shorts and hauls her back. 'I don't think you're in any state to drive,' he says, taking the keys from her.

She stumbles into his arms, laughing as she flips his cap over his eyes. 'Spoilsport.'

He takes a deep breath. She had to deal with him the other night, and now it's his turn to be patient and responsible. But all he really wants is to run up to the row of cottages at the edge of the beach and knock on every single door to see if Summer answers.

'You're incorrigible,' he tells Sally-Ann, keeping his tone light. 'And just a little bit merry.'

'But you love me really,' she says, as she slips a hand around his waist, snuggling up under his armpit.

JULY

Seven months of Summer

49

Kit

Opening night, and he's in the bathroom, cleaning his teeth. The hare sculpture has been transported to the Maltings, where he'd helped position it within a stone's throw of the permanent Henry Moore sculpture. After the hare was settled on its plinth, Kit walked around it, nerves making his stomach contract. He'd never imagined in a million years that he'd be exhibited in the same space as an artist like Moore. The setting is perfect: a flat stretch of lawn, with the mellow red-brick walls of a concert hall and gallery behind, and in front rustling reed beds, stretching into a gleaming expanse.

He wishes Summer could see it; wishes he could share his news with her. He pauses, his toothbrush stilled. An idea occurs to him that's equally terrible and wonderful – could Summer even be at the show this evening? But if she comes, she'll be with her boyfriend, he reminds himself. And he's with Sally-Ann. He spits and rinses, puts the brush back in the pot.

He's put on a clean shirt and tucked some of his cards into his breast pocket. 'It's a busy night,' Benjamin told him. 'Lots of locals come to gossip and browse, but there'll be some heavyweight collectors, too.'

Sally-Ann is picking him up in five minutes. The sound of the pub rises through the floor, a huge beehive vibrating under his feet, an occasional braying laugh punctuating the general noise. Paul and Jenny have got a couple of local part-timers in to cover for him and Sally-Ann tonight. They said they were proud of him when he explained about the exhibition. For the first time in his life, he has a sense of belonging.

He looks at himself in the small mirror above the washbasin. He's put on a tie, but it's strangling him, so he slips it off and undoes the top button of his shirt.

'Hello?' Sally-Ann's voice calls up from the hall. 'You coming? Don't want to be late to your own opening!'

He stands at the top of the stairs. She's waiting below, wearing a floaty violet dress that adds a feminine softness to her thin frame, the sweetheart neckline just low enough to hint at the shape of her small breasts. Her inky hair lies in a glossy mane over her shoulders, and she's clipped one side back with a fabric rose.

'You look . . . really . . . nice.'

Expectation flits across her face, followed by disappointment. He should have said beautiful. Gorgeous. Stunning. Nice? he berates himself. She deserves better.

He goes down. 'Shall we?' he asks, holding out his arm.

She grins and slips her hand through the crook of his elbow.

The noise of the pub is louder here, with just a door between the hall and the crowded bar. They've reached the back door when the phone in the hall starts up. The loud jangling stops them. Kit glances back.

'Oh, leave it,' Sally-Ann says.

Kit has his hand on the doorknob, but the insistent ringing prevents him from pushing into the balmy evening. He lets go of Sally-Ann and strides over to the phone.

'Can I speak to Kit Appleby?' a voice asks.

He swallows, premonition making his pulse race. 'That's me.'

'Margaret Clifton's son?'

At the sound of his mother's name, his stomach shrinks to a knot. The call is from Charing Cross Hospital. He should come immediately, they say, his mother is in intensive care. Her condition is not stable.

A tiny, ugly voice in his head sneers that she always finds a way of ruining everything. But he shuts it out. He looks at Sally-Ann, teetering on her high heels at the threshold.

'Bad news?' she asks, furrowing her brow.

He nods. 'I'm sorry – but I've got to get back to London. It's my mum – she's had a stroke.'

50

Summer

She chooses a simple linen shift she's had for years but never worn because it didn't fit properly. Now it skims her body without pinching, and she can't help admiring the way the clean zing of the lemon yellow makes her tanned skin shine. She slips her feet into flat sandals, runs her fingers through her hair, and fixes a pair of hoops in her ears. She misses her silver hares. One on its own doesn't look right.

When she gets into the kitchen, Dad is there, chatting to Adam, just arrived, handsome in a navy suit, white shirt and patterned tie. 'You look very smart,' she says.

'And you look gorgeous,' he says, putting his arm around her and giving her bottom a secret squeeze.

Loretta knocks on the kitchen window, and they go out to meet her as she waits for them, resplendent in a long fuchsia dress, an orange shawl around her shoulders. She's so different from Mum, who would have looked beautiful but understated in something simple.

It's a short drive to Snape, the sun turning the sky apricot above the line of pine trees, the sweep of fields filled with pigs, the roofs of cottages.

Summer follows a sign for the show, turning off before a bridge into the Maltings car park. The river isn't visible from the car, but the masts of moored barges mark its route. 'What did this place used to be?' Adam asks, as they drive past tall warehouse buildings.

'It was originally used for malting barley,' Loretta says.

'And now it's an exhibition space?' Summer asks.

'There's a wonderful concert hall here, too,' Loretta says. 'And shops and cafés.'

The car park is nearly full, the lawns around the buildings busy with people. Summer finds a space next to an open-top green car that looks like something one of the army doctors in *M*A*S*H* would drive. In contrast, the Maltings appears quintessentially English: across emerald lawns a crowd gathers, women dressed in the kind of summer dresses and hats usually worn to weddings, men in suits making a sober backdrop to clashing florals.

Loretta leads them over the grass to a large, airy gallery – inside, the noise of chatter and clinking glasses is deafening. The walls are covered in paintings of all sizes, in all styles; Summer goes to look. There aren't many portraits.

Adam appears at her elbow with a glass of fizz. 'The free drinks are the best part,' he says a bit too loudly.

She shushes him with a frown but tilts her glass to clink against his. 'Cheers,' she says.

Looking across the room to try and locate Dad and Loretta, her gaze falls on a pretty girl in a violet dress. Summer's sure she's seen her before – that inky fall of hair, the way she flicks it across her shoulders – but she can't place her. The girl seems to know lots of people. She's chatting as she moves amongst the crowd, ignoring the paintings.

After they've wandered around the room, Loretta tells them that she and Donald are going outside to get some air. 'They often have sculptures on display in the grounds,' she tells them. 'And there's a wonderful Henry Moore by the reeds – it's full of holes – you can climb through it.'

Summer and Adam stroll across the lawn together. 'There's the Moore,' Adam says, pointing to three metal abstract blocks. 'And there's another sculpture that looks like . . . a rabbit.'

'Not a rabbit,' Summer says, moving towards the sculpture. 'A hare.'

The creature is almost abstract, just a collection of lines and curves that give the illusion of a hare in flight. Looking closely, she can see that it's been made from something that might once have been a plough. It's clever, she thinks; but more than that, it's beautiful, poetic. She leans down to see the name of the artist.

As she reads the words on the little plaque, all the breath leaves her body.

She glances at Adam, but he's seemingly unaware of anything, gazing around him, looking bored. She reads the name again. The letters dance and blur.

'Want another drink?' Adam's saying. 'Better get them in before the free stuff runs out.'

She can hardly hear him; she's remembering Kit gesturing towards her silver earrings. She'd laughed and corrected him. 'They're hares,' she'd said.

With a jolt, she understands that he's here. It's his opening night. She stares around, expecting to see him behind her. Her legs are shaky, the breath caught in her throat as she turns, searching for him. She starts to walk, looping around the whole of the gallery, pushing her way through the crowd. She goes outside and checks the shops and cafés, but they're closed. She returns to the lawn and his sculpture. He's not here. She finds the main desk; a young man with an inflamed complexion sits behind it, reading a novel. She clears her throat to get his attention and asks for the information on Kit Appleby. An irrational part of her is afraid that he'll refuse her, tell her that Kit has said on no account to give his details away to her. The young man behind the desk hands her a piece of paper with a bored expression. She looks down at a photo of the sculpture and a short biography of Kit, with his telephone number and address printed at the bottom. The Anchor in Orford. She frowns, remembering the tawny hair that had caught her attention that night she'd had a drink with Adam.

'He … doesn't seem to be here?' she says, as she slips the paper into her handbag. 'Kit Appleby?'

'Isn't he?' the young man says. 'Sorry. I'm just on the desk. I don't know anything.'

'Right. Thanks.' She turns and bumps into Adam, looking hot and irritated, clutching two glasses of prosecco. 'Where have you been?' he says, thrusting one of the glasses at her. 'I've been searching for you for ages.'

'Sorry,' she says. 'I … needed to nip to the Ladies.'

She sips the drink. It's flat and warm. Her mind is spinning. She touches the paper in her handbag, checking it's still there. His contact details seem to vibrate under her fingertips.

Her cheeks are hot, her heart thumping inside the linen shift. Can't Adam sense that something is wrong? Can't he tell what's happening?

‘Come on, babe,’ he tugs at her arm. ‘Let’s find your dad and Loretta.’

He has no idea, she realises, as she lets herself be towed along beside him. He’s unsuspecting, completely unaware of the deceiving thoughts in her head. He doesn’t deserve her betrayal. But her heart swells with the knowledge that Kit hasn’t forgotten her. She knows it now. The hare is like a message to her – a secret message. She stumbles, her foot catching on a tuft of grass, her drink spilling over her hand, darkening her yellow dress.

51

Kit

Hospital corridors remind him of when he was stuck in a bed in India. More than the remembered pain of his injuries, it's the pain of knowing in retrospect that those weeks marked the end of his relationship with Summer. His heart contracts. He's on the wrong floor and gets back into the lift. He has to stop and ask three times how to get to the ICU. Nerves scatter his ability to think and process directions.

His mother looks like a stranger in the bed; shrunken, surrounded by machines. He's shocked by the ashen grey of her skin, the way the right side of her face droops, cheek and jowls hanging loose, her lower eyelid pulled down to show the red, wet inner rim.

He sits beside her. She'd be upset to see herself like this – she's taken care of her appearance all her life, been proud of her elegant legs and creamy skin. He touches her inert hand, speckled with age spots. The sight of a cannula taped into her fragile skin makes him wince.

Her gaze passes across him, but there's no flicker of

recognition. 'Mum?' he murmurs. 'It's me. Kit. You collapsed. But you're going to be fine – you're in hospital and they're going to take care of you.'

He has no idea if she can hear him, or if he's telling her the truth. All he knows is what the doctor told him – that she's had an ischaemic stroke. She's on medication, and they are running tests to see the extent of the damage to her brain.

He sits for a while longer, hoping she knows he's there, that in some way she might take comfort from his presence.

When he leaves, he finds a nurse and asks what happens next. The woman says his mother will probably be in ICU for at least a week.

'But – she's going to be all right?'

'We'll be starting rehabilitation as soon as possible,' she says briskly. 'We start early, even in ICU, to minimise muscle atrophy. Her consultant will know more tomorrow.'

He opens the door to his old home, stepping into the familiar smell of pine and bleach. The dancers give him disapproving stares as they hover on pointed toes, cold arms raised. He wonders where Terry is – and why he wasn't at the hospital. When he gets into the living room, he stops. A nest of tables is lying on its side, broken shards of green and white china spread over the carpet. He kneels down, touching puddles of darkness soaked into the fibres of the carpet. He smells coffee. She must have fallen here. Someone had called the ambulance. Terry, he presumes. Kit rights the little tables, stacking them on top of each other, and then takes a bowl of soapy water and a cloth from the kitchen and clears up the broken cup and saucer, trying to scrub the coffee from the carpet. He can't get it out completely. She won't be happy about the mark. He kneels with the wet cloth balled in his fist. A thought strikes him. Will she even get to see the stain? Will she be able to return to this house, resume her normal life?

He tips the shards into the bin, drops the cloth in the sink, and goes upstairs to his mother's room. Even now, he feels strange about entering it. The room is immaculately tidy. The bed made neatly, with cream scatter cushions in place, the crochet bedspread pulled tight. He thinks that perhaps he should bring some of her things into hospital tomorrow. Her dressing table is spread with a bewildering array of pots and jars. He finds one that says 'anti-ageing'. He picks up a hairbrush, wisps of grey stuck to the bristles. He ignores the aerosol can of hairspray but adds a bottle of rose water to his collection. He doesn't know what she'd do with it, but it sounds nice.

In the bathroom, he pauses, noticing there's only one toothbrush in the pot. He opens the medicine cabinet. A packet of Clairol Nice'n Easy hair colour in Rich Mahogany. Bottles of painkillers. Dettol. Savlon. Unwrapped soaps. A packet of plasters. But where is the razor, the shaving cream, the cologne? He goes back into the bedroom and opens the wardrobe. No suits or shirts. He spins around. There's no sign of a man living here. He frowns, anger lodging in his chest. The bastard has done a runner.

He sits on her bed. The evening has turned to night. There's the sound of a pipe clicking, a car reversing in the street. Aching loneliness enters him at the thought of her life in this house: the endless cleaning, the desperate attempt to keep her looks, her figure, and for what? She has few friends. No husband or partner, and a son who tries to stay as far from her as possible.

He stands up, wondering where to find her nightdress. He slips a hand under her pillow but there's nothing there.

Reluctantly, he opens a drawer, finding it full of folded lacy things. He stalls at the thought of investigating further, rooting through her undergarments. With finger and thumb he plucks out something silky and finds himself holding a purple slip. He has a flashback to Sally-Ann in her violet dress. She'd been stalwart in her disappointment of the cancelled evening, offering to drive him to the station – she took him in the Moke, saying she'd always wanted to drive it. He's lent it to her on the proviso that she picks him up from the station. Has she gone to the show without him? He tries to imagine the scene at the Maltings: chatting crowds with drinks in their hands; people stopping to look at the metal hare – what would they say? Has it been admired, or ridiculed?

He gets onto his hands and knees and looks under the bed. Once his mother is on her feet, she'll need slippers. He finds her old blue pair, worn and shiny where her heels have rubbed the fabric; further back, two boxes crouch in the shadows. He pulls them out, curious. He takes the lid off the smaller one, an old shoebox, and his fingers touch folded paper, tied with ribbon: he realises they're letters. His conscience pricking, but unable to resist, he undoes the ribbon and picks the top letter up, scanning the words. It's covered in his mother's writing and addressed to his father. He flicks through the rest, checking. They are all from his mother to his father. But if they're here, she can't have sent them. Unless they were returned to her? He reads the first one:

Darling Alan,

Please don't do this – I know I was angry, but I didn't mean the things I said – I love you – you know I do. It's just that sometimes the loss makes me feel so dark . . .

She must be talking about the loss of her career. He flicks through to another one:

Alan,

How can you be this cruel? Your silence is killing me. I went to hospital, but the news is the same. The consultant says I can't dance again, and that it's not safe to have any more children. But I can bear it, all of it, if I have you and Kit.

He keeps reading. Years of letters. He's certain they were all returned to her. In them, she begs his father. She threatens. She rages. She tells him that Kit has stopped speaking. There are one or two letters that refer to them meeting – and then she's filled with hope. *If we can be a family again, I know we can be happy. Kit will talk again.* But hope soon turns to despair. In the last letter, she writes that he should be ashamed of himself for abandoning his son. And then, no more letters. He looks at the date on the last one. She stopped writing when he was five. Five years of waiting and hoping.

He looks at her bedside table, the surface cluttered with the usual collection of pills. It hits him then, that she must have suffered some kind of physical injury when she gave birth to him – and that it stopped her from carrying on with her dancing. He knew she blamed him for the end of her career, but it never occurred to him that in giving him life, she'd somehow been irrevocably damaged. He grew up with her taking pills – he was forbidden to touch them; it was normal for him to see that quick flick of her head, the dry swallow. But if she's suffered from pain all her life, it would explain her moods – her bursts of anger, her depression. Why did she never tell him? She was always coy about talking about anything she considered private – no toilet humour for her, no mention of sex or periods or the menopause. She didn't even speak of illness or money.

He puts the letters back in the right order, and investigates the other tall, round box, probably once used for a hat, he thinks. Under the lid, he finds something wrapped in white tissue paper. Inside rustling layers, he uncovers a pair of soft leather baby shoes. There's a baby's rattle and a hand-knitted shawl in cream wool carefully folded; underneath that, a lock of wispy brown hair kept safe in more folds of white tissue, with a label saying, 'Kit: one year.' He opens a silk pouch and tips out two tiny milky teeth. At the bottom, kept flat, are some of his first drawings. There's also a piece cut out from the local paper, with a picture of him holding a medal he'd won at an art competition, aged twelve.

He stares down at the contents of the box. His mother loves him. She has always loved him. The understanding squeezes his heart.

He sleeps badly in his own bedroom and wakes to the sound of London. Distant sirens, strange bleepings, the roar of a motorbike, the constant hum of traffic. The noise is unsettling after the peace of Orford.

He makes himself a black tea and drinks it as he wanders into the sitting room and puts the radio on. The morning news carries the comfort of normality, even the bad parts. There's a bookshelf crammed with romance stories, but none of what he'd call proper novels. A couple of women's magazines lie on the coffee table. Under the glass top, he notices photo albums, arranged in piles. He sits down and takes a couple onto his lap, turning the shiny pages, peeling with age. There are pictures he's seen before of him as a baby, a chubby toddler sitting on a plastic tractor, a gangly child, grinning. There's one with him in his mother's arms when he must have been just a few months; she's gazing into his sleeping face. There's another of his mother with his father; she's in a smart blue suit and heels, he's standing close to her, but his gaze drifts away to the left of the picture, as if he's already contemplating his escape.

He's not familiar with the next album he opens. All the photographs are of dancers – elegant girls standing with bouquets of flowers, smiling at the camera, wearing frothy tutus or simple leotards. They are beautiful, dark-haired, like a little girl's dream of a ballerina. With a start, he understands that they're not separate individuals, they are the same person. His mother glows with happiness. Her expression is free of the bitter, disapproving look he knows so well. He touches one of the photos, understanding that, before his birth, she was a different person.

'Mum,' he holds her hand on the bed.

She mumbles, her mouth sagging. He thinks he glimpses frustration in her eyes. And recognition. She knows him.

'I spoke to the doctor, just now,' he tells her. 'And there's every possibility that you can make a really good recovery – with rehabilitation and help,' he adds. He holds her fingers. 'I love you, Mum,' he swallows. 'I didn't understand how much you loved me. I don't think we've been very good at talking to each other.'

He takes a tissue from a box placed there for the purpose and wipes the drool from the side of her mouth, dabbing gently.

'Remember when I couldn't speak?' he says. 'But my voice came back. And so will yours. I'm here, Mum. I'm going to help you.'

A tear slips from the drooping corner of one eye. He's not going to say anything about Terry. Maybe she's guessed.

'I'll have to go back to Suffolk for a night,' he tells her. 'I need to sort a few things out. Then I won't leave you again.'

She tries to speak, her face twisting with exasperation, and he waits, holding her hand. Words emerge, blurred and distorted, but he understands their meaning: 'love' 'you'.

52

Summer

Adam had football practice first thing Saturday morning, so he'd returned to Cambridge straight after they got back from the art show. She'd hardly managed to kiss him goodbye, her lips like wood. Why hadn't Kit been at his own opening?

Waking alone next morning, she rolls over and fumbles on the bedside table, checks the time. Six o'clock. She picks up his details and reads them again. When she'd first held the paper, she'd been overcome with a desire to contact him. But now she's full of doubt. She lies on her back, staring at the ceiling. The right thing would be to forget about him. Burn the paper. Pretend she doesn't know he's living in Orford, just a few minutes away, and hope they don't cross paths again.

She flips onto her side, resting on her elbow, and rereads the number, rubs her finger over the address. It would take no time at all to get there in the car.

She'll wait until, say, nine o'clock before she makes up her mind – it's too early to phone or call on anyone now. To pass the time, she walks a surprised Friday across the fields, then feeds him and Annabelle, and goes for a swim. The water is icy, despite the morning sunshine. The shock revitalises her. Energy fires through her body. Over the past months, she's become a better swimmer, can even do a respectable front crawl – it's all about the breathing, Loretta told her.

After she comes out, she goes back to the cottage wrapped in a robe and finds a note from Dad telling her that he's popped over to Loretta's. More wedding planning. She takes a quick hot shower, throws on some clothes and puts Kit's contact details in her pocket.

She pauses by the telephone in the sitting room, and picks it up, listening to the tone. But she doesn't dial his number. She needs to see his face, not just hear his voice. She doesn't have a choice, she thinks – she has to try and talk to him one more time. She scoops up the car keys, and heads out of the door, leaving Friday and Annabelle in the cottage.

When she gets to the car park at The Anchor, it's nearly empty, except for a Land Rover and a small, green car, like an army vehicle, that seems familiar. As she walks towards the building, she catches her breath at how close she'd come to meeting him here, that night in the crowded bar; the groups of noisy sailors, the glimpse of the back of his head.

The front door of The Anchor is locked. She retraces her steps around the building to the car park and sees the kitchen door is open. She peers into the gloom, rapping on the wood, 'Hello?'

The muted sound of barking starts up – a booming racket that must come from more than one large dog. It's a working kitchen, with gleaming surfaces. It looks scrupulously clean. She smells the bite of bleach. There's a silver deep-fat fryer, boxes of vegetables piled on a big wooden table. She swallows, takes a small step over the threshold and calls again.

A figure appears out of the shadows. A young woman carrying a large container of something that might be margarine. When she sees Summer, she puts it down on the side, and frowns. 'Yes?'

It's the dark-haired girl she met outside the village shop. As Summer makes the connection, two German shepherds come bounding over, barking. She stands still, waiting for them to settle and sniff her. One of them licks her hand.

The girl frowns again and snaps her fingers, and they pad over to her, tails swinging. 'You two,' she tells them, pointing. 'Out.' Obediently, they disappear into the interior of the pub.

'Hi,' Summer smiles. 'I think we've met before?'

'I know who you are,' the girl raises her chin. She's watching Summer intently, as if she thinks she might have come to steal or cause trouble.

'Oh,' Summer is taken aback by the girl's hostile attitude. Blood booms in her ears. 'You do?'

'He told me about you,' the girl says. 'Kit.'

The atmosphere is tight. Summer swallows. Her mouth is dry. She's not sure what's going on. 'That's why I'm here,' she says, with another smile, raising her palms. 'Is he around?'

'He's away,' the dark-haired girl says, putting her hands on her hips. 'But even if he were here, he wouldn't want to speak to you.'

She is winded, her mind blank, 'But—'

'You lied to him,' she goes on in an angry voice. 'He told me.'

Summer blinks in confusion. Her face burns. 'That's ... that's one of the reasons I need to speak to him – I think there's been ... a kind of mistake—'

'I told you. He's not here.' The girl takes a step closer, eyes narrowing. 'What happened between you two in India – it's in the past. Doesn't matter now, because he's with me. We're together – and we're happy. So, you need to leave.' Her eyes move to the door and back to Summer.

She's pretty, this nameless, fierce young woman; her features small and neat, her shining hair caught up in a ponytail. She has extraordinary pale skin. Kit's girlfriend.

Loss swirls in Summer's belly, heavy and dark. She nods, unable to speak, and backs out of the door. She hears it close behind her with a bang.

In the car, she sits without starting the engine. She bites her lip. 'Shit.' She grips the steering wheel. 'Shit.' She drops her head, unable to move. It's a shock. But it shouldn't be. It's been months since India. She's with Adam. Why wouldn't he have moved on, too? It's over, she thinks. Really over. And the irony of it is that they live only minutes from one another.

She turns the key in the ignition with shaking fingers, and leaves the car park, indicating right, pulling onto the road that leads out of the village.

53

Kit

In the hallway of his mother's house, as he's getting ready to leave, it occurs to him that he should probably let his father know what's happened.

His father picks up immediately and is surprised to hear Kit's voice. Kit skips any pleasantries to give him the facts. There's a short pause. 'I'm sorry,' his father says.

'I know you won't visit her,' Kit says. 'But I thought you ought to know.'

'And you,' his father goes on. 'Are you all right?'

'It's a bit late to ask that, don't you think?'

'Kit . . .' There's the sound of breathing. 'I know you blame me. But . . . your mother was impossible to live with.'

Kit swallows. 'Really?' He hopes his father gets the twist of sarcasm in his voice.

'I didn't want to leave you behind, but I had to get away. I had no choice, because if I'd kept on seeing you, she would have used it as an excuse to stay in my life.'

'So, you abandoned me?' Kit says.

'I thought it better to make a clean break. For all of us.'

Anger blinds him for a moment, and he has to concentrate on forcing air into his lungs. 'You had a relationship with her, got her pregnant . . .'

'She told me she used birth control. She did it to trap me.'

'That's . . . that's not what she says.'

'She's a liar, Kit. Pathological.'

'But she didn't run away from her child.'

There's a beat, and a loud exhale. 'I paid childcare all the way through till you were eighteen.' The righteous tone in his voice makes Kit clench his fists.

'You don't get a medal for that.' He sinks onto the chair by the hall table. 'You have a whole other family. A wife. A son who lives with you.' He leans forward over his knees, 'They don't know about me, do they?'

Silence.

'Coward.' Something in his chest unsticks, a flood of sorrow and anger gushing out. 'You're pathetic.' His eyes prick. 'I used to torture myself, wondering what I'd done to make you leave – but I was just a kid – it was you. You're the guilty one.'

'I thought it was for the best,' his father sounds almost irritated. 'Didn't want to mess you around by coming and going. Look, maybe we can meet up sometimes, man to man. Have a drink. And if you need money—'

'It's too late,' he says into the receiver. 'I don't want to see you if you're going to hide me from your other son. My half-brother,' he lets out a breath of frustration. 'And I don't want your money.'

'The offer stands, if you change your mind.'

He wants to cut the conversation off. 'I . . . I'm going to get going – I have a train to catch. Things to sort out in Suffolk.'

'Kit,' his father says, 'I nearly forgot. Some girl rang here for you.'

He stops, his body tingling. 'What? When?'

'It must have been about four months ago. Said she'd met you on holiday.' He sucks in air. 'What was her name? Autumn?'

'Summer.'

His father is still speaking as Kit puts the receiver down. His mind is alight with relief. She must have remembered him telling her his father lived in Wokingham. She's been trying to find him. It hasn't just been him searching for her. It's true that she has a boyfriend, he reminds himself, but maybe it's not serious. He squeezes his eyes shut. They'd missed each other, perhaps by moments, like trapeze artists, fingers skimming past before the tumble into the net below.

He has to find her. Talk to her. Properly, this time.

He arrives at Woodbridge Station, but there's no car. Damn. He'd forgotten Sally-Ann's borrowed the Moke. He was supposed to call her before he caught the train. He may as well jump in a cab, he thinks, as wait for her to drive over and pick him up. His mind is full of Summer. He has one afternoon to find her before returning to London.

The cab drops him at The Anchor, and there's no Mini Moke in the car park. He swears under his breath. How is he going to make the most of the next couple of hours without transport? Paul appears from the storeroom carrying a crate. 'You're back, are you?'

Kit nods. 'For now – but Mum's very ill.' He realises that he should have called Paul and Jenny as soon as he understood the severity of his mother's condition – it was obvious he wouldn't be able to return to work any time soon. But he hadn't been thinking straight.

'Sorry to hear that.' Paul pauses, adjusting his grip on the crate.

'I'm afraid I have to go to London again tomorrow.'

'So soon?' Paul frowns.

'I won't be coming back. I'm really sorry. I can work tonight, but then I'll pack my things and go … I know I'm letting you down.'

'Right – well,' he sighs. 'Can't be helped. And we have Jack to call on. Don't worry.'

'Thank you,' Kit swallows. 'Where's Sally-Ann?'

Paul's shoulders lift a fraction. 'Your guess is as good as mine.'

Kit stands for a moment, thinking. He only has a few hours. He needs a plan. He's annoyed with Sally-Ann, although it's his own fault. He should have phoned. He runs upstairs to his room and dumps his rucksack on the bed. He'll pack the rest of his stuff and get some of his painting gear together tonight, and somehow lug it all on the train tomorrow. Blue or Sally-Ann could probably drop him at the station. He can't take the Moke to London; it belongs to Gerald. He'll need to return it to the farm; maybe Blue would like to use it. He chews his thumbnail, thinking of his studio. The rent is minimal. He doesn't want to give it up yet.

He pulls the old bike out of the cobwebby shed, checks the tyres, and pushes it onto the road.

Ever since seeing her father on the beach, he's had a gut feeling about Shingle Street. As far as he remembers, the 'street' only has a few cottages; he'll knock on every door and ask for her.

The bike's rusty frame complains as he pushes on the pedals. Out of the village, his spine prickles as he cycles along narrow lanes, ears alert for the sound of engines, the roar of rubber against asphalt. As each car passes, his heart thumps. The hiss of a van braking behind makes him sweat and shake. He grips the handlebars tightly, but keeps going, head down, as the vehicle grinds past.

At the Martello tower, he finds a fence to lean the bike against. The sea sparkles with light. There are a few people on the beach, windbreaks arranged around picnic rugs. A little white and tan terrier bounds back to his owner, ears flapping, and drops a ball at his owner's feet. The dog yaps, head tilted, waiting for the game to continue. He longed for a terrier like that as a boy. His mother worked five days a week as a secretary, juggling her job with running the house and looking after him. Of course they couldn't have a dog.

He strides across the shingle, deciding to start at the far cottage and work his way back to the tower. The line of white shells is still intact, and seems to be longer than before, a shining marker in the landscape. As he steps over it, he looks up, counting eight cottages. The further he gets from the car park, the fewer people there are. Soon it's just him and the seagulls, although there's someone out in the water. He stands and watches, his blood slowing as his gaze pulls details into focus. He walks closer to the edge of the water, shielding his eyes from the glare. She's turned for the shore and rises out of the waves as her feet find purchase on the bottom. Is it really her? She's wading out, and he watches her emerge slowly, thighs, shins, her arms moving to keep balance. She's wearing a red costume.

Her short hair is a sleek wet cap around her tanned face. She's wincing over the pebbles, heading for her towel left on the ground. He takes a couple of steps and picks it up, and she jerks around in surprise. Her eyes open in shock as they come face to face.

He can't speak. His head is full of words, but none of them

are right, none of them will say what he needs to say. He holds out the towel.

She snatches it from him, wrapping it quickly around her wet body. 'Kit,' she says, a tremor in her voice. 'What . . . what are you doing here?'

'Looking for you.'

'How did you know . . .?'

'I saw your dad here – took a guess this is where you live.'

'Dad?' She frowns, 'Oh. You saw him with me at Framlingham?'

'Yeah.' Heat rises into his face. His ears burn. 'Framlingham. That was . . .'

'Horrible?' she suggests. 'Embarrassing. Weird?'

He gives a half-smile. 'All of that.' He stares at her face, trying to read her expression. 'It was difficult . . . you being with . . .'

'Adam.' She wipes her face with the corner of the towel. 'It did make it difficult. To talk.'

They stare at each other. The air seems to tighten around them, shutting them off from the rest of the world. He attempts another smile, 'Well looks like it's just us now . . . so . . .'

She takes a shuddering breath, 'I don't know if there's any point. We've both moved on, haven't we?'

He shakes his head. 'Summer,' he holds out one hand as if to a wild creature. 'I've been looking for you since I lost you.'

Her mouth trembles, she bites her lip.

'And I know you tried to find me too. My dad told me.' He wants badly to pull her to his chest, feel her against the length of him, press his lips into her wet hair, kiss her mouth.

She turns away, rubbing herself dry. When she turns back, her expression has closed. Her luminous eyes have become grey and flat. 'That was before I started seeing Adam again.'

'Again?'

'We were in a five-year relationship. It ended ages ago – but he was still . . . important to me.'

'Five years?' His insides crumble. So, it is serious, he thinks.

She's looking down at the shingle; he can't see her expression. 'How . . . how long have you been in Suffolk?' he asks, to break the silence.

'We came in March. After my sister died, we rented—'

Shock flares through him. 'Your sister died?'

'Yes. The operation. I told you.'

'No.' He's blank, shaking his head. 'You never told me anything . . .'

'The note in the hut. I left it by our bed. Explaining.' She's staring at him, a new understanding widening her eyes, her mouth opening.

'I didn't get back to the hut – not for weeks.' He sinks down onto the pebbles and, after a second, she sits next to him. 'I never came back that day. Someone took the note – or threw it away. It wasn't there.'

'Why didn't you come back?' Her voice is small.

'I was involved in a pile-up on the road to Kollam.'

She clasps both hands over her mouth. 'Were . . . were you hurt?'

'Enough to keep me in hospital for a while. I couldn't even phone you. And when I did, they said you'd left the same day as the accident.'

'My dad called me at the hotel,' she says. 'My sister needed me. I was her kidney donor. I had to leave – I waited and waited for you, and then I left you one more note at reception, to tell you to find me at the airport.'

'That was the only one I got – but weeks late.'

Tears fill her eyes. 'Kit . . . all this time . . . did you think I'd left for no reason?'

'I knew something had happened. Just didn't know what.' He pushes his fists into his eye sockets, making sparks fly. 'Jesus. You went back to donate your kidney?'

She's silent. Then she looks at him. 'I didn't know what to think when you disappeared,' she hangs her head. 'I couldn't understand why I didn't hear from you . . .'

'I was afraid of that,' he murmurs.

A tear makes its way down her cheek. She licks it away. 'But you came to Suffolk?'

'You made it sound so perfect.' He holds her gaze. 'I went to Cambridge first . . . I called the magazines and newspapers you said you worked for. I went to pubs to see if you sang in any of them.'

'Kit,' she glances away, biting her lip, hunching her shoulders. 'God. I'm so sorry.'

She looks anguished, and he feels guilty; but before he can change the subject, she's speaking. 'I can't really explain it,' she's saying, her voice husky. 'I suppose I didn't want to have to admit I've done nothing with my life – so I told you my dreams and ambitions . . . made it sound as if they were real.' She hugs her knees. 'But the truth is, since Mum died, I've spent my life caring for my sister. Effie was sick when she was born. Only one kidney – and that didn't work properly. Dad isn't the practical type, and he had his head in work. So . . . it was up to me to take Mum's place. There wasn't room for much else.'

'Effie,' he repeats her name, wondering how old she was. There are so many questions, he doesn't know what to ask next. Panic tightens his chest. 'I didn't even know you had a sister,' his voice wobbles, and he takes a breath. 'I would have understood. Would have . . . admired you. Your commitment . . .'

She looks up, eyes glistening. 'It's hard to understand now but, at the time, being there, with you – it was as if we were in another world. I didn't want to talk about things that were . . . difficult. I didn't want to spoil it. Or make you pity me.'

'I'm sorry . . . that she died.'

Her forehead crumples, her mouth working; she closes her eyes, dropping her chin, curling into herself.

He extends his hand towards her arm, but she flinches. 'No,' she says, moving away. 'It's too late.'

He has an image of the dark man, his arms wrapped around her waist in the pub.

'I met your girlfriend,' she's saying. 'At the pub where you work.'

'What?' Rocks tumbling from a height. Crushing him. 'You spoke to Sally-Ann?'

She nods. 'She was pretty clear that you and she are an item – and that I should back off.'

'I'm sorry . . .'

'No. She had every right.' She looks sad, defeated. 'And it's true. I am with Adam. We're . . . we're making plans . . . he loves me.'

He screws up his courage, 'You love him?'

She sniffs, wipes her nose on the towel. 'Yes.' She looks straight ahead. 'I do. I love him.'

He stares out to sea, to the horizon. She's here, sitting right next to him. He glances sideways, noticing the texture of her cold, wet arm, the puckered skin of her fingers. Dribbles of water run down her neck. His elbow is only inches from hers, yet she seems further away than ever before. A dull sense of hopelessness enters him. 'How did you know I lived at the pub?'

'I went to the art show at the Maltings and saw your hare.'

'You did?'

'It's beautiful – but you weren't there?'

'My mother had a stroke. I had to go back to London.'

'I'm sorry,' she says quietly.

He can't sit next to her any longer, it's too painful. She'd felt the same as him, wanted him too. Maybe they'd be together if it wasn't for his accident and her sister's illness. They'd been separated by circumstances, by bad timing.

Sorrow crashes through him, taking away his breath; he doesn't want to cry in front of her. He gets to his feet, and she struggles up, clutching the towel.

They look at each other. 'I'm sorry I was too late,' he says.

She swallows, nods. 'Me, too.'

He's going to have to walk away from her. 'Goodbye, Summer,' he takes a step. 'I . . . I . . . hope you'll be happy.'

'Where are you going?' Her words twist.

Was that desperation in her voice? He stares at her. But she's got that shielded look again. 'I have work tonight, and tomorrow I'm catching the midday train to London.' His hands are shaking. He pushes them into his pockets. 'Mum's still in hospital.'

It seems as though she wants to say something, then changes her mind.

He can't look at her, his gaze drops. 'I'm . . . I'm not coming back, Summer.'

He feels her flinch. But then she nods. He turns and trudges away, struggling up sliding banks of pebbles, not letting himself look over his shoulder.

*

He cycles slowly, his legs heavy. Cars pass him, full of smiling people enjoying the sunshine, on their way to beaches and campsites. Five years. He wonders how they got back together. Perhaps she needed someone after the shock of her sister's death. Adam had been there at the right time, while Kit had been blundering around looking in all the wrong places.

There are so many things left unsaid between them. There were questions he didn't get a chance to ask. She'd been tense and distant. Their conversation brief and stilted, and he hates himself for handling it badly – maybe he could have said something that would have relaxed her, got her to understand how important their relationship is, to reconsider. Except, he has no right to presume what's best for her. They've only had days together, not years. She's gone through so much. He can't imagine losing a sister. To suffer that after enduring a transplant operation. No wonder she seems different.

He has to end things with Sally-Ann. He and Summer might never see each other again – but he can't be with another person until he's free of his feelings for her. Sally-Ann deserves to be with someone who wants her wholeheartedly.

Thoughts are thick in his head and he's not concentrating on the road, not listening out for vehicles like he usually does. One minute he's the only living creature in the narrow lane, and the next there's a horse galloping right at him – he catches the white of its eyes, the flare of its nostrils – at the same time, there's the distant rumble of a vehicle approaching from behind. There isn't a moment to think. Kit throws himself off the bike, and lunges for the horse's trailing reins. The animal sidesteps him in a dappled blur of withers and flank. But his fingers have closed on leather, and he tightens his grip, bracing himself with bent knees. There's an almighty jolt as the reins snap tight, the muscles in his arms and neck locking. He's nearly pulled off his feet, is towed a couple of steps, but manages to hold on, slowing her to a halt.

'Texas,' he gasps. 'Whoa, girl.'

Grabbing the bridle, he hurries her onto the verge as a lorry rounds the corner, grinding past, straight over the abandoned bike. Kit hears the crunch of metal. But Texas is safe. He is safe.

Elation expands like wings, rising inside him. 'I've got you,' he tells the trembling animal, his hand on her hot neck. 'It's all right. I've got you.'

54

Summer

As she watches him walk away, she makes a soft, involuntary whimper. Her body folds inwards, as if her bones have dissolved. She slumps to the ground. She'd managed to hold it together while he was here, but now the tears come, rinsing the sea from her face. She tries to remember what he'd said – she could hardly focus, she'd wanted to run into his arms, smell him, feel him, kiss him.

She frowns, going over their conversation, extricating the important bits.

He didn't abandon her, didn't forget her. He's been looking for her all this time. She was the one who lost faith. She was weak and hasty, letting herself fall into an old story, letting Adam catch her, instead of standing on her own feet. And now Kit's with someone else. She's lost him.

She struggles to her feet, clutching the damp towel as she makes her way slowly towards the cottage. When Kit asked her, she'd said she loved Adam – but it wasn't true. She'd needed to release Kit. Now he can be with his girlfriend without guilt.

Saying the words aloud made her understand exactly how wrong they were. She feels trapped by Adam, by his need to move their relationship forwards. She has to end things between them. But the timing couldn't be worse. It's her father's wedding tomorrow. She can't ruin that. And Dad is so happy she's with him. He'll be upset, disappointed. She shivers, her teeth chattering. Adam's coming in the morning. He's planning to move job and home for her. Shit. She stops, squeezing her eyes shut.

Kit was in an accident. God. She can't let herself think about it. The horror of it. He could have been killed.

If only she'd known. If she hadn't had to leave the hotel so suddenly, she would have become worried and made enquiries or been told by one of the staff – she would have found out about the accident and gone to see him in hospital. Stop. There's no point in doing this, she tells herself. What-ifs won't help her now.

He went to Cambridge to find her.

Her face flames with embarrassment. All those stupid lies. She'd jinxed everything the moment she hadn't been honest.

As she approaches the cottage, Friday comes running to greet her, his tail wagging. She crouches down and scoops him into an embrace, pressing her wet face into his untidy, rough coat. She sniffles, kissing his soft ears.

'Summer!'

She lifts her head. Loretta is waving at her. 'The flowers have arrived. They're beautiful. Come and look.'

She stands, straightening her shoulders, rubbing her eyes. She goes inside, Friday trotting behind.

The flowers are beautiful, armfuls of stocks, roses and delphiniums delivered by a friend of Loretta's. 'Here,' Loretta says, handing a heap to Summer. 'Let's take them to my place, put them in water somewhere cool until tomorrow.'

Summer hides her blotchy face inside a mass of scented petals. She uses the excuse of the chore to recover, standing in Loretta's kitchen, snipping stems, running water into vases, wiping her nose and eyes on kitchen towel. The marquee people arrive, and Loretta directs them to her decking, where poles clatter, and cats scatter, as two men erect a white canopy over the wooden boards. Dad and Loretta are inside folding up rugs to be laid on the beach the next day – the plan is that there will be tables with food and drink in Loretta's living room for people to help themselves, and then guests can spill out into the shade of the marquee, or into the sunshine with their glasses and plates and make themselves comfortable on rugs, placed near the cottage and far from the plants.

Dad is happy sorting through records, choosing the right music, mellow jazz to drift out into the afternoon, helping people relax. She knows he's written a speech – she's seen him taking it out of his pocket to read, lips moving as he practises the words. It's wonderful to see him excited and full of hope. She's written one too. She's planning on reading it straight after her song.

At her feet are buckets of local oysters and mussels, ready to be scrubbed clean. She opens the fridge to find it full of bottles of champagne. 'The weather forecast is great,' Dad shouts from the sitting room. 'I think we'll start off with some Ella.' He's humming the tune of 'They Can't Take That Away from Me'.

Friday clings to her side, glancing at her anxiously, tail hanging limp. She ruffles his fur. 'It's okay,' she tells him.

Summer calculates the number of hours before the wedding. She has to pull herself together. She can't let anything ruin Dad and Loretta's day.

Dad has dropped a record on the turntable in Loretta's living room. Dave Brubeck. Summer leans against the door frame, watching him get up from his knees with an oomph of effort. 'Oh, I love this,' Loretta says, taking his hand and leading him around the furniture in a stumbling dance. Dad has famously got two left feet, but he tries his best. He spins her, turning her under his arm, red hair flying out.

'And I didn't even step on your toes,' he says, as they stop, out of breath and laughing. He looks younger, healthier since coming to Suffolk. His body strengthened by regular swimming; skin browned by the sun. But it's love that's made the real difference.

'I'm popping home,' she tells them, attempting to sound light-hearted. 'I've got to make up a bed for Laura. She'll be arriving soon.'

She leaves them, walking slowly along the beach path, Friday trotting in front, nose up to scent the air, hopeful for a whiff of rabbit. The blue sky and sparkling sea betray her feelings. She can hardly breathe for the dark weight that swells against her ribs, a wave drowning her from the inside out.

'Summer!'

She turns. Her father hurries after her. 'Are you all right?' he asks.

Her lips form a smile, 'Of course.'

He touches her arm. 'I know you better than that,' he says quietly.

She looks out towards the horizon. 'Really. I'm fine.'

'Are you worried about the cottage?' he asks. 'Because if I move in with Loretta, then of course you can stay on. We'll only be a stone's throw from each other.'

She shakes her head. 'I'm not worried about that. I guessed you'd move in with Loretta.'

'Then what—' he stops. 'You know you can tell me anything. Now you've got me worried – aren't you pleased about me and Loretta?'

'Dad. Of course I am. I'm really glad for you both. It's not that . . .'

He looks at her.

She sighs. 'I . . . I don't know if I'm doing the right thing with Adam,' she admits. 'He's changing his life for me – looking for jobs in Suffolk. And he's talking about us moving in together.' She shakes her head. 'I've sort of agreed. Only . . . now, I'm not sure.'

'It's natural to have doubts,' he says. 'But you have plenty of time to work out how you feel.' He touches her arm. 'You are happy with him, aren't you?'

Her father is looking at her expectantly, a slight crease between his brows. She wishes she could give him a simple answer – the one he wants. 'I don't know. The thing is . . . everything feels different because . . . I met someone when I was in India . . . Kit.' She allows herself to look at him. 'He's here, in Suffolk. He came to find me.'

'He came here?'

'Yes.'

'You like this . . . Kit?'

'We fell for each other straight away. I spent a few days with him in Varkala before I had to leave.'

'But you didn't stay in contact?'

'We lost one another. He's been searching for me, Dad. He hadn't given up on me like I thought.' She bites her lip, 'He came to Suffolk because we made a plan in India for him to move here. It's so ironic – we've been living just a few miles apart.'

'So . . . you mean . . . he wants to resume your relationship?'

'He's not free any more. He wanted to talk to me – find out what happened when we got separated.' She shakes her head. 'He's got a girlfriend here who's passionate about him.' She takes a shuddering breath, her mouth dry, 'Only . . . I know it sounds crazy. But from the moment I met him, I . . . I had this feeling . . . that we belonged together. And even if I can't be with him . . . it's making me realise it's not right between me and Adam.'

'Summer . . . dearest,' he makes a sound of distress at the back of his throat, shaking his head. 'I can see how difficult this is.' They begin to walk again. 'When I'm in a quandary,' he says slowly. 'I find it helps to write things down. A list, if you like, pros and cons. Or sometimes, I just spill my thoughts onto paper.' He takes her hand. 'A kind of stream of consciousness.' He squeezes her fingers. 'I just want you to know, whatever you do, I'll support you.'

'But . . . I thought you wanted me to be with Adam?'

'I only want what makes you happy.' He stops and kisses her forehead. 'I'll be at Loretta's if you need me.'

She watches him tramping back across the beach to the blue cottage.

At the kitchen table, she gets out Effie's old notebook and turns past the pages she's filled with her feature ideas. She finds a clean space and begins by writing out how she feels about Adam.

Adam is my friend. We have so much history. I know we'll make a good team. He can be silly – but he's serious about me. He's good at his job.

He's passionate about history. I like his kiss. There are no surprises.

She thinks of Kit. She stares at the paper, imagining his slow smile and tiger eyes, and then she's scribbling without thought:

I love him I love him I love him I love him...

55

Kit

Blue appears around the corner of the lane at a run. His reddened face collapses with relief when he sees Kit with the horse. 'Jesus Christ,' he pants, coming over to them. 'I was expecting the worst.'

Texas gives a low whinny as Blue reaches her. He bends over with a grunt, his hands on his knees, gulping air. When his breath comes more easily, he wipes the sweat from his face with the edge of his shirt and takes the reins, looping them over his arm. 'You silly mare,' he whispers to the horse. 'Scared me to death.' His hand is gentle on her muzzle.

'Thanks,' he says to Kit. 'I owe you. Don't know what I'd do if she'd been hurt.'

'I was in the right place at the right time.' Kit rubs the back of his neck, 'What happened?'

'I was riding her bareback down the lane. Must have got stung by a horsefly. She tipped me off the back with a rodeo buck, and went hell for leather, kicking her heels.'

'You okay?'

'Yeah.' Blue looks down at his jeans, scuffed and ripped over one knee. 'I'll live. Bloody lorry swerved past, beeping his horn. Idiot.' He shrugs. 'But he missed you both. Bike got a bit bent up, though,' he nods towards the crumpled frame, front wheel mangled.

Kit makes a low whistle when he sees the damage, but it doesn't touch him. He's thinking, it's just a bit of flattened metal. 'Better the bike than me or Texas.'

'My feelings exactly.'

Kit holds out his hands, wonderingly. 'Look. Hardly a tremor.' He shakes his head, 'I should be a mess after a near miss like that. Since the accident in India, every time I've ridden a bike, I've been . . . terrified.'

Blue pats him on the back, 'Maybe it was a kill-or-cure situation – you know, a kind of . . . what do they call it . . . aversion therapy.'

They walk slowly in the heat. Texas plods next to them, swinging her big head. A swarm of flies gathers around her sweat-soaked neck; Blue swats them away with his hat.

Back at Gerald's farm, they trudge past the barns and down the track to the caravan. 'You go inside,' Blue says. 'I'll give her some water, rub her down, make sure she's tethered in the shade.'

Kit goes into the cool of the caravan and slumps on the bench, leaning forward, resting his forehead on his arms. He'd thought that finding Summer would be all it took, that this time they'd walk off into the sunset hand in hand. A Hollywood ending. Idiot.

Blue comes in and pours them both a drink. It's a little early in the day for tequila but, under the circumstances, Kit accepts it gratefully.

'Cheers,' he says, throwing it back with a grimace. He's beaten his fear of cycling and lost the girl he loves all in one afternoon.

'What were you doing on a bicycle anyway?' Blue asks, 'Where's your Moke?'

'Sally-Ann's borrowed it.' Kit licks stinging lips. 'I didn't have time to wait around for her – I had to get to Shingle Street.'

Blue frowns. 'Why the hurry?'

'The girl I told you about.'

Blue looks at Kit questioningly.

'She lives there.' Kit stares down at his glass. 'But she's with someone else.'

Blue inhales, 'You still love her?'

He nods, miserably.

'And Sally-Ann?'

'Damn.' Kit groans and pushes his face into his hands. 'I feel like a shit. I don't want to hurt her but . . . I have to be honest. We can't be together.'

'And what are you going to do about Summer?'

'Let her go. I don't have a choice.'

'I wouldn't be so hasty to come to that conclusion,' Blue says. 'How does she feel about you?' He puts his hands flat on the table. 'Let's face it. If she isn't married, stable door's still open.'

Kit frowns, 'I don't know how she feels.'

'You don't?' His eyes are steely, searching.

'I think . . . she loves me. She's never said the words,' he bites the inside of his lip. 'Neither of us has.'

He remembers her saying that she loves Adam. He closes his eyes briefly, presses the heels of his hands into them.

'Love's a fool's game,' Blue leans across the table, his face creasing earnestly. 'But you got to try and win it – if this girl is the one for you – someone who'll be a friend and a lover – then you got to get back in the saddle.'

'It's no good. I'm leaving Suffolk. I have to go back to London. My mum's had a stroke.' Kit pushes his head into his hands. 'I don't know when I'll be back. Maybe never.'

'You're staying in the city?'

Kit looks at Blue, opening his mouth to say 'yes' and then closing it as a thought occurs to him. He has to care for Mum, but why can't he do that here? When he saw Summer in the pub in Framlingham, surrounded by her family, by people who love her, for a moment he'd felt like a loner, before he'd realised that's not true. This is his home. He's made a life here. He has friends. His studio. He doesn't want to leave.

'If Mum sells her house . . . she could buy a place here,' he tries his thoughts aloud. 'It would be good for her. Sea air, a change of scene.'

Blue nods, encouragingly.

'She might need to go into some kind of care home, a rehabilitation centre, at least for a while . . .' He's working it out as he speaks. 'But I could find one here, couldn't I? And when she's well enough to come home . . . I'd be there to look after her.'

Blue pours out two more shots and clinks his glass with Kit's.

'I'll have to talk to her, when the time is right. There's a way to go before I'll know what state her health will be in when she comes out of hospital . . . I don't want to force her into any decisions.' He taps his finger against the table. 'I'll wait until she's well enough before I talk to her – but . . . I can't see that there's anything to keep her in London.'

They drink. Kit puts his glass down. 'No more for me. I'm working tonight.'

He thinks of his mother and her life in that barren house,

full of unhappy ghosts. The more he thinks of it, the more certain he is that she should move. He'll go back to London if he has to, he's not going to desert her, but Suffolk is where he belongs – and perhaps she could belong here, too.

56

Kit

Jenny is in the kitchen, preparing some fish, a knife sliding through a silver belly. She looks up, 'There you are. I'm sorry to hear about your mum.'

'Thanks,' he kisses her rough, red cheek. 'And I'm sorry for leaving you in the lurch.'

'Don't be daft,' she says, getting back to gutting the fish. 'We've got Jack, and there are plenty of others who'll be glad of a job. But we'll miss you.' Tiny scales spangle her blunt fingers. 'Sally-Ann will miss you most of all,' she adds.

He winces. He's got to tell her that it's over between them before the pub opens and he loses his chance. He takes the stairs two at a time. In his room, he tugs off his sweaty T-shirt, and roots in his drawer for a clean one. The door swings open behind him, and he turns, bare-chested. Sally-Ann comes in, shutting the door behind her. 'Mum told me.' Her mouth wobbles. 'You've leaving? For good?'

'Yes.' He pulls the shirt over his head. 'My mother's in a bad way. She's going to need looking after – there's lots to sort out in London,' he says, doing up buttons.

'But . . . what about us . . .?'

'I'm sorry.' He wrinkles his forehead. 'I've loved the time we've spent together, but I'm not ready for another relationship. Seeing Summer again has made me realise that. I'm so sorry.'

'I could come to London . . . I could—'

'Sally-Ann . . .' He lifts his hand and lets it fall.

'You wouldn't have a job without me, wouldn't have a place to paint,' her tone hardens, 'or any subjects to paint, for that matter.'

'I know,' he says quietly. 'And I'm grateful. So grateful. You're a wonderful person . . . but I should never have let this happen . . . it's my fault.'

'It's not fair.' She sniffs, and a tear trickles down her cheek. 'I never had a chance.' She sits heavily on the bed, head hanging, as she picks at an invisible thread on her jeans. 'It's because of her, isn't it?' she says quietly. 'The girl in the painting. You've been weird ever since you saw her in Framlingham. I think I've sort of known . . . that I was losing you . . . just didn't want to admit it.'

His insides twist. 'I fucked up,' he rubs his face roughly. 'I was a selfish idiot, and I'm sorry. But I'd like us to be friends . . . one day . . . when you're ready.' He takes a step towards her. 'Unless . . . unless you don't want to see me again?'

She looks up at him, sniffs again, searching up her sleeve for a tissue, 'Don't be a pillock.'

He smiles, 'Look, I'll give you my number in London. You can call me anytime.'

'All right.' Her voice trembles. 'I will, if you're lucky.' She clears her throat, swallows. 'When . . . when are you going?'

'Catching the midday train tomorrow.'

'I'm glad you're leaving. It'll be easier.'

He looks at his shoes. 'I am sorry. I really am.'

'You're not the only man in the world, Kit Appleby,' she says, tossing her hair over her shoulder. 'Oh, and that bloke Ben rang again,' she says, crumpling the tissue into her pocket. 'You've sold the sculpture. He wants to talk to you.'

It takes a second to sink in. The words are simple, the meaning huge. He stares at her, mouth open, and she shakes her head at his expression, a twist of a smile appearing, 'Yeah. You're a genius. Obviously. Found your box.'

He clears his throat. 'Thanks. For telling me.'

'That's what friends are for, right?' Her tone is only mildly ironic. She gestures to the door. 'Let's get to work – Dad will have our guts for garters.'

He follows her down the stairs, thoughts whirling – his hare sculpture, sold! He longs to get back to Blue's workshop and begin on another idea; but he'll have to put it on hold until his mother has recovered enough for him to make arrangements. He'll call Benjamin when he gets to London. As he reaches the hall, the sound of the first customers comes through the open door to the snug.

57

Summer

The first thing she sees when she wakes is her dress hanging on the wardrobe door. Loretta is going to be a vision in her multicoloured robes, so Summer has chosen something bold but plain – a scarlet silk sheath to her knees.

The cat is fast asleep across her legs, pinning her down. She moves, tumbling Annabelle to the side. Unfazed, the cat stretches, opening her small pink mouth, tongue curling. Laura is already awake, sitting up in the put-up bed. 'Morning,' she grins at Summer, rubbing her face. 'Think we've overslept – must have been those drinks you forced down my throat last night.'

Summer smiles and pushes her feet onto the floor. She opens the curtains and looks out on a perfect day. Bright, clean sunshine scours the pebbles, making them gleam. The sea and sky are one sweep of blue. She takes a breath. She can be happy, and grateful. She can count her blessings.

'Toast?' She turns to Laura, who's already standing up. 'Tea? Coffee?'

'Please. And coffee, definitely. I need to wake up,' she nods towards the door. 'Just going for a pee.'

'See you in the kitchen.'

Her tactic last night had involved opening a bottle of wine as soon as her friend arrived, launching straight into asking about Charlie, Laura's girlfriend, who can't make it to the party because she's in New York for work. Laura's been trying to get Summer to open up about what happened in Framlingham, and she has no idea that Kit came here, to Shingle Street. And although Summer tells Laura everything, she's not ready to talk about this yet – it feels private; unfathomable.

Downstairs, she flips the kettle on and sticks two slices of bread in the toaster. Effie's notebook is still lying on the table. She moves it into her handbag.

The door opens and Adam comes in, fresh faced, his hair wind-blown. 'Adam?' She blinks in confusion, 'But . . . you were supposed to be here later? After football training?'

He comes close and hesitates before he pecks her cheek. 'I've been here a while.' He sits at the table. 'Got someone else to cover for me. I couldn't wait for the day to start – couldn't wait to see you.' He blinks at her. 'Thought it would be a nice surprise.'

'It is . . . but where have you been?'

'Your dad let me in. I realised you weren't up yet, so I made myself a cup of tea and wandered over to Loretta's to see if I could help with last-minute preparations. Your dad's there. The caterers have arrived.'

She rolls her eyes at him. 'Now I feel guilty.'

'What have you got to feel guilty about?' He holds her gaze.

'Well . . .' she smiles, struggling to maintain eye contact.

'Here I am just out of bed.' She turns her back and starts buttering the toast. 'Do you want something to eat? I'm making breakfast.'

Laura comes down the stairs and gives Adam a hug.

The three of them sit at the table, munching toast and drinking tea, talking about which guests are coming and whether there's enough room for people to dance on Loretta's decking. Summer has to force mouthfuls down. There's a dull ache in her heart, and she resists the urge to press her hand against her chest. Adam seems quieter than usual.

'Never thought I'd see the day when you run out of jokes,' Laura says as she reaches for the marmalade.

'Not in a joking mood, I suppose.' He lights a cigarette and takes a deep drag. 'I didn't get the position,' he says, as he blows out smoke. 'The one in Ipswich.'

A ripple of relief rushes through Summer. 'I'm . . . I'm sorry,' she frowns, trying to hide her reaction. She touches his hand. 'They're the ones who're missing out.'

'Yes, it's their loss,' Laura agrees. 'There'll be other jobs.'

Adam flicks his ash into a saucer. Summer wishes he wouldn't smoke in the house but doesn't want to say anything. He looks beaten, dejected. She raises her shoulders apologetically, 'I need to give Friday a quick walk.' She puts her plate in the sink, grabs her hat from the back of a chair. 'Want to come?' she turns to Adam.

'You two go,' Laura says. 'I'll pop over to Loretta's and see if I can be useful. What time are people arriving?'

'Midday,' Summer says, whistling for the dog.

Friday gets out of his bed, bony bottom pointing up, dinosaur toes flexing. He yawns, showing his teeth in a wolfish grin. She and Adam follow him as he trots along the beach path.

'We'd better head for the fields,' she says. 'Keep to the shade. It's already hot.'

They walk through long grass, Friday darting after smells, lingering over old rabbit trails. She wishes she could live in the moment like him. There's a tension between her and Adam but she isn't sure if he feels it too. She needs to tell him that it's over. She should do it now, she thinks. Or would that be worse for him? Maybe she should wait till after the wedding? But then it would be awkward all day, impossible to act normally.

She ducks as a wasp circles her head, and straightens, squeezing her fingers together to stop the scrawl of panic. She doesn't know the right thing to do. Tell him, or wait?

'Are you all right?' Adam asks.

'Yes.' She pretends to watch Friday snuffling through some bushes. 'Why?'

He stops and kicks out at some cowslips, green sap bleeding under his shoe, 'Because I read your notebook.'

Shock makes her hot, then cold.

'I flipped through it for something to do while I was waiting downstairs,' he says in a dull voice. 'I didn't know it was private. And then, at the end. The bit about me . . . and him.'

'Oh, God,' she stands, aghast, hands over her mouth.

'Apparently you and I are going to make a good team,' sarcasm sharpens his words, 'but you love him. Over and over you wrote it, Summer.'

Her chest is hollow. She wants to touch him, reassure him, but he deserves her honesty. 'I was trying to work out how I felt.' She meets his gaze. 'I . . . I was confused. Kit came to see me.'

'When?' His voice cracks. 'When did you see him?'

'Yesterday.'

'I thought – I thought you wanted to be with me.'

She hears the hurt in his voice and her stomach contracts, 'I did . . . I . . . I believed we could make it work.'

'But now you don't?' Two spots of pink flame in his cheeks.

Her heart is thumping. 'I'm sorry,' she whispers.

His eyes darken, 'What are you saying?'

'I was wrong . . . I still care about you, but . . . I don't think we should have got back together.'

'You've changed your mind because of him?' His expression has hardened. 'Because he's come back into your life?'

'No, it's not just about him. I was already having doubts about . . . us. We used to fit together so well . . . but I'm not sure that we do.'

'So . . . it's over between us?' A muscle works at his jaw.

'Yes.' She takes a deep breath, 'I'm sorry.'

He lets go, forehead and mouth quivering, 'You're dumping me at your dad's wedding?'

'I didn't plan this . . .'

He draws himself up, tilting his chin. 'You didn't want to finish with me today because it would ruin the wedding.' His words are laced with bitterness. He stares at her. 'Well, screw you. I'm leaving now.'

'Adam,' she swallows. 'No . . . it's not . . . I'm so sorry . . . I don't want you to leave like this.'

He looks at her coldly, 'Your dad will have to find someone else to be best man.'

'Adam . . .'

Miserably, she watches him stalk across the field, shoulders set. He stops, ducking his head, cupping his hand to his mouth, and she realises he's lighting up. He keeps going without looking back. It's over. It happened so fast. She never wanted to hurt him, but she had no choice. She stands in the grass, winded, bullets of loss and regret lodged in her chest. But then something shifts; lightness enters her. Relief fills her lungs, balances her – this is what the truth feels like, she thinks. It's a sensation inside her body, a strength at her core. She hadn't realised how much she's been lying to herself.

She waits for Adam to disappear, and then whistles for Friday.

She trudges through the treacly heat back to the cottage. She has to break the news without worrying Dad and Loretta and ruining their day. She has to find a new best man.

'I'll do it,' Laura offers as soon as she hears the news. 'I have my white linen trouser suit to wear.'

'I don't know what to say to Dad,' Summer bites her nail. 'About Adam. I don't want it to spoil the day.'

'Tell him the truth,' Laura says. 'It's always the best way.'

When she breaks it to her father, he doesn't flinch, just takes her hand and asks her if she's all right. She nods, 'I feel like an idiot for going along with it – I knew deep down I should never have gone back to him. He was so angry . . . so upset.'

'He'll be all right.' Dad puts a finger under her chin, tilting it up. 'It will save both of you both a lot more pain later on.' He smiles. 'And I like the idea of Laura as my best man.'

The sound of 'The Time of My Life' drifts out of the cottage. She and Dad have agreed to play it in honour of Effie. The music brings her sister close, as if she brushes past them, as Summer walks Loretta through the gathering of smiling friends towards Dad and Laura, waiting under a garland of bright flowers. As they arrive, Loretta and Summer pause, and she kisses Loretta's cheek before she lets the older woman step forwards to stand next to Dad.

She watches her father's face, how it softens as he turns to Loretta, how he takes her hand with a calm certainty. She never had that kind of conviction with Adam.

The music fades away and there's a brief ceremony with the local vicar officiating, gulls wheeling overhead. As Dad slides the ring onto Loretta's finger, a splatter of white lands on Loretta's turban. She looks up, 'You birds know how to pick your moment!' She shrugs, grinning at Dad, 'It's good luck.' She calls into the sky, 'But one lot's enough, thanks.'

There's a ripple of laughter through the guests. Dad produces a large hanky from his pocket and deals with the mess, and then they are kissing, and everyone claps.

'A couple that can deal with seagull shit on their wedding day,' Laura whispers, 'is a couple that's going to stay together.'

At that moment, Loretta turns around, her face shining, and presses the spill of roses, anemones and tulips into Summer's hands. 'For you,' she says. 'My life changed for the better the moment you ran my bike over.'

Summer holds the flowers to her chest.

'We're looking forward to hearing you sing,' Dad adds, as he kisses her cheek.

Kit must be on his way to catch his train to Liverpool Street by now. She imagines him getting down from the carriage, shouldering his bag, and walking off through throngs of travellers, disappearing from her life. She rubs her eyes and looks around. Guests are gathering in groups, chatting and clutching their drinks and food. The knowledge that he's gone is a numb pressure on her solar plexus. She fixes a smile to her face.

It's time she sang. She doesn't feel nervous – this is a gift to her father and Loretta. She will celebrate their love, even if she's lost hers.

Laura announces her, and everyone stops talking and gathers around, expectantly. She holds the flowers tightly in both hands and lets her voice fly, the words of an old song mixing with the sound of sea birds, the thrum and whisper of waves.

58

Kit

Blue has offered to take Kit to the station in the Moke. He arrives twenty minutes early at the car park of The Anchor, but Kit's ready. The Fisks gather at the door to say goodbye, Paul shaking Kit's hand, Jenny hugging him and Sally-Ann holding herself back, but at the last minute reaching up to kiss his cheek. 'You'd better come back and see us,' she says. 'Or else.'

Kit nods, 'Of course I will,' as he jumps into the passenger seat of the car, dumping his rucksack in the back. 'Goodbye,' he calls, waving to them. 'Goodbye.'

'Woodbridge station here we come,' Blue says, putting it into gear.

'Actually, change of plan,' Kit says, as they turn into the road. 'Can we swing by Shingle Street?'

Blue shoots him a glance. 'You'll be cutting it fine.'

'I know – but I can't go without seeing her one more time.'

He's grateful that Blue doesn't ask any questions, just puts his foot to the accelerator and drives.

He doesn't know what he hopes to achieve, only that he can't leave for good without telling her how he feels. He won't ask her to abandon Adam – he can't expect that – but he needs to say the words that throb like a wound inside him. He loves her.

Blue parks up near the phone box, next to an old cream Bentley with satin ribbons tied to the door handles and a trail of tin cans attached to the bumper.

'Looks like someone's getting married,' he says.

'I'll be quick as I can,' Kit says, hardly noticing. His mind is on her. On finding her. He has to hurry.

'Good luck,' Blue calls.

Kit sprints across the pebbles – not knowing which is her cottage. Will he have time to knock on doors? Will she be in the sea again? Perhaps she won't be here at all. Blood bellows in his ears.

There's a party going on outside one of the far cottages. A marquee flutters. People are gathered around on the shingle as if they're listening to someone. He remembers the Bentley, and his lungs squeeze shut. It's a wedding. As he draws closer, he glimpses her in between gaps in the crowd. She's standing under an arch of flowers. Her dress is like a single flame, and she's holding a bouquet of brightly coloured blooms. She's giving a speech, he realises. He approaches carefully, sliding through some of the guests, staying at the back, straining to hear, but failing.

There's a bout of clapping and everyone is raising their glasses, and there's laughter. 'They make such a great couple,' someone close by says.

'Yeah,' agrees another voice.

'After all these years – worth waiting for the right person,' another chimes in.

There's the murmur of agreement, the onward chatter of conversation. But he doesn't hear anything else, because he understands. Shock pins him to the spot. This is what she meant when she said she was making plans. A bolt of misery shoots through him, and his legs begin to shake. He's gate-crashed her wedding. He blinks into the glare of light. At any moment, Adam will appear, and take his place by her side: her husband. He doesn't want to watch her with him. He couldn't bear it.

This is why she was closed to him on the beach, why she wouldn't even look at him properly. His chest heaves as he tries to get air into his lungs. He can't stop his hands from trembling and shoves them into his jeans pockets. Guests in party clothes mill around, sipping drinks and chatting. A waft of jazz music floats from the blue cottage. A rough-coated dog with a yellow bow around his neck comes up to him, tail wagging. Everywhere he looks, he sees happy people. He feels exposed on the beach, even inside a crowd. He is the intruder here. He has to get away before she sees him. He stumbles in the opposite direction, almost stepping on the long winding line of white shells. As he picks up his feet to go across it, the line seems to mark out the division between himself and Summer, between the life he wants, and the one without her.

On a brink of shingle, he turns and searches her out – drinking her in, her gleaming hair and open face. The way she stands with her back straight in her fiery dress, chatting to people, being congratulated. She looks so beautiful. Then she's lost in a sea of people.

59

Summer

After she finishes her speech, there's applause and clinking of glasses. She clutches the bouquet tighter. It had taken all her strength to sing and then give her speech, but she had to do it, for Dad and Loretta. The happy couple rush forward to hug her, and a few of the guests gather around. 'Beautiful words,' they say. 'Well done. Great speech.' Her face aches with smiling, with keeping from collapsing into a howl of misery.

Someone has turned the music up and people are dancing under the marquee, or reclining on rugs under parasols on the beach, eating chocolate cake and drinking champagne. Friday trots around, being petted by people.

Laura appears through the crowd, a strange expression on her face. She comes close, 'Something weird just happened.' She lowers her voice, 'I think . . . I think I just saw Kit.'

'Kit?' Her heart cuts loose, flaps at her ribs

'Yeah. I'm sure it was him.' Laura glances around. 'Can't see him now though.'

'But . . . he's supposed to be on a train. Going to London.'

'Well, I might have got it wrong,' Laura says, a slight frown between her eyebrows. 'But I think ... I'm pretty sure it was him ... I recognised him from the other night, at the pub.' She touches Summer's arm. 'He caught my attention because he wasn't dressed like a wedding guest, and he was staring at you.'

Summer puts a hand over her mouth. 'When?'

'When you were giving your speech.'

He's come back, she thinks, with a burst of joy. 'I have to find him.' She presses the flowers into Laura's hands.

'I'll help,' Laura says. 'I'll go this way.'

Summer hurries in the opposite direction, circling the guests, craning her neck. She can't see him. Laura appears again, face flushed. 'He's not inside, or in the marquee.'

'Maybe he's further along the beach ...' Summer begins to run towards their cottage. As she stumbles over the shingle, she scans the shoreline. He's not here. Why did he come – and then leave without speaking to her? Folds of silk brush across her legs, sticking to hot skin as she pushes on, struggling up the sliding pebbles. Maybe Laura got it wrong. Maybe it wasn't him.

Then she sees him. A tall figure outlined against the sky, about to turn off from the beach path. The Martello tower looming behind him.

'Kit!'

She knows he hears because he stops abruptly and turns, but she can't see his expression because his face is in shadow. He stands waiting as she hurries closer, her feet slipping awkwardly in her sandals. She can tell that he's holding himself carefully, his shoulders angled, his body stiff, and she reminds herself that he's with Sally-Ann. But he came to see her. There had to be a reason.

'Where ... where are you going?' she pants.

'I have a train to catch.'

She's within touching distance now, and she looks into his closed face, 'But . . . you came to see me?'

'It was a mistake,' his forehead furrows, 'I'm sorry.'

'You wanted to say goodbye?'

'Something like that.'

She half-raises her hands. 'I'm not with Adam any more.' It comes out in a rush.

'But . . .' He's looking at her as if she's spoken in a foreign tongue. 'But . . . I don't . . . you've just married him?'

'What? No.' Understanding falls through her. 'You thought. God. No. That was my father's wedding . . . to Loretta.'

The outlines of his body seem to dissolve, chest folding, knees sagging. 'Your father?' he repeats, shaking his head.

'Yes,' she says. 'Adam wasn't there. We split up his morning – I couldn't be with him – not . . . not with the way I feel about you.' Her words stumble and spill.

'What way is that?'

'I think you know.'

'Say the words,' he says in a low, aching voice.

'I love you, Kit.' Her chest releases with the truth. 'I love you.'

He scoops her towards him. Her nose in his T-shirt, smelling his familiar musty, lemony smell. His arms tight around her ribs. The weight of him, the solid shape of his body against her. She tilts her chin, and his hand moves to the back of her head, running his fingers through her hair. They're kissing hungrily, finding themselves inside each other.

'God, I've missed you,' he says, when they break off.

'But . . . what about Sally-Ann?' she makes herself ask.

He grimaces. 'We're not together. I got it wrong.'

There's the sound of a car horn beeping.

'That'll be Blue,' he glances over his shoulder. 'He's waiting in the car. My train,' he looks panicked. 'I'd miss it but I'm meeting Mum's consultant at the hospital.'

She clutches his hand. 'When can we see each other again?'

'I have to stay in London,' he says. 'Maybe permanently.' He chews his lip. 'Write your number down, quick.'

Her hands skim the folds of her dress. She has nothing with her. Not even a pencil. 'To hell with it,' she says. 'I'll come with you to the station.'

Blue grins when he sees Kit rounding the corner, hand in hand with Summer, but throws a meaningful look at his watch. He drives with his hands tight on the steering wheel, Kit and Summer crammed into the back seat, the wind whipping their hair in their faces. The Moke screams to a halt in the station car park and Kit leaps out, grabbing his bag. He and Summer run onto the platform. The train is there, people pushing past to get on. Doors slam. The whistle blows. He puts one foot up onto the train. 'Goodbye,' he says, looking anguished.

He leans down and kisses her one more time, a brief, hot kiss, and releases her, moving back into the corridor. Without thinking, she follows. They're standing together, people elbowing past to find seats.

'It's going any second,' he warns.

'I'm coming with you,' she says, certainty flooding her.

'To London?' He looks worried. 'I've got to go straight to the hospital. There's nothing to eat in the house, and—'

She puts her finger to his lips. 'I can shop for food while you visit your mum and see the consultant. Unless . . .' she hesitates, 'you don't—'

'No,' he holds her shoulders. 'I want you to – more than anything. I can't stand the thought of being apart from you.'

'Well then,' she says, as the train lurches forwards, throwing them against each other. 'Looks like I'm coming.'

Blue is on the platform searching the windows of the train, and she hangs out of the window, waving. 'Could you go to Shingle Street?' she shouts. 'Tell my dad I'm all right. Donald Blythe. The groom. Tell him I'll call when I'm in London.'

Blue holds up his thumb, his weathered face creasing into a smile.

She thinks of another train journey; it seems a million years ago and only yesterday all at the same time. She hardly knows Kit any better than she did then, and yet she's never been so clear about anything in her whole life – she just wants to be with him, whatever that entails, whatever the difficulties.

He puts his arm around her shoulders as they stand in the corridor, swaying with the movement of the carriage, wheels rattling beneath them. They look out of the window at the masts of boats against the blue sky. She'll tell him about Effie, she thinks. She'll tell him everything. They'll both recall what they've been doing in the lost months between then and now, but there's no rush. They have time.

A voice over the tannoy apologises for the delayed arrival of the train. 'Lucky for us,' she says. 'Not used to cutting it so fine. But I remember you telling me how you're always late for appointments. Buses. Trains.'

'Ah,' he smiles. 'True. But today was an exception. After India, I've never been late again. I'm a new man.'

'Not too new,' she says. 'I like the old one.'

'I have something for you.' He roots through his pocket and

fishes out his wallet. 'Here,' he opens her hand and tips an earring into her palm.

She gasps, 'Where did you find it?'

'Between the floorboards in the hut. I went back to try and find a clue.'

She stares at the little silver creature. She didn't think she'd ever see it again. It's been seven months.

On a pebbly beach, people are celebrating a wedding; she'd still be there too, if Laura hadn't seen Kit. A shiver runs through her at the thought of how close they came to missing each other again. And she wonders how different things would be if she and Dad hadn't come to Suffolk in the first place. Or if she and Kit hadn't been separated in January. She looks at him. All that matters is this. She's in the right place now.

EPILOGUE

Christmas Eve, 1993

Early that morning, Summer walked through the frosty oak woods with Friday padding at her side, while the new puppy barked excitedly, jumping up at the branches of holly and mistletoe Summer held over her shoulder. Now it's six o'clock, and she wipes floury hands on her apron, looking around the room, pleased with how festive the mantelpiece and dark beams look with the swags of greenery and ribbons she arranged earlier. She breathes in the smell of hot mince pies she's just taken out of the oven, the spicy mulled wine warming on the stove, and throws another log on the fire.

Hope, a rescue with collie eyes, terrier legs, and the silky coat of a retriever, turns around three times and settles by the fire with a satisfied sigh. Annabelle, now a bruiser of a cat, has taken it upon herself to teach Hope some lessons in feline respect, and the puppy is no longer in any doubt who's the boss.

Upstairs, in her bedroom, Summer has arranged a small desk and her new sleek electric typewriter in the corner. She sits under the eaves to work, Friday lying at her feet, and just yesterday she finished an article about the white shell line. It's the most personal thing she's ever written, and she thinks, deep down, it's her best. She checked with Dad and Loretta before she began – because it's their love story, starting with the whelk shells that marked the inauspicious start of their relationship, and finishing with the shell line that bonded them, and that goes on, day after day, celebrating their union. It's become a landmark, much photographed and written about by others, and after gathering her own set of pictures of it, Summer wanted to write about the unlikely connection between a cynical romantic novelist and a grieving ex-maths professor, to talk about the symbolism of the line, how hope and perseverance are resonant in its fragile tracing across the landscape of the beach.

So far, Kit is the only person who's read it. She waited downstairs in the kitchen, biting her nails with nerves; and when he came down slowly, looking serious, she was certain he hated it; but he took her hands and held them tight, and she realised his eyes were shining. 'It's beautiful,' he said quietly. 'I'm so proud of you.'

The memory evaporates as her ears pick up the crunch of shingle outside on the path. The door opens, and Kit comes in, supporting his mother on his arm. Both of them are pink-cheeked from the icy wind; Summer hurries forwards to help Margaret out of her coat and get her comfortable in the armchair by the fire, taking her stick and placing it by her.

Kit answers Summer's silent question with a kiss. 'It's a good day,' he mouths, meaning his mother. The stroke had been severe, and Margaret's right arm is still paralysed, walking difficult. She struggles with memory, and her speech hasn't yet fully come back. She has aphasia, and can manage only a few words at a time, but some days are better than others.

Summer puts a glass of mulled wine on a table next to her left side, and Margaret gives her lopsided smile, and looks around, 'Pretty. This.'

Annabelle leaps into her lap and settles, purring, and Margaret's left hand fondles the cat's ears.

The doorbell rings, and Summer welcomes her father and Loretta into the cottage; behind them, Colin and his boyfriend appear out of the darkness with a bouquet of white roses. Just as Kit is getting them all drinks and handing around the mince pies, the door opens again, and Laura and Charlie arrive, with Blue, his guitar slung on his back. The next to arrive is Benjamin with his sister, Kate, who's become a friend of Summer's.

The small room has quickly become packed. In the kitchen, Summer opens the window, letting in a shock of cold air, pausing to notice the dark sky vivid with stars, before she arranges the roses in a vase. As she bends to get more food out of the oven, Laura comes in, holding Hope in her arms. 'She was getting under everyone's feet.'

'She'll be better off in here,' Summer agrees, unable to resist popping half a mince pie into her mouth.

'Where's Friday?'

She eats the other half, licking sugar off her lips. 'Snoring on my bed. He doesn't like crowds.'

'Kit's mum seems cheerful, despite everything,' Laura says. 'Does she like the place she's living?'

'She does,' Summer nods. 'You know Kit suggested she use her London house money to buy a place so that he could look after her, but she refused. Said she wouldn't do that to him.

Anyway, the money means she's got her own lovely room in the home, a physiotherapist and speech therapist to see her every day, and then there's the choir.' Summer grins, 'She loves the choir.'

'A choir?' Laura looks confused, 'You mean . . .? But . . . how?'

'Different part of the brain,' Summer says, tipping sausage rolls onto a plate. 'Extraordinary, isn't it? Actually, turns out she's got a nice singing voice.'

'Well. Good for her.' Laura picks up the plate, 'Shall I offer these around?'

Summer nods, 'Please.'

In the other room, Kit is talking to Blue and Benjamin; he slips his arm around her waist as she arrives at his side, his broad hand settling on her hip. 'Ben's just telling me about a new commission,' he says. 'I've been asked to make a permanent piece for Snape Maltings – something large, a horse or a bull, perhaps. I'm going to discuss ideas with the committee in the New Year.'

'That's amazing,' she squeezes him tightly. 'Well done.'

The door swings open, letting in Sally-Ann and a gust of chilly night air. She's carrying two bottles of champagne, and shivers theatrically, 'Wouldn't be surprised if it snowed tonight. I can't be long,' she adds, handing over the bottles. 'Told Mum I'd be back soon. The pub's packed.'

'Can I pour you a glass?' Summer holds up one of the bottles, but Sally-Ann shakes her head, making a face, 'Got pissed on the stuff once. Is that mulled wine I can smell?'

It had taken a couple of months, but Summer and Sally-Ann have become friends, bonding over dogs and cold-water swimming. As Summer goes into the kitchen and ladles out wine, Sally-Ann appears behind her. 'So, Peter couldn't make it this evening?' Summer asks. Peter is Sally-Ann's new boyfriend – a giant of a man, with red hair and a kind heart. He's from Bury St Edmunds but keeps his sailing yacht moored in Orford and stays on it every weekend.

Sally-Ann shakes her head. 'He's coming to us on Christmas Day though.' She takes a sip of wine. 'And you'll spend it with your family and Kit and his mum?'

'Yeah, Loretta's offered to host.' Summer nods. 'I'm grateful, because the last months have been a bit of a blur with so much toing and froing between here and the hospital, selling the house and sorting things out. It was an upheaval until we got Margaret comfortable. But now . . . I think we've done the hard bit and we can start to feel settled.'

'I'm glad,' Sally-Ann says quietly.

Back in the busy front room, Loretta pulls her to one side. 'Lovely party,' she says. 'I'm looking forward to tomorrow. I have a surprise for your dad. I've dedicated my latest book to him – I'm going to give him a copy as part of his present.'

Summer squeezes the older woman's hand.

A ringing sound makes everyone look up. Kit is tapping his glass with a spoon, and the conversation quietens down. He stands in the middle of the room and smiles at Summer. 'A toast to our hostess,' he says, holding up his glass, 'who also happens to be the woman I love. And, for those of you who don't know, I'm about to move in with her.' He glances at her, grinning. 'I can't wait.'

'What about making an honest woman of her?' Loretta calls.

'Watch this space,' Kit throws over his shoulder as he kisses Summer on the mouth.

She comes up for air and gives him a wry look. 'Maybe next chapter,' she murmurs, before she pulls his face down to hers and kisses him back.

'Blimey, can you two get a room?' Sally-Ann's voice complains.

Everyone laughs and Summer reluctantly lets go of Kit, tucking her shoulder-length hair behind her ears. 'I think we should all sing something,' she suggests. 'A traditional Christmas carol. That okay with you, Margaret?'

Kit's mother nods enthusiastically. Blue gets out his guitar and begins to strum the chords to 'Hark the Herald Angels Sing'; there's throat-clearing and shuffling as they gather around Margaret's chair. The words to the rousing tune fill the room, Benjamin not quite hitting the right notes and Charlie trilling in a surprising soprano. Annabelle jumps down in disgust and stalks from the room, hissing at Hope as she bounds in, barking.

'And now let's hear you sing, Summer,' Laura says, as she lifts the wriggling puppy into her arms.

'Yes, please,' Dad adds.

She nods, summoning the words to 'Silent Night', imagining her sister's shining face, remembering how seriously she took Christmas Eve, the ritual of playing their record of carols from the King's College choir as they decorated the tree and hung their stockings on the mantelpiece.

All is calm, all is bright.

She touches Kit's watch, looped around her wrist. When she'd tried to give it back, he said it belonged to her now; like the silver hares at her ears, it feels part of her.

After she finishes, nobody speaks. There's a pause in time, just the crackle of the flames in the grate, the sound of someone taking a trembling breath and letting it out in a sigh. Summer's eyes search for Kit. He holds her gaze. Looking at him, she wonders at the heart's ability to break and mend and, like a broken bone, grow bigger and stronger.

Just as well, she thinks, as she steps across the room and into his arms; her heart needs to be huge, with so much to fit inside it.

ACKNOWLEDGEMENTS

I owe a huge debt of thanks to my publisher, Hannah Wann, and editor, Emma Beswetherick, for their unfailing support and brilliant suggestions. Without them, this book would not exist. Many thanks as well to all at Little, Brown and Piatkus, especially Andy Hine, Helena Doree, Kate Hibbert, Sarah Birdsey and Beth Wright. Also, to Penny Isaac for forensic copyediting.

I'm lucky to have writer friends who looked at the many drafts this book went through, and I'm so grateful for their advice and comments: Sara Sarre, Alex Marengo, Mary Chamberlain, Viv Graveson, Laura McClelland and Cecilia Ekback.

Thanks as always to my wonderful agent, Eve White, for her years of friendship and good counsel. And to Ludo Cinelli.

A big thank you to Geoff Hanson for talking me through the mysterious working of engines and cars. And to my brother, Alex Sarginson, for sharing his knowledge of cameras and photography. Any mistakes are entirely my own.

As always, thank you to my family: Hannah, Olivia, Sam, Gabriel, Ana, Alex and Alex. The line of white shells that Loretta and Donald create on Shingle Street is inspired by a real line of shells made in 2005 by childhood friends Lida Cardozo Kindersley and Els Bottema. Reflecting on their recent cancer treatment, the two women started placing shells on the shingle and so began the line that's become a local attraction and the subject of photographs, a film, and a book. For many, it's a symbol of courage, survival and friendship.

Anyone who knows coastal Suffolk will recognise place names like Orford, Leiston, Woodbridge, Framlingham, and Shingle Street, and be familiar with certain landmarks like the Martello Tower and Orford castle. However, this is a work of fiction, and I have re-imagined parts of the landscape and area, so there is no geographical accuracy. I have also completely invented certain places and changed the layout of others to suit my fictional purposes. But I hope I have remained true to the beauty of this part of the world – a landscape that lives in my heart.